the da-da-
de-da-da
code

the da-da-de-da-da code

Robert Rankin

GOLLANCZ
London

The Da-Da-De-Da-Da Code © Robert Rankin 2007
All rights reserved

The right of Robert Rankin to be identified as the
author of this work has been asserted by him in accordance
with the Copyright, Designs and Patents Act 1988.

First published in Great Britain in 2007 by Gollancz
An imprint of the Orion Publishing Group
Orion House, 5 Upper St Martin's Lane,
London WC2H 9EA
An Hachette Livre UK company

A CIP catalogue record for this book is
available from the British Library

ISBN 978 0 57507 0 110 (Cased)
ISBN 978 0 57507 9 908 (Trade Paperback)

3 5 7 9 10 8 6 4 2

Typeset by Deltatype Ltd, Birkenhead, Merseyside

Printed in Great Britain by Mackays of Chatham plc,
Chatham, Kent

The Orion Publishing Group's policy is to use papers
that are natural, renewable and recyclable products and
made from wood grown in sustainable forests. The logging
and manufacturing processes are expected to conform
to the environmental regulations of the country of origin.

www.orionbooks.co.uk

For
my beautiful
Raygun
With all my love

Thank you for
the inspiration
the love
and the music

and the shoes

mmmm

1

A headless corpse was floating on the ornamental pond.

It troubled the view and it troubled the ducks and it troubled the two park rangers.

The rangers stood, uncomfortably, upon the north shore, before the Doric temple. The elder of the two was smoking a cigarette; the younger was trying very hard to keep his breakfast down.

'Now, *that*,' said the elder of the two, puffing smoke and speaking through it, 'is the thin end of the wedge. Bikes and baby buggies, crates and shopping trolleys – I don't know how they sneak the stuff in through the park gates. Nor why they feel the need to chuck it in the pond when they do. But *that*,' and he pointed with his cigarette, 'is too much. Much too much, that is. And,' he continued, 'it's wearing a park ranger's uniform.'

The younger of the two men, who had lately returned from Tierra del Fuego for reasons known only to himself, was sick into a mulberry bush. Which is more difficult than it might at first appear, because it is generally understood that mulberries grow upon trees.

'Yes, you get it up, lad,' said his companion. 'Better out than in, that is. Egg and bacon *and* beans. At least your mother loves you.'

From the middle to the near distance came the sounds of police-car sirens.

'At long last,' said the ranger who still retained his breakfast, stubbing out his cigarette.

The route that must be taken by vehicles from any of Gunnersbury Park's gates to the shores of the pond is a complicated one, and it was quite some time before a single police car appeared at the crime scene.

Siren shriek and blue light flash and car doors opening up.

And policemen, numbering two, looking somewhat tired and harassed.

These officers of the law approached the rangers; one had on a helmet, the other a cap.

'Kenneth Connor?' asked the wearer of the cap.

'*Ranger* Connor,' said the elder of the two rangers. 'Not to be confused with the other Kenneth Connor.' And he put out his hand for a shake.

'Other Kenneth Connor?' The wearer of the cap declined the offer of the hand.

'Star of the *Carry On*—'

'So where's this body, then?' asked the officer who wore the helmet. Wore the helmet and carried a truncheon, too.

Kenneth Connor, not to be confused with the other Kenneth Connor, viewed this truncheon with suspicion. 'It's a *dead* body,' he said. 'It won't need truncheoning down.'

'One can never be too careful,' said the bearer of the truncheon. 'The dead don't always stay dead. Sometimes they turn into vampires, or zombies, or booger men.'

'Put it away, you oaf,' his capped superior told him.

'Booger men?' said Ranger Connor.

The constable sheathed his truncheon in the manner known as huffy.*

'Inspector Westlake,' this superior continued, addressing his words towards Ranger Connor. 'Here on secondment from the Bramfield Constabulary, having travelled far. This enthusiastic officer is Constable Justice.'

'Justice by name and—'

'Shut up, you oaf.'

'Yes, sir.'

'And your man here?' said Westlake, indicating the younger ranger, who had now finished his business with the mulberry bush and was making sheepish faces towards all concerned.

'Ranger Charles Hawtrey,' said Ranger Connor. 'Not to be confused with—'

---

* Which is not to be confused with Buffy.
Who slays vampires, zombies and probably booger men, too.

'The Lone Ranger?' Constable Justice sniggered.

'Never,' said his superior, with a voice of stern authority, 'never *ever* snigger in my presence again.'

'No, sir!'

'So where *is* the body?' Westlake asked.

'*I* asked that,' said Constable Justice, 'and got no response. Should we run these villains in for concealing evidence, Guv?'

Inspector Westlake cuffed the constable lightly around the head. 'Return to the motor,' he told him, 'get the other cars on the blower and aid them in reaching our present location.'

'But Guv, the body—'

'Car,' said Westlake. 'Now!' said Westlake. 'Do it!' said Westlake, too.

Grumble-grumble-grumble went the chastened constable. And grumbling so he slouched off to the car, muttering the words 'booger men' underneath his breath.

'Children,' said Inspector Westlake, shaking his head in sadness. 'They are sending us children nowadays.'

Ranger Hawtrey made a face. 'Surely that is illegal,' he said.

Inspector Westlake yawned and stretched. 'And so,' he said, 'perhaps not the best way to begin a bright spring day, but where *is* the body?'

'Floating there.' Ranger Connor lit another cigarette and pointed with it. 'Headless and horrible and messing up the pond.'

Inspector Westlake peered. 'Indeed so,' he said, cocking his head from side to side. 'You've a body there and no mistake.'

'Your lads will have it out before the park opens, won't they?'

Inspector Westlake shook his head. 'The park won't be opening today,' said he.

'But it must,' said Ranger Connor. 'Even Hitler's Luftwaffe couldn't close the park. The park closes on Christmas Days only.'

'It was closed yesterday, as you know full well,' said Inspector Westlake. 'And it will be closed today also, and that is that. The pond will have to be dragged in search of the head, and the entire park searched also, inch by inch, by trained specialists in the field.'

'Them at the Big House won't like this,' said Ranger Connor.

'Them at the Big House will have to lump it, then.' Inspector Westlake patted at his pockets. As was ever the way with police inspectors, he was in the process of giving up smoking. 'You couldn't spare a fag, I suppose,' he asked.

'No,' said Ranger Connor, 'I could not.'

The headless body bobbed in the pond. An inquisitive duck peeped in at its neck hole.

At length three further police cars appeared and a white van with the words 'Scientific Support' emblazoned in red upon its colourless sides. From this issued a number of men, clad in environmental suits.

'Spacemen,' said Ranger Hawtrey, who was standing with his back to the pond.

'Scene of Crime Investigators. Specialists in their field,' said the inspector. 'Forget about Horatio Caine and all that *CSI Miami* toot. You don't solve crimes by having ginger hair and standing about in a brown suit with your hands on your hips. Or putting on sunglasses and then taking them off again.'

'Or speaking *very* slowly,' said Ranger Connor, who was a secret fan of *CSI Miami*.

'Quite so. Scotland Yard has the very crème de la crème of Scene of Crime Forensic Investigators in the known world.'

'What are they doing?' asked Ranger Hawtrey. 'What is that they're pulling out of their van?'

'I'll have to ask you to move along now,' said Inspector Westlake. 'The public are not permitted to watch ... at work.'

'...?' said Ranger Hawtrey. 'What is ...?'

'It's the name of the unit. They are so elite that even their acronym is top secret.'

'It's a barbecue,' said Ranger Hawtrey. 'They've got a barbecue out of their van. They're not Crime Scene Investigators, they're a catering unit.'

'Move along now, sir,' said Inspector Westlake, 'or I shall be forced to let my officer employ his truncheon.'

'They're getting out a garden umbrella and folding chairs now.'

'Move along please, sir.'

'And a crate of beer,' said Ranger Connor. 'And alcoholic beverages may not be consumed within the park's environs without express permission from the management.'

'You too, sir,' said Inspector Westlake. 'Job for the professionals now, this. Thank you for your cooperation. Please go about your business.'

'But this *is* my business.' Ranger Connor stood his ground. *His* uniform was every bit as impressive as that worn by Inspector West-lake. His even had medal ribbons sewn into it. *And* his shoes were more highly polished. And this was *his* territory. He'd worked in this park for twenty-seven years. He wasn't going to be bullied by some bumpkin bobby. Bramfield was a village in Sussex – he'd once passed through it by mistake while on his way to the Bluebell Line (Ranger Connor had a thing about steam trains). *And* he'd had a very trying week, one way and another. *And* there was the matter of the landmines that had been sown on the pitch-and-putt, but he wasn't going to go into *that* at the moment.

'I'm not leaving,' said Ranger Connor. 'It would be irresponsible of me to do so. I know every inch of this park and it's my job to see that not an inch is abused. I'm not having your mob trampling my flower beds.'

'You tell him, Ken,' said Ranger Hawtrey.

'I will,' said Ranger Connor, who hated being called Ken. 'And furthermore—'

'Constable,' called Inspector Westlake to Constable Justice, who was sitting on the bonnet of their police car, smoking a cigarette. 'Come over here and arrest this gentleman, will you?'

'Arrest?' said Ranger Connor. 'Arrest *me*? On what charge?'

'For being a ruddy nuisance. There's a dead man in that pond and I don't have time to bandy words with you.'

'Who wants hitting?' asked Constable Justice, hurrying up and unsheathing his truncheon.

'The big one,' said the inspector. 'If he still refuses to move.'

'I *do*,' said Ranger Connor. 'And I am obliged to warn you, before any attempts are made to hit me in any fashion, that I am an exponent of Dimac, the deadliest martial art in the world. That my hands and feet are deadly weapons and that I am master of Poison Hand, a cruel, disfiguring and mutilating technique, which—'

'Threatening an officer of the law,' said Inspector Westlake. 'That's as good as smiting. Strike this malfeasant down, Constable.'

Constable Justice hesitated. 'Dimac?' he said in a doubtful, wary tone.

'Dimac,' said Ranger Hawtrey. 'Schooled in Chicago by Count Danté himself. Deadliest man on Earth, Count Danté. I've seen Ranger Connor's certificate – he has it up on the wall in the rangers' hut.'

'You have your own special hut, then?' asked Constable Justice. 'How interesting.'

'Constable!' roared Inspector Westlake. 'Take these two men into custody *now*. I'm charging them with impeding the course of justice.'

'I'm sure they'll move along if you ask them nicely, Guv,' said Constable Justice.

'*Ask them nicely?* I'm a police inspector. I don't have to ask *anyone* nicely.'

'Excuse me, sir,' said a member of the Scientific Support unit, ambling up in his environmental suit (sans helmet). 'Is there a socket somewhere that we can run an extension cable to? We need to plug in the candyfloss machine.'

'Not now!' bawled Inspector Westlake, growing most red in the face. 'Constable, arrest these men at once.'

Constable Justice raised his truncheon and dithered with it raised.

'I really wouldn't,' said Ranger Hawtrey. 'It's not worth the months of hospitalisation. And learning to walk again can be a very painful business.'

'Right.' Inspector Westlake snatched the truncheon from the constable's hand, raised it swiftly over his own head . . .

And . . .

Accidentally struck the wearer of the environmental suit a really cracking blow to his helmetless head.

Which was witnessed by the environmental suit wearer's similarly clad fellow workers, who were struggling to erect what looked for all the world to be a tombola stall.

Constable Justice sniggered once again.

Inspector Westlake hit him with the truncheon. 'I warned you not to snigger,' he said.

And then the inspector swung at Ranger Connor, and things took a serious turn for the worse.

2

One Week Earlier

Most, if not all, of Mankind's problems stem from Man's natural inability to accurately predict future events. Think about it, do, just for a moment. Imagine how things might be if we were gifted with the ability to accurately foretell future events. And know, in advance, what would be the result of any particular course of action we were thinking to take. How simple things would be, then. We would never make any mistakes and there would be love and laughter all around and nation would speak peace unto nation and there would be no crime and we'd all live happily ever after.

Although ...

What *is* certain is that a lot of thought would go into each particular action. So much so, in fact, that society would probably grind to a halt.

Discuss.

It is absolutely certain, however, that in the case of Jonny Hooker, had he been granted the gift of precognition, he would not have taken the course of actions that he did, a course that would lead inevitably to him floating headless and lifeless in the ornamental pond at Gunnersbury Park, a short seven days into the future.

Jonny was not aware that this was what Fate had in store for him, and even if he had been, it is doubtful whether he would have cared.

For Jonny wasn't a happy man. Very far from it, in fact. Jonny was a tormented soul, tormented in so many ways.

We learn quite early on as children that life isn't fair. That the world is composed of the haves and the have-nots and that the have-nots greatly outnumber the haves.

But we *are* also taught that if we work hard and do our best, we will receive our fair share and be right up there with the haves. And most of us learn sooner or later that, sadly, this is a lie.

Jonny had been taught many things, but had learned very few. He *had* learned that he was a have-not and that life wasn't fair, so he had at least grasped the essentials of life. Above and beyond these, he had been granted a basic knowledge of the English language, a natural ear for music and an extraordinary talent as a guitarist (a talent that in keeping with the unfairness of life, would sadly go unrecognised until after his tragic early death). Jonny had acquired a few friends and, to his mind, too many enemies.

So Jonny wasn't a happy man.

And today being the day that it was, there was a farmers' market.

Thirteen stalls, local produce, numerous varieties of cheese, free-range eggs, home-made yoghurts, beeswax candles, quiches and flans, and pies made from prime porker pigs.

And as ever the market was being held upstairs, in the loft above Jonny's bedroom.

Jonny lay upon his old rotten cot, his hands clamped over his earholes, his teeth gritted, his eyes tightly closed. He lay in what is known as the foetal position.

The sounds of chatting farmer lads filtered down to him through the ceiling's yellowed plaster. Bucolic ribaldry, hail-fellow-well-mets, palms all spat upon and smacked together to signify fair transactions. A goat went bleat. The porker pies were silent.

Jonny shifted his position and took up a kind of 'praying in the direction of Mecca' sort of posture. Removed his hands from his earholes, drummed them on his pillow.

Raised his head and shouted, 'Do shut up!'

Arose from his bed and stamped his feet and shouted, 'Go away!'

Chitchat went the farming lads. A lady in a straw hat bought some cheese.

Jonny yelled abuse at the ceiling, stalked to his bedroom door (a short stalk, as the room was not over-large), threw open his bedroom door, stalked onto the landing, snatched up the rod with the hook on the end that opened the loft hatch, opened the loft hatch with it, ducked aside as the loft ladder crashed down (as it always did), took a deep breath and shimmied up the ladder.

Jonny stuck his head up through the loft hatch and shouted at ...

Nothing.

There were no farmers in his loft, no stalls, no lady in a straw hat, no pies made from porker pigs. There were dusty boxes, a bicycle frame, some kind of telescopic clothes-drying jobbie, some unlaid rolls of loft insulation.

Jonny took another deep breath, coughed from the dust, slunk back down the ladder and returned to his bedroom and his bed.

Of course there was no farmers' market up in his loft. Of course there had never been a farmers' market up in his loft. *Would* never be a farmers' market up in his loft. He was having one of his 'episodes' again because, as his mother told her chums at the bingo, Jonny, her one and only son, was not very well in the head.

'No farmers' market,' said Jonny Hooker. 'Never was, isn't now, never will be!'

'Somewhere over the rainbow,' said Mr Giggles the Monkey Boy, 'bluebells fly. Or so I have been unreliably informed.'

'And there is *no* Mister Giggles the Monkey Boy,' said Jonny, striking at his left temple with his left fist and covering his eyes with his right one.

'No need to go all *One Flew Over the Cuckold's Nest* on me,' said Mr Giggles. 'It's not my fault that you're not very well in the head.'

'You do *not* exist,' said Jonny. 'You are a fragment of my mash-up mind.'

'And me your dearest friend. Perhaps you mean a "figment".' Mr Giggles reached out a hairy hand and patted Jonny's head with it.

'And please do *not* do *that*.' Jonny sat upon his bed wearing a very glum face.

'Let's go to the swimming baths,' said Mr Giggles, 'peep in the ladies' changing rooms and spy their furry bottoms.'

'I can't swim,' said Jonny. 'And I'm not talking to you because you don't exist. You are the product of my imagination. You are an imaginary friend.'

'You know I don't like that term,' said Mr Giggles, a-twiddling his furry thumbs. 'You know that I prefer to be known as an NCC – a non-corporeal companion.'

'Whatever,' said Jonny. 'But you still don't exist.'

'If I don't exist,' said Mr Giggles, 'how come I can do this?'

Jonny ignored Mr Giggles.

'And this, too.'

Jonny ignored Mr Giggles again.

'And what about this?'

Jonny was prepared to ignore Mr Giggles once more but was distracted from so doing by the sounds of his mother beyond his bedroom door, tripping over the loft ladder and falling into the bathroom.

'Well,' said Jonny to Mr Giggles, 'if you're so real, you can prove it by taking the blame for that.'

Jonny looked up at Mr Giggles, but Mr Giggles had gone.

Jonny Hooker grumbled and mumbled and buried his face in his hands. He was truly sick of Mr Giggles. Mr Giggles had been Jonny's imaginary childhood friend. Jonny had been something of a loner as a child. The other children hadn't taken to him because he was a bit odd and not very well in the head. So Jonny had been grateful when Mr Giggles turned up in his bedroom one night. Mr Giggles said that he had run away *from* the circus. Mr Giggles wore a fez and a brightly coloured waistcoat. He had a suitcase full of treasure and he knew one hundred songs. Jonny got on very well with Mr Giggles.

The only problem was that when Jonny reached puberty, a time when imaginary friends say farewell and vanish away for ever to make way for actual friends, generally of the opposite sex, Mr Giggles had refused to depart. He liked Jonny far too much, he told Jonny, and as Jonny didn't appear to be making many other friends, he'd stay around for a little longer to keep him company.

And Jonny was now twenty-seven and Mr Giggles still hadn't gone away. And the problem for Jonny was that Mr Giggles was just *so* real.

But then so was the farmers' market. Although Jonny could only *hear* the farmers' market. He couldn't actually see the farmers. He could only see Mr Giggles.

In the past, when a lad, Jonny could see and hear all manner of things that others could not: noisy ghosts and bad witches, fairies and spacemen and dragons and pirates and all.

He could no longer see these things, but some of them he could still hear. And those he could hear tormented him.

He'd been through all the usual diagnostics. He'd been prescribed, and had taken, all the usual antidepressants and uppers and downers and so forth.

Chlorpromazine, clozapine, haloperidol and risperidone. Pimozide, which had worked a treat on his Tourette syndrome.

Then there were all the old favourites: methylphenidate (Ritalin), lithium (priadel), anticonvulsant drugs, carbamazepine (Tegretol), valproate semi-sodium (Depakote), gabapentin (Neurontin) and lamotrigine (Lamictal), antidepressants (such as bupropion (Wellbutrin) or sertraline (Zoloft)), neuroleptics e.g. haloperidol (Haldol) and benzodiazepines e.g. lorazepam (Ativan).

And aspirin, for when he had a headache.

And Jonny had learned, through bitter experience, what to say during counselling sessions in order to remain 'at liberty'.

Jonny sighed and ground his teeth and listened to the sounds of his mother floundering around on the bathroom floor. She had clearly fallen belly-up, and, tortoise-like, was quite incapable of righting herself.

'Jonny,' wailed his mother.

And Jonny went to help.

Having reconfigured his mother into the vertical plane, Jonny dusted her down, straightened the hem of her Paisley housecoat, which had ridden up above her surgical stockings, and sought her upper set of false teeth, which had gone adrift in the tumbling. He located these behind the toilet, took them to the sink, rinsed them under the tap and returned them to his mother. The old one slotted the artificial railings over her sunken gums, thanked her son and asked, in as polite a manner as she considered it merited, whether it had indeed, as she suspected, been his intention to have her murdered to death by leaving the loft ladder in the down position when he was well aware that she could not see it due to a sight defect she had acquired (whilst riding to hounds with the Berkshire Hunt) that had severed the optical nerve that allowed people to see ladders.

'It wasn't me,' Jonny suggested.

'Was it Mister Giggles?' his mother enquired.

'It *was* me,' said Jonny. 'I'm sorry, Mum.'

'You're a good boy, Jonny,' said his mother. 'Even if you do try to kill me dead upon every occasion that arises. I came up here to bring you a cup of tea and a letter that has your name upon it. The tea went down the toilet; the letter, I think, went out of the window.'

Jonny glanced into the toilet. There, half-submerged, was his favourite mug. The one with 'THE WORLD'S GREATEST SON' printed upon it.

'Out of the window?' said Jonny, glancing now in that direction.

'Flew like a bird from my hand.'

Jonny lowered the toilet lid and then lowered his mother onto it. 'I'll pop down to the garden and see if I can find the letter,' he told her.

And that is what he did.

Jonny did not exactly bounce down the stairs. Although there was a very slight spring in his step. A letter addressed to *him*? This was something new, something different. Perhaps his luck was about to change. Perhaps some half-forgotten uncle had died and left him a fortune or something.

Jonny reached the foot of the stairs and paused.

What *was* he thinking? Optimistic thoughts?

What had put these into his head?

Why would *he* be thinking that something good was about to occur? How weird was that?

But Jonny *did* feel optimistic. Suddenly optimistic. He didn't know why and he didn't know how, but he did.

It was a very strange feeling.

Almost as if there was something fateful about this letter.

Something life-changing.

In the back garden Jonny found the letter.

It was floating on the ornamental pond.

3

As Jonny fished the letter from the ornamental pond, he noticed something very strange about the garden.

It was very, very quiet.

It had never been a noisy garden, but there was always *some* noise to it, some ambient sounds, as it were.

Traffic rumblings, a neighbour's radio.

Birds a-twitter, washing swinging to and fro.

Scurrying of beetles.

Bells in distant steeples.★

And pretty maids all in a row. Ho ho.

But not today. Not at this particular moment.

Jonny paused in the shakings of wet from his letter. There was absolutely *no* sound. It was as if all sound, the very sound of the world itself, had been suddenly switched off. The power plug pulled from the socket, as it were. A great and terrible silence.

Jonny rooted a finger into his ear. It was a horrible silence. Jonny did not like this silence one bit. Jonny shook his head about.

'It's quiet, ain't it?' said Mr Giggles. 'Is that letter for me?'

'It's not for you, it's—' And 'ouch' went Jonny as all the sounds in the world came rushing back.

'What was *that*? What was *that*?'

'That, my friend, was a pregnant pause,' said Mr Giggles. 'Something significant is about to occur.'

'In this garden?'

Mr Giggles shook his furry head. 'I very much doubt that,' he said. 'I can't imagine a dullard like yourself ever doing anything significant, can you?'

★ Poetic licence. Beetles and steeples, you're allowed that sort of thing.

Jonny ignored Mr Giggles once more and addressed himself to the address upon the envelope that he now held in his hand. It *was* his address. And above it *was* his name – Jonathan Hooker, Esq.

'Open it up, then,' said Mr Giggles.

'I'm ignoring you,' said Jonny. 'I'm not talking to you.'

'Fair enough,' said Mr Giggles, tilting his fez to the angle known and loved as 'rakish'. 'So open up the envelope and let's have a look at the letter.'

'Whatever it is, it is none of your business.'

'Well, obviously not, as I clearly do not exist.'

Jonathan Hooker opened the envelope. As the envelope was soggy, he made quite a mess of this and managed to tear the letter within and generally spoil things. Generally. With difficulty he withdrew, unfolded and read the letter.

Dear Mr Hooker (he read)
Your name has been selected by
our Competition Supercomputer to be a
WINNER WINNER WINNER
If you wish to claim your prize,
Please present yourself to—

'Blah blah blah blah,' went Jonny.

'Present yourself to *where*?' said Mr Giggles.

'Blah blah blah blah,' said Jonny. 'That's what it says here. If I was going to tell *you*, which I'm not.'

'Naturally,' said Mr Giggles. 'Give us a butcher's at the letter.'

Jonny gave Mr Giggles a butcher's.

Mr Giggles read from the letter. 'It's not "blah blah blah blah,",' he said, 'it's "da–da–de–da–da!"'

'And what is *that* supposed to mean?'

'It means what it is,' said Mr Giggles. 'It's musical. You're a musician – you know what it means.'

'As in the way that most tunes go "da–da–de–da–da"?'

'Exactly. Like "Walltzing Matilda" – the tune of each verse goes "Da–da–de–da–da. Da–da–de–da–da. Who'll come a-Waltzing Matilda with me?"'

'So what does this letter mean?'

'Why are you asking me? I don't exist, remember?'

Jonny checked his wristlet watch. He had forgotten to wind it the night before, and it had stopped.

'What time is it?' he asked Mr Giggles.

The Monkey Boy consulted a rather decorative chronometer that he drew from the pocket of his colourful waistcoat. 'Ten-thirty of the morning clock,' said he. 'Sun over the yardarm, time for a pint of wallop.'

'Ten-thirty,' said Jonny. 'Fair enough, I give up.'

'You always do. I don't know why you go to all the trouble. Every day you try to persuade yourself – and also *myself* – that *I* do not exist.'

'And every day I give up at ten-thirty,' said Jonny.

'It's best to.' Mr Giggles smiled upon Jonny. 'Why don't we go down to the pub and try to fathom the meaning of your most peculiar missive?'

'Will *you* be getting the first round in?'

Mr Giggles raised a hirsute brow upon his hirsute forehead. 'You say that every single day,' said he. 'Which curiously I find strangely comforting.'

Mr Giggles followed Jonny through the garden gate.

Upstairs, in the bathroom, Jonny's mother, who had slipped from the toilet lid, floundered once more upon her back making sounds that oddly resembled those of a seagull.

The pub was called The Middle Man. It stood in Pope's Lane, one hundred yards before the northern entrance to Gunnersbury Park. It had been standing there for more than one hundred years and no one so far had told it to move.

Within the pub and standing behind the bar counter stood O'Fagin the publican. He had been standing there for five minutes. His wife had told him to move three times already this morning. O'Fagin felt certain deep down in his bones that she was sure to ask him to do so again.

But O'Fagin was just like the rest of us when it came to his abilities regarding accurate prediction of the future. His wife would never again ask him to move, because later in the day she would run off with a sales rep who travelled in tobaccos and had only entered the pub with the intention of introducing its incumbents to a new brand of cigarettes known as Dadarillos.

Sometimes love, it seems, conquers all.

At other times, who can say?

'I say good morning to you both,' said O'Fagin the publican.

'To myself *and* Mister Giggles?' Jonny Hooker enquired.

'Sun's over the yardarm and all is right in God's Heaven,' said O'Fagin. 'And although I can't actually see or hear Mister Giggles and only know of his supposed existence because every time you're really pissed, you blather on and on about how he's your bestest friend.'

Jonny Hooker groaned.

'But anyway,' continued O'Fagin, 'I had an imaginary friend myself when I was a kid.'

'I know,' said Jonny. 'I went to school with you. And I was the friend that you had.'

'I've never quite understood that,' said O'Fagin, 'because, clearly, I'm much older than you. I'll ask my wife about it later. She knows all kinds of things. She went to boarding school and can impersonate ponies and everything.'

'Good morning, barlord,' said a well-clad fellow who had but lately entered the bar. 'I would like to take this opportunity to introduce you to a new brand of cigarette.'

'Would you mind introducing my wife to it?' said O'Fagin. 'She's through that door over there.'

'Fair enough,' said the fellow. And with that he was gone.

'Nice chap by the sound of him,' said O'Fagin to Jonny. 'But then what do I know?'

'You know how to draw a pint,' said Jonny, miming the pulling of one. 'Best stick with what you know, I suppose.'

O'Fagin applied himself to the pump handle and drew off a pint of King Billy. He presented this to Jonny and said, 'And what is Mister Giggles having, then?'

'Mister Giggles is buying his own.'

'Cheap shot,' said Mr Giggles. 'A tot of rum and a bag of nuts will see me fine.'

'A bag of nuts,' said Jonny.

'Dry-roasted, honey-roasted, salted, plain or fancy?'

'Fancy nuts?' said Jonny.

'Not really,' said O'Fagin. 'I prefer crisps.'

The sun went behind a cloud and a dog howled in the distance.

'Which reminds me,' said O'Fagin. 'did you hear that really big silence earlier?'

'You heard that, too?' Jonny asked. 'Or failed to hear everything else.'

'Quite so. It fair put the wind up me. I was just about to open a letter and my wife was just about to tell me to move, when the world went silent. I thought my hearing aid had packed up.'

'But you don't wear a hearing aid.'

'Of course I don't. Do I look like a homosexual?'

'Not in the slightest.'

'So how do they look? In case one comes in here and I don't recognise him.'

'You're confusing me,' said Jonny.

'Confusing you with whom?'

'Search me,' said Jonny.

'Why – are you hiding something?'

The clock chimed behind the bar and a dog howled in the distance.

'I must get that dog fixed,' said O'Fagin. 'Now, what were we talking about?'

'Silence,' said Jonny.

'But I thought you enjoyed my conversation.'

'You said that the world went silent when you were about to open an envelope.'

'So I did,' said O'Fagin. 'What a coincidence.'

'Do you have the letter? Might I have a look at it?'

'I do and you might. Have you decided yet upon what variety of nuts you'd like to purchase? Only I get a bit anxious if things are left hanging in the air.'

Jonny said nothing.

A moment passed.

'I was hoping you'd ask me, "What kind of things?"' said O'Fagin. 'I have quite a list. You'd be surprised by some of the items on it.'

'No, I wouldn't,' said Jonny. 'But they'd probably make me more miserable than I already am. I thought things were going to perk up when I heard that I'd got a letter. I got almost excited—'

'Me, too,' said O'Fagin. 'But that was a long time ago. On my wedding night.'

'Then things went altogether quiet and I didn't like that at all.'

'Exactly the same as my wedding night.'

'Dry-roasted nuts will be fine,' said Mr Giggles.

'We don't have any dry-roasted nuts,' said O'Fagin.

'Eh?' went Jonny.

'Sorry,' said O'Fagin. 'Only thinking aloud. Tell you what, I have to serve that strange-looking fellow over there who's been bobbing up and down for the last five minutes. This is the letter, have a look.'

And with that said he thrust the letter at Jonny and went off to serve the bobber.

'Are you a homosexual?' Jonny heard him ask.

'Same letter?' asked Mr Giggles.

Jonny examined the publican's letter. 'Same letter,' he said. "Present yourself to da-da-de-da-da." Just the same as mine.'

'We'd better get a head start on him, then,' said Mr Giggles. 'We don't want to be last in the line when there's prizes to be had. If you've had this letter and he's had this letter, then probably damn near everyone else in the borough has had the same letter, too. You'd better get a move on if you want to be a winner.'

'So what is this "da-da-de-da-da", then?'

Mr Giggles sighed. 'I would have thought it was pretty obvious,' he said. 'In order to win the prize, all you have to do is work that out.'

'So the letter is itself the competition?'

'Precisely. And all you have to do is work out the answer – crack the code, as it were.'

'Crack the Da-da-de-da-da Code?'

'In a nutshell, yes.'

Jonny Hooker mulled over the concept. It was possible that every household in the borough *had* received such a letter. It was possible that someone in every household would attempt to crack the code and win whatever prize there was to be won.

And so what might possibly make *him*, Jonathan Hooker, twenty-seven years of age and, as his mother reliably informed the vicar each week after the Sunday service, 'more stone-bonkered than a handbag full of owls', think that *he* would have the remotest hope of winning whatever there was to possibly be won?

Absolutely no chance whatever, was the obvious conclusion.

Jonny Hooker mulled it over and, having done so, arrived at a decision that would inevitably prove fatal.

'I'll do it,' said Jonathan Hooker. 'I'll crack the Da-da-de-da-da Code.'

4

'So how do we go about cracking this code?' asked Jonny, a few minutes later. In the company of his non-corporeal companion, Mr Giggles the Monkey Boy, three-quarters of a pint of King Billy and a packet of fancy nuts, which O'Fagin had discovered hanging upon a card that he never knew he had (so to speak). Jonny had repaired to a dark and mysterious corner of The Middle Man's saloon bar.

'It's rather dark and mysterious in this particular corner,' observed Mr Giggles, settling his hairy self upon a barstool. 'There are many legends attached to this public house, and this particular dark and mysterious corner in particular, as I'm sure you know.'

'I don't care,' said Jonny. 'In fact, I'm not interested at all.'

'It is a fact well known to those who know it well,' continued Mr Giggles, 'that it was in this very dark and mysterious corner that the legendary blues singer Robert Johnson recorded his thirtieth composition.'

Jonny Hooker supped at his beer. 'Robert Johnson, the King of the Delta Blues, never came to England and he never recorded a thirtieth composition. He recorded twenty-nine compositions and *that* is a fact well known to those who know it well. And I am one of those who do.'

''Twere it only so,' said Mr Giggles, helping himself to nuts.

''Tis so,' said Jonny. 'Now give me some of those nuts.'

Mr Giggles passed them over. Or appeared to. Or didn't at all, because he didn't exist. Or whatever.

'They're a tad too fancy for my taste, anyway,' he said. 'But this is definitely where Johnson made his final recording. You can still see his initials faintly visible, carved there in the table top. Beside the burn marks.' And Mr Giggles crossed himself and kissed an invisible rosary.

Jonny Hooker glanced at the table; there were many scratchings to be seen upon its sullied surface. A couple of them did look a bit like an 'R' and a 'J'.

'He never came to England,' said Jonny.

'He did too,' said Mr Giggles. 'I knew him well.'

'I thought you were *my* imaginary friend,' Jonny said. 'I thought *I* thought you up.'

'You thought me *back*,' said Mr Giggles. 'I've been around on and off for many a year.'

'Madness never dates, eh?' Jonny downed the last of his beer.

'I go where I'm needed,' said Mr Giggles. 'And I haven't always looked like this. When I knew Johnson, I was a great big buck-toothed n★★★★r.'★

'I don't think you're supposed to say "that" word anymore,' said Jonny.

'Oh, pardon me, do. But n★★★★r I was, and my dental work was a veritable disgrace.'

'Is this really leading anywhere?' Jonny asked. 'Because I thought we were setting to to crack the Da-da-de-da-da Code, so that I might avail myself of whatever wealth there is for the taking.'

'Money can't buy you happiness,' said Mr Giggles.

'That is a supposition I would like to test through experience,' said Jonny. 'And seeing as I am really miserable now, I do not believe that a great deal of money could possibly make things worse rather than better.'

'So,' said Mr Giggles, 'about Robert Johnson.'

'I don't want to hear about Robert Johnson. Robert Johnson cannot possibly have anything to do with me cracking the Da-da-de-da-da Code.'

'I would hardly have brought him up if he wasn't relevant.'

Jonny Hooker tapped his empty glass upon the table. 'You are a liar,' he declared. 'All you ever do is distract and confuse me. I try to think straight, to get my life on track, to be like other people—'

Mr Giggles giggled.

★ It is to be suspected that Mr Giggles is using the dreaded racist 'N' word. But this of course is *not* the case. Because I, for one, have no wish to do what is now called a 'Jade Goody' (allegedly).

'And you interrupt me!' Jonny glared. 'Like that! You're in my head, talking your toot, keeping me out of kilter.'

'I'm like the brother you never had.'

'But I *do* have a brother. Only he won't speak to me because I'm a nutter who's always talking to himself.'

'I'm like a *different* brother that you never had. A far nicer one, with a smiley face.' Mr Giggles smiled at Jonny, his pointy teeth a-twinkle in the gloom. 'So do you want to hear the legend, or not?'

'And it's relevant, is it?'

'Bound to be,' said Mr Giggles. 'Bound to be.'

Jonny Hooker returned to the bar, where he purchased a further pint of King Billy, then he returned to the dark and mysterious corner.

'Are you sitting comfortably?' asked Mr Giggles.

Jonny Hooker sat down and nodded.

'Then I'll begin.'

And with that he did.

'As you must know,' said Mr Giggles, 'the legend of Robert Johnson runs to this. He was a not particularly good blues singer and guitarist way down in the Delta in the US of A, way back in the nineteen thirties. And, as legend has it, he went down to the crossroads at midnight with a black cat's bone in his hand and sold his soul to the Devil. The Devil appeared, in the shape of a big, well-dressed black man, and he retuned Robert Johnson's guitar. And after that Robert Johnson became the greatest blues guitarist of them all. When Keith Richards first heard recordings of Johnson, he asked who the other fellow was who was playing guitar accompaniment. But Johnson did the whole lot on his own, in one take with no overdubs, which Richards considered impossible because you can't finger all those notes that he did at the same time. But then, you see, after Johnson had sold his soul to the Devil, he always played with his back to the audience. And folk who were backstage and took a little peep swore that he now had six fingers on his left hand.'

'But he never came to England,' said Jonny.

'Did too,' said Mr Giggles. 'Please listen, if you will. The accepted story is that Robert Johnson recorded just twenty-nine songs during his lifetime, before dying mysteriously at the age of twenty-seven.

But this is not so. Robert Johnson recorded thirty songs. He was contracted to do so by the Devil. Like Judas's thirty pieces of silver, so Johnson had his thirty pieces of shellac.'

'So whatever happened to the thirtieth recording?' Jonny asked.

'Aha,' said Mr Giggles. 'Listen and you'll learn. After Johnson had recorded twenty-nine songs, he knew he had just one more to do and then the Devil would come for his soul. So he did a runner – he fled from America and came here to England. He stayed upstairs at this very pub.'

'Go on,' said Jonny. 'He didn't, did he?'

'He did,' said Mr Giggles. 'He convinced himself that he had outsmarted the Devil. Had outrun him. That the Devil would never find him here in England. But he did have his weaknesses. You see, he liked to drink and he liked the ladies. And one night, in nineteen thirty-eight, he was sitting here half-gone with the drink, carving his initials on a table, when a beautiful young woman walked in. She was a wonderful creature and Johnson was entranced. He wanted her and he engaged her in conversation. To cut a long story short, she agreed to have sex with him on condition that he sang her a song that she didn't know. So he took up his guitar and sang one of his songs. But she sang along with it – she knew it. So he tried another and she knew that, too. He ran right through all of his twenty-nine songs. She knew them all. And she got up to leave. But he couldn't let her, there was something about her that fascinated him too much. So he said, "I'll sing you a song that you don't know. You can't know it, because I've never sung it before." And he sang his thirtieth song.'

'And when he'd finished she turned into the Devil and whisked him off to Hell,' said Jonny Hooker. 'Even *I* could see that one coming.'

'Oh,' said Mr Giggles. 'Was it *that* obvious?'

Jonny Hooker nodded. 'It's still a good story, though,' he said.

'That's not the end of it,' said Mr Giggles. 'You see, I was here on that terrible night – I was Johnson's non-corporeal companion. And when he sang the thirtieth song, I recorded it.'

'*You* recorded it?' Jonny did blinkings at Mr Giggles. 'You mean that you actually have Robert Johnson's thirtieth recording? It must be worth millions of pounds. Where is it?'

'Ah,' said Mr Giggles. 'I don't have it any more. And I'm glad that I don't, I can tell you. You see, there's something on that recording that shouldn't be on any recording. Terrible thing, so it is.'

'Go on.'

'Well, as *you* figured out, the beautiful young woman was really the Devil in disguise and when Johnson finished his song, the Devil claimed him. And as he claimed him, the Devil laughed. A hideous, inhuman, ghastly, godless laugh. And it got recorded on the record.'

'The Devil's laughter?' Jonny shivered.

Mr Giggles nodded hairily. 'Now,' said he 'as you are probably aware, it is the habit of legendary musicians to die at the age of twenty-seven. Johnson died at twenty-seven. And after him we have Johnny Kidd, out of Johnny Kidd and the Pirates, Pig Pen out of the Grateful Dead. Brian Jones, Jim Morrison, Janis Joplin, Jimi Hendrix, Kurt Cobain – the list goes on. They all died aged twenty-seven. It is *not* a coincidence. You see, they all had one thing in common: they were all Robert Johnson fans. And each of them, in their twenty-seventh year, got to hear something that they shouldn't have heard. They got to listen to Robert Johnson's thirtieth record. And they heard the Devil's laughter. And if you hear the Devil's laughter—'

'You die,' said Jonny Hooker. 'You die.'

'That's what you do,' said Mr Giggles. 'Horrible business, eh?'

'Horrible,' said Jonny. 'But wait,' said Jonny. 'What about the recording?' said Jonny. 'Where is it now?' said Jonny, also.

'Where indeed? It wasn't to be found amongst the personal effects of the late Mister Cobain, or so I am informed. I am also informed that a certain secret government agency set out to find it. This certain agency has apparently been searching for it for years.'

Jonny Hooker shook his head. 'I will just bet,' he said, 'that there is not a single word of truth to any of that. I really, truly hate you, so I do.'

'No you don't, you love me, really.'

Jonny Hooker shook his head again and found that his glass was empty once more. Although unaccountably so, as he did not recall emptying it. Grumbling grimly, he returned once more to the bar counter.

O'Fagin was affixing up a poster to the wall.

'What's that?' asked Jonny, feigning interest.

'Blues Night on Tuesday,' said O'Fagin. 'Local bands. You should come along – you play guitar, don't you?'

'I do,' said Jonny. 'Regularly, in here, on Heavy Metal Nights. But I don't know of any decent blues bands round here.'

'I never said they were decent,' said O'Fagin. 'I only said they were local.'

'I never even knew you had Blues Nights here,' said Jonny, offering his glass for a refill.

'Haven't for years,' said O'Fagin, receiving Jonny's glass. 'My daddy started them back in the nineteen thirties, but there was a bit of bother, so he stopped them.'

'Bit of bother?' said Jonny. 'Fights in the bar and suchlike?'

'Something like that,' said O'Fagin, crossing himself and drawing Jonny's pint. Which was no mean feat, as he did both with a single hand. 'But all the greats played The Middle Man. See that faded photo up there?' And he did head-gesturings. 'That's my daddy here in the bar. And Robert Johnson with him.'

5

'You left that beer undrunk,' said Mr Giggles. 'Right there on the bar counter, you left it.'

'I paid for it,' said Jonny, and he strode on up the road.

'But why did you leave it? Why did you leave it?' Mr Giggles danced at Jonny's side.

The sun shone down and birdies gossiped in the treetops. A lady in a straw hat, waiting at the bus stop, watched the young man striding by and talking to himself.

'Sad,' said she, to herself.

'Just leave it, Mister Giggles,' said Jonny. 'Just leave it.'

'But why did you leave your pint?'

Jonny ceased his striding and glared at Mr Giggles. 'You did it,' he said. 'I know you did it.'

'Did what? What?'

'Blues Night at The Middle Man! That photo behind the bar! I've drunk in that pub for years and I've never seen that photo before.'

'So you're implying that *I* somehow brought it into being?'

'It's what you do to mess me up. Why won't you leave me alone?'

'Because you need me, Jonny, that's why. You need me, Jonny, you do.'

'I *don't* need you. I don't *want* you. I just want my own mind. I want to think my own thoughts, make my own choices.'

'You wouldn't be able to manage on your own.'

'Other people do!'

'Other people are not like you. Let's go back to the pub.'

'No,' said Jonny. 'I'm going to the park.'

'I don't like the park,' said Mr Giggles. 'The grass smells bad because the dogs all wee on it.'

'Then I will go on my own. *Please* let me go on my own.'

'You might get lost or something. I'd best come along.'

'One day,' said Jonny, 'one day I will drive you out of my head.'

'I really hope for your sake that you don't.'

'And what is *that* supposed to mean?'

'It means,' said Mr Giggles, 'that *I* am the lesser of a great many evils. If you were to drive me out, there's just no telling who or what might take up occupation in my absence.'

Jonny felt a nasty shiver creeping up his spine.

'I'm going to the park,' he said.

Gunnersbury Park is a beautiful park. Just off the Chiswick round-about, if you're coming up the A4, it boasts many facilities: two miniature nine-hole golf courses (pitch-and-putt), two bowling greens, five cricket pitches, one hockey pitch, thirty-six football pitches, six netball pitches, three rugby pitches, one lacrosse pitch, two putting greens, fifteen hard tennis courts, a two-and-a-half-acre fishing pond, an ornamental boating pond, a riding school, dressing rooms and refreshment pavilions.

Add to this the 'Big House', a museum packed with many wonders, a Japanese garden, a Doric temple, an orangery and several Gothic follies.

And it's open every day of the year except Christmas Day, and you can even get married in the grounds. *And* visit Princess Amelia's Bath House. But more about her later.

So it's well worth a visit.

Jonny sat by the ornamental boating pond smoking a hand-rolled ciggy and wearing the Trinidad and Tobago World Cup football shirt he had purchased from a charity shop, but which, along with any description of himself, had escaped previous mention. Across from him, on the west shore, a park ranger named Kenneth Connor (who was not under any circumstances to be confused with the other Kenneth Connor) dragged a shopping trolley up from the water's edge and muttered swear words underneath his breath.

'All that Robert Johnson stuff,' said Jonny, 'all that *was* just a story, wasn't it? There isn't really a thirtieth record with the Devil's laughter on it, is there?'

'Don't you believe in the Devil?'

'I've never really thought about it.'

'Now who's the liar? You think about things like God and the Devil all the time.'

'I don't think the Devil exists.'

'Tricky one, that,' said Mr Giggles. 'You know what they say: that the greatest trick the Devil ever played was to convince people of his nonexistence. That and to get Boy George to the top of the charts, of course.'

'So is the story true, or is it not?'

'It depends what you mean by "true".'

'Does it? Well, let us accept that what I mean by the word "true" is "what actually happened".'

'Sounds a bit ambiguous,' said Mr Giggles, crossing his eyes and sticking out his tongue.

'It is not ambiguous,' said Jonny. 'Something either happened, or it didn't.'

'If only it were as simple as that.'

'It is,' said Jonny. 'And by your prevarication, I think it safe to assume that it was *not* a true story.'

'Well, you'd know,' said Mr Giggles, 'because if I don't exist, it means that *you* made up the story. So *is* it true, or not?'

Jonny Hooker ground his teeth.

'We should go back to the pub,' said Mr Giggles. 'You could get very drunk and we could have a really good metaphysical discussion. Talk some really splendid toot. And you could tell me how I'm your bestest friend, again.'

Jonny fished a scrunched-up piece of paper from his pocket. 'I am going to apply myself to this,' he said. 'The curious silence that both myself and O'Fagin experienced. The pregnant pause. It must mean something. I have nothing else to do with my life, so I will apply myself to this.'

'Bravely said.'

'And since you will not leave me alone, you can help me.'

'I already did. I identified "da-da-de-da-da" as music and I told you a pertinent story about Robert Johnson.'

Jonny Hooker rumpled his brow and puffed on his cigarette. 'Blues music is particularly da-da-de-da-da-de-da-da-de-da-da-de-da-da-da-da-da.'

'Then you're definitely on the right track. You'll probably have it sorted by teatime.'

'You think so?'

'Oh look,' said Mr Giggles, 'there appears to be a small child there, drowning in the pond. He must have fallen out of a paddle boat.'

'Why would you want to distract me?' asked Jonny. 'I thought you were really trying to help.'

'There really *is* a small child drowning,' said Mr Giggles. And he pointed.

Jonny followed the direction of the hairy pointer. Somewhere near the middle of the pond and quite out of reach of the nearest paddle boat, someone small was splashing frantically.

'It *is* a child,' cried Jonny. 'Someone's drowning there,' he shouted. 'Man overboard,' he bawled at the top of his voice. 'Someone do something.'

But nobody did. The paddlers kept on paddling and the strollers-past strolled on.

'A child's drowning!' shouted Jonny. 'You in the boat, there – behind you.'

'You'd best dive in,' said Mr Giggles, 'swim out there, save that child.'

'You think so?'

'No, *I don't*. You're a rubbish swimmer, you'd probably drown.'

'But someone has to do *something*.' Jonny Hooker was kicking off his shoes.

'Oh no,' said Mr Giggles. 'Don't be silly now, Jonny.'

'You drew my attention to it.'

'I thought it would cheer you up.'

'What?'

'*Schadenfreude*. It's always cheering when someone's in a worse state than you are. No, hold on.'

But Jonny was now in the pond. He was wading and shouting, stumbling and falling.

Rising and stumbling on.

It wasn't deep, the ornamental pond. It only went down about three feet, even in the middle where the struggling child was. But a man can drown in two inches of water, or so we are told. And a swan's wing can break a grown man's arm and the Great Wall of China can be seen from outer space.

The boaters were now taking notice of Jonny. They were clapping their hands and laughing. None of them appeared to be noticing the drowning child at all, though.

Jonny struggled onwards, stumbling, falling, rising, pointing. Shouting, 'Drowning child!'

At last he reached the middle of the pond.

The drowning child was nowhere to be seen.

'Oh my God,' cried Jonny. 'The child's gone under. The child's gone under.'

And Jonny dived. And dived and dived again.

Ranger Connor was quite apoplectic. It didn't take much to get him going nowadays. His temper wasn't what it had been. He always seemed to be on the edge.

And now he'd got himself all wet.

And so had Ranger Hawtrey.

It had taken the two of them to drag Jonny Hooker from the pond. And Jonny had put up quite a struggle. He'd punched Ranger Connor right on the nose. Ranger Connor had retaliated with a move that Count Danté (the world's deadliest man) called the Strike of the Electric Dragon (which was named after the lightning on Venus, apparently).

Jonny Hooker was hauled ashore unconscious.

And Jonny Hooker awoke in hospital.

It was Brentford Cottage Hospital that Jonny Hooker awoke in. It's mostly for private patients now. Special patients, really.

Jonny Hooker awoke to find himself struggling. Memories returned to him. The child in the ornamental pond. A park ranger with an attitude. A vicious blow to Jonny's groin, one sufficient to put him beyond consciousness.

'Ow,' wailed Jonny. And then, 'help!'

Because he could not move. He had been secured to the bed. He was indeed held within a straitjacket.

'Help!' shouted Jonny. 'Somebody help me, please.'

A door that was closed then opened. A doctor appeared with a chart. This doctor approached Jonny's bed and viewed Jonny doubtfully.

Doubtfully?

Jonny viewed the doctor. 'Help me, please,' he said.

'We're doing everything that we can to help you,' said the doctor. And he tapped at his chart in a professional manner. 'Everything that we can.'

'I'm all tied up here,' said Jonny. 'Could you release me, please?'

'There will be time enough for that later, I'm sure.'

'The time is now,' said Jonny.

'No,' said the doctor, 'regrettably not.'

'*Not?*' asked Jonny. '*Why* not?'

'Attempted suicide,' said the doctor. 'Throwing yourself in the ornamental pond like that and assaulting the park rangers who tried to rescue you.'

'I did no such thing. There was a child drowning.'

'There was no child. There was no one but you in the pond.'

'There *was* a child.'

'*No* child.'

'Let me free,' said Jonny. 'Please let me free.'

'You do have a bit of a history of this sort of thing, don't you?' said the doctor. 'I haven't brought your notes – there are so many of them. Phew, really heavy.' And the doctor mimed carrying some really heavy notes. 'We did call your mother, though. Apparently the police had to break into your house. You'd left her upturned on the bathroom floor. But she isn't pressing charges.'

'Charges?' Jonny said.

And there was fear in his voice.

'No charges,' said the doctor. 'But she did agree that you have become a danger to yourself, and to others. And so she has had you sectioned.'

'Sectioned?' Jonny Hooker said.

'Sectioned,' said the doctor.

6

Jonny awoke the following day to find that things were quiet in his head.

Very quiet indeed.

Jonny lay, without restraints, upon a nice, neat hospital bed. It was in the 'Special Wing' of Brentford Cottage Hospital. The wing that housed the 'special cases'. Jonny had been in such wings before. He had been in *this* wing before.

Jonny rolled over and blinked towards the window. Sunlight peeped in through it. There were no bars at the window.

'Up and away, then,' said Jonny, rising from the bed and making for the window.

'Or perhaps I'll stay,' he continued, as he viewed the steely fixings and the 'High Security' etchings on the glass. The plaster around this secure window looked quite fresh and new. It had recently needed replacing when a patient, a large Red Indian, had thrown the water cooler out through the previous window.

But that was another story.

Jonny tried the door and found it locked. He returned to the bed and sat down upon it.

And then he became fully aware of just how very quiet things were inside his head.

'Mister Giggles,' said Jonny, 'are you there?'

But answer came there none.

'Mister Giggles?'

Silence. In his head. Light traffic sounds from without the window. Within the room and within his head, silence.

'Oh,' said Jonny. And then he said, 'Damn!'

'Damn, damn, damn,' went Jonny. 'Damn.'

He'd been drugged. Done up once more with the old anti-psychotics.

Jonny glanced all down at himself. Now fully *fully* aware, he was fully aware of his attire. The foolish do-up-the-back hospital smock. The identity wristlet. The – Jonny checked his left arm – the Elastoplast, beneath which he would find the puncture marks.

'I have to get out of here,' said Jonny. Taking very deep breaths. 'I'm still up for winning that prize, me,' he continued, rather startling himself as he did so, for having a sense of purpose in his life was something new to him. 'Yes, I *do* want to win that prize,' he furtherly continued. 'In fact, I am determined to do so. And in order to do so, I must certainly get out of here.'

There was a kind of simultaneous knocking, unlocking and opening of the door and a face peeped in and a voice said, 'Were you talking to somebody in here?'

'Ah,' said Jonny. 'No,' said Jonny. 'Not me, never at all.'

The face entered Jonny's room. It entered upon a head, which was secured at the neck to a body, to which in turn two pairs of standard appendages were attached. The entire ensemble was of the female persuasion. The young and sightly female persuasion.

Jonny looked up from his bed as the figure entered his room. It *was* a sightly figure and no mistake about it. Short black hair and bright-green eyes and the sweetest nose imaginable, the—

'Have to stop you there,' said the nurse, for such was she.

'Stop me where?' asked Jonny.

'You were looking at my nose and you were smiling foolishly.'

'It's a very sw—'

'Please don't say it.'

'Sweet?'

'You said it,' said the nurse. 'The bane of my life, this nose. You can't imagine what trouble it gets me into.'

'No,' said Jonny. 'I don't think I can.'

'What about my mouth?' asked the nurse.

'Very nice,' said Jonny. 'Very silent-film star, that mouth, rather Theda Bara, in fact.'

'And my tits?' The nurse drew back her shoulders and thrust her breasts forward.

'Very nice, too,' said Jonny. 'Very pert.'

'I've nice legs as well and a nice bum. And I have a tattoo on my bum.'

'This is all very good to hear,' said Jonny, who now was most perplexed. 'You are actually a nurse here, I suppose, not a patient.'

'You naughty boy. I am Nurse Hollywood. I *was* a patient, but that was years ago. I am now a fully qualified nurse, and I can assure you that there is a great deal more to me than a sweet nose.'

'I'm sure there is,' said Jonny. 'We've already touched upon the tits and the bum.'

'We'll take this no further,' said Nurse Hollywood. 'I *am* more than just a sweet nose and that is that.'

Jonny felt that this was probably very much the case, as women who boast of having tattooed bums the first time you meet them are probably, as they say, 'up for it'.

'Oh,' said Nurse Hollywood, 'and don't you go getting any ideas about me being up for it just because I mentioned that I have a tattoo on my bum.'

'As if I would,' said Jonny. 'Could you tell me where my clothes are, please?'

'I could,' said the nurse, 'but I won't. There'd be no point as you will not be allowed to wear them for a while. You're having tests this morning.'

'Are you here to test me?'

'No,' said the nurse, 'I'm here simply to introduce myself, as I will be your personal carer during your stay here. And to ask you what you'd like for breakfast.'

'Ah,' said Jonny. 'I'd like the full English if that is on the go. Two sausages, two bacon, two eggs, two toast, black pudding, beans and a fried slice.'

Nurse Hollywood clutched one of those hospital clipboards to her pert bosoms. She took up the pen that was attached to it by a string and made certain notes.

'Am I getting the full English?' Jonny asked. 'Or did I just fail one of the tests?'

'We don't like to use the "F" word here,' said Nurse Hollywood. 'Nobody fails. It's just that some take longer to succeed than others.'

'I am a very fast learner,' said Jonny. 'You'd be surprised at all the things I've learned so far. For instance, I've learned that life isn't fair, that I am a have-not and that I have absolutely no skills at all when it comes to predicting the future. However, I do remain cautiously optimistic.'

Nurse Hollywod made further notes. Something told Jonny that he was not making a particularly good first impression and that the chances of seeing that bum tattoo were getting smaller by the minute.

'I'd like you to have this,' said Nurse Hollywood, peeling an underpage from her clipboard and presenting it to Jonny.

'Your phone number?' Jonny asked.

'A questionnaire of sorts. While I fetch your breakfast, I'd like you to fill it in. Do you think you could do that for me?'

'Not without a pen,' said Jonny.

Nurse Hollywood presented Jonny with a crayon.

'No pointy objects,' said Jonny, pointedly. 'I know the drill.'

'Yes,' said the nurse, 'you do have something of a history, don't you? But things have changed quite a lot since the last time you were admitted. I think you will find that the new techniques and treatments will have a positive effect.'

Jonny said nothing, but nodded as if he agreed.

'Well, we'll see. Do what you can with the questionnaire and I'll be back with your breakfast.'

And with that she left, sweet nose, green eyes and tattooed bum to boot. As it were.

Jonny rose quietly and listened at the door. Assured that she had gone, he tried the handle. Well, there was always an outside chance that she might have forgotten to lock it.

'Naughty, naughty,' came the voice of Nurse Hollywood. Jonny returned to the bed.

Sighing and cursing by turn, he viewed the questionnaire. Of course, if Mr Giggles had been there he would have been a great help. Mr Giggles just loved such questionnaires. He was capable of coming up with some most inspired answers.

Although.

Jonny recalled the last time he'd been sectioned – five years before, and also because of his mum. He'd been given a form to fill out then and he'd taken Mr Giggles' advice. Things hadn't gone too well for Jonny after that.

But then, for now, there was no Mr Giggles. Mr Giggles' chatter had been suppressed by the drugs that now saturated Jonny's thinking parts. That chemically altered his perception. It was a *very* difficult business for Jonny, this, because although he did hate Mr Giggles (well, some of the time (well, *most* of the time)), he *really* hated being drugged up against his will. Because he knew, just *knew*, that with the drugs inside him, although he felt certain that he was thinking *straight*, he was *not*.

The drugs don't work, they make things worse.

Jonny sang this softly.

At length and at not too long a one at that, Jonny perused the questionnaire. He knew better than to ignore it, or screw it up, or eat it. Compliance was the name of the game. As it so often is, when one is all locked up.

'"List five things that you like about yourself"?' Jonny read. To himself. *Not* aloud.

Jonny could not think of *one*. So Jonny tried to think of someone that he liked, so he could list five things that he liked about them.

'This questionnaire is really beginning to depress me,' said Jonny to himself. And he thought once more of Mr Giggles. And he shrugged and made notes upon the questionnaire.

And at a length that was neither too long nor too short, but somewhere comfortably in between, there was another simultaneous knocking, unlocking and opening of the door.

And a face peeped in, and then all the rest made an entrance.

Jonny smiled up, then stopped smiling. 'Who are you?' he asked.

'I am Nurse Cecil,' said Nurse Cecil. Nurse Cecil was a very large nurse, of the *male* persuasion. He had that broken-nosed 'useful' look about him that bouncers (or door-supervisors, as they prefer to be known) have about them. He carried a tray. It did not look like a breakfast tray, as there was no breakfast upon it. Just a sort of a napkin that bulged slightly in the middle.

'Oh,' said Jonny. 'I was expecting Nurse Hollywood.'

'Nurse *who*?' said Nurse Cecil.

'Nurse Hollywood – black hair, green eyes, sweet nose. You must know the nose.'

'Know the nose,' said Nurse Cecil. Thoughtfully.

'She's getting me the full English breakfast,' said Jonny.

'I'll just bet she is,' said Nurse Cecil. 'And she'll probably want to sing "Somewhere Over the Rainbow" while she feeds it to you. Don't you think?'

'I don't think so,' said Jonny.

'No,' said Nurse Cecil. 'And nor do I. Because we do not have a Nurse Hollywood. We have no female nurses here.'

'But she gave me this questionnaire.'

And Jonny reached for the questionnaire. Which was there on the bed.

But which wasn't.

'I think we're going to have to up your medication,' said Nurse Cecil. And he removed the napkin from his tray to reveal a large and lethal-looking hypodermic.

7

It was late afternoon when Jonny next awoke. Not that he knew for certain that it *was* late afternoon. It could have been any time really for Jonny, because the room in which he now awoke did *not* own to a window. It was a windowless room.

In fact, it was more of a cell, really.

In fact, it *was* a cell.

A padded cell.

Good and proper.

Padded walls and padded door and padded floor as well. A single light bulb somewhat above. And all hope sinking fast.

'Oh great,' said Jonny. 'This is *just* great.' And he said it loudly, then shushed himself. The cell was probably bugged – most of them were nowadays.

Well, at least he wasn't in restraints.

He wasn't in a straitjacket.

Which was something. Although not very much, considering. Jonny's stomach rumbled loudly. Jonny tried to shush it. But he *was very hungry*.

Jonny, who had been lying where he'd been left, flat on his back in the centre of the cell, rose unsteadily to his feet. He had that terrible post-medication hangover effect: all the pain, whilst not having previously experienced all of the pleasure. Jonny's knees were shaky and his mouth was dry. Things really weren't going his way at the moment. Not that they ever really went his way, but what had brought all this lot on was anyone's guess. *He* hadn't done anything. *He* had tried to rescue a drowning child. *He* was an innocent man. And given that this was a loony wing – although of course they would never use the 'L' word – he really didn't qualify to be here. He was no more loony now than he ever had been. And the amount of loony that he ever had been was insufficient to merit him being banged up in here now. So to speak.

It wasn't fair. It just wasn't fair.

And then Jonny recalled that he had already learned that life wasn't fair. And so this unjust confinement was not teaching him anything he didn't already know.

But, God, was he hungry.

Jonny took himself over to the padded door and addressed the little sliding shutter jobbie. 'Excuse me,' he said, in as polite a fashion as he could manage, 'is there someone there? I'd really like to speak to a doctor, if it would be convenient for one to speak to me.'

The little shutter shot instantly open. The face of Nurse Cecil grinned through it.

'Hello, Sunshine,' said Nurse Cecil. 'Up and about again, are we?'

'Could I please speak to a doctor?' asked Jonny.

'But of course,' said Nurse Cecil. 'I'll see to it at once.'

And he slammed shut the grille.

And he turned off Jonny's light.

And time can pass slowly in a padded cell with the light off.

But presently, when afternoon had become evening, although Jonny was not, of course, to know this, the door to Jonny's padded cell opened and he was beckoned to accompany Nurse Cecil on a little walk to somewhere.

Although sadly *not* the canteen.

These offices are always the same, no matter the hospital. A desk, two chairs, bookshelves with the inevitable textbooks. A file of Rorschach ink-blots. The big, big file of the patient. An object of interest or two, perhaps a plastic human skull or a phrenology head (out of the reach of the patient, of course).

And a certain smell. A certain medical smell. Which somehow conjures images of Nazi concentration camp experiments. Somehow.

Jonny shivered as he was thrust by Nurse Cecil into this office. Behind the desk sat an earnest-looking fellow in a white coat. He was tinkering at the keyboard of that other thing that all these offices, indeed all offices everywhere, has nowadays.

The computer.

'I'll never get the hang of this,' said the earnest-looking fellow. 'Do sit down, please,' and he consulted the big, fat file upon his desk. 'Mister Hooker.'

Jonny Hooker sat down.

'You may leave us, Nurse Cecil.'

'Wouldn't hear of it, sir,' said the male nurse. 'Leave you alone with this raving maniac? It's more than my job's worth.'

'I'm sure Mister Hooker is not going to cause any bother. Are you, Mister Hooker?'

Jonny Hooker shook his head. 'Definitely not,' he said. 'Do you think that Nurse Cecil might go to the canteen and fetch me something to eat? I haven't eaten in twenty-four hours, at least.'

Moonlight shone through the uncurtained window. Jonny's timing guesswork was right.

'Please get Mister Hooker some supper, would you, Nurse Cecil?'

Nurse Cecil grunted in the affirmative and grudgingly left the office, slamming the door behind him.

'A willing enough fellow, really,' said the chap behind the desk, 'but not the brightest star in the firmament. My name is Doctor Archy. You may call me Doctor Archy.'

'Pleased to meet you,' said Jonny. Who wasn't.

'I have you in here,' said Dr Archy, tapping some more at his computer keyboard. 'The trouble is that I just can't get at you. You're on the database. You'd be surprised at all the information there is on here about you.'

No I wouldn't, thought Jonny. 'Really?' he said. 'Might I have a glass of water?' he continued. 'My mouth is really dry.'

'Of course, of course. There's a machine thing over there with paper cups, help yourself.'

Jonny turned in his chair and noticed the other thing that these offices always have: the little water cooler jobbie. They also have the box of tissues, for when you're having a good cry. But Jonny hoped that he would not be needing the box of tissues. He rose from his chair, passed by the open window – making a mental note of just how open it was, and how open it would need to be for him to shin out of it – and took himself over to the water cooler.

'So much information,' said Dr Archy. 'Too much, some might

say. Or the wrong information. Or information parading, indeed masquerading, as information when it is anything but. If you understand my meaning.'

Jonny turned from his water-cup filling. Eyes met across the office.

Jonny shrugged in as non-committal a way as he could manage. 'Thank you for the water,' he said, and he drank from the cup and refilled it.

'I understand your feelings,' said Dr Archy when Jonny, with water-filled cup, had returned to the patients' chair. 'You're being cautious. You do not wish to say anything that might incriminate you in any way. Give the impression that there is something, how might I put this, *wrong* about you.'

'Politeness costs nothing,' said Jonny. 'That's what my mum always says.'

'Ah yes,' said Dr Archy. 'Your mother. Tell me about your mother.'

Which rang a bell somewhere.

'I think,' said Jonny, 'that I must be a terrible disappointment to her.'

'You love your mother?'

'Everyone loves their mother,' said Jonny.

'Interesting reply.' The doctor tapped some more at the keyboard of his computer. 'This business with the drowning child,' he said. 'How do you feel about that now?'

'I can't say,' said Jonny.

'Can't?' said the doctor, raising his eyes.

'I have been medicated,' said Jonny. 'I cannot be certain of anything.'

'Nurse Cecil told me that you hallucinated a female nurse this morning.'

'Apparently so,' said Jonny. 'I can't explain it. She did seem very real.'

'But now you know that she was not?'

'How can she have been?'

'Good,' said the doctor.

There was a knocking and an opening. Nurse Cecil appeared, bearing Jonny's supper on a tray. He placed this tray on Jonny's lap.

'Salad,' he said. 'You did say that you were a vegetarian.'

'Did you?' asked the doctor, raising his eyebrows.

'Yes,' said Jonny, who knew better than to argue. 'Just this week. You won't have it on your records.'

'Enjoy,' said Nurse Cecil. And, grinning, he left the office.

Jonny Hooker viewed his supper. Lettuce and uncooked vegetable stuff and a glass of tomato juice.

'Mm,' went Dr Archy. 'Looks yummy. Do tuck in.'

Jonny Hooker tucked into his salad. As a hungry man will do.

'Ah,' said the doctor, still tapping at his keyboard, 'something coming up here, I think. Ah yes – it says here that you have developed a recent compulsion to enter competitions.'

Jonny Hooker looked up from his salad, a spring onion stuck between his lips like a green cigarette. 'What?' he mumbled, with his mouth full.

'You are apparently trying to crack the Da-da-de-da-da Code. What would that be all about, then?'

Jonny Hooker's jaw hung slack.

'That's not a very good look,' said Dr Archy. 'I think you should swallow before you open your mouth like that.'

Jonny munched and then swallowed. '*That* is on your computer?' he asked. 'That *I* have entered a competition? But I haven't done it officially. I have decided to do so, that's all.'

'I told you that you'd be surprised by what's on here. You do *look* surprised.'

'I'm amazed,' said Jonny. 'And also rather concerned.'

'Why so?'

'Because—' Jonny paused before saying more. Indeed, he now intended to say no more. He knew full well, because. Because it meant that he had been 'observed', 'listened in to'. That he was under surveillance. How else could that piece of information about himself be on the doctor's computer?

'Because?' said Dr Archy.

'Nothing,' said Jonny. 'Do you think I might have a look at this computer entry about myself?'

'Not permitted, I'm afraid,' said Dr Archy.

'No, I rather thought not.'

Jonny forked the last of his salad into his mouth and munched upon it. Plastic knife and fork, he noted. No weapon potential there. Dr Archy smiled towards Jonny. Jonny smiled back at the doctor.

And then Jonny leapt from his chair, paper plate and cup of juice all spilling to the floor. He swung the computer monitor around. The screen was blank. The computer wasn't switched on.

And Jonny cocked his head on one side and smiled at the doctor. And then swung his fist with a good wide swing and clocked that doc full-face. And the doctor fell back in a flurry of case notes.

And Jonny leapt out of the window.

8

Jonny Hooker awoke with a head full of noise.

A head full of noise and a very damp constitution.

He blinked in the daylight and took in the leaves and the grass and the sky and the hedgehog. The hedgehog sidled away and Jonny clasped at his naked arms and felt a little confused.

Slowly, but shuffled and dealt as if playing cards, memories of the previous evening returned to him. Jonny sorted these memories into their separate suits.

The Special Wing of the hospital. Nurse Hollywood. The padded cell. Nurse Cecil. The interview with Dr Archy. Dr Archy's knowledge of Jonny's doings. Jonny's escape through the window. A horrid chase up the Ealing Road. The outrunning of his pursuers. The scaling of the gates of Gunnersbury Park. The hiding out in the mulberry bush.

The waking up in the morning now, all damp, in the mulberry bush.

And a head full of noise, noise, noise.

'Da–da–de–da–da! Da–da–de–da–da! Da–da–de–da–da!'

'Stop it!' shouted Jonny, and he pressed his fists to his temples. Then, 'Keep it down,' he told himself. 'But stop with the "da–da–de–da–das".'

'Would you prefer a couple of fol–de–rols and a twiddly–diddly–de?' asked Mr Giggles the Monkey Boy. 'This is rather rubbish accommodation, even for you.'

'The drugs have worn off, then,' said Jonny Hooker, 'and I am cursed once more with you.'

'And you should be glad to have me. See the trouble you get yourself into when you're on your own? Medication and a padded cell and a nice plate of salad for your supper.'

'I escaped,' said Jonny. 'I didn't need your help. And it was all your fault that I ended up there in the first place. Drowning child? There *was* no drowning child!'

'You saw the drowning child with your own eyes.'

'We both know that I cannot trust the evidence of my own eyes.'

'I suspect that you're being personal again. But no matter. It's a beautiful day – how do you plan that we spend it?'

Jonny Hooker made an exasperated face. 'Look at me,' he said. 'I'm wearing nothing but a hospital smock. I am officially an escaped mental patient. They'll have my picture in the papers and on the news.'

'You'd better keep your head down, then. That would be my advice.'

'Oh, sound advice, thank you very much.'

'I do detect a certain tone in your voice.'

'I'm starving,' said Jonny. 'I'm starving and I'm freezing to death.'

'Then you must be fed and warmed. My advice would be to hide out here in the park until things calm down a bit. Back in the days when Sir Henry Crawford owned the mansion here, he employed an ornamental hermit to adorn the grounds. The hermit was allowed a Bible for his spiritual sustenance and access to the kitchen garden for vegetables, which he was required to consume raw. He wore a rabbit-skin surcoat and boots made from bark and—'

'Please be quiet,' said Jonny. 'I have no wish to live the life of a hermit, ornamental or otherwise.'

'You were pretty much a hermit anyway. Living rough and foraging for your own food will be character-building. And you know what they say: a healthy body makes a healthy minefield.'

Jonny had long ago given up on the thankless task of taking a swing at Mr Giggles. 'Perhaps,' said he, 'I will just return to the hospital. The bed was comfy enough and I'm sure I could come to some arrangement with Nurse Cecil that would involve me being fed at regular intervals.'

'A tree house,' said Mr Giggles.

'What?'

'You could build a tree house, here in the park, high up a tree and camouflaged. And there's loads of fish in the ornamental pond. You could catch fish at night. And you could rig up ropes between the trees, swing from one to another, like Tarzan.'

Jonny had always liked Tarzan.

'I've always liked Tarzan,' he said.

'Really?' said Mr Giggles. 'Fancy that.'

'No,' said Jonny. '*Not* a tree house. Although, perhaps ... I wonder what time it is.'

And, as if in answer to his question, the distant clock on the spire of St Mary's chimed the seventh hour.

'I have an idea,' said Jonny.

The park rangers' hut was nothing much to look at from the outside. It was one of those horrid Portakabin affairs, of the variety that working men rejoice to inhabit on building sites. There is always the suggestion about such huts that dark and sinister things go on inside them.★

The park rangers' hut lurked behind trees to the north of Gunnersbury House. The trees were many and various. There were the standard oak, ash and elm, sycamore and horse chestnut, but this being Gunnersbury Park, a park which, it must be said, had, over the years, been owned and landscaped and planted and tended by one rich weirdo after another, some of the trees that prettified the place were of the 'odd' persuasion. You don't see moosewood every day – well, not hereabouts anyhow – nor too much in the way of monkey puzzle. And there were sequoias, cornels, dogwoods, ilex, sal and Papuan minge trees, in considerable abundance.

The monkey puzzle having been planted during Princess Amelia's residence, the minge trees during that of Sir Henry Crawford. Who, being a member of the aristocracy, was never averse to a bit of minge in his ornamental garden.

Jonny drew Mr Giggles' attention to the monkey puzzle tree.

Mr Giggles pointedly ignored it.

The park rangers' hut was locked.

'You'll have to smash a window,' said Mr Giggles.

'Which is where you are wrong,' said Jonny, and he rooted

★ No? It must just be me, then.

around and about the door. Presently he upturned a flowerpot to disclose the keys that were hidden beneath. 'Nice as ninepence,' said Jonny.

'What?'

Jonny opened up the door and had a peep within. 'Splendid,' he was heard to say, and he made his way inside.

And presently, at a time not too far distant from his entrance, Jonny Hooker emerged from the park rangers' hut wearing the uniform, cap and boots of a Gunnersbury park ranger. 'How about *that*?' he said to Mr Giggles.

'Positively inspired,' said the Monkey Boy. 'Now I suggest that you run like the wind before the real park rangers arrive.'

'No,' said Jonny. 'I won't.'

'They will catch you and bring you to book.'

'They won't.'

'They gave you a pretty sound walloping when they dragged you out of the pond.'

'They won't recognise me,' said Jonny.

'What?'

So how exactly does it work, or rather why does it not? You can go into that shop week after week, month after month, and get served by the same person, or be on the same bus every day and have your ticket clipped by the same bus conductor. But pass the shop assistant or the conductor in the street, when they are out of uniform and not in the environment that you have come to associate them with . . .

And you don't recognise them!

What is *that* all about?★

But whatever it *is* all about, it works the other way round.

Put someone you know well into a uniform and you hardly recognise them. Freaky, isn't it?

'So your theory is that you will not be recognised because you are wearing a uniform?' said Mr Giggles.

★ Oh come on! It's not just me, surely?

'In as many words,' said Jonny. 'Although, of course, I do not recall uttering any to that effect.'

Jonny dusted down the sleeves of his uniform and squared up his shoulders. The uniform fitted him rather well, and it rather suited him, too.

'I think I cut something of a dash,' said he.

'It's a shame the Village People split up,' said Mr Giggles. 'You'd have looked right at home amongst them. So much the bum-bandit, you look.'

'Bum-bandit?' said Jonny. 'How dare you.'

'I dare,' said Mr Giggles. 'I use the word "n****r". Trust me, *I dare.*'

'Aha,' said Jonny, hastily relocking the hut door and returning the key to its flowerpot bower. 'I hear approaching footsteps.'

And so Jonny did. The approaching footsteps of Messrs Kenneth Connor and Charles Hawtrey. Charles was whistling 'Birdhouse In Your Soul' (the They Might Be Giants classic). Kenneth was accompanying the whistle by laying down a percussive track involving a rolled-up newspaper and his right trouser leg.

And then.

'Well, hello,' said Kenneth Connor. 'Who is this?'

Jonny Hooker stood to attention. 'David Chicoteen, *sir*,' said he. And he offered a salute.

'At ease, Mister Chiocteen,' said Kenneth Connor, but he couldn't help but return the salute.

'David Chicoteen?'★ said Mr Giggles. 'Who he?'

'Student,' said Jonny to Ranger Connor. 'Studying for a degree in—' He paused. 'Park rangering,' he ventured. 'Sent here for work experience, told to report to you directly. To take my orders directly from you and you alone.'

'Me?' asked Ranger Connor. 'Me, personally?'

'The senior ranger,' said Jonny, choosing his words with care. 'You carry yourself with authority. I am certain that I have the right man.'

Ranger Hawtrey made a face. Ranger Connor did some puffing up.

•

★ Cheeky little anagram involved here, if you can be bothered to work it out.

'Well,' said he, 'you do indeed have the right man. Splendid. I have asked them at the Big House again and again for another man. But what do I get? Cutbacks here, cutbacks there. You are a veritable blessing, young Chicoteen.'

'Chicoteen?' said Ranger Hawtrey. 'What kind of name is that?'

'A rubbish one,' said Mr Giggles.

'Dutch, I think,' said Jonny, for who has it in for the Dutch?

'I went to Holland once,' said Ranger Hawtrey. 'They have a museum there, dedicated to poo.'★

'Did he just say what I think he just said?' said Mr Giggles.

Ranger Connor had unpotted the key. He opened the hut door and ushered Jonny inside. 'Our little cottage in the woods,' he said.

It *was* elegantly furnished, Jonny noted, now that he had time for more than a quick look around. There was a very nice George III mahogany sofa-table, with rounded twin-flap top and ribbed trestle supports. A delicious William IV walnut footstool with scrolling legs and brocade-padded seat. A magnificent Empire rosewood cabinet with foliate marquetry veneers. Several exquisite Queen Anne dining chairs, on shell-carved cabriole legs, and a host of other antique bits and bobbery, which lent the hut's interior the look of Lovejoy's lock-up.

Jonny viewed all this as one who had not viewed it before. 'Very nice indeed,' he said.

'Commandeered,' explained Ranger Connor, 'from the museum basement. No point leaving it all to rot down there when it can be put to good purpose here.'

'Quite so,' said Jonny.

Ranger Hawtrey switched on a small television that stood upon a Swedish ormolu-mounted kingswood, walnut and parquetry bombe commode, with a saleroom value of six to eight thousand pounds.

Ranger Connor said, 'That's odd.'

'Odd?' said Jonny.

'The armoire door is open.'

'Armoire?'

'Clothes cupboard, if you like. The French provincial-style one over there, with the cross-banded top and the boxwood stringing.

★ They do indeed. But sadly the gift shop is a bit disappointing.

We keep the spare uniforms inside it. The door's open. Odd.'

'Blimey,' said Ranger Hawtrey,' settling himself down upon one of the Queen Anne chairs. 'If you think that's odd, check *this* out.'

He pointed to the television screen. It was one of those first-thing-in-the-morning news shows. The ones hosted by uncomfortable-looking male presenters whose suits are a little too tight, and very attractive female presenters with heaving bosoms and sexy spectacles.

'Odd?' said Ranger Connor. 'What very sexy spectacles that woman's wearing,' he continued.

'Listen and look,' said Ranger Hawtrey.

'Again, this breaking news,' said an uncomfortable-looking male presenter whose suit was a little bit too tight. 'Doctor Roland Archy, head of the psychiatric unit at Brentford Cottage Hospital, was viciously murdered last night. Police are seeking escaped psychopath Jonathan Hooker, aged twenty-seven. The public are warned that this man is armed and dangerous. Do not under any circumstances approach this man.' And up flashed Jonny's photo on the screen. A nice, crisp, detailed photograph that Jonny did not recall having taken. 'If you see this man, report his whereabouts immediately to the police.'

'Ugly-looking customer,' said Ranger Kenneth Connor.

'Viciously murdered?' whispered Jonny Hooker.

'Psychopath,' said Mr Giggles. 'You're in trouble now.'

9

Ranger Hawtrey brewed a morning cuppa.

'Ranger Chicoteen' held his cup between trembling hands and supped and supped at its contents. His stomach grumbled loudly for the lack of a filling and illicited some sympathy from Ranger Hawtrey, who offered the stomach's owner half of a fresh bacon sarnie.

'Thank you,' said Jonny, chewing at the sandwich but finding the swallowing hard.

'South America would be your man,' said Mr Giggles. 'That's where all those Nazi war criminals retired to. Perhaps you could make a few subtle alterations to the uniform, pretend you're a merchant seaman and sign on with a cruise liner, or something. Then, when you get there, a few more subtle alterations and lo, you'll pass for a young Martin Bormann.'

Jonny Hooker said nothing to Mr Giggles. But Jonny's brain was buzzing like a beehive.

Viciously murdered? Jonny thought. *I only gave him a bit of a smack. This is all some terrible mistake. It's all been a terrible mistake. All of it. Everything from the arrival of that letter. Ever since I determined to crack that Da-da-de-da-da code, my whole world has turned to dirt.*

'It was dirt anyway,' said Mr Giggles, 'but it's quite exciting dirt now. I wonder what is going to happen next.'

'Switch off that television,' said Ranger Connor. 'If we see that lunatic in this park, I'll give him the hiding of his life.'

'It's *him!*' cried Ranger Hawtrey.

And Jonny's blood froze.

'It's who?' asked Ranger Connor.

'That loon,' said Ranger Hawtrey. 'The one who was in the pond the day before yesterday. The one you did the Electric Dragon move on.'

Jonny Hooker slowly crossed his legs.

'Damn me, you're right,' said Ranger Connor. 'Of course, they carted him off to the Cottage Hospital. If I'd known he was a serial killer, I'd have given him the Dimac Death-Touch.'*

'It didn't say on the news that he is a serial killer,' said Jonny, keeping his cap on and his head down.

'He probably will be by the end of the day,' said Ranger Connor. 'He'll probably go on what the Yanks refer to as a Goddamn killing spree.'

Ranger Hawtrey nodded enthusiastically 'A nun-raping, child-slaying, cocaine-fuelled, coprophiliac—'

'Eh?' said Jonny.

'Baby-strangling—' said Ranger Hawtrey.

'What?'

'Puppy-buggering—'

'Now stop it,' said Ranger Connor. 'You'll get yourself feeling all unnecessary and I'll have to throw a bucket of water over you.'

'Hanging is too good for those types,' said Ranger Hawtrey.

'Did they bring back hanging?' Jonny asked

'I wrote to the Prime Minister, suggesting it,' said Ranger Hawtrey.

'I'm seeing a rather unexpected side to you here,' said Ranger Connor. 'Off with that television and let us get down to the job in hand today.'

Ranger Hawtrey switched off the television.

'Obviously we must be particularly vigilant today and on the lookout for this maniac. We will keep in constant radio contact with our walkie-talkies. And travel in pairs.'

'But there's only three of us,' said Ranger Hawtrey.

'Improvise, boy,' said Ranger Connor.

'I'm loving this,' said Mr Giggles. 'And these lads think that *you're* a loon.'

'We'd best tool up,' said Ranger Hawtrey. 'Electric truncheons are what we'll need.'

'And you know where we can acquire electric truncheons?' asked Ranger Connor.

* Not to be confused with the Vulcan Death Grip.

'Actually, yes. I'll make a call on my mobile.'

'No, you will *not*.' Ranger Connor waggled his teacup at the younger ranger. '*I* do not need tooling up because *I* am skilled in Dimac. *You* cannot legally carry a weapon. *Although*—'

'Although?' said Ranger Hawtrey.

'It is something of a grey area, because we are on private property. You could actually carry a sword, if you wish, but not if you conceal it. Funny old thing, the law. Do you have any martial arts training, young Chicoteen?'

'Me?' Jonny, head-down, shook his head. 'But if there is any trouble, I do know how to run.'

'Hm,' went Ranger Connor. 'So, we travel in pairs, except for myself. You can carry a cudgel, Ranger Hawtrey.'

'There are some very tasty swords in the museum,' said Ranger Hawtrey. 'I could commandeer one of those.'

'A stick,' said Ranger Connor.

'*A stick?*'

'A stout stick. But enough chitchat. It is time to get off on the morning round. Master Chicoteen, you will accompany Ranger Hawtrey – he'll show you the drill today. Tomorrow I will find specific tasks to set you.'

Jonny Hooker nodded 'neath his cap.

'Right, then,' said Ranger Connor. 'Up and at it, lads. Up and at it.'

Down shone the sun and it was a beautiful day.

Jonny had never been in the park so early, and the trees and grass all dew-hung and glistening really rather moved him. When you are very ill, or very harassed, or both, you can truly see beauty in simple things. It's something to do with their purity.

Jonny Hooker sniffed at the air. 'What a wonderful smell,' said he.

'Yeah,' said Ranger Hawtrey. 'It *is* good, isn't it? There's something really special about walking around the park first thing, before it's opened to the public. It's, well, it's *untainted*, if you know what I mean.'

'I do,' said Jonny. 'Have you worked here long?'

'Five years,' said Ranger Hawtrey. 'I left school and applied to the police, but I failed the entrance exam. Have you ever wondered why people become traffic wardens?'

'Actually, yes,' said Jonny. 'I can't imagine why anyone would want to do a job that consists of little other than making people miserable.'

'They're folk who've failed the police entrance exam. The examiners know that they are not bright enough to be policemen, but they do so want a job that involves wearing a uniform and bullying the public, so—'

'So how come you didn't become a traffic warden?'

'I failed that exam as well.'

'They have an exam for *that*?'

'I didn't try very hard. Next down the line is park keeper, or park ranger as we are now rather romantically called. And I love it. Ken is a bit of a nutter, but he's got a good heart. And where else are you going to get all this?' And Ranger Hawtrey gestured all around and about.

'It *is* beautiful,' said Jonny. 'You think you'd have a go at this psycho, then? If you came face to face with him again?'

'Not without a very big sword. I'd run like a girlie.'

Jonny chuckled. And then Jonny paused. He'd just had a little chuckle there. A moment of lightness, considering the direness of his situation.

But then, perhaps that's what it was. In this beautiful park, in the earliness of the morning. Just for one moment.

'Surely you're a bit old to be a student,' said Ranger Hawtrey.

And the moment was gone.

'Failed the police exam,' said Jonny.

'No way!'

'No,' said Jonny. 'I don't really know what I'm doing with my life. I don't seem to be in control.'

'Oh, don't say that,' said Ranger Hawtrey. 'You sound like my mad brother.'

'Your mad brother?'

'Everyone seems to have a mad brother, don't they? I think it's a tradition, or an old charter, or something.'

Jonny Hooker nodded.

'My brother has this thing about machines. All kinds of machines, or appliances, really. Anything that plugs into the electric and does something. Radio, TV, iron, hair-straighteners. He gets the messages.'

'The messages?' said Jonny. Slowly.

'He says that messages are being beamed into his head through the electrical appliances. They've got his frequency.'

'They?'

'The controllers. The ones who control the folk who control us. My brother says that he's onto them, so they torment him day and night, beam these voices and images into this head.'

'He's a paranoid schizophrenic,' said Jonny.

'That's what the doctors say, yes.'

'But you don't agree?'

'I don't know. There's stuff he says that makes a lot of sense. Stuff he knows.'

'Is he your older brother?' Jonny asked.

Ranger Hawtrey nodded. And spied a stick on a grassy knoll and picked it up and waved it.

'What kind of stuff does he know?' Jonny asked.

'Mad stuff,' said Ranger Hawtrey. 'But it does make some kind of sense. He reckons it's all to do with holes. He reckons that there's another world, one that for the most part we can't see or hear. But the folk of that world can see and hear us and they love to torment us. But mostly they can't because human beings are born with these inbuilt mental screens to keep them out. It's an evolutionary thing. But some people, so-called paranoid schizophrenics, they have little holes in their mental shields and so these beasties, or demons, or whatever they are, are able to squeeze through and torment them. Drive them to do mad things. That's his theory, anyway.'

'It's a popular theory,' said Jonny.

'*It is?*'

'Amongst a certain fraction of society.'

'It's feasible,' said Ranger Hawtrey, 'if you are prepared to adopt a medieval overview of life – that the insane are indeed Devil-possessed. The thing is that that theory works just as well as any theory of mental imbalance.'

'So you believe him?'

'I don't know what to believe. But I don't think I really believe that messages are being beamed into his head via the pop-up toaster.'

They ceased their perambulations and sat down upon a bench.

Ranger Hawtrey took out a small, white contrivance from his pocket. 'New iPod,' he said. 'You can store two thousand tracks on this. Do you like They Might Be Giants?'

Jonny Hooker shrugged. 'I'm a big fan of The Lost T-shirts of Atlantis,' he said.

'Check this out.' Ranger Hawtrey stuck the tiny earbuds into his earholes, tinkered with his iPod, pulled the ear-bead jobbies from his earholes, passed the whole caboodle to Jonny and said, 'Check this out,' again.

Jonny slotted the ear-bead jobbies into the ears that were his and then pressed the appropriate button.

There was a moment of silence. In stereo. And then a voice said, 'We know where you are, Jonny. You can't hide from us.'

It was a dark and horrible voice.

It wasn't Mr Giggles.

10

Jonny Hooker tore the tiny earphones from his head. He handed back the iPod to the ranger.

'That was a bit quick,' said Ranger Hawtrey. 'You'll want to listen longer than that before you make up your mind.'

'Make up my mind.' Jonny Hooker said these words slowly. If he could make up his own mind, he would make it up out of concrete and surround the thing with steel.

'Are you all right?' asked Ranger Hawtrey. 'You seem to have gone somewhat pale.'

'I'm fine,' said Jonny, who was anything but. 'That iPod is yours, is it?'

'My brother's, actually. I gave it to him as a birthday present, but he heard the voices speaking to him from it at once. So he gave it straight back to me.'

Jonny Hooker gave Ranger Hawtrey what is known as 'the Old-Fashioned Look'.

'*What?*' said Ranger Hawtrey. 'Well, all right, yeah,' said Ranger Hawtrey. 'I'd always wanted an iPod.'

Ranger Hawtrey now took off his cap. He mopped at his brow with an oversized red gingham handkerchief. The cap lay in his lap with its insides upwards, as it were. And Jonny spied these upward innards.

'Tinfoil,' said Jonny Hooker. 'Your cap is lined with tinfoil.'

'No it's not,' said Ranger Hawtrey. Hastily replacing the cap upon his head.

'It is,' said Jonny. 'And you know it is and you know *I* know that it is.'

'Look,' said Ranger Hawtrey, 'like I say, I don't know whether my brother is mad, or whether he really *is* persecuted by hidden enemies. And if he is being persecuted by hidden enemies, whether these enemies are ghosts, or devils, or transdimensional space beings, or the bloody Air Loom Gang itself—'

'The *what*?' said Jonny.

'The Air Loom Gang. Surely you've heard of the Air Loom Gang.'

'Curiously, no.'

'No, I suppose not. I only came across them by chance when I was trawling the Internet for information about my brother's supposed medical condition. And it did all happen a very long time ago, In the seventeen nineties, as it happens, but it's interesting stuff and it made me think.'

'Go on,' said Jonny.

'There was this mental patient,' said Ranger Hawtrey, settling himself back on the bench and tucking away his oversized red gingham handkerchief. 'His name was James Tilly Matthews and he had been an English secret agent. A kind of James Bond of his day. Well, somehow or other, and I'm not entirely sure of all the details,★ he got it into his head that a certain gang had managed to actually get inside his head using a piece of equipment called the Air Loom. This contraption was an amazing bit of kit, designed and built by someone named Count Otto Black and operated by someone known as the Glove Woman. It was fuelled by all manner of noxious fumes and gases, and by the careful manipulation of its keyboard, a kind of magnetic flux or ray could be projected through solid objects like walls and suchlike into the head of their intended victim. And then his thoughts could be manipulated.'

'And this was in the seventeen nineties?' said Jonny.

'Apparently so. The first documented case of a mental patient who was convinced that his thoughts were being tampered with by an "Influencing Machine". They threw him into Saint Mary of Bethlehem Hospital, the original Bedlam. He was in there for twelve years. Lucid for most of the time, but, as with most mental institutions, if you're not mad when you go in, you'll be mad by the time they let you out. If they ever let you out.'

★ If you would like to read all the details, type *Illustrations of Madness* by John Haslam (1810) into you search-engine jobbie.

'What about your brother?' said Jonny.

'He's in the Special Wing at the Cottage Hospital,' said Ranger Hawtrey. 'And I'll tell you this: if I ever meet that loon who did for Doctor Archy, I'll shake him by the hand. That doctor treated my brother very badly.'

What a very small world it is, thought Jonny. 'But tell me more about this Air Loom,' he said. 'I'm fascinated by this. It's at least a hundred years before its time. You can almost picture someone actually building something like that in the late Victorian era, but the seventeen nineties, no way to that.'

Ranger Hawtrey shrugged. 'And so I have tinfoil inside my cap just to be on the safe side. Perhaps there was an Air Loom, perhaps the CIA and the British Secret Service have modern-day equivalents. I just don't know. I'd like to believe that my brother isn't mad, but then wouldn't anyone?'

Jonny Hooker nodded. 'Actually I have heard of Count Otto Black,' he said. 'He's some kind of unkillable supervillain who turns up again and again century after century. Or so I read somewhere. But I appreciate your candour, confiding all this to me, a total stranger.'

'I trust you,' said Ranger Hawtrey. 'Which is to say that I told you because I knew you wouldn't laugh.'

'You did? How did you know *that*?'

'I just did.' Roger Hawtrey stuck his hand out to Jonny. 'Shake?' he said.

'Shake,' said Jonny, and he shook the ranger's hand.

'And thank you for killing Doctor Archy,' said Ranger Hawtrey.

'*What?*' went Jonny, and he fell back in horror.

'I won't turn you in.'

'You recognised me?'

'Not you. Well, not at once. It was the uniform I recognised. You're wearing *my* old uniform. I figured that you'd found the key under the flowerpot, gone into the hut, found the uniform, then we turned up, so you concocted the story about being at college.'

'So you knew all along,' said Jonny.

'And I know that you're not a dangerous madman. *Did* you kill Doctor Archy, by the way?'

'No,' said Jonny, 'I didn't. I punched him and escaped through the window of his office, but I certainly didn't hit him hard enough to kill him.'

'I thought not.'

'What do you mean, you thought not? When did you think not?'

'When I saw your face come up on the television. You see, I saw the drowning child, too.'

'You did?' said Jonny. 'You did?'

'I saw it. It was there and then it wasn't. They did drag the pond to make sure, but there was no body. But I did see the child.'

'Then perhaps you're as mad as I am.'

'*I'm not* mad,' said Ranger Hawtrey. 'And nor, I suspect, are you.'

'Ah,' said Jonny. 'Well, we'd probably best not go into that in any detail. But you're not going to turn me in?'

'Certainly not. You're the most exciting thing that's happened in this park since I've been working here.'

'Thanks a lot,' said Jonny. 'But what about your boss?'

'Ranger Connor wouldn't recognise his own face in a mirror. And I reckon he's going to get sacked pretty soon. He's a bit too free with his fists. Always looking for an excuse to employ his Dimac.'

'I can vouch for that,' said Jonny.

'He's instigated a dress code for people using the park,' said Ranger Hawtrey. 'Quite unofficially, of course. If he sees some young bloke in sportswear he chucks them out of the park.'

'But surely a park is the kind of place were you *can* wear sports-wear?'

'You'd think so, wouldn't you? But he hates chavs.'

'Who doesn't?' said Jonny.

'So the park is pretty much a chav-free zone. And if they show up again after he's barred them, he gives them a sound roughing-up.'

'Part of me is starting to really like him,' said Jonny. 'Shall we stroll on?'

'Are you sure you don't want to listen to They Might Be Giants some more?'

'No,' said Jonny. 'Thank you very much. And thank you for not turning me in and thank you for your conversation. You've given me much to think about.'

★

Ranger Hawtrey and 'Ranger Chicoteen' strolled on together.

And there was quite a ruckus going on in Jonny's head. An internal dialogue, unheard and unguessed at by Ranger Hawtrey.

'We'd best get out of here,' said Mr Giggles. 'This young loon will turn you in at the first possible opportunity.'

'No he won't,' said Jonny.

'Oh yes he will. He's just waiting until they've posted a reward.'

'I'm not worried about it,' said Jonny. 'It's that voice on his iPod that worries me.'

'And what voice was that?'

'Interesting.'

'What?'

'You didn't hear it.'

'Didn't hear what? A voice? What voice?'

'I'm sure that if I find out, you will be the first to know.'

'What did it say, this voice?'

'I'm not telling you.'

'You can't have secrets from me, Jonny.'

'It would appear that I can.'

'Tell me, did you get one of these?'

'What?'

'One of these?' The voice belonged to Ranger Hawtrey.

'One of *what*?' Jonny asked.

'One of these.' And Ranger Hawtrey fished an envelope from a jacket pocket. He seemed to have *so* many things in his pockets: iPod, oversized red gingham handkerchief and now an envelope. Golly.

'It's a competition thingie,' said Ranger Hawtrey. 'Although I can't understand how exactly you win whatever it is that you win.' He opened the envelope and displayed its contents to Jonny.

Jonny laughed, which was something he rarely did. '*That*,' said he, 'is, indirectly or directly, I'm not certain which, the reason why I'm in all the trouble I'm presently in. I determined that I would crack the Da-da-de-da-da Code and win whatever there was to be won, and my life, crap as it was, has become ten times as crap since then.'

'The Da-da-de-da-da Code,' said Ranger Hawtrey. 'That would make a good name for a book.'

61

'Yeah, right,' said Jonny. 'With *me* as the hero.'

'Well, I don't know about that. But what do you think about the letter?'

'I think that I *will* crack the code,' said Jonny. 'I think that, given all that's happened to me so far, it might even be important that I do crack the code.'

'Good on you,' said Ranger Hawtrey. 'Perhaps we could work together on it.'

'No,' said Jonny. 'I don't think so. It's not that I'm greedy for whatever the prize is and unwilling to share. It's just that you could get yourself into as much trouble as me.'

'You cannot attribute your troubles directly to your search,' said Ranger Hawtrey. 'It could just be coincidence.'

'I'm not sure that I believe in coincidence.'

'All right. If you don't want my help, tell me at least how you intend to go about cracking the code.'

'Do the obvious,' said Jonny. 'Trace where the letter was printed. That might be all that's necessary to win the prize.'

'Do you really think so?' Ranger Hawtrey looked all excited.

'You look all excited,' said Jonny Hooker.

'Well, of course I do,' said Ranger Hawtrey, 'because *I* know where it was printed.'

11

'All right,' said Jonny Hooker. 'Perhaps I am prepared to give the concept of coincidence the benefit of the doubt. *You* know where the letters were printed. How do *you* know that?'

'Because they were printed right here in the park. In the museum.'

'How do you know that? Did you see them being printed?'

'No, but I recognised the typeface – it's very distinctive, I'm sure you agree.'

'It's somewhat old-fashioned,' said Jonny. 'I noticed that.'

'It was done on the Protein Man's printing machine.'

'The Protein Man?' asked Jonny. 'He's not one of the Air Loom Gang, is he? A minion of Count Otto Black?'

Ranger Hawtrey made a face. 'His name was Stanley Owen Green,' said he, 'and he was a pamphleteer. Born in nineteen fifteen and died in nineteen ninety-three. He was famous in his way. He had this bee in his bonnet about sex, about how too many people were having too much of it too often, and why. He developed this philosophy that he called "Protein Wisdom". It was based on this simple principle: that children need protein in order to grow, but adults don't, and the excess protein in their systems fuels excess sexual activity. His slogan was "Less Lust from Less Protein" and he took to the streets of London to preach his message.'

'And I bet he didn't get too many converts,' said Jonny.

'Not too many. Especially as he began his preaching in nineteen sixty-eight, in the heyday of the swinging sixties. He used to walk up and down Oxford Street, wearing sandwich boards and distributing his pamphlets, which were entitled 'Eight Passion Proteins With Care". And he did that right through until nineteen ninety-three, when he died. And when he died, his relatives bequeathed his printing machine to the museum. The moment I saw this letter I recognised the type – there's samples of his stuff in the basement store. There's no mistake, I'm sure.'

'Incredible,' said Jonny. 'Incredible.'

'Stuff and nonsense,' said Mr Giggles. 'Let's make our getaway now.'

'Do you think I could see this machine?' Jonny asked.

'If we can come up with some legitimate-sounding reason for going into the basement.'

'Getting into the basement will not be a problem,' said Jonny.

'So we're going to work on this together, then?'

'We'll see,' said Jonny. 'We'll see.'

Jonny hadn't been into Gunnersbury Park Museum since he was a child. As is often the way with folk and museums. But the beauty of museums, well, *some* museums, is that they withstand the slings and arrows of outrageous management and remain the same.

Tiny magical time capsules.

You were there and you are there again and virtually nothing has changed. A few bits of necessary renovation, updated security systems, a new ticket booth, something 'hands-on' for the modern kiddies. But for the most part—

'Unchanged,' said Jonny. And he stood before the transport collection (having sneaked past the lady on the desk with his head down), gazing up at the hansom cab. 'It's just the same. The hansom cab. Did you know that this cab was still in service in Ealing up until nineteen thirty-three?'

'I did,' said Ranger Hawtrey, who did.

'And the pony phaeton,' said Jonny. 'Don't you just love the pony phaeton?'

'Not as much as I love the Rothschilds' town and travelling carriages.'

'It's wonderful.' And Jonny was entranced. There had been a time, oh so long ago, when he had been happy. When he had been a child and when his daddy had still been alive. His daddy had always loved museums. In fact, every time the Hooker family went on holiday, to some English seaside resort or another, it would inevitably turn out that the *real* reason for this particular resort being chosen by the daddy was because the daddy had ascertained that there was some particularly interesting private museum or another that he felt would be interesting and educational for his family to visit.

And Jonny had loved those visits.

He had loved his daddy, and his daddy's enthusiasm for the wonders of old museums had worn off on his son.

And his daddy had a certain technique.

Jonny's daddy knew, as most people who know anything about museums know, that only about one-third, if that, of a museum's collection is ever on display to the public. The rest languishes unseen in storerooms beneath. In fact, that is where the really interesting stuff is. And Jonny's daddy had this technique.

On the Monday of the holiday he would take Jonny to the museum. He would lead Jonny around, speaking with knowledge of all those things that he had knowledge of. And then he would fall into conversation with the museum's curator. And employ his silken tongue. Because the daddy did have a silken tongue. Something that Jonny did not appear to have inherited. The daddy would speak of his son's interest in museums and the sad fact that so much of a museum's collection remains forever unseen by the public.And how future generations must learn the wonder of museums, and how much it would impress itself upon the mind of his little son here (the lad) if he could be granted a glimpse of the hidden collection that lay beneath.

And it was a very hard and ill-favoured curator who was not moved by the daddy's words and who, at least by the Wednesday, had not granted the daddy and the lad a private viewing of the wonders that lay in the storerooms beneath.

Jonny could recall with perfect clarity a museum in Bournemouth where he had not only viewed, but been allowed to hold ('the lad would really like to hold that') a shrunken human head. The product of the Jivaro tribe of the Amazon. The head was supposedly that of a Jesuit missionary, but Jonny had suspected that it was nothing of the sort because it had pierced ears. Pierced ears. The shrunken head had pierced ears. And that had stuck in Jonny's memory, that and the way the hair felt. Human hair on a dead shrunken head. Jonny remembered how, after his father had profusely thanked

65

the curator for taking him and 'the lad' below, they had left the museum and walked out hand in hand into the bright summer sunlight. Travelling from one world to another.

Heavy stuff.

'Are you okay?' asked Ranger Hawtrey. 'You've gone all faraway and misty-eyed.'

'Memories,' said Jonny.

'A museum will do that to you.'

'It certainly will.'

'We'll have to ask Joan on the desk if we can borrow the keys for the basement.'

'You have a cover story then, do you?'

'Not as such,' said Ranger Hawtrey. 'I'm not very good at this sort of thing.'

'You could get her chatting and I could steal the keys.'

'It's some sort of a plan, I suppose.'

'Or we could just go down into the basement without nicking her keys at all.'

'Don't quite follow you there,' said Ranger Hawtrey.

'We could go down the secret passage.'

'Really not following you *there*.'

'You mean you don't know about the secret passage?'

Ranger Hawtrey made another face. 'Clearly not,' said he. 'But then if it *is secret*—'

'Sound point,' said Jonny. 'The curator who showed it to me and my dad when I came here as a child wasn't very good at keeping a secret. Or at least he wasn't very good at keeping one from my daddy.'

There's always a secret passage. Or a priest hole. Or a skeleton walled up in a cellar.

There always is.

And that *is* a tradition, or an old charter, or something.

The secret passage in Gunnersbury Museum is ...

'Well, I never expected *that*,' said Ranger Hawtrey. 'Who'd have suspected that the entrance to the secret passage would be *there*?'

'Who indeed?' Jonny led the way. He shone the torch along the brickwork.

'Where did you get that torch?' asked Ranger Hawtrey.

'Out of your pocket,' said Jonny.

'Good call,' said Ranger Hawtrey. 'Where does this secret passage lead to?'

They emerged from the secret passage.

'And who would have expected *that*?'

'The secret is probably knowing when to stop,' said Jonny.

And it probably is.

'Please lead me to the printing machine,' said Jonny.

And Ranger Hawtrey did so.

They had the storeroom lights on now, and much was as Jonny remembered.

There were the boxes that contained the remains of wooden stakes that had been driven into the bed of the Thames at Brentford as part of the defences against the army of Julius Caesar. Some beautiful swords that were crafted in Hounslow, in the days when Hounslow was famous for the crafting of swords. There was a famous parrot in a glass dome and a painted portrait of the first man ever to open an umbrella in London, a famous Brentford man. And there was also all that remains of the Lucozade sign – the famous one that had the bottle pouring into the glass and all done with light bulbs. Each of which was famous in its way.

The printing press stood at the far end of the room, between a crate that contained the mummified remains of a two-headed giant and a working model of a perpetual motion machine.

'Behold the printing press,' said Ranger Hawtrey.

Jonny beheld the printing press. He beheld it up close and in detail. 'I think you're right,' he said. 'It has been used recently, And yes—' He rooted about amidst the mechanical gubbins and brought to light a screwed-up piece of paper. '—one got stuck in the works. So the letters were printed here. But why here and by whom?'

Ranger Hawtrey shrugged.

'And there's nothing else here,' said Jonny. 'No box of chocolates or sign saying, "You have found the printing press, you are the winner." Mind you, how difficult can it be to find out who did the printing? They must surely have done a lot of printing. That takes time and deliveries of paper and ink. Lots of coming and going. Someone must have seen something. The lady on the desk must have seen them.'

'Let's ask her, then,' said Ranger Hawtrey.

'I think it best that *you* ask her,' Jonny said. 'She might recognise me.'

'This is really exciting,' said Ranger Hawtrey. 'Secret passage and everything, brilliant.'

'I'm happy that you're happy.' Jonny did some thinking. 'So this is what I want you to say to the lady on the desk,' said he. And he whispered.

'Why are you whispering?' Ranger Hawtrey asked.

Jonny sighed. 'Because it makes it even *more* exciting,' he said.

'Ah, yes, you're right. Carry on.'

And Jonny did so.

'Good plan,' said Ranger Hawtrey. And they returned to the secret passage. And from there to the museum proper. And from there to the entrance hall.

Joan, the lady on the desk, sat at the desk. She was a fine-looking lady, was Joan. Jonny admired her looks, but he did so in a furtive fashion with his cap drawn down to hide his face.

Joan the desk lady was watching TV. She had a little portable jobbie. It was her own – she'd brought it in to watch the tennis at Wimbledon. Which must have meant that it was *that* time of year. Well, one of *those* weeks, actually.

Ranger Hawtrey went over and had a word with Joan. Actually, he had quite a few words. More words, Jonny felt, than were strictly necessary. But then, Joan the desk lady was a fine-looking woman.

At due length Ranger Hawtrey ambled over to Jonny and then led him from the building.

Out into the sunlight.

In a rather firm kind of a way.

'Stop pushing me,' said Jonny. 'What did you learn?'

'Quite a lot,' said Ranger Hawtrey. 'But nothing good.'

'Go on.'

'Well, it appears that the printing was carried out under the in-structions and supervision of a Mister James Crawford.'

'Go on.'

'A descendant of the Sir Henry Crawford who once owned the house and grounds back in the eighteenth century. Sir Henry's sons gambled away the family fortune, so by the time James was born there was no money left. But apparently he did some work, research or something about the Big House here, its history. And in return, the curator allowed him to use the printing machine for some private project he had.'

'So we have him,' said Jonny. 'Good work. We have the man who printed the competition letters.'

'Well, not exactly.'

'We don't?'

'Not exactly, no. Which is why I led you from the Big House. There's been another spot of bother.'

'Go on,' said Jonny in a low and sorry tone.

'Joan was watching the TV and the news was just on. James Crawford has been murdered. This very morning.'

'This very morning? Oh no.'

'Oh yes,' said Ranger Hawtrey. 'And apparently *you* did it.'

12

'What are you going to do?' asked Ranger Hawtrey. 'Give yourself up?'

'Give myself up?' and Jonny made the face that Ranger Hawtrey was so good at making. '*That*, I have to say, is not an option.'

'Perhaps, then, you should leave the country. We might alter the uniform you're wearing, make you look like a merchant seaman and—'

'No,' said Jonny, in as firm a manner as he could manage. 'I am *not* guilty of these crimes. And I'll prove it. All this is connected somehow. Me, the competition, Doctor Archy, James Crawford – this is all part of something big.'

'I'm not altogether certain how you reached that conclusion.' Ranger Hawtrey took to steering Jonny off into some bushes.

'Just stop pushing me about.' Jonny made resistance. 'This *is* something big, I feel it, I know it. Don't ask me how, but I do. Will you lend me some money?'

'How *much* money?'

'How much do you have?'

'What do you want it for?'

'Please just give me some money.'

Ranger Hawtrey parted with what money he had and Jonny thanked him for it. And then Jonny asked, 'Do you by any chance know the late Mister Crawford's address?'

'Joan will know it.'

'Then might you ask her for it?'

And so Ranger Hawtrey did, and he returned to Jonny with the address upon a slip of paper. Jonny thanked him and then he said goodbye.

'You'll be back, won't you?' asked Ranger Hawtrey.

'I hope so.'

'You can sleep in the hut. I won't tell anyone, you can trust me.'

'Thank you,' said Jonny. 'I really appreciate all this.'

And the two shook hands.

'Oh, thank you, Ranger Hawtrey, I *really* appreciate all this, kiss kiss love love love.'

'Shut your face,' Jonny told Mr Giggles.

'Well, it's pathetic. I think that Ranger Hawtrey is not so much a park ranger, he's more of an uphill gardener. He definitely fancies you.'

'Please be quiet,' said Jonny.

'And so now you're going to go to James Crawford's house and immediately get arrested by the police?'

'No,' said Jonny. 'I'm going to the pub.'

'Thank the Gods,' said O'Fagin as Jonny Hooker entered the bar, collar up and cap-peak down and really in need of a drink.

'Thank the Gods for what?' asked Jonny in an Irish accent.

'Ah, even better,' said O'Fagin. 'A *Jewish* police officer, splendid.'

Jonny Hooker mounted a barstool and spoke further words from beneath the cover of his cap. 'Can I help you in some way, sir?' he asked.

'I didn't think they were going to send anyone,' said O'Fagin. 'When I made my report at the police station they just kept sniggering. I didn't think they'd taken me seriously.'

'Perhaps you'd better begin at the beginning,' said Jonny. 'And please draw me a pint of King Billy whilst you do so.'

'Absolutely.' And O'Fagin applied his hand to the pump and his tongue to the telling of stuff. 'T'were a dark and stormy night,' he began.

'And I'll have to stop you there, sir,' said Jonny. 'Was this a recent dark and stormy night?'

'No, this was back in nineteen thirty-eight. The night that the Devil took Robert Johnson's soul, in this very bar.'

'Right,' said Jonny. And he sighed. Sorrowfully.

'Ooh, what sorrowful sighing,' said O'Fagin. 'That would fair have me going if it wasn't for the fact that I'm as hard as a marble headstone, me.' And he passed Jonny Hooker his beer. 'On the house,' he said. 'I hope it cheers you up.'

'Thank you very much,' said Jonny. 'Carry on with your story.'

'And then they threw me out of the police station,' said O'Fagin.

'No,' said Jonny. 'Carry on from the point where you left off. In nineteen thirty-eight.'

'You're sure you don't mind?'

'Not in the least. I have my beer now and I probably won't be listening anyway.'

'That's a shame,' said O'Fagin, 'because I'd be prepared to share the wealth.'

'Omit *nothing*,' said Jonny. '*What* wealth?' he continued.

'Well,' said O'Fagin, 'Robert Johnson spent the last couple of years of his life living here in this pub. He lived here with this big buck-toothed n****r – his brother, I think.'

'I really don't like that word,' said Jonny. 'Nobody should use that word any more.'

'It's all right to call another n****r, a n****r, if you're a n****r yourself.'

'So I have been unreliably informed,' said Jonny. 'But you are *not* a n****r, as it were.'

'Oh yes I am,' said O'Fagin.

'Not,' said Jonny.

'Am too.'

Jonny looked O'Fagin up and down. Well, as much up and down as he could from beneath the cover of his cap. 'Oh,' said Jonny. 'Well blow me down, so you are. I never noticed before'.

'People rarely do,' said O'Fagin. 'That's what I love about West London – class, colour or creed mean nothing. A man is accepted for what he is inside.'

Jonny nodded thoughtfully.

And didn't laugh at all.

But the sun *did* go behind a cloud and a dog *did* howl in the distance.

'So,' continued O'Fagin, 'that bucktoothed ... black chap, he recorded Johnson's thirtieth song right here in this pub.'

'And *you* saw this?'

'No,' said O'Fagin. 'I was somewhat handicapped from doing so by the fact that I hadn't been born then.'

'Just testing,' said Jonny.

'For what?' asked O'Fagin.

'Oh, look,' said Jonny. 'My beer is finished already. I wonder how that happened.'

'Probably something to do with the way you've chucked it down your gob.'

'Same again, please.'

O'Fagin took Jonny's glass and returned to the beer engine in its company. 'Anyway,' he said to Jonny, 'he was in here last night. Asked after my dad. Pointed to that picture back there.' O'Fagin gestured. Jonny peeped. 'That's him, with my dad. And he hasn't changed at all. How does that work, you tell me?'

Jonny shook his head. He had never noticed *that* photo behind the bar before. Next to the one with O'Fagin's dad and Robert Johnson, it was. Of O'Fagin's dad and what could only be described as a black man with large teeth. A black man with large teeth who wore a fez and a brightly coloured waistcoat.

'Hold on,' said Jonny. 'He looked *exactly* the same?'

'Didn't seem to have aged by a day. He said he was looking for Jimmy.'

'Jimmy?' Jonny asked.

'James Crawford, the old drunk fella who wore the long, black coat with the astrakhan collar.'

'Him?' said Jonny, who had seen that particular old drunk many a time. 'That chap was James Crawford?'

'Never a happy man,' said O'Fagin, 'what with his great-great-great-granddaddy doing the family fortune on the roulette wheel at Monte Carlo. He used to spend most of his days drinking cider in the park and bleating to passers-by that all the park should have been his.'

'Right,' said Jonny. 'And in all truth I don't blame him for it. I'd be pretty pissed off if I'd had rich ancestors and they'd wasted away the family fortune before I'd had a chance to do it myself.'

'Oh,' said O'Fagin. 'Then no one's ever told you about your —'

'What?' said Jonny.

'Nothing,' said O'Fagin. 'I must be thinking about someone else. Because you are a Jewish policeman I've never met before. So where was I? Oh yes. The blackamoor with the expansive dentition. He wanted to know where Crawford was. Said that Crawford had something of his and he wanted it back and if Crawford didn't hand it over, he'd kill him.'

'Golly!' said Jonny.

'I'm sure that's not politically correct,' said O'Fagin.

'Do you know where this character is now?'

'The schwartzer with the big railings?'

'The very same.'

'On the run from the police for murdering Jimmy Crawford, I should think. Isn't that why you are here?'

'Just trying to get *all* the relevant information,' said Jonny.

'Whatever happened to your Jewish accent?'

'Acclimatisation?' Jonny suggested.

'And that's a very strange police uniform.'

'Special branch,' Jonny suggested.

'It says "Gunnersbury Park Ranger" on your breast pocket.'

'It says "Calvin Klein" on my knickers,' said Jonny, 'And "Kelogue" on my cornflakes, but I'm sure that's a misspelling.'

'Gunnersbury park ranger,' said O'Fagin.

'Special Branch,' said Jonny. 'Trees have branches, special trees have special branches, and there's loads of special trees in Gunnersbury Park. Even one that involves the word "minge". I'm sure you'll agree about that.'

'I'm always agreeable,' said O'Fagin. 'You'd be surprised at what I'll agree to after I've had a few gin and tonics.'

'I thought you black lads drank rum,' said Jonny.

'You racist bastard,' said O'Fagin. 'If there was any justice they'd bring back the birch.'

'I didn't know it had been away,' said Jonny.

'Two weeks in Benidorm,' said O'Fagin. 'God, I love this job.'

'First-class toot,' said Jonny, 'but I don't know whether it's helping.'

'Talking the toot always helps,' said O'Fagin.

The sound of police car sirens reached the ears of Jonny Hooker.

'See,' said O'Fagin, 'I told you.'

'What?'

'That talking the toot always helps. I saw you through the window as you were approaching the pub – recognised you at once. There's a reward on your head, so I called the police on my mobile. I've kept you talking the toot in order to give them time to arrive. I expect they'll have the place surrounded by now. I'm really looking forward to spending the reward money.'

'How much reward money?' Jonny asked.

'One thousand pounds,' said O'Fagin. 'That was the wealth that I mentioned. That I was prepared to share. I lied about being prepared to share it, though.'

'*One thousand?*' said Jonny. 'For one thousand pounds, I'll turn myself in.'

'You can't do *that*!' O'Fagin fell back. In alarm.

'You just watch me,' said Jonny and he put up his hands.

'But that's not fair,' said O'Fagin. 'I made the phone call.'

'I'll give you the money for the call,' said Jonny. 'That's only fair.'

'Thanks,' said 'Fagin. 'No, hold on, that's *not* fair. I want the reward money, all of it.'

'Sorry,' said Jonny. 'It's mine. Although—'

'Although *what*?'

'Well,' said Jonny, 'it's only a thought. I don't know whether you'd be interested.'

'I would,' said O'Fagin. 'I really would.'

'Well,' said Jonny, once more, 'if I were to make an escape now, maybe bop you over the head to make it look as if you tried to stop me – I bet they'll raise the reward money.'

'Do you really think so?' O'Fagin scratched at his head.

'They'd double it, I'd bet,' said Jonny. 'Then you could turn me in at a later date and make twice as much money.'

'Right,' said O'Fagin. 'We have a deal.' And he put out his hand for a shake.

And Jonny Hooker shook it.

'I'll show you the secret passage,' said O'Fagin.

13

The secret passage emerged from the far side of the pub's car park. Jonny Hooker emerged from it.

There were police cars all around The Middle Man.

Most of these, however, were unoccupied, their occupants now storming the premises. As it were.

Jonny Hooker took himself over to the nearest of the unoccupied vehicles. He did this in what is called a skulking fashion.

The key was in the ignition.

Jonny Hooker entered the car and, as officers of the law unnecessarily employed one of those big steel cylinder jobbies to smash open the unlocked saloon bar door of The Middle Man, Jonny backed the police car slowly from the car park.

The valiant policemen, having stormed into The Middle Man, would find its landlord prone upon the saloon bar carpet, cruelly struck down by a copper warming pan. The brutality of this new atrocity would elicit a doubling of the reward money.

'You've been ever so quiet,' said Jonny, as he drove along.

Answer came there none to Jonny's ears.

'Oh, come come,' said Jonny. 'Surely you have something to say on the matter.'

Mr Giggles, however, remained silent. And unseen to Jonny at the present also, as it happened.

'All right,' said Jonny. 'Don't talk to me. 'I'm more than happy for you not to talk to me.'

'I know what you're thinking,' said Mr Giggles.

'Do you really?'

'You think that *I* killed James Crawford, and the doctor, too.'

'It does rather look that way, doesn't it?' said Jonny.

'It will never hold up in court.'

'But it *does* look that way. I was in the Special Wing of Brentford Cottage Hospital, drugged up to the eyeballs, your presence suppressed from my mind. So where were *you* during that time? Perhaps you are some kind of shapeshifter, capable of moving from the noncorporeal to the corporeal at will. Perhaps *you* killed the doctor after I left. And you became the large-toothed black man once more and then killed James Crawford.'

'Outrageous,' said Mr Giggles. 'You have no evidence whatsoever to support this outrageous allegation.'

'Perhaps not, but it does fit together rather neatly, doesn't it?'

'I'm Mister Giggles,' said Mister Giggles. 'I'm *not* Mister Homicidal Maniac.'

'I don't know what you really are,' said Jonny, 'but I *will* find out. Oh yes, I *will*. You just wait and see.'

'This is all a bit sudden, is it not?' asked Mr Giggles. 'All this assertiveness. Making decisions for yourself, getting all bold and adventurous.'

'Do you mean taking control of my life?' Jonny asked.

'Where are we going?' asked Mr Giggles.

'To the house of the late James Crawford.'

'Let's go to the shopping mall instead.'

'No,' said Jonny. 'Let's not.'

'Oh, come on, we can play "Mumma or Munter?"'

'"Mumma or Munter?" What's that?'

'It's a game I've just invented. It would make a really great reality-type TV show. You go to the shopping mall and pick out big fat women with big fat stomachs and you poke them with a stick and ask them whether they are pregnant, or simply fat – "Mumma, or Munter"? See. There'd be a prize if they're a mumma, and a forfeit if they're just a fat munter. You stomp on their mobile phone or pie them in the face or something.'

'That is appalling,' said Jonny. 'I would *never* think of doing such a thing.'

'But if *I* am a figment of *your* imagination, then you just did.'

'I'll get to the bottom of you,' said Jonny.

'Or "Look Out Behind You",' said Mr Giggles. 'That's another game. You shout "Look out behind you" at people. Now sometimes they will and sometimes they won't, but whatever they do, we do something painful to them. Or there's "Whoops Sorry I Pushed You Into the Path of a Speeding Car". Or "Smack the Commoner". Or we could go to Argos and look through *The Laminated Book of Dreams*. You always like that.'

Jonny Hooker sighed. '*The Laminated Book of Dreams,*' he said. Dreamily.

'But the point is,' said Mr Giggles, 'that that's the kind of jolly good fellow I am. All laughter and jolly japes. How could you ever think that I could murder people?'

'Hm,' went Jonny. And left it at that.

And presently arrived at the house of the late James Crawford.

'All right,' said Mr Giggles, 'if you are determined upon this reckless course of action, the best way to approach the situation is—'

But, 'Shut up!' Jonny told him.

The road was taped across and police constables stood on guard. They carried semi-automatic weapons, because there was always the off chance that this might just have something to do with international terrorism, so you could never be too careful. Numerous newspaper and media Johnnies stood about, smoking cigarettes and making lewd remarks to passing women PCs.

Jonny drove the police car right up to the tape, scattering numerous newspaper types before him. A constable with an AK-47 gestured for Jonny to wind down his window. Jonny wound it down.

'Drop the tape please, Constable,' said Jonny.

'On whose authorisation?' asked the PC

'On whose authorisation, *what*?' asked Jonny.

'On whose authorisation, *sir*!' said the PC

'Drop the tape *at once*,' commanded Jonny.

The constable dropped the tape.

And then saluted.

'Ludicrous,' said Mr Giggles. 'Tell me that that did not just happen.'

Jonny Hooker grinned a wicked grin.

'And stop doing *that*,' said Mr Giggles. 'You're frightening me.'

Jonny Hooker drove slowly down the blocked-off road. Of course, it had been too easy. Ridiculously easy. Impossibly easy. But that wasn't to say that it *was* impossible. Implausible, perhaps. But *not* impossible.

And that, perhaps, was the point.

There was a big white van double-parked before the house of the late James Crawford. The back was open and men in environmental suits were unloading picnic chairs and a table-tennis table. Jonny drove around them and parked up. Then he hooted the horn.

A constable issued from the house of the deceased. He carried a General Electric minigun.

Jonny beckoned to him through the open car window.

'Hurry up, lad,' he called as he beckoned. 'This door won't go opening itself, will it?'

'No, *sir*,' said the constable.

And he opened up the door.

'So what do we have here?' asked Jonny Hooker, inside the house now and in the front room.

'And who are *you*?' asked a certain body.

'Chicoteen, Special Branch, hence the dress uniform. And you?'

'Inspector Westlake,' said Inspector Westlake, 'on special second-ment from the Bramfield Constabulary. I am awaiting information regarding the very special and top-secret assignment that I have been called here to deal with. In the meantime I thought I might as well solve this murder. It is within my compass, as it were.' Inspector Westlake made a certain gesture.

'I see,' said Jonny. And it sounded as if he did. And he made a certain gesture of his own. 'Well, just carry on. I'll take a little look around on my own, if you don't mind.'

'Well, actually I *do*,' said Inspector Westlake. 'Might I see your ID?'

'I trust you noted *that*,' said Jonny, pointing to a stain upon the wallpaper just to the right of the fireplace. 'Suggestive, would you not agree?'

'Eh?' said the inspector.

Jonny considered an 'Eh *what*?' But then thought better of it. 'I'm sure you know your own business best,' he said. 'I'll just leave you to it.'

Inspector Westlake went to examine the stain.

Jonny cast an eye about the room.

Now, some rooms are certainly happy. They have a jolly feel to them. They have cheerful wallpaper and a sunny disposition. One can sit in such a room and feel elevated. Happy. Given to a peacefulness of mind.

This was *not* one of those rooms.

This room was a sorry room. A room given to despair. A lost room, a room that had abandoned all hope. A room that was crying inside. And all around and about.

Glum was this room.

Glum and grim. Of dismal aspect.

'No natural light,' Jonny observed.

'Pardon?' said a constable, who was carrying a rocket launcher.

'No natural light. What is that over the window?'

'Soundproofing,' said the constable. 'It's all over the room – there, there and even up there.' He swung his rocket launcher up towards the ceiling, nearly putting Jonny's eye out. 'This whole room is soundproofed, and double thickness. I know these things, see, because I'm in a band and we've recorded in a real recording studio.'

'Fascinating,' said Jonny.

'Do you really think so? I have one of our CDs here. Perhaps you'd like to hear it.'

'Love to,' said Jonny, and he accepted the proffered CD. 'Dry Rot,' he continued. And a smile appeared upon Jonny's face. It was a sort-of secretive smile, a smile that, if you'd asked it what it meant, would have replied that it meant something that you didn't know but wasn't going to tell.

'That's the name of our band,' said the constable. 'We play at The Middle Man on Metal Nights. You should come along sometime.'

'I'll try,' said Jonny. 'But in the meantime, if you don't start calling me "sir", I will have you court-martialled, or whatever the police equivalent of that is.'

'Pork-martialled?' suggested the PC. 'I'm not really into the respect-for-your-superiors side of policing. I joined up for the weapons and the suspect interrogation. I've got really long hair tucked up inside my helmet.'

'Where is the body?' Jonny asked. 'Has it been removed to the morgue?'

'No, it's over there, behind the upturned armchair. But I wouldn't go looking at it if I were you. It's pretty grisly.'

Jonny glanced some more about the miserable room. 'He had a lot of gramophone records,' he said, sighting many a shelf-load.

'About thirty thousand by my reckoning,' said the constable, 'and some real gems amongst them. I had a little delve. All catalogued, alphabetical order. Pick a band, have a look. I'll bet there's a copy here.'

'I doubt that,' said Jonny.

'Name a band,' said the constable.

'Dry Rot,' said Jonny.

'Oh, that's not fair,' said the constable. 'We only cut a dozen copies on vinyl. They're very expensive to get done. Mind you, a damn fine mini-album, it was, called *Pretence of Strategy*. The best track is "Sides to a Story". But there won't be a copy here. He's not likely to have got hold of one.'

'He might,' said Jonny.

'He won't have,' said the constable.

'Humour me,' said Jonny.

'All right,' said the constable. He pushed past Inspector Westlake, who was studying a stain upon the wallpaper with the aid of a mag-nifying glass, and applied himself to one of the record shelves.

'*Some Call Me Laz,*' he went, 'by Lazlo Woodbine and the Wood-binettes. Blimey, that's rare. And the original soundtrack album for *Plan Nine from Outer Space*. And ... blimey.'

'Blimey?' said Jonny.

'A copy of our demo,' said the constable. 'The *first* copy. I thought *I* had *that*.'

'Where are the Js?' Jonny asked.

'Js?' asked the constable.

'For Johnson, Robert Johnson.'

'King of the Delta Blues?'

'You've heard of him?'

'He was the man,' said the constable. 'He invented it all.'

'Would you check the Js, please, Constable?'

And whilst Inspector Westlake continued to inspect a stain upon the wallpaper and a couple of chaps in environmental suits fussed about at this and that whilst erecting a swingball in the centre of the room, the musically inclined constable checked the Js for Robert Johnson.

'Damn me,' he said. 'Yep, the full complement. A collector's dream.'

'All thirty?' asked Jonny.

'He only recorded twenty-nine,' said the constable. 'See, all numbered, twenty-seven, twenty-eight, twenty-nine—'

'And thirty,' said Jonny, and he pulled a brown card slip-sleeve from the shelf. "Apocalypse Blues," he read. 'Recorded London, August 16th, nineteen thirty-eight.'

'No way!' said the constable.

Jonny put his hand through the hole in the centre of the sleeve. 'Empty,' said he. 'The recording is gone.'

'We're going to move the body now, sir,' came a muffled voice, muffled by the plastic face-mask jobbie on the Scientific Support chap's environmental suit.

'Get to it, then,' said Inspector Westlake.

Jonny peeped on as two of the environmentally suited fellows pulled aside the toppled armchair to reveal the body of Mr James Crawford.

'Oh my goodness,' said Jonny as he viewed it.

'Oh yes,' said Inspector Westlake. 'Very messy business. Same as that Doctor Archy. Head chopped right off the body, and taken away as a trophy by the murderer. We're dealing with a psycho serial killer here. This won't be the last, you mark my words.'

And Jonny marked his words.

14

Jonny Hooker's hand was tightly over his gob.

The sight of a headless body can elicit a degree of queasiness. In fact, most of us go through life without ever seeing a headless body and so our mettle, as it were, is never tested.

Jonny Hooker swallowed and swallowed again. It would not look good, indeed not professional, for him to hurl up his stomach contents over the chaps in the white environmental suits. Questions might be asked.

Questions!

Jonny Hooker had a moment. Took in a moment. Reality seemed to be long gone. He had bumbled along, a no-mark, a nonsuch for all of his life. True, he *was* a talented musician, but it had never taken him anywhere. For *he* had never taken *it* anywhere. *He* had been too wound up in himself. In the problems he had with himself. Simply with trying to be himself. Simply trying to survive.

But this, all this, was as ridiculous as it was exciting. And it *was* exciting. And he *was* involved in it. Involved directly in something for possibly the very first time in his life. He was attached to this. There was something about this that allowed him a degree of control. Which enabled him.

But it was all so absurd. So unreal. You just can't bluff your way into a crime scene dressed as a park ranger but posing as a high-ranking police officer, especially when *you* are the prime suspect.

It simply cannot be done.

Yet.

'Sir,' said the constable with the rocket launcher, 'and please understand me, I do hate to have to call you "sir". But *sir*, as you are evidently possessed of a certain intuition that has clearly not been granted to other senior officers of the law—' He gestured towards

Inspector Westlake with the business end of his rocker launcher and nearly put Jonny's left testicle out. '—I am thinking that perhaps you should have a look at this.' And he did a bit of discreet finger-pointing with his non-trigger finger.

Jonny followed the direction of the pointing, a skill that he was now raising to almost an art form, and spied out the object of the pointing: a book, somewhat bloody about the edges, that lay upon the seat of a woebegone armchair.

The constable now raised his trigger-free hand and spoke behind it in a whispery, secretive manner. 'I was first on the crime scene,' he secretively whispered, 'and I had a little flick through that – it was lying on the floor. You might find it of interest. Perhaps a clue or two lies within.'

'Perhaps,' said Jonny, and then, 'What is *that*?' And he pointed up to the ceiling. It was a loud, 'What is *that*?' and it drew the attention of all who were present in the melancholy room. The men in the environmental suits dropped the headless body.

Inspector Westlake just said, 'What?'

Jonny scooped the book from the armchair and swept it into his pocket.

'*What?*' said Inspector Westlake, once again.

'Ah,' said Jonny. 'Apparently nothing. I thought I saw something, but *no*, it was nothing.'

'As *nothing* as this stain by the fireplace,' said the inspector. 'It's a damp patch, been here for years by the look of it.'

'Bravo,' said Jonny. 'Has anyone checked out the rest of the premises?'

'Of course,' said Inspector Westlake.

'Splendid,' said Jonny. 'I'll just follow up on the details, then. This young officer will accompany me.'

Inspector Westlake waved them away.

'Are we off to the pub, then?' asked the police constable, once he and Jonny had left the room of dolefulness.

'Have *you* checked out the rest of the house?'

'Well, I did have a bit of a snoop about. The bedroom's pretty weird.'

'Weird?'

'Up there, see for yourself.'

The constable led Jonny to the bedroom. He pushed open the door and turned on a light and Jonny peered within. It was not a happy bedroom. Indeed, if the room directly beneath this bedroom had been a heart-sinking and death-wish-leading-to-suicidal-tendency room, this bedroom surpassed it, or possibly undermined it in the field of wretched disconsolateness, or indeed suchlike.

And this was a rather smelly room. A room that was rank indeed.

'Phewee,' went Jonny, fanning at his nose.

'I'd join you in such fanning,' said the constable, 'but I might, like as not, put my nose out with this rocker launcher.'

'You *could* use your other hand.'

'I *could*,' said the constable, 'but I don't want to, all right?'

'Fine with me,' said Jonny. 'So what is with the horrid smell?'

'Same business,' said the constable. 'Window all soundproofed over. All the walls, too, as you can see.'

'I do see,' said Jonny. 'But what is this all over the walls? They're scrawled all over with felt-tip pen or something.'

'Take a close look,' said the constable.

And Jonny did so.

'Music,' he said. 'Musical notation. Lines and lines of music all over every wall.'

'*And* the ceiling,' said the constable, 'and what can be seen of the floor beneath the wank-mags and the used tissues.'

'I don't feel that there was any need for you to mention them,' said Jonny.

'Really? I felt it added a certain shock value.'

'Do you read music?' Jonny asked.

'I'm in a band, aren't I?' said the constable.

Jonny nodded. 'So *do* you read music?'

'Of course not. Who reads music nowadays?'

'Well, actually *I* do,' said Jonny. 'Curious thing – I was able to read music before I was even taught to read and write.'

'That's the first I've heard of that,' said the constable.

'It's the first time I've mentioned it,' said Jonny.

'So do you think it's significant?'

'What do *you* think?'

'I'm not paid to think,' said the constable. 'I'm paid to do what

I'm told. And hopefully be told once in a while to shoot at someone with this here rocket launcher. A swarthy terrorist, hopefully.'

Jonny Hooker sighed.

'And could I offer you some advice, whilst we're on the subject of terrorists?'

'We're not on the subject of terrorists,' said Jonny.

'Of murderers, then, or at least wanted suspects.'

'Go on,' said Jonny, slowly.

'Well,' said the constable, 'and no offence meant, but you really are crap at impersonating a police officer. Don't you think that wearing a Gunnersbury park ranger's uniform is a bit of a giveaway, as it were?'

'*What?*' went Jonny.

'I'm not thinking to turn you in, or even arrest you myself but—'

'*What?*' went Jonny. An even louder '*what?*' than before.

'But I really would hightail it out of here if I were you,' said the constable. 'Before the truth dawns upon Westlake.'

Jonny's mouth went flap-flap-flap, but the word 'what' accompanied by a question mark did not issue from it yet again. After a moment or two, the words, 'You recognised me?' did, though.

'You're kidding, right?' said the constable.

'I'm not kidding,' said Jonny.

'Jonny,' said the constable, 'it's me, Paul – we went to school together, remember?'

'Ah,' said Jonny. 'School together, was it?'

'It was,' said Constable Paul. 'You sat next to me in Mister Vaux's class. And Mister Jenner took us for music and you used to show off because you could read the music to concertos better than him, so he used to make you go outside and stand in the quadrangle, remember?'

'I *do* remember,' said Jonny. 'I remember all too well. Jonny looked Paul up and down. 'I didn't recognise you,' he said. 'It must be the uniform.'

'Really?' said Paul, and he shook his head.

'You're shaking your head,' said Jonny.

'Well,' said Paul, 'I am thinking that the fact that I told you I was the bass guitarist in Dry Rot should have tipped you off.'

'Ah,' said Jonny.

'Ah indeed,' said Constable Paul. 'Seeing as how you are the *lead* guitarist in that very band.'

'Ah yes,' said Jonny. 'But I didn't want to give myself away. Not in front of Westlake. I did give a sort of secretive smile though. You might have pick up on that. Small world, eh?'

'Small world?' said Constable Paul. '*Small world?*'

'Well, it *is* a coincidence. I didn't even know you were a policeman. I recall you telling me that you were something big in rock 'n' roll in the city.'

'Yeah, well, I'm not,' said Constable Paul. 'Oh, and *this* is for you.' And without any warning. Because that is the way you must always do it if you wish to do it successfully. He swung a fist at Jonny and caught him right on the chin.

Jonny fell back, arms all flailing, mouth all going 'Owch' and 'Oooh'.

'You twat,' cried Constable Paul. 'Getting yourself wanted by the bloody police when we're playing a gig on Friday at The Middle Man and O'Fagin was going to pay us and everything.'

'You hit me!' Jonny lay amongst tissues and mags.*

'You're unbelievable,' said Constable Paul, and he looked to be squaring up to administer further hittings should Jonny choose to regain his feet. 'Park keeper's uniform—'

'Park *ranger*,' said Jonny.

'And bloody wanted man! And you turn up *here*. Murderers always return to the scene of the crime, is that it?'

'That *isn't* it. Of course that isn't it. I didn't murder anyone.'

'Then what are you doing *here*?'

'I have to find out.' Jonny didn't try to rise, just sat there looking glum. 'I *have* to find out,' he said once more, 'what is really going on. And something *is* going on, something big. I know it. I just know it.'

'And you're going to solve this ... whatever it is, this something big?'

'I'm part of it and it's part of me. I can't explain, but I know that whatever it is, it's making me *alive* – do you know what I mean?'

---

* This month's copy of *Munters in the Mall* being amongst them.

Constable Paul shook his head. 'You can get up now,' he said. 'I promise I won't hit you again.' And he helped Jonny back to his feet. 'What are you going to do now?' he asked.

'Several things,' said Jonny. 'Three things, in fact. First thing – could you photograph all these walls and the ceiling and what you can of the floor for me?'

'No sweat,' said Constable Paul. 'Can do that on my mobile phone.'

'Second thing – I have to make a swift getaway,' said Jonny.

'Out the way you came and away in the police car you nicked.'

'Brilliant,' said Jonny. 'I'll call you and we'll meet up later, okay?'

'Okay,' said Constable Paul. 'And the third thing?'

Jonny kneed Constable Paul in those oh-so-tender regions.

'Speak to you later,' he said.

15

'Violence!' said Mr Giggles. 'You administered violence.'

'He hit me first,' said Jonny. 'I was simply balancing things.'

'Balancing things? You're growing out of control. Punching that Doctor Archy was bad enough. But as for kneeing Paul in the nuts—'

'He hit me first.'

'All wrong, all wrong. He could have turned you in, but he didn't.'

'What are you getting so upset about?'

'I abhor violence,' said Mr Giggles.

'How strange,' said Jonny, 'as you've put me in positions so many times in the past that have caused folk to mete out violence to me.'

'I never have!' said Mr Giggles.

'Oh really?' said Jonny. 'And yet I recall so vividly the time you persuaded me to play "Point out the Porker" in KFC and that very large woman beating the bedoodads out of me.'

'How was I to know that she knew Dimac?'

'How indeed?' Jonny had ditched the police car. He hadn't wanted to, because it was a comfortable ride and it *did* appear to command a certain degree of respect from fellow motorists, But he had been forced to as he'd heard the 'all-points-bulletin' being put out over the dashboard radio regarding the fact that the car had been TWOCed* and that officers were being encouraged to shoot upon sight the potential terrorist who had done the TWOCing thereof. Or the *said* TWOCing. Or whatever.

Jonny now rode in a black Chrysler Cruiser.

'And that's another thing,' said Mr Giggles. 'You TWOCing *this*

---

* Taking With Out Consent. As if you didn't know!

car. How did you know that the keys from the police car would work in *this* car?'

'Everyone knows *that*,' said Jonny. 'Police car keys are special keys that can work any vehicle.'

'Are you sure that *everyone* knows that?'

'Absolutely,' said Jonny. 'The same as everyone knows that if you leave your hall light on at night when you go out, burglars will think you're in and not attempt to break in and rob you.'

'And everyone knows *that*?'

'Everyone except for burglars,' said Jonny. 'The world is a wonderful place, is it not?'

'What did you say?' asked Mr Giggles.

'You heard what I said.'

'I heard it, but I don't believe that I heard it.'

'I have no comment to make on that,' said Jonny, and he took a corner at speed and had a passing cleric off his bicycle.★

'You're enjoying yourself,' said Mr Giggles.

'I am,' said Jonny.

'That's not right,' said Mr Giggles.

'You don't want me to enjoy myself? I thought that you dedicated yourself to helping me enjoy myself. Encouraging me to enjoy myself. Doing everything within your power to ensure that I enjoy myself.'

Mr Giggles went, 'Hm,' in a 'certain' manner.

'So you must be so happy for me,' said Jonny.

'Oh yes,' said Mr Giggles. 'I am, I really am. So where are we going now?'

'Back to the park,' said Jonny.

'Back to the park?'

'It's lunchtime.'

And, of course, it was. Because time *does* pass quickly when you're enjoying yourself and Jonny Hooker really *was* enjoying himself. And he'd had a busy morning and it was a little after one of the afternoon clock and so he returned to Gunnersbury Park.

And parked the stolen Chrysler in amongst some bushes behind

★ Why does that happen so often?

the public car park and ambled off to the park rangers' hut.

Ranger Hawtrey was very pleased to see him.

Ranger Connor not so much.

'Where have you been?' he asked Jonny.

'Litter patrol,' said Jonny. 'Caught some school truants having a cigarette, formed them into a litter patrol – I hope you approve.'

'I do,' said Ranger Connor. 'Well done, that man.'

Ranger Hawtrey smiled and shook his head. 'It's French omelettes today,' he said, 'seasoned with cinnamon, garlic, galingale and nutmeg, with a salad on the side and crispy fries.'

'Wow,' said Jonny. 'A gourmet repast.'

'My hobby,' said Ranger Hawtrey. 'That and learning to play the classical violin. But that's a bit tricky because I'm left-handed.'

'Why so tricky?' Jonny asked.

'There's no such thing as a left-handed concert violinist,' said Ranger Hawtrey. 'You can't have one in an orchestra because their bowing arm would bump into the other violinists.'

'Well, I never knew *that*,' said Jonny.

Ranger Hawtrey served Jonny up with lunch. As he passed him a Queen's pattern knife and fork, he whispered, 'How is it going?'

'I'll tell you later,' said Jonny. 'Could you pass the tomato sauce?'

Ranger Connor had finished his lunch and settled down in one of the Queen Anne chairs, put his feet up on a Persian pouffe and got stuck in for a bit of a nap.

Ranger Hawtrey pulled a copy of *Southpaw Violinist* from one of his loaded pockets and, despite his eagerness to know what Jonny had been up to, took to the reading of it.

Jonny ate and appreciated his lunch, took the bloodstained book from *his* pocket and gave it a bit of perusal.

It was a leather-bound notebook kind of jobbie of the variety that friends of authors buy for authors as Christmas and birthday presents because 'it's a really nice thing and you can make notes for your next novel in it'. And which authors always put to one side and mean to use and then lose. Although they really *are* nice things. And the gifts of them are *really* appreciated.

On the flyleaf was written, in a shaky hand:

THIS BOOK BELONGS TO JAMES CRAWFORD

And beneath this, James Crawford's address.

And beneath this, what appeared to be the title of the book. And this title was:

ANSWERS?

'Answers?' thought Jonny. 'Answers to what?'

'To the meaning of life, maychance,' said Mr Giggles.

But Jonny ignored him.

Jonny turned the page and read the words:

IF YOU ARE READING THIS BOOK
THEN IT MEANS THAT I AM DEAD.
I DO NOT CLAIM TO HAVE ALL OF
THE ANSWERS. THE ONE WHO COMES
AFTER ME WILL FIND OUT ALL OF
THE ANSWERS. I ONLY HOPE THAT
THIS BOOK WILL PROVIDE
HIM OR HER WITH SOMETHING
TO WORK ON.

'Hm,' went Jonny, and he read on. The writing was all in capital letters and all in violet ink. Neither boded particularly well, but Jonny persevered. After all, if he was looking for a clue, then *this* was definitely it.

'"They are amongst us",' he read. '"There is no telling how many of them there are; one can only guess. What is known from recorded history is that they form themselves into tight covens or gangs. That they hide themselves in secret places. That they construct their machines in secret places and that they man their machines in these secret places. These machines, these Looms that weave the air, the sounds, the music, are used to effect control. The subject chosen for control is magnetised; this can be done at any time. The Magnetiser may disguise himself in a hundred different ways, perhaps as a postman or a house-painter, a dog-walker or a simple passer-by. But however he is disguised, he administers the magnetisation, which is done through electrical contamination. Once the subject is magnetically marked, then the Loom can be tuned to his frequency. An individual Loom's range is not unlimited, but as Looms exist dotted throughout the kingdom, the subject will rarely be out of range of one of them. Once the Loom is attuned to the unique magnetic vibration of the chosen subject, then the keyboard will be manipulated and the notes dispatched as a magnetic flux, or vibrating wave, or carrier signal. This music, which is played upon the keyboard by the member of the gang who is known only as the Glove Woman, passes its rhythms to the subject not as the notes, which they are, but as the words that are in accordance and sympathy with these notes. Which is to say that the scale is also an alphabet of sound. The notes become words when absorbed into the subject's head. The subject hears these words, coming apparently from without. They will be interpreted according to the subject's belief system. The voice of God? The voice of the Devil? The voice of inspiration? An alien life form? An imaginary friend—"'

Jonny paused at this, munched upon a crispy fry and took a sip of tea. And then he read more.

'"Why do these gangs target a particular subject? The reasons are many and various, but all to one end: control. Ultimate Control. To control individuals with a view to controlling all. There is no escape for the subject once marked by the Magnetiser. For not only does the Loom weave its music, but other music all about will conspire with it. The subject cannot escape from the music of others, in the supermarket, in a café, or restaurant, or public house, issuing from the headphones of fellow travellers, or passers-by or from windows, or indeed from their own record or CD collections. Or from the radio, or television, or indeed any electrical apparatus capable of issuing a pulse that might be a regular beat. All this music, indeed *all* music, contains the hidden formula. The hidden code. And all can be activated by those gangs who work the Looms. Such it has been for centuries. And such it will continue to be unless—"'

Jonny Hooker turned the page.

'Unless *what?*'

There was no more text. Jonny flicked this way and that, but that was it. Jonny Hooker closed the book and returned it to his pocket.

Ranger Hawtrey laughed out loud and pointed to a page of his magazine. 'Southpaw fiddle humour,' he explained. 'Don't mind me.'

'Ranger Hawtrey,' said Jonny.

'Call me Charlie,' said Charlie. 'I know I should have said to call me Charlie earlier, of course, but I'm a bit shy.'

'Right,' said Jonny. 'Well, Charlie, remember how you were telling me about your brother? The one you gave the iPod to?'

'I do recall,' said Charlie.

'And he's banged up in the Special Wing at Brentford Cottage Hospital.'

'I prefer to use the expression "receiving treatment", but in truth it amounts to the same thing.'

'Well,' said Jonny, 'I was just thinking – it's a very nice day and everything. What say we pop to the hospital after work and pay your brother a visit?'

Ranger Charlie made a thoughtful face. 'But,' and he whispered to Jonny, 'and no offence to you, believe me, but do you not feel that as a wanted suspect in the murder of Doctor Archy at Brentford Cottage Hospital, you turning up there this afternoon might just be asking for trouble? I mean, a bit like going to the zoo and sticking your head in the tiger's mouth?'

Jonny Hooker nodded, and he grinned. 'Yes,' he said to Ranger Charlie. 'Just like that.'

16

'And you really believe that *this* is going to work.' Mr Giggles' voice had a certain heightened quality to it. And for those dubiously gifted with the ability to see Mr Giggles, it was to be observed that there was also a certain agitation and indeed animation going on with him.

'It is a work of genius, if I *do* say so myself.' Jonny Hooker spoke from the corner of his mouth. In a whispered manner, spoke he.

Because Jonny was back in the park rangers' hut. It was clocking-off time now, five-thirty of the afternoon clock, and those who had the appropriate cards to clock off with (Jonny's, apparently – well, according to Jonny – must have been held up in the post some-where) were doing the said clocking-off.

And Jonny was viewing his face in a Regency wall mirror, with bevelled plate and gradrooned frame, which had previously escaped mention.

'A work of genius,' he said once more as he cocked his head from side to side and viewed. What was to be seen of his face wasn't much and the much there was of it was not of sufficient muchness as to illicit recognition, even, it must be said, by the mother who bore him and who had loved him for much of the subsequent time.

Jonny's face was a cockeyed quilt of Elastoplast dressings.

'What, *exactly*, did you say happened to you?' asked Ranger Connor.

'Allergy,' said Jonny, turning to smile with the visible bit of his mouth. 'Allergy to grass. It will calm down in a week or so.'

'Allergy?' Ranger Connor said this in a sniffy kind of tone. 'I frankly despair for your generation. In my day no one ever had allergies. Polio, we had, and diphtheria, and we were grateful for it. But all this namby-pambying about these days, lactose intolerant? Anorexic?

Obsessive-compulsive? And what's that one where the school kids go bouncing off the walls and have to be subdued with Ritalin?'

'Attention-Deficit Disorder,' said Ranger Hawtrey.

'Stuff and bally nonsense,' said Ranger Connor. 'A good clip around the ear with the business end of a seven-league boot is what they need.'

'Seven-league boot?' said Jonny. And Ranger Hawtrey shrugged.

'The way I see it,' said Ranger Connor, 'indeed, the way it seems to me, is this. Drug companies employ special "experts" whose role is to "discover" all these new syndromes and give them catchy titles, so that the drug companies can cure them with expensive drugs that they just happen to have prepared in advance and are ready for marketing.'

'Actually, I quite like that,' said Ranger Hawtrey. 'As a conspiracy theory, that satisfies on so many different levels.'

'It's the truth, I'm telling you,' said Ranger Connor.

'I thought you said it was the way it seemed to you,' said Ranger Hawtrey.

'Same thing – it's just in the way you say it.'

'I'm still a bit confused about the seven-league boots,' said Jonny. 'But an explanation can wait until tomorrow.'

'Not coming down to The Middle Man for a pint, then?' said Ranger Connor. 'To celebrate your first day on the job.'

Jonny pointed to his face.

'Maybe next week, then. You, Ranger Hawtrey?'

'Sadly no,' said that ranger. 'I'm off to see my brother.'

'The loony or the castrato?'

'Castrato?' said Jonny.

'Ah,' said Ranger Hawtrey. 'I neglected to mention my *other* brother.'

'Castrato?'

'I'd really rather not talk about it, if you don't mind.'

'I don't,' said Jonny. 'So, shall we depart? I'll walk along with you on your way to the hospital.'

'Cheers,' said Ranger Hawtrey.

'I'll go down to the pub on my own, then,' said Ranger Connor. 'It's Quiz Night tonight and I am feeling quietly confident that I will win.'

'How so?' Jonny asked.

'Because I intend to cheat. But only in the spirit of healthy competition, I hope you understand that.'

'Seven-league boots,' said Jonny.

'Exactly.'

As it was such a nice early evening, and as he was in no particular hurry, Jonny did not drive to the Cottage Hospital in the stolen Chrysler. Instead, he strolled, in the company of Ranger Hawtrey.

And a very nice stroll it was too.

There was a police presence at the Cottage Hospital. There was much in the way of 'DO NOT CROSS' tape ringing the entrance around and the parked police cars had their roof lights flashing to maximum effect. A crowd of onlookers were onlooking. Police constables, some armed with Lightsabres and death rays, were keeping this crowd back behind the tape.

'Not more trouble, I hope,' Jonny said to Charlie.

'Let's see,' said Charlie, and he nudged his way into the crowd.

'Look where you're nudging, young man,' said a lady in a straw hat. 'Some of us have been here for hours. You can't just come nudging through.'

'So sorry,' said Charlie. 'What is happening, do you know?'

The lady in the straw hat gave her nose a conspiratorial tapping. 'That's for me to know and you to find out,' she said.

'I could probably find out if you told me,' said Charlie.

'That's true enough,' said the lady, 'but such information is only granted on a strictly "need-to-know" basis.'

'I need to know,' said Charlie. 'My brother's in there.'

'The loony one, or the castrato?'

'Eh?' went Charlie. 'What and who?'

'Don't mind me,' said the lady in the straw hat. 'I get these flashes. In my head. It's my holy guardian angel, I believe, that or Barry the Time Sprout.'

'So what *is* going on?' asked Jonny, who had nudged himself level with Charlie.

'Cut yourself shaving?' asked the lady in the straw hat.

'Leprosy,' said Jonny. 'I'm highly contagious – that's why I need to get into the hospital.'

'Leprosy?' said the lady. 'I don't know what the younger generation is coming to. Rickets and phossy jaw not good enough for you? I caught elephantiasis in the Belgian Congo back in the nineteen fifties. I was running with the rebels then, fighting for the cause with Che. "Don't drink out of the puddles," they told me. But did I listen?'

Jonny shrugged.

'No,' said the lady. 'I did not. So my legs ballooned out like two tracksuit bottoms stuffed up to the crotch regions with pickled shallots. They had to ship me back to Blighty in two separate consignments.'

'Nasty,' said Jonny.

'Nasty indeed,' said the lady. 'So don't think to impress me with talk of leprous sores – I've wept mucus from places where you don't even have places.'

'What *is* going on in the hospital?' asked Charlie.

'Some loony's had his head chopped off,' said the lady.

Jonny looked at Charlie.

And Charlie looked at Jonny.

'My brother,' said Charlie, going all pale in the face.

'Don't jump to conclusions,' said Jonny.

'Some *other* loony, you suppose?'

'I'm sure there's plenty to choose from.'

'There was only the two,' said the lady. 'The special ones.'

'The two?' said Charlie.

'The special ones?' said Jonny.

'That's what I heard,' said the lady. 'I heard from a friend of mine who is the dinner lady on the Special Wing, that all the other loonys had been cleared out months ago because, according to her, who had overheard two interns chatting, something had been discovered that was going to change everything and the two remaining loonys were the key to it. Or something like that. Mind you, she's rarely fully coherent – she's got satellite TV and you know what *that* means.'

Jonny nodded slowly. 'No,' he said.

'Beams and rays from the satellite dish into the head,' said the lady. 'I always cross myself when I pass a house with a satellite dish on it, on the off chance that mankind is the work of a divine creator, rather than simply the product of the "selfish gene" or the swinging sixties. You can never be too sure of yourself, in my opinion. It's always best to adopt a belt-and-braces approach to life, whilst applying Occam's Razor, of course.'

'Of course,' said Jonny.

'I have to get into the hospital,' said Charlie.

'You'd best have an accident, then,' said the lady.

'No need,' said Charlie, and then he took Jonny by the shoulders and took to shouting. 'Make way there, please. Casualty coming through, burns victim, make way, please.'

Of course, no one *did* make way.

'Leper!' cried Jonny. 'Come for my medication.'

And but for the lady in the straw hat, who had once caught elephantiasis by drinking from a muddy puddle in the Belgian Congo whilst running with the rebels in the company of Che, the onlookers *did* make way.

The constables too stood aside.

'Careful as you go there, sir,' said one. 'I wouldn't want you nudging my trigger finger and have me setting off this doomsday weapon that I'm holding in my hand.'*

'I don't recall telling you to break out the doomsday weapons yet,' said a senior officer. 'Return it to the munitions van this minute and re-equip yourself with a phase plasma rifle (in a forty-watt range).'†

Jonny did limpings and Charlie aided him towards casualty.

There were a great many medics in the waiting room of casualty. And a great many policemen, too. And all and sundry were jabbering away and no one seemed particularly interested in Jonny or Charlie.

A lady sat behind the admissions desk. She was not wearing a straw hat. But she did look familiar.

To Charlie.

'Hello, Joan,' said Charlie. 'I didn't know you worked here.'

'I do evenings,' said Joan. 'And I'm prepared to travel, if necessary. If there's a desk to sit behind that is not already occupied, then I'll sit behind it.'

---

* As a running gag, you have probably peaked too early there. (Ed.)
† Hm! (Ed.)

'Splendid,' said Charlie.

'Are you referring to my breasts?'

'I wasn't,' said Charlie, 'but they *are* splendid.'

'Why, thank you very much. Can I help you at all? Or have you just come here to gawp at my breasts?'

'I wasn't gawping,' said Charlie.

'I was,' said Jonny.

'You *both* were,' said Joan. 'But it's acceptable, because I am not on duty at the park, so technically we are not working together. So what do you want?'

Charlie scratched at his cap. 'My brother is an, er, inmate here,' he said. 'One of the two patients in the Special Wing. I've come to visit, but I've just heard that one of the two inmates has been murdered. Please tell me that it isn't my brother.'

'It isn't your brother,' said Joan.

'Praise be,' said Charlie.

'In fact, it wasn't either of the special cases. It was a different loony altogether. An escaped loony. The one who escaped last night. He returned here for some unaccountable, but no doubt loony, reason and got into a spot of bother with a constable who was on duty here guarding the crime scene where Doctor Archy was murdered. There was some kind of altercation and the constable shot his head off with a Prozac.'

'Do you mean a projac?' Charlie asked. 'A science fiction-type weapon favoured by Kirth Gerson in Jack Vance's legendary Demon Prince series?'

'Perhaps,' said Joan. 'But being a woman, I am unlikely to admit to being wrong. Nor indeed to reading science fiction'

'I'm confused,' said Jonny. 'An escaped loony? But I thought there were only two loonys on this ward.'

'I don't make the rules,' said Joan. 'All I know is that it was an escaped loony who returned. The one who killed Doctor Archy. His name was Jonny Hooker.'

17

'Now you're confused,' said Mr Giggles the Monkey Boy. 'You're more confused than a pantomime horse with two back ends and no snout.'

'Horses don't have snouts,' whispered Jonny.

'All God's children got snouts,' sang Mr Giggles. 'Time we were off, I'm thinking.'

'Absolutely not!'

'Sorry?' said Joan, from behind the desk. 'Did you say something? Were you undressing me with your eyes? And have you cut yourself shaving?'

'No on all three counts,' said Jonny. 'What have they done with the corpse of this Jonny Hooker?'

'Some special unit took it away. Chaps in environmental suits, in a white van with "Scientific Support" printed on the sides. They erected an adventure playground for the kiddies—'

'*What* kiddies?' asked Charlie.

'Manners!' said Joan. 'A lady is talking, don't butt in.'

'Sorry,' said Charlie.

'They took the corpse away. Wrapped it up in clingfilm first and then took it away.'

'And the adventure playground?'

Joan shook her head and tut-tut-tutted. 'We're beyond that *now*,' she said. 'This is a corpse we're talking about. Don't go carping back to adventure playgrounds – behave like a man.'

Charlie gave his head a scratch. 'Do you know a lady who wears a straw hat?' he asked.

'My mum wears a straw hat,' said Joan.

'I'm sorry,' said Jonny, 'but I remain confused. How did they identify this corpse as being that of Jonny Hooker?'

'By his clothes and by his wallet.'

'Ah,' said Jonny.

'So what *have* you done to your face?' asked Joan. 'And also who are you? You're wearing a park ranger's uniform, but I've never seen you before.'

'You must have caught a glimpse of me earlier at the Big House,' said Jonny.

'Please don't contradict me – I find it so confusing.'

'I'd really like to see my brother,' said Charlie, 'if it would be all right. I'm sure all this unpleasantness must have upset him.'

'I doubt that' said Joan, 'with the amount of pharmaceuticals he's dosed up on.'

'How do you know about that?'

'Because it's my job to keep him topped up when the doctors slip out to the pub.'

Charlie sighed. And Jonny sighed with him. To keep him company, so to speak. Or offer support, or whatever.

'Can I *please* see my brother?' asked Charlie.

'Of course you may, as it's you. It's outside normal visiting hours, but I will make an exception. As it's you.' And Joan did eyelash-flutterings at Charlie.

'As it's me?' asked Charlie.

'I think—' said Jonny.

'Let him work it out in his own time,' said Joan.

'Oh,' said Charlie. And he took to smiling. A lot.

'Don't get carried away with yourself,' said Joan. 'I'd expect at the very least to be taken out to dinner first.'

'Right,' said Charlie. 'Where would you like to eat? What time do you get off?'

'Oi,' said Jonny. 'We have business to conduct here.'

'*We?*' said Joan.

'I'm with him,' said Jonny, 'come to see his brother. Well, *my* brother, too, as it happens. I'm Charlie's brother.'

'Yes,' said Charlie. 'That's right. He is.'

Joan glanced Jonny up and down.

'The castrato?' she asked.

★

They were given special visitors' badges. Special visitors' badges to admit them to the Special Wing. They were sort of laminated. They had the words 'Special Visitor' printed on the cards that were within the laminate. Although there wasn't really anything particularly special about them.

Except, of course, that they did gain you entry to the Special Wing outside of visiting hours. Which was *a bit* special.

But not much.

'Special badge,' said Charlie, giving his an approving stroke. 'I do like a special badge, me. Or a backstage pass. Now that's *really* special, a backstage pass.'

'Come and see me play,' said Jonny. 'I'm in a band, Dry Rot. We're playing on Friday at The Middle Man. We weren't going to be playing, due to me being wanted by the police, but as I'm no longer wanted, on account of me being dead, I suppose we will be playing on Friday. I'll give you a backstage pass if you want.'

'So I can come backstage?'

'Well, if there *was* a backstage. But as we're playing at The Middle Man the backstage is the gents' toilet. But the pass will enable you to use it.'

'Brilliant,' said Charlie.

'Tragic,' said Mr Giggles.

They strode along a corridor. Here and there they passed constables who carried improbable weapons of the futuristic variety.

'My brother's room is along this way,' said Charlie. 'Do try not to look *too* surprised when you see inside it.'

'Why?' asked Jonny. 'What exactly is in it?'

'Aha,' said Charlie. 'We're here.'

A police constable stood on guard before the door to Charlie's brother's abode. The police constable was not armed. But he *was* a master of the Vulcan Death Grip.

'Stand away from the door, sir,' he told Charlie, 'or I will be forced to maim and disfigure you with little more than a fingertip's pressure.'

Charlie whistled. 'Dimac?' he enquired.

'Amongst many other martial skills. Have you ever heard the expression "there's more than one way to skin a cat"?'

'More than once,' said Charlie.

'Well, I know seven different ways. And I could knock the skin off a rice pudding by sheer will-power alone.'

'You'd be a bad man to cross in a fight, then,' said Jonny.

'The worst,' said the constable, 'because not only am I skilled in all these martial arts, I'm also just aching to use them on some unsuspecting individual who gets my back up over some trivial matter.'

'Didn't I say that martial artists are always looking for an excuse to do that?' asked Jonny of Charlie. 'Or was it you?'

'It might have been me,' said Charlie, 'but since I met you I no longer appear to be able to keep a firm grip on reality.'

'So,' said the constable, 'away on your toes in a sprightly manner or suffer the consequences in the form of badly broken bones that will take months to knit. And then not too successfully.'

'We've special visitors' badges,' said Jonny. 'We've come to visit the patient in this room.'

'We don't use the "P" word here,' said the constable. 'Here we call a loony a loony. Or at least I do. And frankly, who, other than a superior officer, is liable to argue with *me*?'

'Not me for one,' said Jonny. 'So can we go in? Please?'

'Of course,' said the constable. 'A pleasure to talk to you. I do trust that we will meet again sometime, under more violent circumstances.'

'Yes,' said Jonny. 'I *do* hope so.'

'Are you being sarcastic?'

'Absolutely *not*,' said Jonny.

'Shame,' said the constable.

He slid back a bolt, the constable did, and he pushed the cell door open. For such indeed it was. A cell. There's no bandying about in mental wards, and in isolation rooms. An isolation room *is* a cell. A padded one, generally. And they smell of disinfectant. Of bleach and of that certain hospital smell. It's a frightening smell. It stays in your nostrils.

Jonny smelled that smell as the cell door opened. Jonny had smelled that smell before. On far too many occasions. And one of them far too recent.

And Jonny followed Charlie into the cell. The cell that smelled of that certain smell.

And then Jonny smelled more and he saw more also. As one will when one enters a new room for the first time and views the unexpected.

And Jonny's jaw hung slack and Jonny gaped in awe.

And Charlie said, 'Jonny, this is my brother.'

And the constable, who was skilled in martial arts, slammed shut the cell door and slid the bolt home.

And Jonny looked towards Charlie's brother.

And Charlie's brother was as Charlie.

For he was an identical twin.

Which, perhaps, was a little surprising to Jonny, as Charlie had not thought to mention that his older brother was his twin, and therefore older by little more than a few minutes. But, perhaps, as surprising as this was to Jonny, it was not, as it were, the thing that surprised him the most and had his jaw hanging slack and his mouth all gaping wide.

This thing was another thing altogether.

And this thing was the fact that Charlie's identical twin brother was not anchored to the floor of his cell by the force of gravity, as one might reasonably expect. Charlie's identical twin sat in the lotus position, floating three feet above the floor.

And as the draught from the closing door caught him, he fluttered like a leaf on a breeze and fair put the wind up Jonny.

18

'Smoke and mirrors,' said Mr Giggles. 'Seen it all at the music hall.'

Jonny mouthed the words, 'Shut up now,' but did not speak them aloud.

'My brother, Hari,' said Charlie. 'Hari, this is my friend, David, David Chicoteen.'

'I don't think there's any need for that,' said Jonny. 'I'm very pleased to meet you, Hari. My name is Jonny Hooker.'

Jonny edged a little closer to the floater and put out a tentative hand for a shake. But it was only a tentative hand, as there was this fellow, stabilized somewhat now, but still clearly hovering in the air.

'I ...' went Jonny. 'I ... I really don't know what to say.'

'Give me a minute, please.' The arms of Hari were folded over his chest. These arms he now unfolded and stretched wide, clicking his neck and giving a bit of a yawn. And then he uncrossed his legs and extended these to the floor of the cell. And all at once he was standing.

'It wasn't so much the voices that put Hari in here,' said Charlie, and *he* shook Hari's hand and gave him a bit of a brotherly hug. 'It was his constant law-breaking.'

'The law of gravity,' said Hari. 'Never could be having with it, wished like crazy to try to break it, tried like crazy and, as the old saying goes, if at first you don't succeed, you must be doing it wrong.'

Jonny Hooker shook his head and gave a whistle, too. 'You really *were* floating in the air, weren't you?' he said. 'I mean, *that* was really real.'

'Really real,' said Charlie's identical twin. 'But I suppose you could say that it's a bit of a cheat.'

'So it *is* smoke and mirrors.'

'No, I simply found that the only way I could float in the air – fly, in fact – was to do it the same way you do.'

'I don't do it at all,' said Jonny.

'Oh, I think you do. Nearly all of us do.'

'In our dreams,' said Jonny.

'Precisely.'

Jonny Hooker shook his head again. 'But I'm not dreaming now,' he said.

'Which is why *you* can't fly. You are awake and so you cannot dream that you are flying. I, however, am asleep, and so *I* can.'

'That doesn't make any sense,' said Jonny. 'I'm awake.'

'And I'm asleep. Somewhere away from here, all tucked up in my cosy little cot.'

'He's a stone bonker,' said Mr Giggles. 'Good levitation stunt, though.'

'You are in your cosy little cot?' said Jonny.

'And I'm five years old. What a queer dream this is.'

'Ah,' said Jonny.

'And please don't "Ah" me,' said Hari. 'I am *not* a stone bonker. You saw me hovering in the air, did you not?'

'I think I did,' said Jonny.

'Oh, it's "think you did" now, is it? You *know* you did, so don't go trying to fool yourself that you didn't. And if the only way a man can fly, if that man is not *Superman,* is when he's dreaming, then one of us is now dreaming the other. I think you *must* agree.'

'Well,' said Jonny.

'Don't take any guff from this swine,' said Mr Giggles, which rang a bell somewhere. 'He's trying to tie you up in knots. As you're presently into violence, kick him in the nuts – that will prove which one of you is awake.'

'So,' said Hari, 'am *I* dreaming *you*, or are *you* dreaming *me?*'

'Nuts,' said Mr Giggles. 'One in the nuts, then off on our way.'

'I am perplexed,' said Jonny.

'As are we all. Come sit yourself down; let us talk the toot and see which way the blighter goes.'

'Thank you.' And Jonny sat down.

'Not there,' said Hari.

And so Jonny moved.

'Nor there, either.'

'Here?'

'Not there.'

'How about here?'

'There's good,' said Hari. 'But the other places weren't.'

Jonny gave the other places glancings. They all looked good to him.

'Areas of ill omen and bad portent,' said Hari, 'where evil has been done and sorrow felt. I see them, you see, like smears upon a spectacle lens. Where you're sitting now is a good place. It suits you.'

'I'm sitting on the seat of your lavatory,' said Jonny.

'I'm beginning to warm to this clown,' said Mr Giggles. 'But I still feel you should kick him in the nuts.'

'And you're really comfortable there,' said Hari, and he made enigmatic hand wavings.

'Actually, I'm not,' said Jonny.

'Yes, you are, you're *really* comfortable.' Hari waved his hands about some more, but Jonny shook his head.

'Dammit,' said Hari. 'The constable on the door, who is skilled in the Vulcan Death Grip, sold me a wrong'n there.'

'Wrong'n?' Jonny enquired.

'A course in Jedi Mind Control. He said he'd downloaded it off the Interweb.'

Jonny smiled painfully. 'That wasn't very funny,' he said.

'No.' Hari cosied himself upon his bunk. He stretched out his legs and waggled his big toes, for as with most loonys he went barefoot. And as there was now nowhere, but for the floor, for Charlie to sit, Charlie stood.

'Jonny's been involved in all kinds of exciting adventures,' said Charlie to his brother. 'And he wanted to meet you.'

'And about time, too,' said Hari. 'I have been awaiting his arrival.'

'You *have*?' said Jonny.

'He *hasn't*,' said Mr Giggles.

'I might have been,' said Hari. 'I await the arrival of so many people – Members of Parliament, members of the royal household. Are *you* a member of anything?'

'I'm in a band,' said Jonny. 'I'm a musician.'

Ah,' said Hari. 'A musician, that must be it. So who sent you – Project Beta, the Ministry of Serendipity, the Sons of the Silent Age, MJ Twelve, MJ Thirteen, the Minge Tree Appreciation Society?'

'There isn't really a Minge Tree Appreciation Society, is there?' Jonny asked.

'No, but there should be. So why are you here?'

'I'm caught up in something,' said Jonny. 'I don't know exactly what, but it does somehow have something to do with music, of this I'm sure. And people are apparently dying because I have got caught up in it, or so it seems to me. And I am determined to find out what it is and solve what it is, and if there's a prize at the end of it, then so much the better.'

'All sounds terribly vague,' said Charlie's brother.

'Well, when put like that I suppose it does. But *I* know what I mean. And whatever it is I'm involved in *is* terribly exciting and *is* making me feel alive for possibly the first time in my life.'

Hari Hawtrey rolled onto his side and fixed his gaze upon Jonny. 'You've got demons, haven't you, Jonny? Demons and imps, is that it?'

'One in particular,' said Jonny.

'Easy now, please, Jonny boy,' said Mr Giggles.

'Your brother was telling me about the voices you hear,' Jonny said. 'And he *does* take them seriously – he wears tinfoil inside his cap.'

'Wearing it now,' said Charlie, tapping at his cap.

'But you're not wearing any tinfoil,' said Jonny to Charlie's brother.

'I wear it when I'm awake. But what is it you want to know? What is it that you think *I* know?'

'Anything,' said Jonny. 'Anything and everything. Anything that you know or believe.'

'No,' said Charlie's brother. 'You're not ready for that, not yet.'

'I'm as ready as I'll ever be.'

'I'll tell you some,' said Hari. 'I'll tell you some if you promise to do me a favour in return.'

'It's a deal,' said Jonny.

'No, it's *not* a deal,' said Mr Giggles. 'Ask him what he wants in return first. He might be hoping to give you one up the chocolate speedway. Drop anchor in Poo Bay, as it were.'

Jonny Hooker gritted his teeth.

'It's nothing sexual,' said Hari. 'In case that's what you're thinking.'

Jonny Hooker shook his head.

'Then I'll tell you something. As you are a musician, I will tell you something of a musical nature. Have you ever heard of a musician by the name of Robert Johnson?'

Jonny nodded. 'Many times,' said he.

'And so you've heard about his final recording?'

'His thirtieth,' said Jonny. 'The one with the Devil's laughter at the end. Allegedly. "Apocalypse Blues" it was called.'

'You know *that*. I am impressed.'

'I only found out today,' said Jonny, 'but I think it's part of the something I'm caught up in.'

'And so you must have heard the urban legend that all those rock stars who died aged twenty-seven did so because they were played the recording of the Devil's laughter.'

Jonny nodded once more.

'And so did you hear the other legend – the one that balances it, so to speak?'

Jonny Hooker shook his head. 'Go on, please,' he said.

'About the angel,' said Hari. 'The angel and the castrato.'

Jonny Hooker raised an eyebrow. 'Is this about your brother?'

'It seems to be something of an open secret,' said Charlie, shrugging away like a good'n.

'Well, it's not him,' said Hari. 'Although there is a connection. The name of this castrato was Alessandro Moreschi. He was born in Montecompatrio in eighteen fifty-eight and died in nineteen twenty-two. He was reckoned to be the very last castrato. During his professional life as a soloist with the Vatican choir, he was known as the Angel of Rome, because his voice was the very epitomy of polyphonic purity. He was the only castrato ever to make recordings and these were made just after the turn of the twentieth century.'

'I've never really understood about castrati,' said Jonny. 'What *was* the point?'

'Purity of tone. During the golden age of castrati, between sixteen fifty and seventeen fifty, it was reckoned that as many as four thousand boys a year were being castrated in Italy, their impoverished parents hoping that these unhappy lads would find fame and fortune – and there was much fortune to be had for the few who made it to the top. The idea was to preserve the high-pitched voice of the child, and when the voice was projected by adult-sized lungs it produced a sound so beautiful that audiences were known to collapse in tears.

'Moreschi was the last of his kind, and fate it must surely have been that he lived into the twentieth century, into a time when his extraordinary voice could be recorded upon wax cylinders. There were eighteen recordings made at the Vatican and you can even buy a cleaned-up digitally enhanced version on CD.* But there's one recording that isn't on that CD: Moreschi singing Handel's "Ombra mai fu". It is said that his voice was so beautiful, so pure, so heavenly, that folk weep when they hear that recording. But they do more than weep, because so sweet was the voice of Moreschi, so heavenly, in fact, that as he sang, his voice reached up to Heaven and an angel descended to Earth and joined him in the final chorus. And *that* is on the recording.'

Jonny Hooker shook his head, slowly and with thought. 'And do *you* think that's true?' he asked.

'True?' Hari Hawtrey smiled. 'Yes. *I* think it's true. But then *I* would, because *I* have heard that recording.'

'Really?' Jonny Hooker said. 'Really, truly truly?'

'And I soared,' said Hari. 'I soared and I glowed and I was filled with the spirit.' And as Jonny looked on and Charlie looked on, Hari became transfigured. He glowed as if lit from within and he drifted up from the floor.

'And with this,' he said, and his voice came as a wind from his mouth, 'and with this, with the hearing of this, the hearing of an angel's voice, I heard a sound that no man may hear until he is called up into the choirs invisible upon his death. So the gifts were given unto me, that I should hear their voices, the voices of the angels, but also the voices of the evil ones. That I should hear them here in my head. And thus I became an outcast, ridiculed by men, a social

* And I'm not lying. Type his name into your computer and order a copy.

pariah, a loony, doomed to live as a prisoner. Thus and so.' And Hari made the sign of the cross and drifted back to the floor.

And the candle glow dimmed all away and things turned somewhat quiet.

Jonny Hooker suddenly gasped for air, aware that he had somehow forgotten to breathe.

'And relax,' said Hari, and he settled back down on his bunk.

'Wow,' said Jonny. 'I mean, wow, well, wow.' And so well wowed was Jonny that he ignored the contradictory nature of what Hari had previously said, that he was in the Special Wing because he flouted the law of gravity, yet wasn't in the Special Wing at all, because he was really five years old and asleep in his bed somewhere. And Jonny just concentrated on the WOW factor. Because a recording of an angel's voice would have something of a wow factor.

Charlie Hawtrey wiped away a tear. 'I always get a bit of a crinkly mouth when he tells that story,' he said. 'Although I've heard it lots of times before.'

'I give a moving account,' said Hari. 'And so that is that and now you must do me the favour you promised me.'

'Oh yes,' said Jonny. 'Yes indeed, anything you want.'

'Splendid,' said Hari. 'It's not a big thing. I doubt if a young man such as yourself, bound upon a mission that may turn out to be sacred (well, you never know), would have much of a problem carrying it out.'

'Name it,' said Jonny.

'Bust me out of this prison cell,' said Charlie's brother, Hari.

19

'No,' said Mr Giggles. 'No, no, no.'

'Yes,' said Jonny Hooker. 'It's a deal.'

'No, Jonny, listen, please.' Mr Giggles was once more agitated, once more animated. 'This joker is one hundred per cent fruitcake, a fruit-loop, a fruit and nut, a nutty fruit-nut-loopy-cake, a—'

'A loop-nut-fruit-cake-cakey-nut-fruity-fruit-job?' whispered Jonny, without moving his lips.

'And the rest. Get out while you can. Make a run for it now.'

'Pack your bag, then,' said Jonny to Hari, 'and we're out of here.'

Charlie looked at Jonny. Very hard. 'Are you sure about this?' he asked. 'I mean, well, I mean ... '

Jonny Hooker did some shrugging. 'It's fair,' he said. 'I agreed to do him a favour and he told a good tale. I don't know if it's pertinent or not, but it was a good tale. I don't think he should be banged up in here, so I'm setting him free.'

'Top man,' said Hari.

'But you can't just bust him out, just like that.' Charlie put conviction into his voice. 'These things take planning, lots of planning – you can't just spring someone from incarceration on the spur of the moment.'

'Of course I can,' said Jonny. 'It's a piece of cake. A piece of fruity-loop nutty-nut cake.'

'No,' said Charlie. 'It's not. It's really not.'

'Listen to this man,' said Mr Giggles. 'He's a bit of a geek, but he knows what he's talking about on this occasion.'

'Please leave it to me,' said Jonny.

'But you haven't any weapons,' said Charlie.

Jonny shrugged some more. 'Do you still have that print out of the Jedi Mind Control techniques?' he asked Hari.

'No,' said Hari, who was packing his toothbrush. 'I wiped my bum on them and threw them at the constable. He gave me quite a hiding, I can tell you. But I deserved it, so that was okay.'

'Run,' said Mr Giggles. 'Run now and fast.'

'Right,' said Jonny. 'So this is the plan.'

The constable who was skilled in the Vulcan Death Grip, amongst so many other things, released the bolt and let Jonny and Charlie return to the corridor.

'Enjoy the visit to your brother?' he asked Charlie.

'Not much,' said Charlie. 'And it was jolly unsporting of you to sell him sheets of nonsense about Jedi Mind Control.'

'He was very happy with them and you're so happy that he's happy,' said the constable. And he waved his hands a bit. Enigmatically.

'He *is* very happy with them and I *am* so happy that he's happy,' said Charlie.

The constable winked at Jonny.

'No way,' said Jonny.

But the constable grinned.

'Well,' said Jonny. 'Most impressive.'

'What?' said Charlie. '*What?*'

'Nothing,' said Jonny, and *he* winked at the constable.

'Did I ask whether you'd cut yourself shaving?' asked the constable.

'No,' said Jonny. 'I don't think you did. Charlie's brother is having a little meditate now, but he'd like you to awaken him, possibly with a tap to the skull with your truncheon, in ten minutes – would that be all right?'

'I'll do my best,' said the constable. 'We policemen are the servants of the public, after all. It is our duty to do our best for the community at large and the public as a whole.'

Jonny paused.

But the constable didn't crack a smile.

But the setting sun went behind a cloud and that dog howled again in the distance.

'Most impressive once more,' said Jonny, and he bade the constable farewell, and he and Charlie plodded away up the corridor.

'Could we elevate this plod to a bit of a march, or a least a stalk?'

asked Charlie. 'I'd like to be out of this horrible place as quickly as possible.'

'Ever anxious to oblige,' said Jonny, gathering speed.

They left the Cottage Hospital, passed beneath the 'DO NOT CROSS' tape and nudged their way back through the crowd, stopping only to exchange pleasantries with the lady in the straw hat, who might or might not have been Joan's mum. They set off over the Great West Road and via a somewhat crooked route they made for The Middle Man.

The Middle Man wasn't doing much when it came to the way of business. But O'Fagin, who stood as ever behind the bar counter, although upon this night with a bandaged head and an eyepatch, was grateful that the pub was open for business at all, considering the pounding it had taken shortly after Jonny had left it earlier that day.

'Bopped me on the head, he did,' said O'Fagin to Charlie, pointing to his wounded head as he did so. 'Robbed the till,' (Jonny raised his eyebrows to this) 'and had it away on his toes, by some route still unknown. But while I'm out for the count, the police outside start bawling through a loud hailer: "Give yourself up, Jonny Hooker, or we come in all guns blazing." But of course he's gone and I'm out like a dead-dog's eye at a Balinese barbecue.' (Jonny raised his eyebrows once again.) 'So the next thing is they're having at this pub with weapons of mass destruction and the Lord Gary Glitter knows what else. I had to shore up the bog wall with some railway ties I was saving to make a feature of in my back garden. I've had to cancel Quiz Night, which didn't please Ranger Connor. He went off in a right huff.'

O'Fagin presented Charlie and Jonny with the pints of King Billy that Charlie had ordered. 'But that's enough about me for now,' he continued. 'You'll probably be reading about it in the papers tomorrow – "LOCAL PUBLICAN'S HEROISM", I did some interviews with the press, sold them the real story.'

'*Sold* them?' mouthed Jonny, and up went his eyebrows again.

'And now, so I heard on the wireless set this afternoon, Jonny Hooker's dead,' O'Fagin continued some more, 'so his mum will have to pay off the huge bar tab he ran up here.'

Jonny Hooker's teeth now ground together.

'What a life, eh?' said O'Fagin. 'So how *has* your day been, Ranger Hawtrey? And who is this with you and has he cut himself shaving?'

'Allergy,' said Charlie. 'Although surely now—'

'Still an allergy,' said Jonny.

'He's my brother,' said Charlie.

'Really?' said O'Fagin, 'now as the loony one is banged up, this must be the castrato.'

'Indeed it is,' said Jonny in a very high voice, which almost set him to giggling.

'I've always wanted to meet a castrato,' said O'Fagin. 'There's something I've always wanted to ask.'

'The answer is "deep in the heart of Texas",' said Jonny.

'Really?' said O'Fagin. 'I thought it was "somewhere over the rainbow".'*

'Easy mistake,' said Jonny.

Charlie whispered at Jonny's ear. 'Those ten minutes you told the constable who is guarding my brother's cell about are now up,' he whispered, checking his wristwatch. 'What is going to happen now?'

Jonny put his hand to his ear. 'Hearken unto,' he said. And in the not altogether too far distance, the alarm bell of the Cottage Hospital began to ring.

'Now there's a sound you don't hear every day,' said O'Fagin. 'The escaped loony alarm. Although, come to think of it, it seems to have been going off with painful regularity recently.'

'One more pint of King Billy, please,' said Jonny to O'Fagin.

'But you haven't finished that one yet.'

'It's not for me.'

O'Fagin diddled his fingers on the bar counter, as he had never really been one for shrugging. 'As you please,' said he, and he did the business.

Jonny paid up and he and Charlie took themselves off to a darkened corner. *The* darkened corner. That notorious darkened corner.

And presently a policeman entered the bar, made his way to the

* Opinions naturally vary on this.

table of Charlie and Jonny, sat down at it, took up the spare pint and drained it to its very dregs.

'Very impressive,' said Charlie.

'The simplest ones are always the best,' said the policeman. In the voice of Charlie's brother. Because it *was* Charlie's brother. The loony one, *not* the castrato.

'Cheers, Jonny,' said Hari.

'Cheers to you,' Jonny replied.

'Okay,' said Charlie, 'would you please just run this by me one more time. I'm not quite sure what just happened.'

'Oldest trick in the book,' said Hari. 'The old switcheroo. Or was it? You were there, in the cell – you saw it all.'

'I looked away,' said Charlie.

'Ah, so you did. Well, what happened was that Jonny bound me hand and foot with shirts and socks and suchlike and gagged me, too. Then he left with you, telling the constable to wake me from my meditation in ten minutes. The constable entered the cell ten minutes after you'd gone, found me struggling in my bondage, pulled the gag from my mouth and heard me then shout, "Stop him, stop him – it's my loony brother who left the cell. I'm Charlie Hawtrey." Oldest trick in the book.'

'But a classic,' said Jonny.

'Absolute classic,' said Hari. 'And to add weight, I made a real fuss, shouted about my brother stealing my uniform and how my uniform meant everything to me. I put on such a good show that the sergeant in charge, who was chatting up that Joan—'

'She fancies me,' said Charlie.

'And me also,' said Hari. 'That sergeant ordered the martial artist constable to strip to his undies and give me his uniform.'

'Nice touch,' said Jonny.

'I'm not so sure,' said Charlie. 'After all, that constable did make Hari very happy by selling him that Jedi Mind Control stuff, and I am *so* happy that he's happy.'

'Eh?' said Hari.

'What did I just say?' said Charlie.

'Nothing,' said Jonny. 'Continue, Hari.'

'Well, that's about it,' said Hari. 'Oh, I did get the sergeant to make the constable in the underwear drive me here to the pub. The least he could do, considering, don't you think?'

'I certainly do,' said Jonny, and he drained his pint to dregs which were like unto the dregs of the glass that had been drained by Hari. So to speak.

'Your round, Hari,' said Jonny.

'This is nonsense,' said Charlie. 'No one could ever really get away with all that. It's ludicrous.'

'I thought you were enjoying it,' said Jonny. 'I thought you said that it was all very exciting and you were loving every minute of it.'

'Oh yes,' said Charlie, 'I did. So I should just ignore the fact that it's ludicrous, do you think?'

Jonny nodded.

And Hari nodded. And, 'Ah,' said Hari, patting at his constable's uniform. 'The constable's wallet is still in his pocket. Drinks on me, I think.'

'I'll get them in,' said Jonny and he took the wallet. 'If you go up to the bar and O'Fagin recognises you, things could get a bit complicated.'

'He'll never recognise me,' said Hari. 'I'm wearing a police uniform. People never recognise even close friends when they're dressed up in a uniform.'

Jonny made a 'so-so' face.

'Oh, stuff it,' said Charlie. 'Let Hari go. What could possibly happen?'

20

Hari returned from the bar in the blissful company of beers. 'I just love that O'Fagin,' he said. 'Although not in a physical sense, for that would be abhorrent. But for one, such as myself, who is a student of human nature, I have to say that a more singularly unspeakably dishonest individual never drew breath to my knowledge. If one discounts all the well-known criminals, of course.'

'Quite so,' said Jonny, taking up the new beer he had been issued with and going 'cheers' with it. 'What is he up to now?'

'Selling his life story to the Sunday tabloids, apparently. He is of the conviction that this very pub is an epicentre for paranormal phenomena.'

'Upon what grounds does he base this particular conviction?' Jonny asked.

'None whatsoever, I should imagine. The man is a scoundrel.'

'And it takes one to know one, nah-nah-ne-nah-nah,' went Mr Giggles, closely, it seemed, at Jonny's right ear.

Jonny ignored the troublesome Monkey Boy whilst wondering whether or not Mr Giggles fell into the category of psychic phenomena. All too well, he supposed.

'So,' said Hari, 'many thanks once again to you, Jonny, for arranging my escape. I'm wondering whether we might continue to do favours for one another upon a mutually beneficial basis.'

Jonny Hooker smiled through his Elastoplasts.

'So,' said Hari, once more, 'do you have any clear idea about exactly what this quest you seem to be on might be?'

Jonny Hooker scratched his head. 'Not as such,' said he. 'I know that it is something to do with a letter I received, telling me that I was a competition winner. It would appear that in order to claim my prize, I must solve something that I have whimsically named the Da-da-de-da-da Code. Although the man who printed the competition letters is now dead, which, although it might have put the kibosh somewhat on winning the prize, does appear to have elevated the competition to a higher level. There *is* a secret, and some person, or persons, are prepared to murder in order to keep this secret.'

'Is this "da-da-de-da-da" as in music?' Hari asked.

'I am assuming so. As fate takes me from one place to another, I find myself meeting people who tell me tales – of Robert Johnson, of Moreschi the castrato, of an Air Loom that weaves music into words. It all seems to be musically related. But as to where it's all leading? That's anyone's guess.'

'Air Loom?' said Hari. 'Who spoke to you of the Air Loom?'

Charlie made the face of shame.

'It's a good story,' said Jonny. 'I think it has more than a ring of truth to it, being set, as it was, years before such technology could possibly exist. I'm wondering whether this James Tilly Matthews character actually did see some kind of machine. It's possible. I was hoping you might be able to shed some light on the matter.'

Hari took to the sipping of ale.

'Did you by any chance ever meet a Mister James Crawford?' Jonny asked.

Hari ceased supping. 'Why do you ask?'

'Because there is an empty record sleeve on the shelves of his collection marked "Apocalypse Blues" by Robert Johnson.'

'James Crawford allowed *you* access to his collection?'

'Not as such,' said Jonny, and he pulled the small leather-bound notebook from his pocket. The one with the bloodstains on it.

'Oh dear,' said Hari, leaning back on his bar stool. 'If you have his notebook then—'

'I'm sorry,' said Jonny. 'He's dead.'

'Oh dear, poor James. I assume it was not a natural death.'

'Someone cut off his head,' said Jonny. 'Probably the same someone who cut off the head of Doctor Archy and whoever was in the hospital today wearing *my* clothes and carrying *my* wallet.'

'Oh dear, oh dear,' said Hari. 'Things are far worse than I thought. Although I'm glad about Doctor Archy. He was a stinker, him.'

'James Crawford printed the letter that I received,' said Jonny, 'on the Protein Man's printing press beneath Gunnersbury Park Museum.'

'We went there through a secret passage,' said Charlie. 'It was very exciting. I recognised the typeface on the letter – I have to take the credit for that.'

'The credit.' Hari smiled, and it was a smile that lacked somewhat for humour. 'Your discovery and your disclosure of it to Jonny here no doubt precipitated James Crawford's death.'

'Oh,' said Charlie. 'I don't think that can be the case.'

'Have you read the contents of this book?' Jonny asked Hari.

'Naturally. James and I spoke a great deal about the subject of the Influencing Machine. He had become convinced that he had been magnetised and that a nearby machine was being tuned to his vibratory signature.'

'And do *you* believe this?'

'Yes, I do,' said Hari. 'But remember, I have been certified insane.'

'Myself also,' said Jonny. 'Several times, the latest being the day before yesterday.'

'I suspect that you are quite as sane as me,' said Hari.

'Right,' said Jonny. 'So let us say, for argument's sake, that some modern equivalent of Tilly's Air Loom were to exist. And James Crawford had been targeted by the operators. And he sought help by printing the competition letters, hoping that they might mean something to someone, someone who would help him. Then it seems logical that it would be a member of a present-day Air Loom Gang who murdered him. Does that make any sense?'

'It does to *me*,' said Hari. 'How about you?'

'I wouldn't describe myself as warming to the idea, but there is a certain cold-blooded logic to this, assuming that such a machine were actually to exist.'

'You've read *all* the contents of the notebook?' asked Hari.

'I have,' said Jonny. 'He speaks of control: that the Gang seek to control all. And somehow it's done through music, music that is played on the keyboard of the machine and which somehow translates itself into aural messages beamed into the brain of the unlucky targetee.'

'In as much of a nutshell as one requires to house a nut, yes.'

'How would you know?' Jonny asked.

'Know what?' Hari asked.

'Know if you had been targeted, if you had been magnetised?'

'There lies the problem,' said Hari. 'James Tilly Matthews gave exceedingly complex descriptions of the Loom and the Gang employed in its operation. It's all most detailed. But he couldn't *prove* any of it. He couldn't prove that he had been magnetised, or that Members of Parliament were being targeted, although that was what he believed. He couldn't prove it, but he made a real nuisance of himself to the high muck-a-mucks of his day about it and so he was declared mad and spent twelve years in Bedlam. Talk of disembodied voices tends to lead the talker directly to the madhouse.'

'Some things never change,' said Jonny. 'But could there *really* be a present-day Air Loom?' And, for that matter, could it be under the control of the deathless supervillain, Count Otto Black? What do you think?

'Do you have a computer?' Hari asked. 'Check the web, check the conspiracy-theory sites. If the technology didn't exist in Matthews' time, it's odds-on favourite that it does now. And if it exists, you can bet your bottom dollar that someone will be using it.'

'To what end?'

'You know to what end – control.'

'So we're talking about the CIA, or some undercover covert government operation? Beaming voices into people's heads?'

'I did have the constable who dropped me off here take me first to a nearby corner shop.' Hari lifted his police cap. It was lined with tinfoil.

'But I thought you said that you had been given the gift for hearing voices through hearing the recording of the angel singing.'

'There are voices and there are *voices*,' said Hari. 'Nothing is simple, nothing straightforward. One could easily go mad thinking about this stuff.'

Jonny nodded. 'One certainly could.'

'I was wondering,' said Charlie, 'whether, Jonny, you might put us up for the night at your house? I don't think it would be safe for us to go to ours – it's the first place the police will stake out in search of Hari.'

'Oh my sweet Lord,' said Jonny, spluttering somewhat into his beer. '*My* place. *My* mum. She must think that I'm dead, that I was murdered.'

'Then won't she be pleased when she learns that you're not?'

Jonny Hooker shook his head. 'I somehow doubt that,' he said. 'I'm sure that she's heard all the news and I'm sure she's made up her mind that I'm a homicidal maniac. And when it turns out that I'm still alive, I will still be the number-one suspect for the murders, including the one of my bogus self. Which the police will probably reason that I did in order to fake my own death.'

'Difficult times for you,' said Charlie. 'So it's not back to your place, then?'

'No,' said Jonny. 'It's not.'

'But you do intend to continue with this quest of yours?' said Hari. 'It does appear to be coalescing into a quest to seek the murderer and clear your own name. And to uncover the existence of the Air Loom Gang.'

'Yes,' said Jonny. 'It rather does look like that, doesn't it?'

'So where are we staying tonight?' Charlie asked. 'Because I must get a good night's sleep or I will be all grumpy in the morning.'

Jonny did raisings of his eyebrows.

Hari just shook his head.

'We could sneak into Gunnersbury Park,' was Jonny's suggestion, 'hole up in the rangers' hut for the night.'

'Good thinking,' said Charlie. 'Are you up for that, Hari?'

Hari nodded. 'And first thing in the morning I'm on my way.'

'To where?' Charlie asked.

'To anywhere,' said Hari. 'I'm an escaped lunatic, and in the current climate I'll probably find myself being shot on sight by some constable with a photon-torpedo launcher, or something.'

'I was hoping you might help me,' said Jonny.

'Given your record so far, how long do you think my head would remain upon my shoulders?'

'Perhaps I should come with you, Hari,' said Charlie, 'keep you company. Where do you think, Tierra del Feugo?'

'So I have to do this on my own?' Jonny took sup from his pint.

'Think of yourself as the hero,' said Hari. 'A loner, an outcast, but a seeker after truth who will ultimately succeed and make good.'

'And is that how *you* see me?'

'I was suggesting that it was how you should see yourself.'

Jonny Hooker shrugged and nodded a not-too-winning combination.

'All right,' said he. 'I'll go it alone.'

'You're brave,' said Hari. 'I'm sure you'll succeed.'

'You *are*?'

'I do wish you wouldn't keep asking me these leading questions.' Hari fished into the upper-right breast pocket of the uniform that he wore. 'I wonder if they still carry the regulation— Ah, yes, they do.' And he pulled out a small pocket compass. 'This might be of some use to you,' he said, and he handed it to Jonny.

Jonny took the Metropolitan Police-issue compass. 'In case I get lost?' he said.

'No, in case you get—' Hari paused. 'Shall we say that it would probably have helped James Tilly Matthews if he'd thought to carry one.'

Jonny placed the compass gently onto the table before him. He peered down at the glass. The needle was pointing firmly. It was pointing towards Jonny.

But Jonny did not lie (or indeed sit) to the magnetic north of the compass. Quite to the contrary, in fact.

Jonny's jaw went just a little slack. 'Does this mean—' he began.

'It means,' said Hari, 'that you'll probably be wanting to wear some tinfoil under your cap.'

21

Jonny Hooker spent a most uncomfortable night in the hut. It wasn't a physical discomfort, for he slept upon a rather comfortable Regency-style chaise longue, with cabriole legs and a gilded muff trumble. It was a serious mental discomfort. And Jonny was no stranger to this. All his life he had been haunted. Haunted and driven. Haunted and driven by Mr Giggles. Imaginary friend? Audio/visual hallucination pumped into his head from an Air Loom? What?

Jonny now had tinfoil lining his cap.

And Mr Giggles was silent.

Which meant ... ?

Jonny didn't know what this meant. That Mr Giggles' voice had been smothered by a layer of tinfoil? Or that Mr Giggles was simply away for a while? Or lying low, or playing a prank?

And magnetised?

For Jonny *was* magnetised – he had discovered that he could lift pins from a table top without touching them. Which was surely proof, wasn't it?

Proof of the Air Loom's existence.

Jonny knew it was nothing of the kind.

There might be myriad explanations. And if it were proof, then whom could he trust to confide this truth in? He could hardly turn up at a police station and declare himself alive and magnetised. He would once more be the wanted man. The escaped lunatic. The murder suspect. And who would believe him anyway? He had no *real* proof. He wasn't even certain that he believed in the Air Loom himself.

He would just have to wait. Wait until Mr Giggles raised his hairy head again. Wait until he had some hard evidence. Wait until he could prove his innocence.

But then waiting, as such, was out of the question. He had to act. And act now (well, perhaps not right *now*, but certainly first thing in the morning). Act before the forces of law caught up with him. Or even the Air Loom Gang. If the tinfoil cut off their mental probings they would surely know, wouldn't they? And if they suspected that he was onto them, they would kill him.

Or would they? They hadn't killed him so far and he seemed to have found out a lot. But then perhaps they hadn't killed him because they wanted him to take the rap for their murderings. That was more than possible.

In fact, *that* made a great deal of sense.

And so Jonny tossed and turned on the chaise, ever careful not to dislodge his cap.

A victim of his own thoughts.

Here indeed lay madness.

The dawn chorus wakened Jonny, which at least meant that he had managed to snatch a little sleep. It woke him to a view of a clear blue sky, through a window that was somewhat steamed up by the condensed breaths of three sleepers. But the other makeshift bunks were now empty; the brothers Hawtrey had departed. They had, however, left fifty quid on the table for Jonny, which was kind, at least.

'So,' said Jonny, trousering the money, 'that's it. All on my own.'

'Not entirely,' said the voice of Mr Giggles.

Jonny clutched at his foil-lined cap. It was still firmly stuck to his head.

'You didn't believe any of that guff, did you?' Mr Giggles giggled. 'That Hari is dafter than a bucket of blowfish. All he wanted was for you to set him free. And now you can have that on your conscience, too.'

'How so?' Jonny asked.

'You can be *so* dim,' said Mr Giggles. 'Those two were in it all together – surely you reasoned that out.'

'What *are* you talking about?'

'That Hari is a paranoid schizophrenic.'

'Just like me, then?'

'A lot worse than you. I'll bet it was him who did for Doctor

Archy. Or his brother in some previous and foiled attempt to release Hari.'

'That doesn't make any sense.'

'They used you, Jonny.'

'Then why tell me all that stuff?'

'To reinforce your own beliefs. Tinfoil in your cap? Did you really believe that I was being beamed into your bonce by a gang with a magical machine?'

'Hm,' went Jonny.

'I know what "Hm" means.'

'I don't trust you,' said Jonny. 'And I do not believe anything that you tell me.'

'And yet I'm certain it was me who got you started on this quest of yours in the first place. Because it did seem like a bit of a laugh. At the time.'

'Aha,' said Jonny. 'But the things *you* told me tie up with the things *they* told me.'

'Toot,' said Mr Giggles.

Jonny raised himself from the chaise, stretched his limbs, sought the frying pan. Prepared breakfast.

'I love the smell of hash browns in the morning,' said Mr Giggles.

'But I'm not cooking hash browns.'

'No, you're charcoaling sausages. You really should take much more care of your diet.'

'And why should I do that?'

'Because you must look after yourself.'

'And why?'

'To stay healthy. I care about you, Jonny.'

'As if you do.'

'I do, really. You mean everything to me.'

'Yeah, right.'

'Oh, you do, Jonny, which is why you must trust me. I have your interests at heart. I want what's best for you, because what is best for you is best for me.'

Jonny tipped the charcoaled sausages, along with a lot of grease, onto a *famille rose* dining plate, painted with red and gilt at the centre, beneath a coat of arms surmounted with the Crawford family ducal crest (saleroom value four to six hundred pounds). 'Lovely grub,' said he.

'I have to look after you,' said Mr Giggles. 'If not because I care, then because I have to.'

'Are you trying to tell me something?' Jonny spoke through blackened teeth. 'Perhaps these sausages are a tad overdone.'

'You're my last,' said Mr Giggles. 'When your time is done, then *my* time is done.'

'Just what are you saying?' Jonny now picked charcoal pickings from his teeth.

'When you die, I die,' said Mr Giggles. 'I'll never be an imaginary friend to any other after you. I'll just vanish away.'

'You'll die, like me?'

'That's about the shape of it. Which is why it is in my interests to keep you fit and well and alive for as long as possible.'

'Right,' said Jonny, slowly. 'I see.'

'I doubt if you do, but it's true anyway.'

'And so I'm sure you're going to tell me to abandon my quest and head off to Tierra del Fuego after the Hawtrey brothers.'

'Something of the sort, yes.'

'Well, I'm not doing it. I do not intend to spend the rest of my life as either a fugitive or a prisoner. I intend to clear my name, and if there is some sinister underground organisation beaming stuff into people's heads, I'll track them down and expose them.'

'You'll get yourself killed. It's such a bad idea.'

'Well, it's what I'm going to do. So you can either help me out or go on ahead to Tierra del Fuego and wait there in case I change my mind and decide to join you. I would favour you taking the latter option. What say you?'

'I think I'll just tag along for now.'

'What a surprise.'

'I'm thinking of you, I really am.'

'Then,' said Jonny, 'I suggest you maintain a thoughtful silence until you have something really useful to say. Then I will be able to concentrate fully on the job in hand and avoid making some foolish mistake, which might well result in me taking a zapping from the business end of some constable's mega-weapon. What say you to this?'

Mr Giggles offered up a somewhat grudging agreement. 'So what do you intend to do next?' he asked.

'Have a poo,' said Jonny.

'And after that?'

'A wipe?'

'All is lost,' said Mr Giggles. 'We have descended to toilet humour. All is surely lost.'

Jonny Hooker didn't do the washing up. He did have a poo and he did wipe afterwards. He did *not* remove the Elastoplasts from his face and, having no alternative clothes available, he remained in his borrowed park ranger uniform. Which was growing a tad whiffy. As was Jonny, as neither had been laundered for a while.

Jonny left the hut before the arrival of Park Ranger Connor. He exited the park as he had entered it.

Furtively.

It was a beautiful morning. Those birdies chitchatted, the air smelled of flowers, a milk float rattled on by.

Normality was there to be found, all around and about.

Jonny wondered whether, just perhaps, he should go and speak to his mum. He concluded that no, he should not.

I will return to her in triumph, he told himself. *In triumph, or not at all.*

Jonny passed The Middle Man. It occurred to him that he was supposed to be playing there this very evening, with his band Dry Rot. But then Paul, the bass guitarist, must think that he was now dead. So he probably wouldn't be playing there, although he could of course phone Paul, or call round to his house and tell him the joyous news. Things did seem to be getting very complicated. Enough, in fact, as has been said to drive a fellow mad.

Jonny resolved that he would call Paul, so he popped into the nearest phone box to do so. Jonny remembered now that he had no small change for the phone.

So he would call in on Paul instead.

Jonny remembered now that Paul favoured a really large fry-up to begin his day.

Jonny concluded that he would definitely call in on Paul. At once.

And with this conclusion firmly under his cap, so to speak, Jonny set off for Paul's house.

When Paul wasn't being a police constable, Paul was being a musician. A rock musician of the metal persuasion. And one dressed in the manner of the Goth. At Jonny's knock upon his blackly painted front door, Paul opened up said door, all bleary eyed, and blinked about at Jonny.

And Jonny did espy the nightwear of Paul, and it was of the manner of the Goth. The manner of the Goth, those black pyjamas.

'Pyjamas,' said Jonny.

'*Black* pyjamas,' said Paul. 'I dyed them myself. Which isn't gay, I hesitate to add. I was augmenting these otherwise undistinguished pyjamas by staining them the hue which is forever night. Now bugger off, you sticking-plaster-faced parkie nutter.'

'Nicely put,' said Jonny.

'Bugger off,' said Paul. 'No, hang about,' said Paul. 'No, hold on there,' said Paul. 'It's you, Jonny,' said Paul. 'You're supposed to be dead!' said Paul.

Black indeed as the yawning grave itself, the long, dark night of the soul and the bum of the sweeper who chimneys doth sweep was the interior of Paul's abode. If it stood still and could be painted black, then Paul had painted it so. With two coats.

'How do you get your black so black?' asked Jonny.

'I put it on hard,' explained Paul. 'In the case of this sitting room, I simply exploded a ten-gallon can of Dulux ever-black emulsion with a couple of pounds of Semtex that I found in the evidence locker at the police station.'

'Nice,' said Jonny. 'Very cheerful.'

Over a fry-up that would have seen Al Jolson proud, Jonny explained the situation. In fact he told Paul everything. The lot. And he showed him James Crawford's book and advanced his theories, such as they were, regarding the possible existence of the Air Loom Gang. And everything. Really. The lot. He even showed Paul the business with the pocket compass.

And when he was done, Paul threw back his long, black hair and peered at Jonny over a forkload of long, black pudding. 'And you really believe all this?' he asked.

'I'm beginning to,' said Jonny, marvelling at the blackness of the pudding. 'And I intend to find out the truth—'

'And clear your name and make your mum proud, so you said.'

'So, will you help me?'

'Of course not,' said Paul. 'Whatever made you think I would?'

Jonny Hooker shrugged. 'Did you photograph the music that was scrawled all over James Crawford's bedroom, like I asked you?'

Paul shook his darkened head. 'Sorry,' he said. 'I forgot.'

'Thanks for nothing,' said Jonny.

'But you will be playing with the band tonight?'

'If I'm still alive I'd love to,' said Jonny.

'I'll inform the rest of the lads.'

'Do you think they can be trusted?'

'It's a possibility. What are you going to do now?'

Jonny Hooker gave his nose a tap. 'Play it by ear,' he suggested.

'Well, do try not to get in any trouble.'

Jonny Hooker said he'd try. And indeed he would.

But unknown to him, as indeed it was unknown to almost anyone other than those directly concerned, great events were unfolding, great events in which Jonny Hooker would become involved.

Great events and terrible, these events.

Terrible indeed.

22

Inspector Westlake was enjoying his breakfast. He was billeted in a cosy guest house in Abaddon Street, Brentford. The French Quarter, where the wine flowed like water and the trees were gay with the letters of France and full of Parisian promise.

Inspector Westlake was living high-off-la-hog and in-la-fast-lane. Mrs Corbett, who ran the guest house, had this thing about gentlemen in uniforms. It was a *big* thing, because *she* was a big woman. Inspector Westlake had this thing about big women. The only crimes that were going to be involved here were victimless crimes.

'More wine?' asked Mrs Corbett, leaning her prodigious bosoms over the inspector's left shoulder, wine bottle in one hand and tray of Dordogne Delight in the other.

'Not for me, fair lady.' The inspector dabbed at his mouth with an oversized red gingham napkin. 'Too early in the day and me in my uniform.'

Mrs Corbett purred above him. She loomed large and smelled of *Eau de Chateau*. 'Do take some coffee, then. It's all brewed up in a proper copper coffee pot. And it's French.'

'Just a soupçon, then.'

There came a ringing at the doorbell and Mrs Corbett excused herself from the inspector's presence.

Inspector Westlake perused his surroundings. They were heavy on the chintz, the lace doilies and the antimacassars. And the strings of garlic. Up on the mantel shelf, the inevitable Spanish straw pony, wearing a beret. Above this beast, a framed print of a crying child, with a pencilled-on French moustache. Five different choices of jam upon the clothed table, as many of marmalade, including quince. And more croissants than you could bung down your trousers on a midsummer's morn. He had fallen on his feet and no doubt about

it. Called up from Sussex to deal with something of a sensitive nature that required his certain touch, but about which he had so
far heard nothing. The week had been a worrying one, what with
these beheadings. But at least he was away from his wife, a small
and mouse-like being, whom he had married by accident during
an acid trip back in the nineteen sixties, in circumstances that were
far too complicated to go into now in any detail. Although he was
looking forward to dealing with the something of a sensitive nature,
whatever it should turn out to be, he could, in truth, have done
without the beheadings. For without the beheadings, he would have
had little to do and could have spent more time here in his billet.

Mrs Corbett returned in the company of a young constable. The
young constable's name was Constable Justice and to the disappointment of some, but the relief of others, he was presently unarmed.

Mrs Corbett slotted herself into the doorway and the young constable found himself having to squeeze past. To the delight of just
the one of them, and this one not the constable.

'Good morning sir,' said this young, bright bobby, saluting as he
did so.

'Good morning to you and at ease.' Inspector Westlake injected
a toothsome viand into his gob and munched upon it. 'Mmmth
dmmph mm mmt?' he asked.

'What do I want?' asked the constable, who prided himself in his
knowledge of Esperanto. 'I have been dispatched post-haste from
HQ to pick you up in the car, sir. Having first delivered this to
you.'

'And what is this?'

'An official letter, sir. Government-sealed, for your eyes only.'

'Gmmph mmph,' said the inspector, his gob refilled and his interest tweaked.

The constable handed over the official letter and saluted once
more. 'Do you want me to wait in the car, sir?' he asked.

'No, no, no, sit down, Constable, have a cup of tea.'

The constable's eyes turned towards the obstruction in the doorway. A certain look of fear came into those eyes. A bead of perspiration appeared on the forehead, slightly south of the helmet.

'I'll wait in the car, sir, if you don't mind. And sir?' The constable
leaned low and whispered, 'Could you please ask that woman to

move out of the doorway – she pinched my bum when I came in.'

Inspector Westlake shook his head sadly. 'Might I have some more toast, do you think?' he enquired of Mrs Hayward. The lady of the house smiled broadly, did a little curtsy and vanished away to the kitchen.

Constable Justice shivered. Right down his spine that shiver went. 'I'll wait in the car,' he said and again took to his heels.

Inspector Westlake held the envelope up to the light. Watermarked paper, official Government seal. Two seals, in fact, the second being that of the House of Windsor.

This would be his notification of the sensitive something to which he must add his certain touch.

With no greater ado than was required, Inspector Westlake took up an ivory-handled escargot knife, its blade engraved in the manner of Louis XVI, and cut through the envelope's seals.

He opened the envelope, drew out the letter, unfolded it and read it aloud. Softly.

For the attention of Inspector Westlake
For your eyes only

Dear Inspector Westlake

As you must know, affairs in the Middle East have reached a crisis point. Our advisors advise Us that what they refer to as an Apocalypse or Armageddon Scenario is unfolding before Our very eyes and if steps are not taken at the earliest opportunity to remedy this situation, then the Empire, nay, indeed the whole wide world, will be in peril.

Inspector Westlake paused for a moment at this point. 'This letter,' he said, softly and to himself alone, 'is from—' and he turned over the letter and marvelled at – the sovereign's signature.

'Her Majesty, God bless her,' said the inspector, and he felt a shiver run up *his* back. She was a damn fine woman, Her Madge. A damn fine big woman, what with her royal patronage of Ginsters pies and everything. And she was doing *what*? Asking *him* to sort out the crisis in the Middle East? Surely not, because, after all, and let's face it here – at the end of the day and all that kind of thing, there is *always* a crisis going on in the Middle East. Always has been, always will be. Such is the way of the Middle East: it's hot and dry and made of concrete and everyone hates everyone and fights them as and when.

Which might, of course, be considered something of an over-simplification, but, in all truth, it is the opinion held by most folk in the Western nations.

Inspector Westlake read on:

As you will also know, since you have risen to the rank of inspector and are therefore a 24^6 Freemason, the Powers of the World would prefer that Middle Eastern conflict to remain localised and not escalate to a global level. To this end We, Ourself, will chair a meeting of these Powers of the World in the hope that reason can be made to prevail, Armageddon averted and the Empire put beyond jeopardy. Upon the recommendation of your superiors, We are placing you in charge of arranging a suitable venue for this meeting. Due to its sensitive nature, it cannot be held upon either Crown or Government properties. It must be in elegant surroundings. It must be secure. It will be held this coming Sunday. You will arrange everything.

And it *was* signed by the sovereign.

Inspector Westlake folded the letter. He sniffed at the letter and sighed after this sniffing. He tapped this letter upon his forehead. And, assured that he was unobserved, he kissed this letter.

A conference of The Powers of the World. And one that could determine the World's future, or lack of it. And the arrangements for this were being entrusted to him. And to him alone. He was in charge. He unfolded the letter and read that final line once again:

You will arrange everything.

'Yes!' Inspector Westlake made a fist with his free hand and punched it towards the ceiling. This was it, the big one, his *big* chance. If he pulled this one off in the manner known as without-a-hitch-and-A-Okay, there'd be a knighthood in this for him. 'Yes! Oh yes!'

'Yes?' asked Mrs Corbett, re-entering the breakfasting room in the company of toast.

'Yes indeed.' Inspector Westlake refolded the letter, returned it to its envelope and slipped the whole into his breast pocket. 'Oh yes indeed.'

'Good news, then?' asked Mrs Corbett, getting a bit of lean-forward going.

'The best,' said Inspector Westlake. 'But I know not the lie of the land too well hereabouts. Are there any premises nearby where a conference might be held? With elegant surroundings and a degree of security?'

Mrs Corbett stroked at her bosom, as one might stroke at one's chin. 'The only place around here that fits that kind of bill would be the Big House in Gunnersbury Park,' she said. 'It's a museum now, but it was once owned by Princess Amelia and later by the Rothschilds. And I believe they hold private conferences there.'

'The Rothschild's?' Inspector Westlake knew of the Rothschild's. Big in Freemasonry, the Rothschild's.

'Sounds promising,' said Inspector Westlake. 'I've passed the park several times. I'll pop in later. in fact, I'll pop in now.'

'Not before you've finished your toast, surely.' Mrs Corbett grinned a stunning selection of pearly-white teeth. And waggled those bosoms somewhat.

'Well, perhaps a slice or two, thank you very much.'

Mrs Corbett buttered toast. 'So what is it, then?' she asked. 'Police conference? Police ball? Police peni—'

'Strictly hush-hush, I'm afraid.' Inspector Westlake made with a wink. 'All strictly hush-hush. But you know Gunnersbury Park well, then, do you?'

'No,' said Mrs Corbett. 'I've never actually been in that park.'

'But you know of the Big House, as you called it.'

'Yes,' said Mrs Corbett. 'I did, didn't I? Although I'm not altogether certain as to how I do. Perhaps someone mentioned it to me, or put the idea in my head, or something. I don't really know.'

She turned to take her leave once more, and as she did so her hand trailed across the table top in front of the inspector. And to her surprise, as indeed to that of Inspector Westlake, the cutlery followed her trailing hand. As if drawn to it.

As if to a magnet.

23

'Allah be praised!' cried Ranger Connor, falling to his knees and wringing his hands in supplication.

Jonny Hooker looked down upon Ranger Connor. Although only in a physical way. He would always look *up* to a martial artist.

'What is going on here? Why are you praising Allah?' Jonny asked. He was now back in the park rangers' hut. Ranger Connor was in the park rangers' hut. There seemed to be a lot of drama in the park rangers' hut.

'It's Ranger Hawtrey,' said Ranger Connor. 'He left a message with Miss Joan on the desk. He's upped and awayed it to Tierra del Fuego.'

'No?' said Jonny. 'Not really?' said Jonny.

'Indeed and to badness,' said Ranger Connor. 'It seems that he aided and abetted the unauthorised release of his brother.'

'The loony or the castrato?'

'The loony, apparently. Sprung him from the Special Wing of the Cottage Hospital. Even boasted in his message about the ingenious manner by which he effected the escape.'

'Indeed?' said Jonny.

'Indeed,' said Ranger Connor. 'Alas and alack and things of that nature generally.'

'So this would be a bad thing, then?' said Jonny.

'I was grooming that lad for greatness. Such a betrayal this is. Such a disappointment.'

'So why were you praising Allah?'

'At your arrival. *For* your arrival. You are now my only hope. But have no fear – I will treat you like the son I never had.'

'Nice,' said Jonny. Doubtfully. 'Although—'

'Although?'

'I'd really like to learn Dimac. For self-defence only, of course, not so I might go throwing my weight about in pubs and beating nine bells of crap out of anyone who failed to take my fancy.'

'Naturally not,' said Ranger Connor. 'I think we've already covered *that*. Self-defence only. Correct.'

'So, will you train me?'

'Absolutely,' said Ranger Connor. 'In fact we'll start at once. You can begin with the special Dimac Wrist-Flex exercises.'

'Splendid,' said Jonny. 'What do I do?'

'You clean this frying pan that some lowlife scoundrel – no doubt in the shape of that ingrate Ranger Hawtrey – has defiled with blackened sausage. Wax on, wax off, that kind of business. Then you can do the floor, then repaint the outside of the hut, then—'

'Perhaps I don't want to learn Dimac after all,' said Jonny.

Ranger Connor shook his head. 'You can't back out now,' he said. 'You asked me to teach you. That's as good as taking a blood oath.'

'Will I be able to maim and disfigure, with little more than a fingertip's pressure, by lunchtime?' Jonny asked.

'No,' said Ranger Connor. 'Don't be silly.'

'Sorry,' said Jonny.

'Clean the dishes,' said Ranger Connor.

Jonny cleaned the dishes and, as he did so, putting in a lot of vigorous wrist-action, he asked himself the question that others had asked before him, and certain others were asking now.

'Why am I here?' asked Jonny.

As in, 'What am I doing *here*?'

He had decided, had Jonny, that he would lie low for a little bit, maintain a low profile, let the dust settle, keep his head down and so on and so forth. Just go to work as usual and see what there was to be seen.

And, it had to be said, he really quite enjoyed being a park ranger. And to Jonny it appeared that being a park ranger mostly seemed to involve strolling around the park wearing a uniform, and, once he'd learned a bit of Dimac, duffing up any chavs who defiled the park with their presence.

And there was one further thing: Jonny wanted to have another look around the storerooms that lay beneath the Big House. Another look at the Protein Man's printing press. Perhaps James Crawford had left some clues, some something that would lead Jonny to Crawford's murderer. The murderer? The Air Loom Gang? Something.

A knock came at the door of the hut. Ranger Connor answered that knock, words were exchanged and Ranger Connor closed the door once more. 'Well well well,' said Ranger Connor. 'I am summonsed to the Big House. It appears that some bigwigs wish to hold some kind of secret conference. Countess Vanda requests my presence.'

'Countess Vanda?' Jonny asked, up to his elbows in Fairy.

'Curator of the museum. She grants few interviews. The gardeners don't even believe she exists – they say that there's a waxwork and a tin can on a string involved.'

'Strangely,' said Jonny, 'you've lost me there. What about this wrist-action?'

'Nice wrist-action.' Ranger Connor admired Jonny's wrist-action. 'Countess Vanda is photosensitive, or something, so she conducts interviews with the staff in almost total darkness in her office in Princess Amelia's sitting room. The gardeners think that there's no Countess Vanda, just a waxwork dummy, a puppet, and that the voice is done through a tin can attached to a string. The voice being that of a popular children's TV presenter with a high voice and a warped sense of humour.'

'Right,' said Jonny, nodding thoughtfully. 'And people think *I'm* mad.'

'What did you say?' Ranger Connor asked.

'Nothing,' said Jonny. 'Well, you go off and speak to Countess Vanda and I'll finish the washing-up and get stuck into all these other chores, which naturally are not really chores but subtle forms of Dimac training. I've seen *The Karate Kid*, I know how it works.'

'Precisely,' said Ranger Connor. 'Fate has brought you to me and no mistake.'

Jonny splashed on in the sink and Ranger Connor, like Elvis before him, left the building.

Although obviously Elvis didn't leave this particular building.

Obviously.

Jonny whistled 'Heartbreak Hotel', dried his hands and, having given Ranger Connor sufficient time to be on his way, slipped off to the Big House himself.

Through the entrance hall, then down the secret passage to the storeroom. Although—

Jonny slipped through the entrance hall, unnoticed by Joan who was doing her nails and watching daytime TV. He slid back something or other and entered the secret passage. Which was where the 'although' came into it.

Although, thought Jonny, *although I do want a look at that printing machine, I'd also rather like to have a look at this countess curator.* She was obviously a new curator, as the one who had done the curating when Jonny's father had first brought Jonny to the museum had been a big fat fellow called Stan, who smelled of model train sets and carried himself in the kind of fashion that wasn't the fashion any more.

And secret passages lead in all kinds of directions. And all these kinds of directions were remembered by Jonny.

So Jonny crept and skulked along, the light of Ranger Hawtrey's torch tunnelling the darkness before him. Smells of ancient plaster and dust and pigeon poo and rats' muck and mildew. And gently creep and gently skulk along.

And up this time rather than down. And Jonny shone the torch before him and found that little hatchway affair, switched off the torch and removed the hatchway affair. The hatchway affair lay behind a portrait of Sir Henry Crawford, many times great-granddaddy of the recently deceased James. This portrait hung over the fireplace in Princess Amelia's sitting room. And the little hatchway affair removed the eyes from the portrait, to be replaced by the eyes of Jonny Hooker. Just like in those old-fashioned movies, which sometimes starred Bob Hope. And didn't you always want to live in a house with a secret passage and a big portrait with the removable eyes that you could peer from behind, all secretive-like?

You didn't? Well, shame upon you.

Jonny Hooker always had and he was loving this.

He had to do some getting-accustomed: the room was in mostly darkness. A single shaft of sunlight slotted down between the curtains and fell upon the now naked head of Ranger Connor, who had his cap off. Jonny could not see Countess Vanda. He could hear her, though.

'Ranger Connor,' she said. 'One hears good reports of you.'

'Thank you, Ma'am,' said the ranger.

'And one hears so many bad reports nowadays. So much trouble and strife in the world. So dispiriting.'

'Indeed, Ma'am,' said Ranger Connor. 'And so much of it caused by young fellow-me-lads who would benefit from a spell of conscription and a short, sharp shock.'

'One does so agree.'

Ranger Connor nodded his naked head. Sunlight sparkled on his baldy patch.

'And so,' continued Countess Vanda, 'it is with great pleasure that one learns that the Powers of the World are to hold some kind of major peace conference right here in the Big House this very Sunday. One gave one's go-ahead to this at once, of course.'

'Of course,' said Ranger Connor, bowing his sunlit scalp.

'Now, there will be policemen, policemen aplenty, I shouldn't wonder.'

Jonny shrank a little back at this.

'But one does not wish for you to become involved with these policemen, Ranger Connor. Common folk are these. I wish you to form your own security force. How many rangers do you have under your command – twenty, thirty?'

'Just the one, sadly, ma'am,' said Ranger Connor. 'We were cut back, in the last financial year. The choice, I seem to recall, being between rangers and a new car for the chairman of the borough's Parks Committee.'

'Ah,' said Countess Vanda. 'My word,' said she, too.

'It's probably a bit eleventh-hour for me to take on any extra manpower,' said he of the sunbathed bonce, 'but I am skilled in the martial arts and I have a good man under my command. Even if he is a bit of a weirdo.'

'Weirdo?' whispered Jonny.

'Then be my eyes and ears. Stay away from the policemen, but keep an eye out for trouble. The threat of terrorism is ever present. Anything suspicious, report directly to me. Which is to say, to one. Do you understand?'

'I do,' said Ranger Connor. 'I was wondering, ma'am – this conference, it will involve heads of state, will it?'

'It will.'

'Including *our* head of state?'

'Her Majesty?' Countess Vanda paused, and it was a long, silent pause. 'Her Majesty will be present,' she said, when done with pausing, 'which is why great trust is being placed in you. Policemen are buffoons. No threat must come close to the monarch.'

'I see.' And Ranger Connor nodded. 'So will it be permissible for me to tool-up, as it were? Carry a weapon, concealed or otherwise?'

'On this occasion, yes.'

'Splendid.' Ranger Connor rubbed his hands together. 'Can I help myself to something from the stores?'

'As long as it does not leave the park.'

'Splendid.'

'Now leave me, I have much to do.'

'Yes, ma'am, thank you, ma'am.' And backing away and rubbing his hands together once more, Ranger Connor left the room, closing the door behind him.

Jonny Hooker drew back his eyes and prepared to replace the hatch. A flicker of movement caught his attention. Jonny Hooker paused.

Countess Vanda had risen to her feet, possibly from behind a desk, or a table – Jonny was unable to see. But he caught that flicker of movement and now he caught also her profile, caught itself in that shaft of sunlight.

And Jonny Hooker noted well that profile. Because he had seen it before. The darkest of hair, the greenest of eyes and the sweetest of noses. A profile he'd seen so recently.

That of Nurse Hollywood.

24

'Hit the ground running and head for the hills, buddy boy.'

Mr Giggles was most emphatic. Jonny shook his head.

'The peelers,' said Mr Giggles. 'The Bill, the filth, the fuzz, the buggers in blue. They'll be crawling over every inch of this place come lunchtime.'

'You think?' said Jonny.

'I know, buddy boy.'

'And don't "buddy boy" me, please.'

'Away,' said Mr Giggles. 'Sprightly, on your toes.'

This advice was offered in the dark, as the battery of ex-Ranger Hawtrey's torch had given up its ghost and Jonny was now feeling his way about in a secret passage.

'Things couldn't be worse,' said the disembodied voice of Mr Giggles. 'You are oh so so in the wrong place at the wrong time.'

'Really?' said Jonny. 'Really? Do you think?'

'And you're being all too calm and collected.'

'And you don't like that, do you?'

'I have no idea what you mean. My, it's darker in here than your mate Paul's soiled underwear. Let's head for daylight, then up and away.'

'And this would be your considered opinion?'

'Take my advice,' said Mr Giggles. 'I know what's good for you.'

'It's interesting, isn't it,' whispered Jonny, 'the occasions when you choose to speak and those when you do not.'

'You told me to keep quiet unless I had something really pertinent to add.'

Jonny nodded invisibly and continued to feel his way along. 'And you really think that I'm going to run away, do you?'

'A strategic withdrawal is not necessarily a retreat. In fact, a strategic withdrawal can make the love making oh so much sweeter.'

'Please be silent,' said Jonny. 'I have things to think about.'

'No you don't, no things at all.'

Jonny stopped and spoke with a certain sharpness in his voice. 'I think that I *do*,' he said. 'You are not going to suggest this is coincidence.'

'Coincidence? I don't know what you mean.'

'That I am *here* and that what is clearly going to be a most important meeting of, how shall I put this, the "controllers" of the world, is going to take place here on Sunday.'

'And what would such a meeting have to do with you?'

'Oh, come on,' said Jonny. 'That is somewhat disingenuous.'

'Jonny,' said Mr Giggles, 'I really have no idea what is going on in that head of yours. Is it all that gibberish Hari Hawtrey spun you, that you are some lone hero upon a sacred quest? What do you think is going to happen here? Are terrorists going to menace the conference? Are you going to do a Bruce Willis and save them? You don't even own a vest.'

'I didn't mention terrorists,' said Jonny. 'Where did you get the idea of terrorists from?'

'Well, if not terrorists, then what?'

'You're doing all the theorizing,' said Jonny. 'I haven't said anything except that I do not believe that this is a coincidence. Perhaps I am being somewhat self-obsessed, but I do believe that at last my life has some kind of purpose.'

'It does – you're a good musician. Tell you what, go back to Paul's and spend the day there, then do the gig tonight – what do you say to that?'

'And tomorrow?'

'A holiday abroad.'

'I think not,' said Jonny. 'To quote you, "I think I'll stick around for a while." Ah,' and Jonny pushed upon a panel, 'I think we're in the storerooms.'

And they were.

'Now,' said Jonny, entering a storeroom and sliding the secret something that disguised the passage's entrance back into place, 'I'd like to take another look at that printing press.'

'Why?' asked Mr Giggles.

But Jonny didn't reply.

Jonny began to root about amongst the things in the storeroom.

'I don't know why you're wasting your time with this,' said Mr Giggles.

'So you think I should get out of here at once?'

'Absolutely, yes.'

'Then I'll continue to search about.'

'Simply to be contrary?'

'If you have nothing pertinent to add.'

'I know. I know.'

There were a great many packing cases in the storeroom. Jonny took up a crowbar that lay, as they so often do, handily near at hand, and attacked the lid of the nearest.

'What are you doing?' squealed Mr Giggles. 'You'll damage valuable exhibits with your big silly hands.'

'Not exhibits,' said Jonny. 'The labels on the cases say "EFFECTS FROM THE ESTATE OF THE LATE JAMES CRAWFORD BEQUEATHED TO GUNNERSBURY PARK MUSEUM". I'll bet it's his record collection.'

And it was. Amongst other things.

Jonny opened box after box with Mr Giggles tut–tut–tutting as he did so. Eventually Jonny opened a box and said, 'What do we have here?'

'Gramophone records?'

'More leather-bound notebooks,' said Jonny. 'A good many leather-bound notebooks.'

'More paranoid ramblings,' muttered Mr Giggles.

Jonny opened a notebook and read what was written within.

REGARDING THE DEVIL'S CHORD

Jonny read.

And then what was written beneath:

The Devil's chord, also known as the Devil's Interval, also known as the tritone, augmented fourth or diminished fifth, is an exact bisection of an octave. The octave has throughout history been regarded as a symbol of perfection; consequently the Devil's Interval was seen (and indeed heard) to be the most harsh and discordant interval, and as it is the exact antithesis or opposite of perfection (the octave, or God) this interval has gained a reputation of being demonic. In early church music (from which most Western music springs) only the intervals of a perfect fourth, perfect fifth and octave were permitted because they gave a perfect or pure harmony as befitted divine worship and instilled a sense of stability and resolution in the listener. The Devil's Interval gives rise in the listener to a sense of unease, or restlessness, which needs resolution. In modern-day music, the tritone is used ubiquitously and is often utilised as a pivot, to drive the music on into alternative harmonic realms. It is used particularly in jazz, pop and rock, all of which have been denounced at one time or another as the Devil's Music. And, seemingly, it would appear, in the light of this, not without good cause.

'Now, that *is* interesting,' said Jonny.

'Really?' said Mr Giggles. 'In what way would that be?'

'I'm a musician,' said Jonny, 'but I've never heard of the Devil's Interval before. But thinking about it, it's used in all kinds of atmospheric music, like background music in horror films.'

'It's used in the title sequence of *The Simpsons*,' said Mr Giggles.★

'So *you* know all about the Devil's Interval?'

'I know about most things,' said Mr Giggles, 'which is why you should pay attention to what I say to you. You'll find that the Devil's Interval is mostly used in the lower registers of the tonic scale. Your heavy metallers sing in deep, deep voices, don't they?'

Jonny nodded. They did.

'Because big, deep bass notes are associated with evil, way down deep, like the location of Hell. And angelic voices are high – your sopranos and your castrati of, course, voices soaring up to Heaven. And right in the middle, halfway between Heaven and Hell, you have Mankind. Right here on Earth. And where is most music of mankind based? Right around middle C on the piano. Your

★ And it is!

basic pop song has your basic "three-chord trick" – G, C and D seventh. Popular music, middle-of-the-road music, middle-of-the-range music. Music of the common man. And they'll all have your "Da-da-de-da-da" in them somewhere. It's the heartbeat of popular music. A tonal key that opens a musical door.'

'I'm impressed,' said Jonny. 'You're actually talking sense there.'

'It's elementary stuff – any music student could tell you all about it.'

'Then I'm *not* impressed,' said Jonny. 'Thanks for putting me straight.'

'Mind you,' said Mr Giggles, 'there's always a n****r in the woodpile, as it were.'

'Please don't start all that again,' Jonny told him.

'One piece of music that doesn't fit. A piece of classical music with lots of high notes and more Devil's Intervals per bar than any other piece.'

'And what's that?' Jonny asked.

"The Dance of the Sugar-Plum Fairy," said Mr Giggles.*

Jonny was rooting some more in a packing case. 'Well, aha,' said he. 'Or should I say, eureka?'

Mr Giggles feigned lack of interest.

'Laptop,' Jonny said. 'James Crawford's laptop. I'll bet he typed up all his theories from his notebooks onto his laptop.'

'And so you're going to steal it?'

'I'm going to borrow it. But first—' And Jonny took to replacing the packing-case lids and hammering back their nails with the crowbar. '—best not leave any evidence that any crime has been committed here, eh?'

And as luck, or fate, or coincidence, or whatever would have it, just as Jonny had hammered the last nail into place—

'What is *that*?' said Jonny, and he listened.

A key was being turned in the storeroom door.

'Up and away,' whispered Jonny, and he took to the secret passage.

Two men entered the storeroom. One was young and firm and assertive; the other was older, and complaining.

* And he's right, check it out.

'I'm *not* a porter,' this older one complained, and Jonny knew that voice. 'I'm a park ranger,' said Ranger Connor, 'and it's not my job to shift boxes about.'

'How very unpatriotic of you,' said the younger man. Jonny didn't recognise the voice. And he couldn't see the younger man, so he couldn't see that he was wearing a black suit, black tie, white shirt, black shoes and dark sunglasses. He spoke with the accent known as posh. He spoke with the voice of authority.

'I commandeered you as you were leaving the Big House because you carry yourself with military bearing—'

'Yes,' flustered Ranger Connor. 'Well.'

'And I said to myself, this chap looks like a Sandhurst type, probably here on Special Ops.'

'Well,' went Ranger Connor, with a tad less fluster.

'Give him a task that is top priority and a man such as this can be trusted to carry it out. For Queen and country, doncha know.'

'Well,' went the ranger, fluster-free.

'Item in one of these cases required. Very important, security of the Crown and all that sort of thing. Just require you to go through the crates, fish the fellow out and bring it up to me. I have some business with woman on reception desk.'

And I'll just bet I know what kind, thought Jonny.

'Well,' went Ranger Connor, once more.

'Laptop computer jobbie,' said the young toff. 'Whip it out of the crate and bring it up to me.'

Ranger Connor grunted.

'Top man,' said the toff.

Jonny didn't hear him say it, though, for Jonny had made a strategic withdrawal along the secret passage and out of the Big House and was now sitting beside the ornamental pond, opposite the Doric temple, with the laptop open on his lap.

'You'd best throw that in the pond,' advised Mr Giggles. 'You're bound to get caught with it and be taken off to prison.'

'Password,' said Jonny. 'I need the password.'

Mr Giggles whistled "Jailhouse Rock".

'Now what would his password be?' Jonny asked.

'Bum poo?' said Mr Giggles. 'Smelly willy, big hairy bottom burps?'

'And you complained about toilet humour lowering the tone.'

'Just trying to lighten the situation as you're clearly doomed. Throw it in the pond and let's be away.'

Jonny tapped in letters. His guess was rejected.

'You only get three tries,' said Mr Giggles.

'I know,' said Jonny, who thought hard and tried once more. And failed.

'One try left,' said Mr Giggles. 'Get it over with and let's get going.'

Jonny drummed his fingers on the laptop. One more try was all he had. There was no telling what secrets the laptop might yield up. None at all, in all probability. But *no*, that couldn't be right. The chap with the posh voice wanted the laptop. Security of the Crown, he'd said. There had to be answers. Some key that would open some door.

Jonny smiled and tapped letters into the keyboard.

The laptop screen lit up.

And Mr Giggles said, 'Oh.'

'Piece of cake,' said Jonny.

'Luck of the damned, more like.'

'Well, you inspired it,' said Jonny, 'with your talk about popular music. Music of the common man. A tonal key that opens a musical door.'

Mr Giggles groaned.

And Jonny said, 'That's right.'

'Da–da–de–da–da,' said Mr Giggles.

'Da–da–de–da–da,' said Jonny.

25

'Oh my goodness,' said Jonny Hooker. 'Oh my goodness me.'

Mr Giggles peered over his shoulder. Jonny could smell his breath.

Jonny slammed the laptop shut. 'Best put this somewhere safe,' said Jonny.

'The pond?' said Mr Giggles. Jonny shook his head.

'So what did you see? What did you see?' Mr Giggles bobbed up and down.

Jonny Hooker ignored him.

'Come on, Jonny,' crooned the Monkey Boy. 'You have no secrets from me.'

'No secrets?'

Jonny was having a moment. One of *those* moments. Those moments that you sometimes, although *rarely*, have, when all sorts of things seem to fall into place. Everything appears to make sense. All becomes clear. And things of that nature, generally. Jonny was having one of *those* moments. And he wasn't on drugs or anything.

The image he'd seen on the screen, the breath upon his neck: the two had triggered the one of those moments.

Jonny Hooker arose. 'On second thoughts,' said Jonny, 'I think it would be best if I were to keep this laptop safe.' He opened his ranger's jacket and viewed the big poacher's pocket. Park rangers' jackets always have big poachers' pockets. It's so they can carry the rabbits and suchlike that they catch in their snares. It's a tradition, or an old charter, or something.

'So what did you see?' asked Mr Giggles. 'Come on, I won't tell anyone.'

'That's a new approach,' said Jonny. 'I will tell you one thing that's on there, top of the alphabetical list: "Apocalypse Blues" by

Robert Johnson. Someone might have nicked the original recording from James Crawford's collection, but obviously not before he was able to put it on his laptop.'

'Jonny, you're not—'

'Thinking to play it? Listen to find our whether it really does have the Devil's laughter at the end?'

'Don't do it, Jonny. I'm begging you not to.'

'Begging me?' said Jonny.

'You'll die if you hear it.'

'And you really believe that?'

'I do, I really do.'

'I wonder,' said Jonny.

'You will die,' said Mr Giggles. 'You *will* die, you will.'

'But why should I believe you?' Jonny asked.

'Because I'm telling the truth and I don't want you to die.'

'Because if *I* die, *you* die.'

'And that, yes.'

'We'll see,' said Jonny.

'No, we will *not* see. Throw the laptop in the pond. Do it for your own good.'

'You do sound very definite about this.'

'I do,' said Mr Giggles. 'Listen, if I tell you something, a secret something, will you promise me that you won't play the record?'

Jonny thought about this proposition. And it was such a lovely day and the birds were singing and he was having such a good time, such an exciting time, and feeling so alive for the very first time in his life, and everything.

And he *had* just had that moment.

'All right,' said Jonny. 'I'll promise, as long as what you tell me is worth it.'

'I think you'll find it pertinent,' said Mr Giggles, seating himself next to Jonny.

'Go on, then.'

And Mr Giggles did so.

'The dead'ns,' said Mr Giggles. 'Doctor Archy, James Crawford, the mystery man with your wallet in his pocket – I know how they died.'

'They had their heads chopped off,' said Jonny.

'Not chopped,' said Mr Giggles. 'More like atomised.'

'Ah,' said Jonny. 'The suspect will be a police constable, then.'

'The suspect is there in that laptop,' said Mr Giggles. 'Those men died because they heard the Devil's laughter. Too much for the human brain. Kaboom, and head all gone.'

'You're having a laugh,' said Jonny Hooker.

'I wish I was. It's how they found Hendrix and Morrison and all the rest. They covered it up in the sixties, of course. And Kurt Cobain "shot his head off". A likely story, eh?'

'The Twenty-Seven Club,' said Jonny. 'They heard the Devil on Johnson's last recording and—'

'Kaboom,' said Mr Giggles. 'Atomised. Not pretty. So you see, I don't want this to happen to you.'

'And don't you think you might have mentioned this to me earlier?'

'I told you you'd die if you heard the Devil's laughter.'

'But not that you knew how the murder victims had died.'

'What did it matter? We don't know who played them the music. Crawford may have put the recording on his laptop, but he had more sense than to play it. He knew what it could do.'

'Why didn't he just destroy the original recording?'

'Perhaps Crawford did. Perhaps it wasn't stolen. But this is, as I've said, the Unholy Grail of music. Johnson's final recording.'

'Perhaps he cleaned it up,' said Jonny, 'digitally. Removed the Devil's laughter.'

'I wouldn't advise you to check. You saw Crawford's body. His head had been atomised.'

'Hm' went Jonny.

'I don't like that "Hm", and don't go getting any ideas about testing it on a guinea pig in a soundproof room – it won't work.'

'Well,' said Jonny, 'this is all most interesting. And no doubt pertinent. But *I* have a pressing engagement.'

'You do?' said Mr Giggles.

'I do,' said Jonny. 'Big as my breakfast was, I now fancy lunch. And a pint of King Billy. I'm off to the pub.'

The pub was not on Inspector Westlake's schedule. He was all gung-ho and well fired-up and filled with motivation. And he was now at the Big House in Gunnersbury Park and having a word at the reception desk.

'Inspector Westlake,' said Inspector Westlake, 'on special secondment from the Bramfield Constabulary, here to supervise the security arrangements for Sunday's conference.'

'And what conference would that be?' Joan asked as she regarded the inspector in the manner known as coquettish.

'Top secret,' said Inspector Westlake, giving his nose that certain tap.

'Which would be why I haven't been informed of it,' said Joan. 'Would you care for a light-up pencil with a dinosaur on the top? We've just had a delivery of them. And a great many other such items.'

'No, madam, I certainly would not.' Inspector Westlake looked this way and that.

Constable Justice looked the other.

Joan grinned at Constable Justice. 'Saucy,' she said as she grinned.

'A word with your superior, please,' said Inspector Westlake. 'Spoke to her earlier on the blower. Countess Vanda by name, pleasant lady, rather posh voice.'

'I'll give her a little tinkle,' said Joan, and she did so: spoke words, received others and put down the phone. 'She said she'll be down in just a moment.'

'Splendid,' said Inspector Westlake.

'Little balls,' said Joan.

'Madam?' Inspector Westlake raised his eyebrows.

'We have little plastic balls,' said Joan, 'for sale, here, in the museum shop. They're new in, too – transparent, they have dinosaurs inside them.'

'Fascinating,' said Inspector Westlake, whose foot was beginning to tap.

'You have restless legs,' said Joan, 'which must make you posh, I suppose.'

'Must it?' the inspector enquired.

'Your other chap had restless legs and he's posh.'

'My other chap?' Inspector Westlake made a baffled face.

'Police security chap. Very well dressed, black suit, white shirt, really expensive sunspecs.'

'Police security chap? What are you talking about, madam?'

'He's just popped down the corridor to the toilet.'

'Just popped? Who is this fellow? Did he identify himself to you?'

'He said I was to call him Joshua. He left his warrant card with me, said I wasn't to look at it because it was top secret.'

'Kindly show me this card.'

'But it's top secret.'

'Madam, I am an officer of the law. Kindly show me this card or I will have no option other than to have you shot.'

Joan fished the card from her cleavage. She handed it to the inspector.

Inspector Westlake drew out a pistol.

'A gun!' shrieked Joan. 'No, please—'

'A gun indeed,' said Constable Justice. 'An all-chrome Desert Eagle, forty-four long-slide semi-automatic with double-lever action.'

'You certainly know your handguns, Constable,' said Inspector Westlake. And he drew out another such weapon and flung it to his fellow officer.

'Sir?' said that fellow.

'Terrorist threat,' said Inspector Westlake. 'Get on the blower to the station, Constable – we have a situation here.'

Joan began to flap her pretty hands about.

'No cause for alarm, madam,' said Inspector Westlake. 'We are professionals. We are trained to deal with this kind of situation.'

'But he's not a terrorist. He has a posh voice. And terrorists are common folk, foreign, swarthy, with beards. Everyone knows that.'

Inspector Westlake proffered the card. 'This is *my* warrant card,' he said. 'Or rather a copy of my warrant card. Down that corridor there, you say he went?'

Joan pointed, and then she ducked.

As did Inspector Westlake.

But he not only ducked.

He returned fire also.

26

Constable Justice assumed the position. Which is not to say that of the captured villain. This was the down-on-one-knee-with-the-gun-at-arm's-length-held-tightly-between-two-hands position. Constable Justice had assumed this particular position many times in the past, but always in the comfort and privacy of his cosy bedroom. He had not been allowed on the shooting range. He had not been issued with one of the If-he's-looks-a-bit-foreign-looking-and-suspicious-and-likely-to-be-tooled-up-shoot-to-kill licences, which all armed British policemen carry in the interests of national security, but pretend that they don't.

Regarding the matter of being allowed on the shooting range: he *had* signed on for the firearms course and he had been accepted. But there had been a bit of bother when he'd been handed the gun. There had been a bit of, perhaps, light-headedness on his part. The excitement of holding a real firearm, had, perhaps, got the better of him. There had been gunshots. There had been minor injuries. Happily there had been no loss of life.

'Die, motherf★★ker!' shouted Constable Justice, and he let off with the full clip.

The chap in the dark suit did a sort of judo roll from one side of the corridor to the other. The corridor was flanked by a row of marble columns. Fluted, they were, with marble bases, and richly ornamented in their upper regions. They had been designed by Inigo Jones for the occasion of Sir Henry Crawford's wedding. The bullets from Constable Justice's pistol strafed across these columns. Carrara marble flew in blurry chips. Stucco cascaded down.

The chap in the black suit came up firing. Souvenir Taj Mahals decorated with dinosaur motifs exploded and went to ruin.

Inspector Westlake shouted, 'Raise your hands and drop your

weapon.' Then took to ducking once more. Bullets ricocheted and priceless artworks took the onslaught. Down behind the reception desk, Inspector Westlake radioed for back-up.

'Terrorist attack, the Big House, Gunnersbury Park.'

It was a simple message, a mere seven words. It got the job done back at the local constabulary.

'Oh oh oh!' went Constable Mulberry Grape, a young and eager fellow who had a shared love for water sports and Westlife. He pressed the blood-red alarm button and ordered the breaking out of the high-velocity broad-area-havoc-wreaking terror weapons.

'Sir,' said Constable Justice, crawling over to Inspector Westlake, 'I think we have the b*stard pinned down. Do you want me to creep around to the rear of the Big House, smash my way in through a window, creep up behind the b*gger and shoot him in the *rse?'

'Don't think I quite understand you there, Constable,' said the inspector, further ducking as Gunnersbury Park souvenir mugs shaped like Stegosauruses popped and burst above his head and rattled all about. 'Esperanto, is it?'

'I creep round to the rear of the house, sir, and—'

'No, Constable, the words with the "*s" in them.'

'Censored swear words, sir. Police constables are forbidden to swear.'

'And who forbade you to swear, Constable?'

'The Chief of all policemen, sir, in a memo. Sir Robert Newman.'

'Ah,' said Inspector Westlake. 'That c*nt.'

'Oh look, sir,' said Constable Justice, plucking something up from the chaos. 'A souvenir dinosaur in the shape of a dinosaur.'

'Dinosaurs ruled the Earth for ages and ages,' said O'Fagin the landlord to Jonny the customer.* 'They'd be ruling the world today if it wasn't for the fact that they all died out.'

---

* On the rare chance that the reader might be experiencing some confusion as to who O'Fagin presently believes Jonny to be: let's just go with, Charlie Hawtrey's "other" brother and hope that it works out.

'A pint of King Billy, please,' said Jonny.

'Cut yourself shaving?' asked O'Fagin.

'The old ones are always the best,' said Jonny.

'Hence my talk of dinosaurs.'

Jonny watched O'Fagin pull the pint. O'Fagin was wearing a lot of gold jewellery. Several sovereign rings adorned his horny hands. Many chains of gold hung round his ragged neck. A golden earring pierced each ear. An ampallang of gold worried his willy. Although Jonny couldn't see the ampallang. Happily.

'So,' said Jonny, 'dinosaurs today, is it? And I thought that perhaps you would be asking me whether I loved it when a plan came together.'

'Why would that be?' asked O'Fagin, proffering the pint.

'Because you are clearly sporting all this bling as a tribute to Mister T out of the A-Team.'

'I prefer the word "homage",' said O'Fagin. 'But then I've always been a lover of cheese.'

Jonny paid him for his pint with the fifty pound note.

O'Fagin held it up towards a shaft of sunlight. 'So you sold your story to the Sunday tabloids, too,' he said.

'Not yet,' said Jonny. 'But when everything's done and dusted I certainly hope to.'

'Hope springs eternal,' said O'Fagin, ringing up 'no sale' on the cash register, fishing out many pound coins and shrapnel and dutifully short-changing his customer. 'Sadly, however, the dinosaurs did not possess the gift of eternal life.'

'Well done you,' said Jonny. 'Nicely done.'

'Thank you, sir. I do pride myself that once I get some good toot going, I'm a hard man to shift from the subject.'

'So,' said Jonny, 'I see by that poster that you have a band playing here this evening – Dry Rot. Are they any good?'

'They're rubbish,' said O'Fagin. 'I'd far rather have Dinosaur Jnr.'

'Or even a T. Rex tribute band?'

'Not forgetting Terry Dactyl and the Dinosaurs,' said O'Fagin.

'Who could?' said Jonny.

'Or even Captain Beefheart and his Magic Band.'

'Don't quite see the dinosaur connection there,' said Jonny.

'On the legendary album *Lick My Decals Off, Baby* there's a track called "Smithsonian Institute Blues" – it's about dinosaurs.'

'Bravo,' said Jonny.

'And that song contains almost as many Devil's Intervals as "Dance of the Sugar-Plum Fairy".'

'It's a wonderful world that we live in,' said Jonny.

'And a better one without dinosaurs,' said O'Fagin. 'We can all thank our lucky stars that they were too big for Noah to get them on his Ark and so all drowned in the Great Flood.' And he went off to serve a ringmaster and a couple of dwarves who had recently entered the bar.

'Brontosaurus?' Jonny heard him say. 'Don't get me started on that.'

'I'm thinking,' said Mr Giggles, 'that perhaps we'd better have another look at that laptop.'

Jonny ignored Mr Giggles.

'Well, think about it, Magnet Boy – your new super-magnetic powers might well be scrambling the laptop's innards.'

Jonny smiled and said nothing at all.

'This isn't a bl★★dy dry-cleaning service!' Jonny heard O'Fagin shout at the ringmaster. 'Out of this pub this instant and take your two strange children with you.'

The ringmaster left the pub in a sulk. And a top hat and red ringmaster's coat.

'Bl★★dy d★mn ch★★k!' said O'Fagin.

'Pardon?' said Jonny.

'Sorry,' said O'Fagin. 'I do have a tendency to lapse into Esperanto when someone gets my goat.'

'I didn't know you owned a goat.'

'Nor did I.'

'What did he say to you?' Jonny asked.

'The goat?' asked O'Fagin. 'A talking goat? Where? Where?'

'The ringmaster,' said Jonny. 'Chap in the top hat and red ring-master's coat.'

'Oh,' said O'Fagin. 'Ringmaster, was he?, I thought he was a Royal Welsh Fusilier. He wanted directions to Gunnersbury Park. This is a pub, I told him, not a bl★★dy dried-Kleenex server, whatever that is.'

'Slightly puzzled by that one,' said Jonny.

'Gimme a break,' said O'Fagin. 'I can't pronounce "cartographer".'

'Why did he want to go to Gunnersbury Park?'

'Probably to play on the pitch-and-putt like everyone else.'

'Odd,' said Jonny.

'You think *that's* odd?' said O'Fagin. 'Then take a look at *this*.'

But Jonny had left the bar counter. He'd made it over to the front windows, lifted a corner of the nylon net curtain* and was peering out through an unwashed pane.

The ringmaster and the two dwarves were in the car park, beside a white transit van. It did not have a 'circus' look to it and there was no sign of any other performers, nor their distinctive wagons, nor the fairground paraphernalia and freak-show booths that make a good circus a great one. And so on and so forth and suchlike.

The ringmaster was being offered directions by a police constable. Jonny looked on as the police constable, obviously in response to a call on his police radio, spoke into it, listened and then began to jump up and down. And then hustled the ringmaster and the dwarves into the transit van, which then left the car park at speed.

'Double odd,' said Jonny.

'If you think that's double odd,' said O'Fagin, 'then check this out – if I press it here it goes—'

And he passed out.

And Jonny left the bar.

'Got them on the blower, sir,' said Constable Justice. 'They've left the station, proper mob-handed. They'll be here as soon as can be.'

'I thought you were creeping around to the back of the building in what might be mistaken for Esperanto,' said Inspector Westlake.

'Seemed like a good idea at the time, sir,' said the constable, ducking further as further gunshots caused him further to duck, 'but then I considered that I'm not wearing that Teflon body armour that the Special Ops chaps wear and so I might take a round to the chest. And frankly, sir, much as I love the job, I don't love it that much.'

'I suppose that's fair enough,' said Inspector Westlake. 'But tell

---

* Brentford Nylons. Finest nylon in the world.

me, Constable, what exactly is that that you've further ducked your-self into?'

'Only me,' said Joan.

And down Pope's Lane they came in force, those officers of the law. Jonny, who had stepped from the bar to watch the departure of the white transit van, stepped back swiftly into the bar as the police cars all swept by.

'Do-da-do-da-do-da,' went the police car sirens.

'Da-da-de-da-da,' went Jonny.

O'Fagin raised his head from behind the bar counter. 'I'm not doing *that* again,' he said. 'I know that every boy should have a hobby, but you have to draw the line somewhere.'

Things went suddenly silent in the entrance hall of the Big House. But for a gentle sighing that came from Joan, all was peace and quiet.

'Do you think he's run out of ammo, sir?' whispered Constable Justice.

'Why don't you stick your head up above the reception desk and check?'

'Not keen, sir. I could hold a gun to this lady's head and tell the terrorist that if he doesn't give himself up, I'll shoot her.'

'What?' said Inspector Westlake.

'If you think it might work,' said Joan.

'Just stay down,' whispered the inspector, and, doing the 'keep-down' gesture, he climbed slowly to his feet. 'Last chance,' he called. 'Throw down your weapon and come out with your hands held high.'

And then the inspector went, 'Waaaah!'

As he fell back onto Constable Justice, Constable Justice saw why. The figure in black reared over them. He was up on the reception desk and then – and here the 'Waaaah!' became involved – he was up above them. He was across the ceiling, scuttling like a great black spider.

And then he was down and out of the door.

And things went quiet again.

161

27

Constable Paul assumed the position. It was a different position from that previously assumed by Constable Justice. The position assumed by Constable Paul was the Bass Position.

The Bass Position being that assumed by the bass player in a rock band. There are many similarities to the Lead Position, this being the position generally assumed by the lead guitarist, of course. Many similarities, but a few subtle nuances.

Paul was demonstrating these subtle nuances to the constables who sat to either side of him in the back of the Paddy Wagon.★

'This position really dates back to the bass player in Status Quo. He allegedly originally adopted it due to bum burns caused by a dodgy vindaloo.'

'But surely that's a Rock Myth,' said Constable Brian Lurex (who had changed his name by deed poll. From Barry). Like the one that Ozzy is the father of Britney Spears.'

'Or the one that the Rolling Stones eat their own young,' added Constable Durex, who had reason enough to change his name, but hadn't. 'Or that the Post Office Tower was modelled on a plaster cast of Jimi Hendrix's knob.'

'I heard that,' said Constable Rigor-Mortice (of the Sussex Rigor-Mortices). 'And how come you're referred to as Constable *Paul*, while we're referred to by our surnames?'

'Because I play the bass. Now, as I was saying—'

The Paddy Wagon bumped through the car park of The Middle Man. Jonny was back at the bar and so missed that.

'Sorry,' Constable Handbag, the driver, called back over his

★ You don't see too many Paddy Wagons about nowadays. The Ealing Constabulary are the last to actually employ them. But then they do have a tradition to uphold. The entrance to Ealing Police Station was used as the exterior of Dock Green in the TV series.

shoulder through the little hatch-hole jobbie. 'I just wanted to see if this Wagon could survive unexpected contact with a being from another world.'

'Don't ask.' Constable Durex waved a finger at Constable Paul. 'Sometimes it's better not to know.'

'I'll tell you what I'd like to know,' said Constable Paul, un-assuming the position and picking up something large, black and lethal-looking from the floor of the Paddy Wagon. And cradling it as one would cradle a bass guitar. 'What I'd like to know is whether I'm really going to get a chance to use this baby. It's a positronic ionisation rifle, powered by the transperambulation of pseudo-cosmic anti-matter. I'm expecting great things of it. Well, great things of a destructive nature.'

'It's funny,' said Constable Lurex, 'how swiftly things can get out of hand. Without a guiding hand. Without a degree of conscious control. How swiftly everything can fall to pieces.'

'Eh?' said Constable Paul.

'Klingons on the starboard bow,' sang Constable Handbag.

'It says in the manual here,' said Constable Wingnut, 'that the positronic ionisation rifle can dispense a charge of energy equal in heat to five times that of the sun on a very sunny day. And how, when using it on Gypsies or anyone from the North wearing clogs, the operator is advised to wear special mirror-lensed spectacles.' He took up the special mirror-lensed spectacles and slotted them onto his head.

'Cool,' said Constable Paul. 'I didn't get a pair of those.'

Bump and bump went the Paddy Wagon.

'Almost there,' Constable Handbag called back. 'Just had a bit of a Gerry Anderson moment there. I think the string working my right hand has come loose.'

Constable Durex waved the 'don't ask' finger once more at Constable Paul.

'But—' went Constable Paul.

'He'll be all right when his medication kicks in. Just don't let him near any of the weapons.'

'Whoa!' went Constable Handbag, and he slammed on the brakes. Constable Paul and all other constables in the back moved forward at speed and reassembled untidily in a big heap at the front.

'Look at that. Look at that!' cried Constable Handbag. 'It's Ziggy Stardust, or one of the Spiders from Mars.'

Constable Paul had quite a good view: his head was now stuck right through the little hatch in the partition that divided the cab from the rear of the wagon. It was quite difficult to breath though, what with all those other constables all piled up around and about and above and below him. But he had quite a good view.

Constable Handbag and Constable Paul viewed the scene before them. It was a scene that was not devoid of interest.

There were five police cars all swerved to a halt. And many policemen about these. And these policemen were discharging their weapons in the general direction of the Big House.

Happily the bolts of hypersonic energy and the effusion of sub-atomic knub-knub particles were mostly missing the Big House and striking instead the trees and the parked cars. A stray round of plasma passed between the trees and took out the park rangers' hut.

Which was a shame because Ranger Connor's spare duffle coat and pack of Serial Killer Top Trump cards were in there.

Explosions erupted from the trimmed lawn. A statue of Sir Henry Crawford became nothing but memory.

But.

The target towards which this other-worldly fire power was directed was clearly no easy target. For although time and time again little red dots of laser light flickered upon his person, he out-manoeuvred every blast and volley. Sometimes on four limbs and sometimes on two, the being in black moved swiftly.

And then from the Big House issued Inspector Westlake, waving his hands and calling for a ceasefire.

WAP! WOOMPH! KAPOW! And KABLAM!

'I said to cease fire!'

The constables in the Paddy Wagon looked on in awe as the figure in black leapt over a gun-toting constable, somersaulted over a police car, ran, jumped and dived and—.

'Aaagh!' went Constable Handbag as the being in black passed through the windscreen of the Paddy Wagon and dropped down into the passenger seat beside him.

'Get out,' said the being.

Constable Handbag got out.

The being moved into the driver's seat and slammed shut the driver's door. 'Withdraw your head,' he told Constable Paul.

'I can't,' wailed Constable Paul. And it *was* a wail.

'Withdraw it or I will tear it from your neck.'

Constable Paul had one of those moments. Not one of the those-moments that Jonny had recently had, but rather one of those *other* those-moments. The ones where there's a car accident and the car's resting on the legs of a child and a little old lady lifts the car and the child gets rescued. One of those superhuman moments.

Constable Paul fell back into the rear of the Paddy Wagon taking knotted constables with him and descending into another untidy heap.

Made worse by the sudden acceleration of the Paddy Wagon.

And made doubly worse by the WHAMS, BAMS, WOOMPS, KABOOMS and CRASH-BANG-WALLOPS of police shellings that were now being directed towards the rear of the Paddy Wagon.

'Cease your bloody fire!' cried Inspector Westlake.

And, chastened by such abominable language, the constables holstered their weapons.

'And bloody get after them, you f★★ckwits!'

'Phew,' said Constable Justice. 'Can I come, too? I can drive the car.'

'Look at my bloody car!'

The inspector's bloody car was in bloody ruination.

'You can take mine,' said Joan, straightening her attire and issuing from the doorway. 'Mine's a Smart Car and it appears to have escaped the carnage.'

'Thank you, madam,' said Inspector Westlake, accepting the keys.

And off up the drive went the Paddy Wagon and out of the park gates and into Pope's Lane. And after it went the police cars. And after them a blue and grey Smart Car. Which although, perhaps, not as brisk as the turbo-charged police cars, *was* very light on petrol and kind to the environment.

'Oh woe, help,' and, 'alas,' bemoaned the writhing mass of constables in the rear of the Paddy Wagon.

'Get the f★ck off me!' shouted Paul.

'So I said, "Get the duck off me,"' said O'Fagin, 'Because frankly it's not a good look at a Masonic ball.'

'At least it wasn't a dinosaur,' said Jonny, sticking out his empty glass in search of a refill.

'Dinosaur?' said O'Fagin. 'It was a duck. Have you been drinking?'

'Yes,' said Jonny, 'and I'd like some lunch. Do you have any Peking duck?'

'Stegosaurus,' said O'Fagin.

'That's easy for you to say,' said Jonny.

'Not as easy as you might think. But the Peking duck is off, because it had stegosaurus in it.'

'Do you mean streptococcus?' asked Jonny.

'Do *you*?' asked O'Fagin.

And then there came to the ears of Jonny and the ears of O'Fagin what can only be described as a growing cacophony. Of police-car sirens and screaming engines.

'They're coming back,' said Jonny.

'Tank tops?' said O'Fagin. 'I do hope not.'

'Tank tops?' said Jonny.

'Oh no, hold on there.' O'Fagin checked something beneath his counter. 'Blues musicians,' he said, 'dinosaurs, no, it's seventies fashion tomorrow.'

'What *is* that?' Jonny asked

'The table of toot,' said O'Fagin. 'All publicans are issued with one monthly. Tells you what toot to engage your customers with. I don't know what I'd do without it.'

A whistle of missiles was clearly to be heard. That Doppler effect whistle. The one that varies in tone as the something that is causing the whistle, a missile in this particular case, gets nearer and nearer.

'Incoming!' shouted O'Fagin, and he took a dive to the floor. On his side of the bar counter Jonny did likewise as two things struck The Middle Man.

The first was a small ground-to-ground Harbinger missile, fired in anger by a constable named Agamemnon towards a swerving Paddy Wagon.

The second was the swerving Paddy Wagon itself.

It's unwelcome entry into The Middle Man being made somewhat easier due to the gaping hole that had just opened before it.

There was that rending of brickwork, that splintering of plaster, that tumbling of lintels, that ruination of pub chairs and tables and articles and artefacts and artless artworks, and with a roar as of a rogue elephant and the mash of a train wreck, the Paddy Wagon came to a halt.

Amidst smoke and dust and chaos.

28

Jonny Hooker raised his head from rubble. He felt at himself, although not in the biblical sense, and declared himself sound enough in mind and limb and still upon the plane of the living. Although somewhat bruised and battered all about.

Coughing dust, as one does in an aftermath, he rose, a-patting at his person and spitting somewhat, too.

'Are we the last survivors?' O'Fagin's head appeared above the bar counter. 'Was that the holocaust? Oh blessed be.'

'It's a Paddy Wagon,' said Jonny, pushing laths and plaster away from the Paddy Wagon's rear door. 'Somewhat embedded in the gents.'

'Not the nuclear holocaust, then?' O'Fagin made the sign of the cross, the Sign of the Four, the sign of the times and the times they are a-changing, all over his chest and upper body regions generally. 'And there was me thinking that you and I would have to mate to repopulate the Earth and stop it from being taken over by monkeys.'

'Not dinosaurs?' said Jonny.

'Been there, done that. What is that funky noise?'

The funky noise in question came from the rear of the Paddy Wagon. It was a funky groaning, moaning noise. A collection of noises, a group, a covey, a shoal, a bevy, a—

'What is that gallimaufry of noises?' O'Fagin asked.

'Policemen, I think.' Jonny struggled with more laths and plaster, struggled with the Wagon's rear door.

There was a struggle and a yank and an opening and a rush.

And suddenly Jonny was engulfed by policemen.

A blue serge horde poured out and about him.

Jonny went down in the blur.

'Jonny, mate.' Hands were laid upon him and Jonny was raised aloft.

'Paul?' Jonny could see Paul's helmetless head, his fine head of hair all caught in a shaft of sunlight. Which now flowed into the public bar through a large hole in the ceiling.

'Jonny, mate, I'm sorry, I could have killed you.'

'*You* could of killed me?'

'I grabbed him round the throat. An act of bravery. There'll no doubt be a medal in it for me. I hope it has a black ribbon. I—'

'What *are* you talking about?' Jonny fanned away Paul's hands, which were patting and poking at him. Groaning constables were rising to their feet. Others were now peering in through the big hole in the front wall.

These others had mighty weaponry.

Jonny Hooker put his hands up. 'I surrender,' he said. 'I'll come quietly. Don't shoot, G-men, clap the cuffs on me, Copper, it's a fair cop.'

'Have you lost all reason?' Paul took to patting Jonny's hands down again. 'They're not here to arrest *you*.'

'Oh,' said Jonny. Which sometimes says so much.

'I wonder if he's still alive?'

'Who?' asked Jonny. 'Who?'

'The madman who jumped into the cab. He flew in through the windscreen.'

'Flew?'

Constables with big, bad guns were creeping into the bar.

'Did you get the bastard?' one of them asked.

'Bastard?' said Jonny.

'Man in a black suit,' said Paul, patting all over himself. 'Black sunglasses, Gunnersbury Park, shoot-out, not human, blimey.'

Jonny Hooker shook his head. 'The driver in the cab?'

'Driver,' said Paul. 'Man or monster or something.'

'Really?' Jonny Hooker looked along the Paddy Wagon: it was pretty firmly embedded into the wall. There didn't look to be a lot of chance of reaching the cab.

'Little hatchway,' said Paul, 'between the cab and the rear – let's go and have a look, eh?'

'You're being terribly brave,' said Jonny, 'considering that you didn't have the bottle to throw in your lot with me.'

'Well, that's only because you're such a loser. No offence meant.'

'None taken, I assure you.'

'Friendship is a wonderful thing,' said O'Fagin. 'Red and white flock paper, I think, and one of those super-jukebox jobbies that works through the Interweb and has a million tracks on it.'

Jonny looked at Paul.

And Paul looked at Jonny.

'Is it worth asking him?' Paul asked Jonny.

Jonny shook his head.

'I'll tell you anyway,' said O'Fagin. 'Notice how unnaturally calm I am, even though my livelihood is in ruination? Well, that's because it's a police Paddy Wagon and I am a Freemason. And I expect a very large cash payout for all of this damage. And it will be worth another instalment in the Sunday tabloids and probably further headlines in tomorrow's gutter press and—'

'Quite,' said Jonny, and to Paul, 'Little hatch, go on, then.'

And Paul climbed into the rear of the Paddy Wagon.

'Want to have a look, too?' he asked.

'Wouldn't miss it for the world.'

Jonny climbed in after Paul and the two made their way forward. With a degree of care. A certain caution. A certain anticipatory caution.

They reached the little hatchway and Jonny whispered, 'Go on, then.'

Paul hesitated. 'He might well still be armed and dangerous,' he said.

'My feelings entirely, which was why I marvelled at your bravery. Or, should I say, bravado.'

'I'm brave enough,' said Paul, and he took a small peep, then a big peep and then a bigger peep still.

And then he ducked back his head and went, 'Not again.'

'Not again?' asked Jonny, and then *he* peeped.

But *again* it certainly was.

The driver sat there, bolt upright in the driving seat, both hands upon the wheel. But this was not a man in a black suit, white shirt and black tie. This was a man in a dusty eighteenth-century frocked coat, with quilted sleeves and lacy frillings. Golden rings adorned his slender fingers.

And as to the 'again'—

This was also a man who lacked for a head.

'Clear a path there, step aside.' Inspector Westlake entered the punctured premises. Pistol held high and big striding gait, he shuffled constables to the right and left of him and called into the rear of the Paddy Wagon.

'Is he alive?' he called.

'No, *sir*,' replied Constable Paul. 'His head's all gone, just like Mister Crawford and the rest.'

'Another? Damn and blast.' Inspector Westlake entered the Paddy Wagon. 'I want this area sealed off,' he told Constable Paul. 'And I want Scientific Support here at the hurry-up. And *you*—' He pointed the business end of his pistol at Jonny. '—I want *you* out of here.'

'Yes, *sir*,' said Jonny.

Jonny Hooker whispered certain words to Constable Paul. Constable Paul made a doubtful face. Jonny whispered further words and Constable Paul said, 'All right.'

'I told you to get out of here,' Inspector Westlake said.

Jonny grinned and saluted. 'Yes sir, sir,' he said.

'Yes, your ladyship?' said Joan. She had re-established herself behind what was left of the reception desk and she had answered the ringing telephone.

It was an internal call, from Countess Vanda.

'Excuse me, your ladyship, for just a moment.' Joan plucked something that did not even remotely resemble a dinosaur from her left earhole and returned the telephone receiver to it.

'What was all that ungodly racket?' asked Countess Vanda.

'We had a bit of an incident, your ladyship. A terrorist – there was a lot of shooting. I think I might have piddled myself.'

'I really do not wish to hear about that.'

'Which part, your ladyship.'

'Any of it. I trust there hasn't been any damage done to the museum.'

Joan did some bitings of the lower lip. Most of the dust had settled now and the ruination was fearsome.

'There has been *some*,' she said. And then she went, 'Waah!'

'Waah?' asked Countess Vanda.

'Ranger Connor just pinched my—' Joan raised a saucy eyebrow at the ranger.

Ranger Connor stared all around and about. 'What happened *here*?' he asked.

Joan put her hand over the telephone receiver. 'Terrorist,' she said.

'Terrorist?'

Joan shushed him. 'Yes,' she said to Countess Vanda. 'I'll call the conservators on the phone. I'm sure they'll be able to, er, patch things up. Goodbye.' And she replaced the receiver.

'Terrorist?' said Ranger Connor. 'Oh no and I missed it.'

'You wouldn't have liked it,' said Joan, primping at her hair. 'Not very nice at all, it wasn't. He ran across the ceiling.'

'The ceiling?'

'Man in a black suit.'

'A black suit?'

'And a white shirt.'

'White shirt?'

'Please don't keep repeating what I say.'

'What I say?'

Joan smacked Ranger Connor.

'Thank you,' said the ranger. 'But you're saying that the man in the black suit, chap with the posh voice— ' Joan nodded. '—that he was a terrorist?'

'Probably still is.'

'But he asked me to find—'

'To find?'

'Don't *you* start.'

'What did he ask you to find?'

'A laptop. Amongst the effects of the late James Crawford. But it wasn't in the boxes.'

'Well, all's well that ends well, eh?'

'Are you doing anything at lunchtime?' Ranger Connor asked.

'Eating my lunch?' Joan replied.

'I was wondering, perhaps if you'd care to join me for a sandwich in the rangers' hut.'

'Ah,' said Joan. '*About* the rangers' hut.'

'About the rangers' hut?'

Joan smacked him again.

'Has something happened to the rangers' hut?'

'It got sort of blown up,' said Joan.

'*Sort of blown up?*'

Joan withheld her smacking hand. 'It must come as a bit of a shock,' she said. 'I'm sorry.'

'*You're sorry?*' said Ranger Connor, going all pale. 'That new Ranger Chicoteen – I left him in the hut.'

'Ranger Chicoteen', Elastoplast-speckled, dust-spattered also, had left the devastated bar of The Middle Man but had not, as such, left altogether. He hovered about amongst the growing crowd that was now being held back behind the hastily strung lengths of 'DO NOT CROSS' tape.

'Stand back please, sir,' Constable Paul advised him.

'Don't be a twat,' said Jonny.

'Show a little respect for that constable,' said a lady in a straw hat. 'He's only doing his job. And it can't be any fun looking like that.'

'Like that?' said Constable Paul.

The lady in the straw hat smacked him.

Lads from Scientific Support, in their nice white environmental suits, were milling all around and about. Two were assembling a coconut shy. Two more were manhandling a body on a stretcher through the yawning maw that had so recently been the front wall of The Middle Man.

Jonny Hooker did cranings of the neck.

The stretcher passed him near at hand and as it did so the crowd made a bit of a surge forward. There was some jostling involved and some muffled and censored swear words issued from within the face helmets of the men in white.

Jonny bumped up against the stretcher. Something tumbled from it and fell onto the ground.

Constable Paul demanded some order. 'Back!' cried he. 'I'm

arresting this lady in a straw hat for striking a police officer.'

'You'll never make it stick, rat boy,' cried the lady.

'Rat boy?' said Paul.

And the lady smacked him again.

Jonny stooped swiftly and picked up the something that had tumbled from the stretcher.

It was a key. A brass key. Jonny turned it over on his palm and gave it a furtive once-over.

It was an antique key for sure. Upon it were engraved certain words and a date. Jonny read these words and he read that date, and Jonny Hooker smiled.

The words engraved upon the key were:

THE ACME AIR LOOM COMPANY

The date was:

1790

29

'Whenever I hear the words "Culture Club", I reach for my pistol,' said O'Fagin to Jonny.

It was a little after noon now and some semblance of normality had returned to The Middle Man. Not a great deal, but *some*.

The Paddy Wagon had been dragged from the building's innards, winched onto a low-loader and driven away. Steel acros had been positioned all around and about to support the failing ceilings and walls. The rubble had been swept away, along with the broken furniture and art-for-art's-sake artery. Plastic sheets were now taped over the great big hole.

Jonny Hooker had a brass key in his pocket. A brass key that really meant something. Exactly what that something was, Jonny was not precisely sure. But it was a reality. A confirmation. That he *was* on the right track. That the Air Loom really had existed. What to do next, of this Jonny wasn't so sure. So for now he drank ale with O'Fagin.

'And don't get me started on Spandau Ballet,' said O'Fagin.

'Is there an Eighties Night in the offing?' Jonny asked.

He sat on one of the two remaining barstools, before what was left of the bar counter. O'Fagin had his arm in a sling. Someone had mentioned 'compensation for injuries received' to him. He also sported an eyepatch.

'The show must go on,' said O'Fagin. 'Apparently at the first hint of any kind of disaster, these nineteen-eighties bands, that you'd hoped were long forgotten, turn up to do a benefit night.'

'That's very sad,' said Jonny.

'Sad but true,' said O'Fagin. 'And I haven't heard anything from Metallica. I'd be happy to have them.'

'Is the show going on tonight, then?' Jonny asked.

'Absolutely – we'll be having that Dry Rot. A gay band.'

'Gay band?' said Jonny.

O'Fagin slapped him.

Jonny punched O'Fagin.

'I don't think it's supposed to work like that,' said O'Fagin, clicking his jaw back into place. 'Do you have something against gay bands?'

'Dry Rot is *not* a gay band. It's a heavy-rock band.'

'Heavy rock or mincing pansy – it's all the same when you come right down to it.'

'It is *not*,' said Jonny. 'Not the same at all.'

'Oh yeah, you're probably right,' said O'Fagin. 'I must have misread the instructions on the box. I think I have concussion. I wonder how much I can claim for that?'

'So Dry Rot will still be playing tonight?'

'Damned right,' said O'Fagin. 'As I told that Duran Duran. Go back to Russia, you simpering fairy, I told him, we'll have none of your commie music here.'

'Quite so,' said Jonny.

'Quite unlike anything I've ever seen in my life.' The words came out of the police pathologist's mouth and entered Inspector Westlake's ears.

'Go on,' said the inspector.

'Well,' said the police pathologist, 'observe this.'

They were in the County Morgue. Because every English county has a County Morgue. And it was one of your proper morgues, too, with the big aluminium filing cabinet jobbies for putting the stiffs in. And the table with the blood gullies in it for carving up the stiffs on. And all the equipment and paraphernalia that anyone could hope to find in a place where stiffs are carved and stored away.

The police pathologist, whose given name was Dickey, but whose nickname was the Gall-Bladder-Sandwich Man, drew back the sheet that covered the headless corpse and drew Inspector Westlake's attention to the gory neck hole. 'Just like the others,' he said.

'I have not as yet received the reports on the others,' said the inspector, pointedly. 'Perhaps they have got lost in the post.'

'No need to adopt that tone, old chap. You haven't received the reports because I was told to hand them over directly to Inspector Westlake.

'I *am* Inspector Westlake,' said Inspector Westlake.

'No,' said the pathologist, 'you are *not* Inspector Westlake. Inspector Westlake is a young chap who wears a black suit, white shirt, black tie, black shoes and sunglasses. He took the previous reports with him. Who *are you*, anyway?'

'I am Inspector Westlake!' roared Inspector Westlake, producing his warrant card and thrusting it in the pathologist's face. 'That man *there*, on the slab – that is the terrorist who has apparently been impersonating me.'

'I think *not*,' said the pathologist.

'I think *so*,' said the inspector. 'He was killed during a high-speed chase. 'A young officer will be receiving a commendation over it.'

'*Not* the man,' said the pathologist. 'Can't be.'

'And why can it not be?'

'Nicely put,' said the pathologist. 'I'd have had to smack you if you'd repeated me.'

'Why?' asked Inspector Westlake.

'Who knows?' said the pathologist. 'These things come into fashion, they're a sort of running gag, they're here and then they're gone. Who can say?'

'About the body?' said Inspector Westlake.

'Now that is quite another matter. That is not a here-today-and-gone-tomorrow sort of body. It's more a here-yesterday-but-shouldn't-be-here-today kind of affair.'

'How so?'

'This body,' said the pathologist, 'is not the body of a man who died today.'

'It certainly is,' said Inspector Westlake.

'I do hate to keep contradicting you,' said the pathologist. 'Well, as a matter of fact, I *don't*, but this man did *not* die today. By the state of this body, by the mummification process—'

'The *what*?'

'This body is mummified. This body is a museum piece. The clothes are authentic, the jewellery, the shoes. This is the body of a Regency dandy. This body is more than two hundred years old.'

★

'Two hundred years old,' said Mr Henry Hunter. Master conservator, with no nickname. 'The pillars date from around seventeen ninety, as does much of the interior work.'

Joan smiled up at Henry Hunter. He had arrived post-haste in his bright blue van with his bright young assistant Sparky. Sparky had taken a shine to Joan. Joan to Henry Hunter.

'Tragic business,' said Henry. 'Shoot-out, you say? Anyone injured?'

'Only the portrait of Sir Henry.'

'That old rogue. Not the first time someone took a pot shot at him.'

'I suppose you know all about the Big House,' said Joan, adjusting her bosoms onto the temporary top of the shored-up reception desk.

'Father and son for many generations,' said Henry, averting his gaze from the bosoms. 'A long and strange history this place has. Rogues and rascals and weirdos. If these old walls could only speak, eh?'

'Sexual intrigue?' Joan asked.

'I'm sure you've read all the guide books.'

'Scandal?' asked Joan.

Henry had his special wooden work-case jobbie. He shifted certain reproduction prehistoric animal facsimiles aside and eased it onto the temporary counter top. Flipping the catches, he opened the lid. 'We'd best get to work,' he said.

'You can talk as you work,' said Joan. 'I know, I do it all the time.'

Henry took out pots of gunk and tubes of glue and balls of string and a cardboard box containing a number of professional-looking brushes, of the type used by conservators when they do delicate restoration work. Badger-pelt swabbers and fox-fur floggers.

'About the scandals?' said Joan.

Henry gave his nose a tap with a hamster-hair handicrafter and nearly put his eye out. 'Discretion,' he said.

'Oh, go on.'

'Well.' Henry took to directing Sparky.

Sparky grudgingly removed his gaze from Joan's breasts and steered it towards the job in hand. 'This is going to take months,' he said.

'Years,' said Henry.

'Hours,' said Joan.

'Hours?' said Henry.

Joan didn't smack him.

'Hours?' said Henry once more.

'Twenty-four hours,' said Joan. 'I have just received a call from Buckingham Palace.'

'Buckingham Palace?' said Sparky.

And Joan smacked him.

'Buckingham Palace,' said Joan once more. 'Apparently there's to be a special conference of big wigs held here on Sunday. What with all this kerfuffle, I thought they'd move it somewhere else, but apparently not. Buckingham Palace were appraised of the situation, but apparently they still want the meeting to go ahead here. So you have to have the place all spruced up and well again within twenty-four hours.'

Sparky almost said, 'Twenty-four hours?'

Almost.

'Would you like me to make you both a cup of tea?' Joan asked. 'British workmen thrive on tea. Tea and fellatio, or so I've heard.'

'Madam,' said Henry. 'Madam, excuse me, please.'

'You are excused,' said Joan. 'Third on the left down the hall.'

'No, that is not what I mean. Are you telling me that some kind of international conference is to be held *here*, on Sunday?'

Joan nodded. Prettily.

'And that Her Majesty the Queen, God bless her, will be attending?'

Joan winked. 'I think so, yes.'

'Oh no,' said Henry. 'Oh no, no.'

'No?' said Joan.

'No,' said Henry. 'Not here, that must not be.'

'Are you all right, Spunky?' Sparky asked.

'No, I am *not*! And don't call me "Spunky". I do *not* have a nickname.'

'Spunky?' said Joan.

'No,' went Henry Hunter once more. 'Her Majesty must not come here.'

'She came once before,' said Joan, 'during the Millennium

celebrations. We had a brand-new toilet installed for her, just on the off chance that she *does* go to the toilet, like the rest of us.'

'And did she?' Sparky asked.

Joan put her finger to her lips.

'I know she came here before,' said Henry. 'I helped to install that toilet – a reproduction Thomas Crapper, cost an arm and a leg, but it was worth it. But months of planning went into that visit. Security men were here for months, one on permanent twenty-four-hour watch inside the toilet itself. When was this latest visit planned?'

'Just today, I think,' said Joan.

'No! No! No!' Henry Hunter grew quite red in the face. 'It's far too dangerous. I advised against it last time and I advise against it now. Why wasn't I informed?'

'Perhaps because the countess knew you'd advise against it.'

'The countess?' said Henry.

'The new curator.'

'New curator? What happened to Stan?'

'Vanished,' said Joan. 'Apparently. Ran away, or something.'

'No!' Henry fairly shrieked this 'No'. 'Her Majesty must *not* come here again,' shrieked Henry. 'If she does, she will surely die.'

'Surely die?' said Joan.

And Henry smacked her.

30

Henry Hunter 'no'd' some more.

So Joan gave him a smack.

'Thank you,' said Henry. 'And I'm sorry that I … well, I don't know what came over me.'

'That's all right.' Joan smiled. 'I quite enjoyed it really. But why are you getting yourself in such a lather? What makes you think that the Queen might be in danger if she comes here?'

'I must speak to the new curator.'

'I'll pass the message on.'

'This is important,' said Henry. 'Very important.'

'Oh, all right.' Joan made deep-breasted sighings. 'I'll give her a call, but she won't be pleased. She usually likes to have a little lie down in her hyperbaric chamber at this time of the day.'

'Her what?' said Sparky.

'I can't smack you if you don't do it properly,' said Joan.

'Eh?' said Sparky.

'Please call her now,' Henry said.

Joan did phonings and words passed this way and that. Joan re-placed the receiver. 'She says you can go up now. And while you're up there you can shift some of the furniture about. The conference is to be held in her office – Princess Amelia's sitting room.'

'No. No. No,' said Henry Hunter. And then took to issuing orders to Sparky to mix up some gunk and begin the restoration work by mopping the grime from what remained of Sir Henry's portrait with a small yellow item that closely resembled SpongeBob SquarePants. Because Henry *was* a professional and he *did* have a reputation. He stalked up the sweeping staircase, along the gallery and did big knockings upon a certain door.

'Come,' came the voice of Countess Vanda.

Henry entered the room.

'And please shut the door.'

'But it's dark.'

'I am sensitive to the light.'

'But,' went Henry. 'But—'

'There is a chair, just there, before you. Yes, that's right, lit by the shaft of sunlight.'

Henry dropped into the chair. He had a bit of a sweat on, did Henry. And a bit of a shake going, too.

'I understand you have an objection that you wish to voice,' said Countess Vanda.

'In the strongest possible terms,' said Henry, wiping a bead of perspiration away from the end of his nose. 'Her Majesty the Queen must not return to this house. It is not safe. It must not happen.'

'Mister Hunter,' said Countess Vanda, in a voice as soft and sweet as a Thelwell pony. 'Mister Hunter, we have not as yet been formally introduced. I am aware of your work here at the Big House, and that you're of the latest generation of conservators, and that your family has a connection with this park that stretches back several hundred years.'

'Then please listen to me,' said Henry.

'I will,' said Countess Vanda. 'Please state your case. And do so with alacrity, for it is time for me to recharge my batteries, as it were.'

'Madam,' said Henry, 'generations of Hunters have gone before me, working here at the Big House. Generations who have remained loyal to the House and its owners. Over the course of time they have become privy to many confidences and aware of many scandals. And remained tight-lipped.'

'Most commendable.'

'I know things about this house,' said Henry, 'that would shock you to your very soul. Crimes have been committed here – grave crimes, horrid crimes, crimes that have been covered up, swept under the carpet. And things of that nature—'

'Generally?'

'Generally,' said Henry. 'In the seventeen nineties, talks were held here regarding the British position on the French Revolution.'

'Parliamentary talks?'

'Ah,' said Henry. 'No, not parliamentary. The owners of Gunnersbury Park have, throughout the centuries of its existence, shared something in common, something unknown to the general population, indeed unknown to those in Parliament.'

'Go on,' said Countess Vanda.

'I am telling you this because I fear that if the Queen hosts the talks here, her life may well be in danger. Otherwise I would not speak of such things.'

'Go on,' said Countess Vanda once more.

'The Secret Order of the Golden Sprout,' said Henry. 'All who have owned this house through the years have been members of this Secret Order.'

'This Order is unknown to me,' said Countess Vanda.

'It is a secret society, founded, many believe, by a certain Count Otto Black, of evil memory. This order has throughout the ages conspired to control those who rule this land of ours, through fair means or foul. Mostly foul. At the talks in seventeen ninety,' continued Henry, 'was a most remarkable character: an Illuminati by the name of the Count of Saint Germain, a musician, artist, traveller and mystic, a man who claimed that he could improve the quality of diamonds and turn base metal into gold.'

'A charlatan,' said Countess Vanda.

'By no means, madam, although he certainly encouraged those who built legends around him. It was said, for instance, that he had discovered the elixir of life and that he had once walked with Christ.'

'Enough of this now,' said Countess Vanda. 'Please come to the point.'

'The talks were held,' said Henry, 'but something occurred. It is not sufficient to call it a disagreement. Sir Henry Crawford hosted the talks, and Sir Henry Crawford was slain. He and several others, including I have reason to believe, the Count of Saint Germain.'

'Murders and intrigue litter the pages of history,' said Countess Vanda. 'I do not believe that the meeting tomorrow could possibly have any links to something that happened in seventeen ninety.'

'Seventeen ninety,' said the pathologist. 'Somewhat significant, do you not think?'

Inspector Westlake, to whom this remark was addressed and who was still in the morgue with the pathologist, although he would have preferred to be in the pub with his lunch, asked, 'In what way?'

'In the very manner of this,' said the pathologist. 'This is a case for Mulder and Scully, to be sure.'

'It's a queer one and no mistake,' said the inspector. 'But by applying Occam's Razor, I think a simple solution should be forthcoming.'

'Oh, do you really?' said the pathologist.

'Indeed. It is a case of substitution. Clearly the mummified body of a man who has been dead for two hundred years did not commandeer and drive away that Paddy Wagon. This body was clearly substituted by the driver. A being who, I must confess, is possessed of certain abilities suitable for inclusion amongst *The X Files*. I confess that I did not examine the body when it was removed from the Paddy Wagon, so I cannot say when the substitution was made.'

'Substitution?' The pathologist blew onto the end of his bone-saw, raising a fine cloud of bone dust. 'Someone did what? Dug this body from some vault? Put it behind the driving wheel, in a public house surrounded by policemen, for what reason? A joke, perhaps?'

'Perhaps,' said Inspector Westlake. 'Believe it or not, there is a class of person in this country who derives considerable pleasure in thwarting the forces of the law. Criminals, we call them in the trade. Perhaps you have heard of them.'

'Most amusing.' The pathologist buffed the bone-saw on his sleeve. 'But let us, for argument's sake, say that you are correct. Then how would you explain *this*?'

He took himself over to the rack of filing cabinet jobbies where the dead were filed in a certain order and yanked out one of the drawers.

'And who's this?' asked Inspector Westlake.

'Jonathan Hooker, if the tag upon his toe is to be believed.'

Inspector Westlake said nothing.

'I believe you attended the crime scene, Inspector. Indeed, I believe you supervised the loading of this particular body into the Scientific Support vehicle once the garden furniture had been removed from it, and directed its transportation here.'

'I did,' said Inspector Westlake.

'And *I* examined the body, made my report and—'

'Gave it to an impostor,' said Inspector Westlake.

'So it appears. However, this impostor never entered the morgue. I placed the body in this cabinet. So kindly explain *this*.' With a suitably theatrical flourish, the pathologist whipped aside the sheet that covered the body to expose—

'A mummy,' said Inspector Westlake, viewing the withered hand that showed beneath a lacy cuff and the sleeve of a green frocked coat.

'Another mummy,' said the pathologist. 'And I mentioned the significance of the year seventeen ninety, only because he had papers in his pocket with that date upon them.'

Inspector Westlake scratched at his head. 'I have to confess,' said he, 'that this is all most perplexing.'

'A word I think one might use without fear of being accused of exaggeration.'

'One thing,' said the inspector, lifting the wizened, spectral hand and letting it plop back down with a dull thump. 'Could it be some disease, or contamination, or – God spare us – some terrorist chemical weapon?'

'That is capable of changing clothes from present day to those of an antique persuasion?'

Inspector Westlake shook his head. 'I have to further confess that I have no idea what this means,' he said. 'Have you drawn any conclusions? Do you have any theories?'

'None that I would wish to put upon record for fear of my reputation.'

'But which you might care to vocalise? In private? Off the record? On the level and under the arch?' And Inspector Westlake did certain Masonic gesturings with his fingers.

'In private and off the record – *strictly* off the record—'. The pathologist returned the inspector's gesturing with certain of his own. '—I believe that this body is the same body you had sent here. How it changed in this manner I do not know. How the clothes were changed I do not know.'

'What makes you believe it's the same body?'

The pathologist lifted the dust-dry right hand. 'We fingerprint every body that comes in here, as soon as it comes in – standard procedure. We fingerprinted the body you dispatched to us. This mummy here – I played a hunch and fingerprinted it again. Even allowing for the process of mummification, which would make any kind of positive identification difficult, in this case it wasn't – the prints are the same. It's the same body.'

'Bodies everywhere,' said Henry Hunter, in the darkness lit only by that little slice of light. 'Here, in this very room. And it doesn't end there. There were further summit meetings held here, and at each something unaccountable occurred. Deaths again and again. Each of these summit talks had a direct effect upon world events. Each was held here with those involved not knowing what had happened here in the past. The only ones who knew were those who organised these summit talks, who orchestrated the murderings, who covered up the truth: the Secret Order of the Golden Sprout.'

'And you believe that this will happen again?'

'I read the newspapers and watch the news the same as everyone else. I, like you, know what is going on in the Middle East and how it could trigger a global holocaust. If this is a summit meeting of those who truly control the affairs of this world, there is no telling what those who seek to control these controllers intend.'

'This Secret Order of the Golden Sprout?'

'The same,' said Henry Hunter.

'It is a fascinating tale,' said Countess Vanda. 'It is also, of course, the king of all conspiracy theories. I confess that I *have* heard of this Secret Order. I believe, however, that there is no positive proof that they have ever existed.'

'Oh, they exist,' said Henry. 'I have seen them with my own eyes. Meeting *here* in this very room.'

'And how did you see them?'

'I would prefer not to say. But I have. And they *do* exist. They have the tattoo, here.'

'Where is that?'

'Here.' Henry held his left forearm in the shaft of sunlight. 'The golden sprout above the triangle.'

'Well, thank you, Mister Hunter. Your tale is indeed interesting, but I do not have any reason to believe that Her Majesty is in danger. We will be honoured to have her attend the meeting here and I have every confidence in Inspector Westlake's ability to handle the security.'

'No,' said Henry Hunter. 'No. No. No.'

'Yes, yes, yes,' said Countess Vanda. 'Your concern is noted. Now please return to your work. We'd like the reception area returned to its former glory as quickly as possible.'

'No,' said Henry Hunter. 'No.'

'No?'

'My conscience will not allow it. I will inform Inspector Westlake. And if he does nothing, I will inform the press.'

'Oh dear no.' The voice of Countess Vanda surprised Henry Hunter. Because it did not come from before him now. It came from behind.

Softly and above his left shoulder.

'The talks *must* go ahead. *Here,*' she said.

And then Henry felt two hands upon his neck.

And there was a twist and there was a sickening crunch and Henry Hunter toppled sideways into darkness.

And just for a moment, just for a flash, the naked left forearm of Countess Vanda was to be glimpsed in the shaft of sunlight.

And there was a tattoo upon it.

That of a triangle with a golden sprout above it.

31

Jonny Hooker shuddered.

'Someone walk over your grave?' asked O'Fagin.

'As if I'd know,' said Jonny.

'Anyway,' said O'Fagin. 'I'm glad your nuts grew back.'

'What?' asked Jonny, and not without reason.

'Well,' said O'Fagin, 'being a publican you have to remember people's names and faces and all kinds of minutiae about them, so you can name them and mention details and stuff, so the punters think that since you remember these things, you must like them. Which, of course, you don't, you only want their money.'

'How candid,' said Jonny. 'How charming.'

'We aim to please, sir.'

'And the point?' Jonny asked.

'Well,' said O'Fagin, once more, 'you were introduced to me yesterday as Charlie Hawtrey's castrato brother. But you're not speaking in a high voice now, so I assume that your nuts must have grown back.'

'Ah,' said Jonny. 'Right,' said Jonny. 'That would probably be it,' said Jonny, also.

'See, I don't miss stuff,' said O'Fagin. 'I'm on the ball, me, all the time. On the ball, get it?'

'Not really,' said Jonny. 'If you're so good on continuity,' said Jonny, 'perhaps you can tell me whether I've had my lunch here yet?'

'No, you haven't.' O'Fagin flourished a menu. 'Don't get me going on pub grub,' he continued.

'I'll try not to.' Jonny perused the menu.

'Do you ever feel,' asked O'Fagin, whilst Jonny was engaged in this perusal, 'that everyone, except yourself, seems to be having a really interesting life and that somehow you've been left out?'

Jonny looked up from his perusal. 'All the time,' he answered. 'Well, up until recently. Well, yes, I suppose so, yes.'

'So,' said O'Fagin, 'what's it like, then? Because me, I live on the cutting edge, life in the fast lane and all that kind of business.'

'I think I'll have a cheese sandwich,' said Jonny.

'Oh, *very* adventurous.'

'Yes, you're right,' said Jonny. 'I'll have the cheese *and* pickle.'

'Do you sometimes think that life is going on all around you but somehow you're not taking part?'

'Isn't that the same question you just asked?'

'There are subtle differences. I think the problem with life is that most of us never get out of life what we'd like to get. We don't even ask for much. But things always conspire, people always conspire to cheat, or trick, or fool us out of what we want.'

'You think so?' said Jonny.

'I know so,' said O'Fagin. 'Let's use this sandwich as an example. Cheese and pickle, you said.' O'Fagin got his notepad out. 'Was that on white bread, or brown?'

'White,' said Jonny.

'Butter or margarine?'

'Marge,' said Jonny.

'Cheddar or Jarlsberg?'

'Cheddar.'

'Branston or Major Grey's?'

'Branston.'

O'Fagin did tickings. 'The cheese and pickle are off,' said he. 'The bread is all stale, we're out of margarine and the cat ate all the pickle. I can do you a steak pie and chips.'

Jonny Hooker grinned and turned his menu towards O'Fagin. On it the steak pie and chips were circled.

'Did you scrawl that on my menu?' O'Fagin asked.

Jonny nodded. 'While you were just explaining to me what the problem with life is,' said he. 'With this souvenir pen with the top shaped like a dinosaur.'

'Was all of this supposed to mean something?' O'Fagin asked.

'I think so,' said Jonny. 'Recent events have taught me that *everything* means *something*.'

Everything must be done as I want it done,' said Inspector Westlake into a telephone receiver. 'If *something* goes wrong after that, then I will take the blame. But I will only carry the can if it's *my* can. Do I make myself understood?'

At the other end of the line was the Extra-Special Operations Unit, that Above Top Secret Special Operations unit that deals with all the high-security whatnots that come up and someone has to deal with when all the usual Special Operations Units are saying 'that's not within our jurisprudence'. The man in overall charge of the Extra-Special Operations Unit was an English gentleman. He wore a grey pullover, a checked shirt and a knitted tie. He sported a curious beard and smoked a pipe. He had appeared regularly on the Open University during the nineteen eighties when the Open University was a channel only watched by British spies who knew all the codewords and what the *Open* University was *really* all about.

Of course, we *all* know now.

The gentleman's name was Thompson. These gentlemen are always called 'Thompson'. There have been generations of them, all doing the same job. Father to son, father to son. Since around 1790. Apparently.

'Give me the "gen" one more time, me old cock-sparra,' said Thompson.

'I want a ring of steel placed around Gunnersbury Park,' said Inspector Westlake. 'Important talks are to be held there this Sunday. Some queer occurrences have come up and I want to be one hundred per cent certain that those at the talks will be completely secure.'

'Which is why you called the Extra-Special Operations Unit,' said Thompson. 'For the record, how did you get our number? Was it from a card through your door, a card in the newsagent's window or *Yellow Pages*?'

'I'm a Freemason,' said Inspector Westlake. 'Couldn't you tell by the way your telephone rang?'

'Only testing,' said Thompson. 'We have to be very careful in this game, I can tell you. We have to know who's who and what's what. So, have you made a list?'

'I've faxed you a map,' said Inspector Westlake. 'The layout of

Gunnersbury Park, the location of the Big House and the room within where the talks will be held.'

'I have it here,' said Thompson. Who did. 'It looks reasonably straightforward. We'll run a fence around the entire perimeter, twenty feet high, electrified, of course.'

'Of course.'

'We'll lay down minefields, laser trips, braggers and flame wasps. I'll have fifty men in full camo dig in around the perimeter. We'll put a couple of silent birds above.'

'Silent birds?' Inspector Westlake asked.

'Stealth helicopters. You can't see them, but they can see you.'

'Splendid.'

'And who will be footing the bill for all this?'

'Just put in your invoice,' said Inspector Westlake. 'All expenses will be covered.'

'And you wish to take overall control of this operation yourself? We can supply a management team.'

'It is my call,' said the inspector. '*My* watch. Nothing and no one is going to mess with this operation. Nothing and no one is going to enter that park without my approval. Nothing and no one is going to endanger the lives of those at this meeting. Do I make myself clear?'

'Utterly clear,' said Thompson. 'All forces and security procedures will be in place within twelve hours. You have nothing to fear, Brother Inspector – nothing and no one will penetrate security. Nothing and no one will be allowed to enter the park that could in any way endanger the talks or those engaged in them.'

Parked behind the Big House, under the shade of a tree, unblemished by the earlier gunfire, unnoticed by all concerned, was a white Ford Transit van. The side doors and indeed the rear doors of this van were open and at the behest of a chap dressed in a top hat and red ringmaster's coat, two dwarves were unloading a number of boxes.

The dwarves had an odd look to them. There was something quaint and old-fashioned about their attire. In fact, it had a positively antique look to it, as if these dwarves had stepped straight out of the Regency period.

About, say, 1790.

'Hurry along now,' said the ringmaster, an odd-enough body himself at close quarters, what with the made-up face and the peri-wig that showed beneath his top hat. 'Down the secret passage and into the storerooms beneath.'

The dwarves made haste, but not without difficulty, for the boxes they carried were heavy. Heavy, wooden, dusty and very old-looking, they were. And printed with antique lettering upon the sides of these cases were the words

ACME AIR LOOM COMPANY.
THIS WAY UP.

32

'Well, I haven't said too much for a while.' The voice of Mr Giggles was once more at Jonny's ear. Jonny didn't welcome this voice and did what he could to ignore it.

Jonny supped upon further beer.

Mr Giggles prattled away. 'Get that down you and let's be going,' prattled Mr Giggles. 'Whatever the situation is, it is approaching that time when it becomes out of control. Put your faith in me, buddy boy, Tierra del Fuego awaits.'

'Now that I remember it,' said O'Fagin to Jonny, 'did you want to buy a ticket?'

'I know I am putting what is left of my sanity at risk by asking,' said Jonny, 'but a ticket for *what*?'

'For tonight's benefit gig. Dry Rot are playing – they're a girls' drum and fife band. Should be worth watching.'

'Dry Rot are heavy rock,' said Jonny. 'I think I did mention this before.'

'Possibly,' said O'Fagin, 'but it's odds-on that I wasn't listening. Tickets are a tenner, by the way. Or four for fifty quid.'

'I won't need a ticket,' said Jonny.

'You will if you want to get in.'

'I am in the band,' said Jonny.

'Nobody told me it was a transvestite drum and fife band. This puts an entirely different complexion on things. I'll have to charge you twelve pounds.'

'I'm with the band,' said Jonny. 'Dry Rot – I'm the lead guitarist.'

'Jonny Hooker is the lead guitarist,' said O'Fagin, 'which I find confusing, because I'm sure I heard that he's dead.'

'I'm his replacement.'

'Ah, very pleased to meet you.' O'Fagin stuck his hand across the bar counter for a shake. So Jonny shook it. 'And allow me to thank you for your generosity.'

Jonny Hooker shook his head now and said, 'What?'

'For donating your fee to the pub rebuilding fund. The five hundred pounds will come in very handy.'

'Five hundred?' said Jonny. 'You only ever pay fifty. Well you always promise to, but you always say that you don't have any change and that you'll pay next time.' Jonny paused. 'Well, at least that's what I've heard. From a *very* accurate source. You've certainly never paid any band five hundred pounds.'

O'Fagin did that nose-tapping thing. 'I have according to my accounts and tax returns,' said he. And he went off to serve a gaunt gentleman of aristocratic bearing who wore a long, black beard and a curious young woman with bright-red hair who wore long rubber gloves.

'It's a pity—' said Jonny.

'Are you addressing *me*?' asked Mr Giggles.

'Let's say yes,' Jonny said, 'I am, and it's a pity that the solving of the Da-da-de-da-da Code business seems unlikely to bring me any financial reward. Because if it did, I would most certainly use it as a deposit on buying a pub. It seems there are fortunes to be made in that game.'

'You'd hate it,' giggled Mr Giggles. 'Always starts well in the early evening, when folk are pleasant and sober. But by chucking-out time, these same pleasant and sober folk have turned into foul-mouthed drunks who don't want to go home at all. You'd hate them in no time.'

The reconstructed saloon bar door opened to admit the passage of Paul. He strolled over to Jonny and leaned upon the bar counter. 'I love all the plastic sheeting,' said Paul. 'It looks as if Christo has turned this pub into an installation.'

'Any luck?' Jonny asked.

'Regarding what?'

'You know *exactly* what. What I whispered to you about when Inspector Westlake told me to leave the pub.'

'Following the body?' said Paul.

'That's what I asked you to do. And to find out what the pathologist said.'

'Yes,' said Paul. 'And it could well have put my job at risk.'

'Paul,' said Jonny, 'I never knew exactly why you decided to join the police force.'

'For the uniform and the violence,' said Paul. 'Same as everyone else.'

'Perhaps. But I do not see you as a copper, as it were. You are a musician. You *know* you are.'

'You're right.' Paul took off his helmet and placed it on the bar counter. As he did so, Jonny noticed that the interior of Paul's helmet was *not* lined with tinfoil. Jonny straightened *his* headwear. He had no intention of taking that off.

'You are right,' Paul continued. 'I joined for the uniform, but it turned out to be dark blue, not black. I'd always thought they were black. Even the body armour is dark blue. Apparently you have to be in Special Ops to get a black uniform. And as for the violence – it's like sex.'

'Not the kind of sex I usually have,' said Jonny.

'You usually have *no* sex,' said Paul. 'But what I mean is that sex is great. I love sex, but sex every day?'

Jonny sighed.

Mr Giggles sighed.

'*Every* day,' said Paul. 'You get tired of it. You really do. It's not a treat any more. After a few weeks of laying into Joe Public with my extendible truncheon the novelty began to wear off.'

'I'm so sorry to hear it,' said Jonny. Who wasn't.

'So you augment it with a bit of torture down in the cells. Or "interrogation", as I believe it's otherwise called. But eventually you get bored with that. So then you're into your vigilante Mad Cop Street Justice scenarios – arresting drug lords, taking them into the woods and executing them, that kind of thing. But then that pales and what are you into then?'

'Cannibalism?' said Jonny.

'Exactly. But soon you find yourself getting bored with that, so—'

'Stop,' said Jonny. 'Please stop.'

'Exactly,' said Paul. 'So I'm thinking of stopping being a policeman.

I thought perhaps I'd become a doctor, or something.'

'A doctor,' said Jonny. Without enthusiasm.

'Well, I expect you'd get the chance to perform radical new procedures and insane medical experiments on people. Once you'd got bored with taking out appendixes, of course.'

'Did you follow the body?' Jonny asked.

'To the morgue? I certainly did.'

'And?' said Jonny.

'I listened at the door. Then later I slipped in and nicked stuff.'

'Top man,' said Jonny. 'What did you nick?'

'A ham sandwich,' said Paul, 'and a Thermos flask. I haven't opened that yet, so I don't know what's inside. But it's at least half-full.'

Jonny Hooker gave Paul a certain look.

'Don't ever look at me like that again,' said Paul, 'or I will be forced to forget the long years of our friendship and experiment on you with a really horrible-looking piece of medical kit that I also nicked.'

Jonny Hooker sighed.

'All right,' said Paul. 'I listened and this is what I heard.'

And Paul related unto Jonny all that he had overheard of the conversation between Inspector Westlake and the pathologist. All that stuff about mummified bodies, antique clothing and the fingerprints matching and everything.

'About those fingerprints,' said Jonny. 'Did they say whose fingerprints they were?'

'Not on file, apparently. And they did a DNA test. Did you know that everyone's DNA is put on file when they're born? With or without their parents consent. It's been going on for the last twenty years.'*

'I can't say I'm surprised,' Jonny said. 'But no match, I assume?'

Paul shook his head and, with his helmet now off, got his long hair trailing in Jonny's beer. 'Which reminds me,' said Paul, removing his hair and wringing it out, 'buy me a beer.'

'Did you bring me anything?' Jonny said. 'Apart from sandwiches and a Thermos flask?'

---

* And it has!

'They're not for you. But I did nick this.' Paul drew out one of those plastic evidence bags with the sealy-up tops. 'Contents of the pockets of the deceased.'

'Splendid,' said Jonny and he unsealed the sealy-up bit and tipped the contents onto the bar counter.

'Beer?' said Paul.

Jonny hailed O'Fagin.

'A pint of King Billy for Paul,' said Jonny.

'Excellent,' said O'Fagin. 'And many thanks to you, Paul, for your generous contribution to tonight's fundraiser.'

Paul opened his mouth to reply.

But Jonny stopped him.

O'Fagin pulled Paul's pint. 'Weird old couple over there,' he said as he pulled, throwing in a small shoulder shrug in the appropriate direction. 'Chap with aristocrartic bearing and a long, black beard and some spaced-out redhead with long rubber gloves on. They smell like an old dog basket and talk like characters out of a *Carry On* movie.'

'Which one?' Paul asked.

Jonny shook his head. 'Silly boy,' he said.

'Well,' said O'Fagin, 'now that you ask – what was the one that had that bloke in it?'

'I liked that one,' said Paul. 'But wasn't that bloke in two of them?'

Jonny Hooker ignored the coming conversation and examined the items that lay upon the bar counter. A lace handkerchief with the initials 'S. G.' embroidered upon it. A horn snuffbox, its lid inlaid with the same initials in silver. Jonny opened the snuffbox and took a little sniff. Then sneezed all over Paul.

'Pardon me,' said Jonny.

There were a number of coins – a silver sovereign, some pennies and halfpennies. All looked new, but all dated from the seventeen eighties. Jonny pocketed these coins. There was a wad of what appeared to be some kind of sweetmeat, wrapped in waxy paper. And a brass something or other.

Jonny examined this something or other.

It looked a bit like a miniature flute. A slim brass cylinder with a hole at one end and a kind of flattened mouthpiece at the other with a narrow slit above it, or *below* it, depending upon which way up you held it.

Jonny held it with the narrow slit upwards, put the mouthpiece to his lips and gave it a little blow.

No sound issued from the slim brass tube. Jonny blew once more and once more no sound came. Jonny took a really deep breath and gave a really big blow.

And every optic behind the bar counter, and every empty glass stacked and racked upon stacker and racker and every single window that had escaped the assault of the Paddy Wagon—

Exploded.

'Wah!' went O'Fagin, ducking and cursing and spitting and effing and blinding.

Paul looked towards Jonny Hooker.

Jonny Hooker shrugged and went off to the toilet.

Inspector Westlake returned from the toilet. The toilet at the police station. He returned to his office. Returned to his office, locked the door, sat himself down at his desk.

Inspector Westlake had one of those sealy-up-topped evidence bags. His had papers in it. Papers that had been taken from the pocket of a frocked eighteenth-century coat that clothed a mummified body. The one in the wall-cabinet jobbie. The one with the Jonny Hooker toe tag.

Inspector Westlake spread the papers before him on his desk. And examined them through an overlarge magnifying glass.

'Tiny, tiny writing,' said Inspector Westlake. 'Although ... ' He held the paper up to the light. 'The watermark is clear as clear, as if the paper is brand-new. But it's dated seventeen ninety. Curious indeed.' He further examined and 'hmmmed' and 'indeeded' as he did so. 'A musical score,' he said. 'Complete notation for a single instrument. What, though? Ah, an organ, by the look of it. And the libretto. But surely not a song as such. These words do not scan. It is more as if the music underscores a spoken text. Ah, spoken by several different speakers, according to the notation. I see. I see.'

And Inspector Westlake read the text aloud.

And then he read the text aloud again.

And then Inspector Westlake cried, 'No. No. This must not be.

This must not come to pass. Oh no, such evil, such evil.'

And for a moment his voice cracked and tears welled up in his eyes.

And then he cried, 'No! The End of the World. The Apocalypse! Oh no!'

33

O'Fagin did weeping and wailing. And also gnashing of teeth. Which did have a suitably apocalyptic quality about it. 'Woe unto the House of O'Fagin,' cried O'Fagin, rending his garments also, 'for it is un-done. What have I done, oh Lord of the old button hole?'

'Lord of the old button hole?' said Jonny, who had lately returned from the gents.

Or, more accurately the hastily ordered Portaloo that had been deposited at the rear of the pub to temporarily replace the gents that had been destroyed by the Paddy Wagon.'*

'It's a publican thing,' O'Fagin explained. 'But what of my glasses? Oh no!'

'Juggernaut,' said Paul. 'Rattled the glasses off the shelves.'

'*Juggernaut?*' O'Fagin made fists of his fingers and threatened the sky with them. 'Not bloody juggernauts. This was a sign, a sign from the heavens.'

Paul looked at Jonny.

Jonny just shrugged.

'What is it, Lord?' O'Fagin asked, his fists now praying palms. 'What has your humble servant done to displease you? What? What?' O'Fagin did cockings of the ears.

'Is he getting an answer?' Jonny asked.

'I think he is,' said Paul.

'I wonder—' said Jonny.

'Oh yes, Lord, yes,' said O'Fagin. 'Raise the entry charge and put up the price of the pints, I understand.'

'Precisely what I was wondering,' said Jonny.

'While I'm on the hotline to God,' said O'Fagin to Jonny, 'do

---

* It's always best to be precise about these matters, in order to avoid any confusion.

you want me to ask him to clear up your skin condition, so you can take off all those Elastoplasts?'

'No thanks,' said Jonny. 'I can manage.'

'You might have a word with your God about getting him a girlfriend,' said Paul. 'Does your God arrange things like that?'

'I could ask,' said O'Fagin. 'Let's use this ashtray as an offering plate — bung in a fiver and I'll phrase a request.'

Paul did not oblige and O'Fagin took himself off in search of the broom.

'You did that,' said Paul.

'I never did,' said Jonny.

'You did *too* with that brass whistle.'

'Don't be silly,' said Jonny.

'I'm not,' said Paul. 'I already had a little blow of it in the squad car driving over here. It blew out the windscreen.'

'Why didn't you tell me?'

'What, and miss all this?'

Jonny Hooker checked his pint. It appeared to be free of glass chippings.★

'What are we going to do?' he asked Paul. 'I assume that we *are* playing here tonight.'

'Damn right,' said Paul. 'We're getting paid fifty quid for it.'

'Ah,' said Jonny.

'Ah?' said Paul.

'Never mind,' said Jonny. 'So we *are* playing. Are we meeting the rest of the lads here, or what?'

'Here,' said Paul. 'They'll be here in an hour.'

'And in rock 'n' roll time?'

'Two hours,' said Paul.

'Six hours,' said Thompson of ESOU. 'Six hours from now. Which will be?'

'Midnight, sir?' said a young and eager constable. He was, *however*, a Special Operations constable and so he wore a black uniform.

'Correct, Constable. And what is your name?'

★ It *was* only the empty glasses that shattered. In case you were wondering. You weren't? Fair enough.

'Constable Cartwright, sir.' The constable saluted.

'Cartwright, eh? As in *Bonanza*? "Da-da-de-da-da-de-da-da-de-da" *Bonanza*?' Thompson da-da-de-da-da'd that legendary theme.

His team da'd on with him.

'No, *sir*,' said Constable Cartwright.

'Shame,' said Thompson. 'I was always a fan of Hoss, myself. Big old gentle giant of a man, played, if I recall, and I do, by Dan Blocker. A fine character-actor. Looked a bit like Tor Johnson. But then so many of them did.'

There was a moment of silence.

'Sir,' said Constable Cartwright, breaking it.

'Yes, Constable?' said Thompson.

'Why *exactly* is this taskforce being put into operation?'

'Good question,' said Thompson. And he did a bit of strutting. He strutted on a tiny stage before an easel affair, which had a cloth-shrouded board upon it. And he did his strutting before an assembled company of Special Operations bobbies, all black-clad and useful-looking. And all in a kind of bunker briefing room deep beneath Mornington Crescent Underground Station.

The assembled company numbered near to one hundred, so it was a fair-sized bunker briefing room. It had a coffee machine at the rear end, next to the door. Beside the fire extinguishers.

'Jolly good question, Constable,' said Thompson. And he did the flourishing whipping-away-of-the-cloth routine. And his whipping-away exposed a map.

Of Gunnersbury Park.

'Ooooh,' went Constable Cartwright.

And 'Oooooeeee,' went all the other constables present. *Special constables*. For they just loved a map.

'Perimeter,' said Thompson, producing a little stick from somewhere and tracking the perimeter with it. 'Fifty men, one-hundred-yard intervals. General Electric mini-guns. Night sights. You will *all* wear night-vision spectacles. Ornamental pond.' He gave the location a tap. 'Three frogmen, two down, one up. Surface-to-air shoulder-mounted missiles. Doric temple, three men, machine-gun nest. Japanese garden, dig in a network of slit trenches here. The pitch-and-putt, I want that sown with landmines. We'll give the Hun a run for his money, eh?'

'The Hun?' asked Constable Cartwright.

'Are you acting as spokesman for the assembled company?' Thompson asked.

'Not as such, sir. It's just that I'm the only constable who has so far been identified by name.'

'And a damn fine name, too. Who's that chap next to you?'

'Me?' asked Constable Cassidy.

'No, other chap?'

'Me?' asked Constable Rogers.

'Next to you.'

'Me?' asked Constable Deputy Dawg.

'Yes, you. Didn't I go to Cambridge with your father?'

'No, that was *my* father,' said Constable Milky Bar Kid.★

'Thought so. So, any questions?'

'Yes, sir,' said Constable Cartwright. '*Why* is this taskforce being put into operation?'

'Glad you asked that, Constable,' said Thompson. 'Here we have a building known as the Big House. It is also known as Gunnersbury Park Museum and has a really nice lady called Joan working on reception. But you will not go bothering Joan. *I* will liaise with Joan directly, myself. Do I make myself understood?'

'Yes, sir,' said one and all. Saluting.

'Regarding security of the Big House: you will disregard anything that might have been relayed to you, via rumour or jungle drums as it were, that Inspector Westlake, on secondment from the Bramfield Constabulary, will be in charge of this operation. You will answer to *me*. Take all your orders from me. Do I make myself clear? Any questions?'

'Yes, sir,' said Constable Cartwright. 'Why is this taskforce being put into operation?'

'Good question, Constable. Now, I want a fifty-man squad inside the Big House. You will be the lucky lads testing the new electronic camouflage suits. Our back-room boffins have ironed out most of the glitches and these suits will cloak you in a mantel of invisibility.'

'Ooooooh,' chorused the constables. Who may indeed have been

★ That's enough now. (Ed.)

lovers of a map, but who were brought almost to the point of orgasm at the prospect of invisibility.

'Sir?' said Constable Cartwright. 'Can I be put on duty in the Big House?'

'Good question, Constable. Yes, you can. And take those other aforementioned constables with you. We only have five invisibility suits. I lied about there being fifty, sorry, so the Big House team will be just you five.'

'Aaaw,' went disappointed constables.

'Fab, gear and groovy,' went Constables Cartwright, Cassidy, Rogers, Deputy Dawg and Milky Bar Kid.

'Every constable will be issued with a helmet-mounted night-vision camera so that I can monitor all movements from the control room here, from where I will direct operations. Any questions?'

'Yes, sir. Why is this task—' began Constable Cartwright.

'Yes, *sir,*' said O'Fagin, saluting and marching up and down behind the bar counter.

'Why is he doing *that*?' Paul asked.

Jonny shook his head. 'Let us pray that we never find out,' he said. 'What time is it now?'

'Getting on for eight o'clock. Doesn't time fly when you're hav-ing sex with two Thai girls who think you're the greatest bass player since Herbie Flowers?'

'Oh dear,' said Jonny.

'Oh dear?' asked Paul.

'My guitar,' said Jonny. 'It's at my house. How am I going to play?'

'Paul made grinnings at Jonny. 'I'm one step ahead of you there – just check this out.' And he hailed O'Fagin.

'Yes, *sir*?' said O'Fagin, marching up and saluting.

'Why are you doing that?' Paul asked.

O'Fagin whispered in Paul's ear.

'That is *so* brilliant,' said Paul.

'What?' went Jonny.

O'Fagin grinned.

'Do you still have that guitar?' Paul asked.

O'Fagin grinned some more.

'Do you?' Paul asked.

O'Fagin did some more grinning.

'That's not really working for me,' said Paul.

'Sorry,' said O'Fagin. 'I'm just practising. We have a group called Dry Rot playing later – they're a mime act.'

Paul ignored O'Fagin, but rephrased his question. 'Do you still have that old guitar in the case in the beer cellar?' he asked.

'I do,' said O'Fagin. 'Chap left without it, never came back.'

'Can I borrow it?' Paul asked.

'For the benefit gig?' O'Fagin asked.

'Say yes,' said Jonny.

'Yes,' said Paul.

'Then of course you can.' O'Fagin left the bar, went down into the cellar and returned in the company of an ancient plywood guitar case.

'I don't like the look of *that*,' said Jonny.

O'Fagin placed the guitar case on the bar counter. Paul flipped the catches and opened the case.

A beautiful instrument was brought to light.

'It's a Gibson L-1, an acoustic model made in Nashville somewhere between nineteen twenty-six and nineteen thirty,' said Paul. 'Note the hand-made pick-up and the tortoiseshell "dot" markers on the third, fifth, seventh, ninth, twelfth and fifteenth frets. Note the wear on the fingerboard. Gently stroke the veneer.'

Jonny did so, gently.

'What do you think?' Paul asked of Jonny.

Jonny lifted the guitar from the case. Reverently. With care.

Jonny held the Gibson to his ear and gently fingered the strings. 'It's in tune,' he said. 'What a beautiful tone.'

'Good enough for you?' Paul asked.

'Oh yes.'

Jonny stroked the neck of the guitar. It was a thing of striking beauty. Elegant. Precise.

'I can't believe someone would forget an instrument like this,' he said, 'Just leave it in a bar.'

'He didn't exactly forget it,' said O'Fagin. 'He sort of couldn't come back for it.'

'Do you know whose guitar this was?' Jonny asked.

O'Fagin looked at Paul.

And Paul looked at O'Fagin.

'It belonged to a blues singer,' said O'Fagin. 'His name was Robert Johnson.'

34

'You are so, so *not* going to play that guitar!'

The voice of Mr Giggles came close at Jonny's ear, his breath hot on neck, his hairy hands a-quiver.

Jonny did as Jonny did: ignored the Monkey Boy.

'Oh no, I'm serious this time. Deadleeeeeeee.'

Jonny shook away his imaginary friend and addressed his attention once more to the Gibson.

The guitar that had once belonged to Robert Johnson?

The guitar that the Devil had tuned, down at the crossroads oh so long ago?

Jonny's hands gave a little quiver, too.

'Are you all right?' asked Paul.

'Do you really think it's real?'

'Really Robert Johnson's, do you mean?'

Jonny mouthed the words, 'I do.'

Paul just gave a shrug.

'There's a picture of the man up here on the wall, playing it,' said O'Fagin. 'There with my daddy and some big buck-toothed black chap I never knew the name of.'

'Come on, buddy boy,' crooned Mr Giggles. 'You've had enough excitement now, let's have it away on your toes.'

'Robert Johnson's guitar.' Jonny's voice was filled with awe.

Just as it should have been, really. Because if this *was* Robert Johnson's guitar. And if Robert Johnson *did* go down to the crossroads at midnight so many years ago. And if he *did* sell his soul to the Devil. And if the Devil *did* tune Robert Johnson's guitar. And if this *was* that very guitar.

Then.

Well!

Jonny took the guitar and assumed the position. As in lead-guitar player. It is not necessary to go into all those subtle nuances that distinguish the lead guitarist position from that assumed by the bass guitarist. Deep down in our rock 'n' roll hearts, we all know them.

Jonny found a chord and he strummed it. A simple A-seventh chord. The one Robert Johnson is holding in the famous studio portrait. Holding on the Gibson L-1. And as that sound rose from that guitar, a certain electricity, a certain vibrancy seemed to breathe through the air of The Middle Man. And a shaft of light, angling down through a hole in the roof, caught Jonny to perfection.

Jonny's thumb stroked over the strings and Paul looked on and O'Fagin looked on and the gentleman with the aristocratic bearing, who wore the long, black beard looked on, and the red-headed woman in the long rubber gloves looked on as well.

As well as a bloke from Porlock.

And as all of them looked on, Jonny looked on, too. He looked on at the fingers of his left hand as they ran up and down the finger-board, now figuring this chord and now forming that.

For it was to Jonny as if that's what he was doing.

Merely watching.

As if the fingers dancing up and down the guitar's neck were not the fingers of his own hand. Rather they were those of a maestro, some master guitarist. Jonny was just a spectator.

Jonny Hooker closed his eyes and played.

'Enough!' Paul's hand fell across the strings of the guitar. 'Enough.'

'What are you doing?' went Jonny. 'What?'

'Stop playing now, that's enough.'

'I was just having a little strum – what's the matter with you?'

'The matter with *me*? What's the matter with *you*?'

'Me?' Jonny glanced all around and about. There were a lot of folk now in the bar. A lot, and they were all clapping.

'What?' went Jonny. 'What?'

'You've been playing for an hour and a half,' said Paul. 'And God alone knows what. Stuff I've never heard before.'

'Oi,' shouted a roughneck, all spruced up in an England foot-baller's style vesty number, his muscular arms sporting many patriotic tattoos. 'Watcha stop the music for? Let him play.'

'He'll play again soon,' said Paul. 'As soon as the rest of the band get here.'

'Soon's not good enough. We want more now.' The crowd took to grumbling in surly agreement.

'An hour and a half?' went Jonny, glancing down at his fingers. The tips of those on his left hand were white, while those on his right hand were bloody. 'An hour and a half.'

'Let the park keeper play,' said a lady in a straw hat. 'I haven't heard music like that since my castrato nephew joined the Vatican choir.'

'An hour and a half?' Jonny held the guitar away from himself. Returned it with haste to its case.

'Enough for now, mate,' he called out to the England supporter. 'Have to take a little break, okay?'

There were grumblings and mumblings and Jonny closed the case.

'Get me beer,' he said to Paul. 'Get me beer and now.'

Paul ordered beer from O'Fagin. 'What was all that about?' he asked Jonny. 'Where did you learn all that stuff?'

'I don't know. I'm not even sure what I did. Was it good, what I did?'

'Good? It was unbelievable. Although a bit creepy at times, somewhat heavy on the Devil's Intervals.'

'Ah,' said Jonny.

'We've got to keep that stuff in,' said Paul, 'work it into the playlist tonight. No, stuff the playlist, we'll just follow you.'

Jonny Hooker clicked his neck. He was aching from head to foot. 'I don't think so,' he said. 'There's something not at all right about that guitar.'

'I'm going to make some calls,' said Paul. 'We need a mixing desk and something to record with. Get it onto a laptop. This is *big*, Jonny. Really big.'

And Paul took out his mobile phone and took himself off outside. And a young woman of outstanding characteristics made her presence felt in Jonny's vicinity.

'Could I have your autograph?' she asked.

Autograph? Jonny's mind went boggle boggle boggle. A young woman of *such* outstanding characteristics asking *him* for an autograph. Which meant—

Which meant.

Which meant what it means in the rock 'n' roll parlance.

Jonny Hooker was led out back to receive a boggling blow-job.

Ten minutes later he returned to the bar. He had *that* look upon his face. *That look* that can mean nothing other than what it means. So to speak.

And Paul had returned to the bar before him.

And Paul beheld Jonny.

And Paul beheld *that look.*

And Paul said unto Jonny, 'No. You didn't? You?' For Paul had also beheld the young woman with the outstanding characteristics who had accompanied Jonny on his return to the bar. 'No,' said Paul. 'Say she didn't ... No.'

'You still haven't brought me that beer,' said Jonny.

'No.' Paul pointed to the woman and back to Jonny.

'What?' said Jonny. 'What?'

'You know bloody well what. I was lining her up for later.'

'I've finished with her,' said Jonny. 'For now.'

'No. No. No.'

But it was yes. And Paul brought Jonny a pint of King Billy and Jonny tucked into this pint.

'I can't believe you did that,' said Paul. 'That *she* did that. I can't believe it.'

'Just stop now,' said Jonny. 'I am having trouble believing it also, but I'm pretty damn sure it did happen. So—'

'So?' said Paul.

'So perhaps I *will* give that guitar another little go later.'

'Right,' said Paul. 'Right. Well, you do that. And stuff it – if you manage to get yourself laid, then good luck to you.'

'How very kind,' said Jonny.

'If you can play again how you just played, then you'll deserve anything you get.'

Jonny Hooker regarded his wounded digits. And he was still aching in all sorts of places. Although one place felt rather nice. 'It's possessed,' he whispered to Paul.

'Your plonker?'

'The guitar, you buffoon. I didn't play any of whatever I played. I don't even know what I played. I didn't play the guitar. The guitar played me.'

'I think it best if you just keep that to yourself,' Paul counselled. 'Don't mention it to the record producer or anything.'

Jonny Hooker finished his pint. 'And what record producer might this be?' he rightly enquired.

'I don't know what it is with me,' said Paul, 'but all of my life so far I've never done anything for anyone that has resulted in them owing me a favour. Except for once. I was walking along very late on Christmas Eve a couple of years back and I heard this voice calling for help. It turned out to be this bloke who'd fallen, somewhat drunk, into this hole that the gas men had dug in the road. I helped him out and he said that one day he'd repay me. I still have his business card.' Paul flourished same and Jonny read from it.

ANDI EVANS
Soliloquy Records

'Andi Evans?' said Jonny. 'You pulled Andi Evans of the legendary metal label Soliloquy Records out of a hole in the road?'

'I did,' said Paul. 'And I have hung on for two years, waiting for *the* moment. The moment when I would call in my favour, when it would be worth calling it in. Tonight is that night, Jonny. You will play. Andi Evans is bringing down a mobile mini-recording studio jobbie. You will play, he will record. We will get a record contract and you'll get blow-jobs seven nights a week. Am I a good friend to you, or what?'

Jonny Hooker raised his glass. 'I'd toast to this mighty plan,' said he, 'but my glass appears to be empty.'

At the rock 'n' roll time expected, or at least within a couple of hours of it, the two remaining members of Dry Rot appeared at The Middle Man. These were hairy fellows whose attire bespoke of those to whom black would always be this year's black.

Desmond was the drummer, and also had a barrow in the market-place. And Molly was the singer with the band.

Molly had a small goatee. Which was not a qualification for *her* to join a travelling circus. It was simply that *he* favoured a small goatee.

Molly's dad, Mary, had chosen the name for Molly when Molly had been born. It was something to do with Mary growing up in the nineteen sixties. But just what, no one knew for certain.

And Mary was not available for comment.

For he was on death row in San Quentin, having tracked down and slaughtered his father, Mavis.

Which was sort of rock 'n' roll.

Desmond's stage name was Tom.

And Molly's was Gazz.

Why try to improve upon perfection? Who knows?

'You gonna give us a hand to unload the gear?' Molly asked Paul.

'I'm sure Jonny would love to help,' said Paul.

'Jonny?' said Molly. 'Why is your face covered with sticking plaster? And why are you dressed as a parkie?'

'Do you ever read a newspaper or watch television, Molly?' Jonny asked.

'Never,' said Molly. 'Watched *Top of the Pops* once, but didn't like it. Do read the *NME*, of course, the Andi Evans metal column.'

'Then have you got a big treat coming tonight.'

'Oh, I do hope so,' said Molly. 'because I could do with cheering up. You know my mum reads the Kleenex?'

'Reads the Kleenex?' Jonny did not know of such a thing.

'It's a divination type jobbie. Like reading the tarot or the tea leaves. You blow your nose on a Kleenex and my mum can tell your future by the crumples. And the colour of the snot, I suppose.'

'Boogermancy,' said Mr Giggles. Who hadn't spoken for a while.

'Where is this leading?' Jonny asked Molly.

'Actually,' said Molly, 'I think it's a bit of a misunderstanding.'

'Not quite following you,' said Jonny.

'You see,' said Molly, 'she freaks me out with her weird gypsy stuff, so I never let her do any readings on me. Trouble was, I had a day off work today because I'd bought some bootleg porn DVDs – Nunsploitation movies, every one a classic. And you know how it is when your mum's out and—'

'This is going to involve another use for Kleenex, isn't it?' Jonny said.

'I should have flushed them.'

'*Them?*'

I left them under my pillow. She made up my bed and she read my Kleenex.'

'Nasty,' said Paul.

'Did *you* read them, too?' asked Molly.

'No, I mean, well—'

'Well, nasty it is. According to my mum, something really awful is going to happen. She said that when she saw the stains on the Kleenexes, they spelled out the words "EVE OF THE APOCALYPSE".'

'That's a lot of letters,' said Paul.

'They're very inspiring DVDs,' said Molly.

35

A limo pulled up outside The Middle Man. It was a *stretch* limo. It was a black stretch limo.

So everyone who was inside The Middle Man pushed their way through the plastic sheeting and went outside The Middle Man to see who would be getting out of the black stretch limo.

And can't *that* be a disappointment!

There once were days when only the truly rich and famous were driven about in black stretch limos. Or *the* black stretch limo. For back in the nineteen sixties, there was only one in the country. And if you saw it pull up somewhere, you knew, just *knew*, that someone rich and famous was going to get out of it, helped by the chauffeur, of course, and made a right fuss over.

But then *those* were the good old days. When we had values. When dogshit came in white as well as brown, and cigarettes came in hundreds of colours and hues, and all of them were good for you. And only sportsmen wore sportswear.

But *now*?

Now if a stretch limo pulls up, then like as not it will turn out to be full to the gunwales with a posse of Essex girls in micro-skirts, wearing flashing Devil horns on their heads, all out on a hen night.

And looking for love.

Or if not love then—

Which was probably why all the folk who were inside The Middle Man, went outside The Middle Man at the arrival of the black stretch limo. Well, the blokes all did, anyway.

The chauffeur, a very large black chap with a shaven head beneath his cap, left the cab and opened a rear door. Andi Evans issued from the limo, doing the Devil-horn fingers.

The 'no crumpet' alert sounded and the blokes returned to The Middle Man.

'Plebs,' sneered Andi. Which was, in essence, correct. 'Stay with the limo,' he told Betty,★ the shaven-headed chauffeur. 'I don't like the look of this neighbourhood. Leave the limo for five minutes and we'll come back to find it up on bricks, without an engine. Or, worse than that, full of Essex girls.'

'That's a bit harsh,' said Betty.

'I'll send someone out to bring in the gear. Would you like a drink, or something?'

'Just a ginger beer and an arrowroot biscuit, thank you.'

Andi Evans entered The Middle Man.

And received a cool hello from the members of Dry Rot.

Because you do *have* to be cool. You *have* to. You can't just go rushing up, going, 'Ooh Mister Evans, how incredible to meet you, I've bought every album on your label and I'm your greatest fan.'

It's just *not* cool.

So the members of Dry Rot leaned against the bar counter making cool-sounding grunts and doing that odd punching of fist against fist that is some kind of black ghetto thing. And black ghetto things do have a reputation for being cool.

Jonny Hooker returned from the Portaloo. He had been there alone. He returned alone. Paul introduced him to Andi.

'Ooh, Mister Evans,' said Jonny. 'How incredible to meet you. I've bought every album on your label and I'm your greatest fan.'

Dry Rot members looked on, aghast.

Andi shook Jonny warmly by the hand.

'What a joy,' he said. 'I've been hoping for years that someone would say that to me. One has doubts, you see, regarding one's talent. Has one one's finger upon the pulse, as it were? Is one hip to the scene? Is one the new one, if you know what I mean.'

'I see,' said Jonny.

'Because no one ever tells one that they appreciate one's work.'

'"*One*" is something of a dickhead,' observed Mr Giggles.

'So tell me,' said Andi, 'this band of yours, Dry Rise—'

'Dry *Rot*,' said Jonny.

★ Very possibly Whoa-Black-Betty-Bam-a-Lam.

'Most humorous, yes. It's booga-booga music, is it?'

'Pure Kleenex,' said Mr Giggles.

'No one can hear you but me,' whispered Jonny, behind his hand. 'And *I'm* not listening.'

'Well,' said Andi, 'if you'd all like to chip in and bring in the gear from the limo ...'

'Did anyone bring in our gear from our van?' Jonny asked.

'While you were in the bog,' O'Fagin chipped in, 'most of the women in the bar helped to bring it in.'

'Cool,' said Jonny.

'*And* they set it up and did a sound check,' said O' Fagin.

'While I was in the bog?'

'Time goes fast when—' Paul began.

'I'm sure it does and time is money,' said Andi Evans. 'So if you'll all chip in, it will all be chipper. Togetherness is the new singularity, you know. Pip pip.'

'No one really talks like that,' said Mr Giggles. 'He's faking it.'

'Don't you love the way he talks?' Paul whispered behind his hand to Jonny. 'He's always at the cutting edge. Apparently posh is the new common. Cool, eh?'

'Cool,' said Jonny. 'I'll help unload the gear.'

Loading and unloading. A lot of warfare consists of this. And marching, of course. And waiting for something to happen, or waiting to be ordered to make something happen. Then there's the actual fighting. Then you take a stray round in the head, probably from friendly fire, and then you're dead.

Which is, pretty much, warfare.

But there's a lot of loading and unloading.

And in peacetime, when you're in a militaryish situation, a security situation, which might involve terrorists, there is going to be a lot of loading and unloading.

There just is.

In the great munition stores beneath Mornington Crescent Underground Station, where vast quantities of ordnance stand ready when required, there was a great deal of loading going on.

Constable Cartwright had been put in charge of this.

Because, when asked for a volunteer, *he* had put his hand up.

'You'd think there'd be other ranks involved in this operation, wouldn't you?' he asked Constable Cassidy, as Constable Cassidy helped to load a crate of anti-matter grenades onto a canvas-covered lorry.

'It's egalitarian,' said Constable Cassidy, who had found the word in a dictionary and been meaning to find a use for it. 'We are all constables together, bonded as one against a common enemy, receiving our orders from a single source.'

'I never did get a straight answer to my question,' said Constable Cartwright. 'We're guarding a museum, as far as I can make out, but why and from whom – these are somewhat grey areas.'

'Ours is not to reason why,' said Constable Tennyson.

'You're not in our team,' said Constable Rogers. 'You're supposed to be in that team over there, with Constable Byron, Constable Keats and Constable Wordsworth.'*

Constable Tennyson sauntered away.

'Where are the invisibility suits?' asked Constable Cartwright.

'I've got mine on,' said Constable Deputy Dawg.

'Who said that?'

'It's me, I'm here.'

'Isn't that brilliant,' said Constable Cartwright. 'You can't see him – he's completely invisible.'

'No, I'm just tying my shoelace,' said Constable Deputy Dawg, and he stood up.

'Whoa,' said Constable Cartwright. 'That's a great-looking suit – it's got, like, little solar panels all over it.'

'Shall I switch it on?'

Constable Deputy Dawg switched on his suit. There was a sort of humming sound and then sort of a popping sound. These were followed by a very definite screaming sound. Then the sound and sight of an explosion.

'Well, he's certainly vanished,' said Constable Cassidy.

'The bits of him that I've got all over me haven't,' said Constable Passing Cloud. 'Anyone know which truck my tribe is travelling in?'

★

---

* Don't even think about it! (Ed.)

'I travelled in tobaccos for a while,' Andi Evans told Paul as he tinkered about with the mobile sound-recording console.

'That must have been dull,' said Paul. 'I thought you'd feed all the tracks onto a laptop – surely that's a very big console.'

'Dull as dishwater,' said Andi. 'Don't know why I mentioned it now. And as to the laptop, I can't be having with them. I bought this *big* console from BIG CONSOLES 'Я' US. Big is the new small, you know.'

O'Fagin waggled a finger at Paul. 'It's about time you got started,' he said as he waggled. 'I'll want you done and dusted in less than an hour, then Ghandi's Hairdryer go on. You may be good. But they used to be famous.'

'Ghandi's Hairdryer?' said Paul. 'I thought they went dirt in about nineteen eighty-four.'

'Apparently not,' said O'Fagin. 'Been playing reunion gigs at Butlins every season ever since. And they've volunteered to play tonight to raise money for the rebuilding fund.'

'But *we* were headlining tonight.'

'Only because you were the only band playing tonight.'

'Ghandi's Hairdryer,' said Andi, in an approving tone. 'They used to be a favourite of mine, back in my early days of rock journalism. Is Cardinal Cox still the lead singer?'

'The fat bloke over there with the baldy head.'

Andi glanced over. 'He hasn't changed a bit.'

'Hold on here,' said Paul to O'Fagin. 'This isn't fair.'

'Don't be uncharitable,' said O'Fagin. 'It's all for a good cause. I need a holiday and I could hardly afford the kind of holiday I booked this afternoon on my wages alone.'

'Leave it,' said Jonny to Paul. 'We're better than Ghandi's Hairdryer ever were. We'll make this a gig that no one will ever forget.'

'Yeah,' said Desmond. 'A gig to remember. To a gig to remember.' He raised his pint glass.

'To Dry Rot,' said Jonny, raising his.

'To the future,' said Molly. 'Does anyone have a Kleenex? I think I'm coming down with a cold.'

36

O'Fagin the publican took the stage.

'My lords, ladies and gentlemen,' went O'Fagin. And then he went, 'One-two, one-two, can you hear me?' But as the microphone wasn't switched on, he was ignored to a man.

Paul had his bass guitar out of its case and was strapping the blighter on.

'Make the bloody mic work, if you please,' said O'Fagin.

Paul reached over and switched on the mic.

And oh that glorious feedback.

It drew the attention of the crowd and O'Fagin called for order.

'My lords, ladies and gentlemen,' he began once more, 'I would like to say that it is with deep joy that I gaze down from this raft of a stage across this sea of smiling faces. But, alas, I am a man cast adrift by fate. Doomed like the *Flying Dutchman* to sail on for ever without ever reaching port.'

'He's going for a nautical feel,' said Jonny to Paul.

Jonny had the Gibson out of its case. And he was strapping it on.

'He claims to have once been a lone yachtsman,' said Paul.

'He's a bloody pirate,' said Mr Giggles.

'But by the yo-ho-hos,' O'Fagin went on, 'and the cruel, stormy waters that have battered this landlocked galleon, threatening to drag it down to Davy Jones's locker—'

'Get on with it,' cried a sportswear wearer.

'I'll drink to that,' cried a lady in a straw hat.

'Mighty flood tides,' continued O'Fagin. 'But here, before me, a lighthouse, shining its blessed light through the fog, leading me safely into port through the largesse, oh, the generosity ... ' Words failed O'Fagin, so he wrung his hands and danced a little hornpipe. 'Pieces of eight,' he sang.

'I do believe he's lost it altogether,' said Paul. 'It's been a few years coming, but I knew it would get here eventually.'

'This pub,' cried O'Fagin, tears in his eyes and fire in his belly, 'would go under if it were not for *you*. You, my patrons, whose generosity tonight, on this *benefit night*, will save this dry-docked beer galleon.'

The crowd were growing somewhat restless.

And this restlessness took on a new and urgent form as Jonny Hooker plugged Robert Johnson's guitar into the amp* and strummed out a random chord.

'Oooh' and 'Aaaah' went the crowd.

O'Fagin opened his mouth to speak further nonsense, thought better of it and closed it again. He'd take the hat round later, he thought, that would be for the best.

Gazz the lead singer, Molly to his mum, grasped the available mic. 'Hello, Ealing,' he bawled into it. 'We're Dry Rot and we've come for your daughters. Those we can't f*ck, we eat.'

'He nicked that line,' said the lady in the straw hat. 'From a police constable, I think.'

'First song,' bawled Gazz, 'is "Johnny B. Goode".'

And so should the first song always be.

There are certain great rock 'n' roll songs in this world. *Great* rock 'n' roll songs. 'Johnny B. Goode' ranks amongst the very greatest. And when it comes to *rock*, then you can't best Motörhead's, 'Ace of Spades'.

Jonny Hooker had played rhythm and lead on Dry Rot's opening number at least fifty times. But never before had Jonny played it quite like this. Jonny found his fingers finding notes between the notes, forming figures and chords that transcended anything Chuck Berry could ever have imagined, even in his most lavatorial dreams.

Jonny would be good tonight, and tomorrow would be another day.

'Mount up, gentlemen.' Constable Cartwright stood on the roof of what was to be the lead truck. He was clad in his invisibility suit but

---

* With a lead running from the previously mentioned hand-made pickup. In case there were any doubts.

had not, as yet, switched it on. Within the truck, in the company of much advanced ordnance, sat three other constables. They were wearing their suits. They hadn't switched them on yet, either.

'I want this done by the numbers.' Constable Cartwright was giving a good account of himself. Cometh the hour then cometh the man and all that kind of business. He had acquired an electric megaphone to shout through and he was shouting through it with spirit. 'Let's do what we're paid for, people,' he shouted.

In the control room sat Thompson, before many monitor screens, each displaying the view as seen through a helmet-mounted camera. At least a third of them were fully functional, which Thompson considered a good average. His microphone was clearly working properly, as it conveyed his words directly into the earpiece worn by Constable Cartwright. Who repeated these words, as he had been ordered to do, through his electric megaphone.

Thompson leaned back in his chair and nodded in satisfaction. *So far so good*, he thought.

'There's no cause for worry here,' he said, his hand suddenly over his microphone, his head turned to the figure who sat in a darkened corner of the room. 'I've double the men I need for this type of operation. It will be fine, I promise you.'

The face of Inspector Westlake moved out from the darkness and into the light. It was a somewhat ashen face with dark half-circles under the eyes. The inspector's normally ruddy countenance had undergone a radical and unfetching change in the space of a few short hours.

'You look done in, old chap,' said Thompson. 'What say you get some shuteye? I'll take care of things.'

Inspector Westlake shook his head. 'This is bad,' said he. 'This is very, very bad.'

'Listen, old chap, you showed me those papers that you say were found in the pocket of a man who somehow turned into a mummy. I have read these papers, and I agree that if what is written there were to come to pass, then doom and gloom all round and woe unto the House of Windsor and let's all hunker down for the nuclear winter. But there is no reason to believe that the madness in those papers should ever become reality.'

'But it's them,' said the inspector. '*Them.*'

'The Secret Order of the Golden Sprout?'

'Not them.' Inspector Westlake buried his face in his hands. 'I, like yourself, am of the Brotherhood. We understand how the world really works, who pulls the strings. We know that matters of world importance are far too important to be left in the hands of career politicians.'

'Hush with such words,' said Thompson. 'Walls have ears and all that kind of thing.'

'Even here?'

'There's no telling. Wait, I will engage the anti-bug.' Thompson reached towards his control panel and thumbed switches. 'The Dance of the Sugar-Plum Fairy' welled from a speaker system. Thompson removed his microphone, switched it off and laid it aside. 'Brother Westlake,' he said, 'I know as well as you, as do all within the craft who have obtained to a certain degree, that the Secret Brotherhood or the Parliament of Five, as we more rightly know them, control the controllers. Wise and learned men order our existence, a hereditary chain whose links have remained forged together for over two hundred years. Wars that are waged are waged because it is economically expedient that they should be waged. This world of ours is a closed system; the books must always balance; there is no help to come from outside. It is business. Taking care of business. And, although I hate to use the terrible phase, at the end of the day, all is well. Always has been well, always will be well.'

'But these papers. This music, these words.' Inspector Westlake tore the ancient papers from his pocket and flung them at Thompson. 'This is an overthrow of the system. This is a *coup d'état*.

'It is fantasy,' said Thompson, raking up the papers, which had fluttered down at his feet. 'We know that *our* men, the Parliament of Five, control the controllers of this world. But these papers suggest that the controllers of the controllers are themselves subject to being controlled by another party: a Secret Secret Brotherhood, one that has existed for centuries, unimagined even by the Golden Sprouters. One that can orchestrate the actions of Mankind through what? This music? It is ludicrous, impossible. It is conspiracy theory taken to the point of madness.'

'I have played the music,' said Inspector Westlake.

'You have?'

'On my little banjolele. I always carry it with me when I am away from home.'

Ahem,' went Thompson.

'That music is not the work of man.'

'Whatever do you mean?'

'I mean that it's something more. Something evil. I was only able to play the first couple of bars before—'

Inspector Westlake brought his hands into the light.

They were bound with bandages.

And blood showed through these bindings.

And blood there was on Jonny Hooker's fingers.

But Jonny didn't care.

Dry Rot were done with 'Johnny B. Goode' now. Andi Evans had committed it to the big tape spools on his big tape deck. Andi Evans had the look of a penitent who has unexpectedly been brought into the presence of God. He did have that on tape, didn't he? He had his headphones on. He wound back the tape and he played the last bit again. He *did* have it.

And in his long years as a music journo, as a record producer, as a man-who-would-be-Brian-Epstein, Andi had heard much music, much, much, much. And most of it God-awful crap. And many guitar solos had he heard. But nothing, nothing, nothing on the scale of the one that Jonny Hooker had just played. And *that* was only the warm-up number.

And it was an acoustic guitar!

What would be coming next?

'Thank you. Thank you,' went Gazz into the mic. 'Thank you very much indeed.'

For the crowd was applauding, wildly, madly. Cheering and whooping and such. And the young woman with the outstanding characteristics, who had earlier made Jonny's year-so-far, had been joined in front of the stage by several other such women, all with similarly outstanding characteristics and all most enthusiastic.

'We are rocking here.' Paul nudged Jonny. 'You're doing really amazing, mate.'

Jonny Hooker nodded and did a guitar soloette. The crowd went wilder and the women did blowings of kisses.

'I'd like to take the credit,' said Jonny.

'Then do,' said Paul.

'But,' went Jonny.

'What?' went Paul.

'Well, nothing, I suppose.' And Jonny looked out at the crowd: the yelling, cheering, applauding crowd, the outstanding young women. He'd wanted this all his life – fame, adulation, recognition. He *had* wanted to do it by himself, though. Wanted it to be *his* talent, *his* skill, not some – what was it? – magical guitar? Possessed guitar? The guitar that the Devil had tuned that midnight in Clarksdale, sometime in the nineteen thirties, at the crossroads of Highways 49 and 61.

But then, of course.

Jonny's head was swimming. But there was a 'then, of course'. This 'then of course' was, then, of course, perhaps this wasn't Robert Johnson's guitar at all, just a *really* good guitar. The really good guitar that Jonny had always wanted but could never afford. The one he had always said he would be able to play on like a mad angel, if he'd ever been given the chance.

Perhaps this music was *his* music, born of *his* talent, finally being given its head. Finally set free of his troubled soul, as it were.

'Daydreaming?' Paul asked Jonny.

'Sorry,' Jonny said. 'I was miles away.

'Are you ready for the last number?' Paul asked.

'Last number?' said Jonny. 'We've only just started.'

Paul shook his head. 'We've been playing solid for two hours, mate. I'm done. We're all done – except for you. Andi Evans has almost run out of tape – he says only one more number.'

'One more number.' Jonny Hooker shook his head. 'Two hours of playing? I thought O'Fagin wanted us off in an hour.'

'Leave this to me,' said Paul, and he stepped up to the mic. 'All right,' he said, 'I guess I know that you've all enjoyed yourselves, which is why we did the six encores. But this does have to be our last. Ghandi's Hairdryer want to come on. It's well past time and the bar has to close. So, to finish, we are going to do one of our own compositions. Well, I say one of our own, but we've never actually played it before.'

'Eh?' went Jonny.

'Eh?' went Gazz.

'I've been told by the management, in the form of Mister O'Fagin, to dedicate it to him. Seeing as he says he wrote it. And as I've read the lyrics and checked out the chords, I do have to tell you that I think it's a blinder. It's a twelve-bar-blues. I hope you like it.'

'What the fuck is this?' Gazz asked Paul.

'Trust me,' said Paul. 'And just follow Jonny when he plays.'

'You can't just throw us to the lions by bunging us the music for a number we've never played.'

'You reckon not? It's what we've been doing all evening, isn't it? Drum along,' he told Tom the drummer. 'It's in A.'

'A,' said Jonny, shaking his head in doubt.

Paul returned to the mic. 'So,' said he, 'bear with us, please, and we will give you something you've never heard before, something even more special than everything you've heard so far: a number penned by our own Mister O'Fagin.'

'O'Fagin bowed behind the bar.

The crowd looked rather doubtful.

'But,' continued Paul, 'according to the song sheet the number was in fact written by someone called "R. Johnson".'

Jonny did a double-take as he looked at his score.

'It's called "Apocalypse Blues",' said Gazz.

37

A convoy took to rumbling through the night-time streets of London. It rumbled up from an underground car park somewhere slightly to the north of Mornington Crescent Underground Station and it took to its rumbling with vigour.

In the lead vehicle sat Constable Cartwright, next to the driver, Constable Rogers. Constable Rogers had volunteered for the driving job and as he was the only one in the truck who had a full driving licence, the job was his.

Constable Cartwright keyed 'Gunnersbury Park' into the SatNav. 'Head that way,' he told Rogers.

Constable Rogers came and went. Came and went went he.

'Oh my God,' went Constable Cartwright. 'Would you look at yourself.'

Constable Rogers glanced down at his hands and saw a hands-free steering wheel.

'Eeeek!' he went. 'I thought I was driving. Where have my hands gone? Where has all of me gone? Oh, I'm back now. No, I'm not.'

'It's the invisibility suit,' said the suddenly enlightened Constable Cartwright. 'Every time we go over a bump, it switches on and you vanish. It's really rather good.'

'I don't want to end up like Deputy Dawg. Do you think it's safe?'

Constable Cartwright made so-so gestures with the fingers of his right hand, but as the truck went over another bump, his fingers vanished as well.

Fingers, fingers, fingers.

Fingers of Jonny's left hand upon the neck of the wondrous guitar.

Fingers of Andi Evans upon the big buttons of the big recording desk equipment.

Fingers of Tom gripping his drumsticks.

Fingers of Gazz on the mic.

A finger on the trigger. Two fingers of red-eye from the optic. A finger of fudge is just enough.

What?

There was a bit of hush from the crowd as Jonny fingered the guitar.

History has it that Robert Johnson recorded twenty-nine different compositions. There are forty-two separate recordings of these twenty-nine.

It might surprise many to know that the lyrics to 'Apocalypse Blues', penned in Johnson's own hand, actually exist. They are stored amongst a few of his other personal effects in one of the storerooms beneath the Big House at Gunnersbury Park. In a shoebox, on a shelf next to the Protein Man's printing machine.

These lyrics have never before been published and sadly they cannot be published now. Due to copyright reasons.*

Jonny prepared to play guitar and Gazz prepared to sing.

'Please don't sing,' said Constable Cartwright. 'I'm trying to jig about with the SatNav, but the handbook is very complicated and I'm finding it difficult to concentrate.'

'I'm *not* singing,' said Constable Rogers. 'The music is coming out of the radio.'

Constable Cartwright jigged with the radio. 'But the radio isn't switched on,' he said

'But that's where it's coming from – listen.'

Constable Cartwright put his ear to the dashboard radio and listened. 'It *is*,' he said.

'It's blues,' said Constable Rogers. 'I like a bit of blues, me. Mind you, I like a song about a four-legged friend even more.'

---

* However, for those lucky few who receive one of the limited-edition giveaway CDs that accompany hardback editions of this book, a recording is to be found, sung by the author. One for eBay, that, eh?

'I like anything that goes "Da-da-de-da-da-de-da-da-de-da, Bonanza",' said Constable Cartwright. 'But how can that radio be playing when it's not switched on? And what is that blues song all about?' He listened some more. 'Sounds a bit biblical,' he said.

Constable Rogers came and went.

Constable Cartwright did likewise.

'Ah,' said Constable Cartwright, at length. 'This is an extremely smart piece of SatNav. See what it does here?'

Constable Rogers took a look.

And it only takes a moment, doesn't it?

That lack of concentration, when behind the wheel.

The truck went over a big, big bump and all of its occupants vanished.

'What was *that*?' Constable Cartwright glanced into the wing mirror. 'I think we just ran over a vicar on a bike.'

'Well, you were talking about the Bible.'

'Well, keep your eyes on the road. What I was going to say was that this SatNav must be brand-new military hardware. It's not a computerised representation of the streets. It's actual real-life foot-age, shot from a spy satellite. Look carefully – you can see us going along the road. Clever, eh?'

'Very,' said Constable Rogers. 'Why are we that funny colour?'

'It's night-time. Night-vision camera on the spy satellite, I sup-pose. It's infrared. That's our heat signature.'

'And those?' Constable Rogers did hasty pointings.

'People,' said Constable Cartwright. 'And a dog, look. And you can even see the people in their houses. Here, I think there's a couple having a shag in that house.'

Constable Rogers nearly had the truck off the road.

'Please look where you're driving, Constable. I'm going to do a little fast-forward on the SatNav. Have a look at our objective, Gunnersbury Park. Do you realise that with this we can actually see if anyone is skulking about in the park at night. It will make our job pretty easy, eh?'

Constable Rogers nodded. But as he had momentarily vanished from sight, this nodding went unseen by Constable Cartwright.

★

Unseen by the crowd at The Middle Man, Jonny Hooker's face was not a thing of beauty. It was turned away from the audience. Jonny was speaking urgently.

To Paul.

'We can't play this number,' said Jonny. 'We just can't do it.'

'Of course we can,' said Paul. 'It looks simple enough, the chords anyway. Your standard twelve-bar blues.'

'It's a lot more than that.' Jonny could read music well enough and even the first glance had told him that this was no standard twelve-bar blues.

'This is Robert Johnson's last number,' said Jonny to Paul. 'His thirtieth composition, the one he never intended to play because he knew that once he'd played it, the Devil would come and claim his soul.'

'And he played it here and the Devil *did*,' said Paul. 'I've heard that tale. Everyone's heard that tale.'

'They *have*?' said Jonny.

'They *have*,' said Paul 'But do *I* believe it? No, I don't. Do I believe that this is really Johnson's last composition? No, I don't. Do I believe that you are holding Robert Johnson's guitar?'

'No, you don't?' suggested Jonny.

'No, I don't,' said Paul, 'but something special is going on, isn't it, Jonny? Something special is going on with you. With your life. Things are beginning to mean something for you. You told me earlier that you've never felt so alive in all your life.'

'It's true,' said Jonny.

'Then play the damn song, Jonny. Play like you've never played. Let Andi Evans get it all on tape. Let's do something with our lives, eh, Jonny? Grasp the nettle, go the whole hog, all that kind of business.'

Jonny Hooker thought about this.

The crowd began to boo.

'Are we going to play this number, or what?' asked Gazz. 'The mob is growing surly.'

Jonny looked down at the wondrous guitar.

'We play,' said Jonny Hooker.

★

'It's a bit like playing a really advanced computer game,' said Constable Cartwright, jigging about with the SatNav. 'Ah yes, see here. No, *don't* see here, I'll tell you about it. I've got Gunnersbury Park up on the screen now and, yep, looks clear of people, just some little heat signatures. Here, ah, yes, I can zoom in. Squirrels. Squirrels in the trees. How cool is this?'

Constable Rogers agreed that it *was* cool.

After all, squirrels *are* cool.

Everyone knows that.

They're *not* just rats with good PR.

'Oh yeah,' said Constable Cartwright. 'Really cool. I'm panning back a bit here. Oh, look at th—, No don't look, just listen – there's a lot of activity here. A gathering of people, looks like in a single-storey dwelling. No, not dwelling, pub. It's a pub full of people near the park. A band's playing, too. This is really brilliant.'

'That music is playing again through the turned-off radio,' said Constable Rogers. 'It's louder now and it sounds like a full band rather than just a single singer.'

'Yes,' said Constable Cartwright. 'It does. How odd. But hold on, this is odd, too.' He jigged and he tweaked at the SatNav. 'It's gone on the blink. No it hasn't. It's working okay. But the pub. Damn me, look at that. The temperature is dropping in the pub, dropping right down to zero, it looks like.'

And yes, it was true. Within The Middle Man music lovers were beginning to pat at themselves, hug at their arms and marvel at their breath as it steamed from their mouths.

Andi Evans 'hh'd' upon his fingers. 'Someone leave the fridge door open?' he asked of no one in particular. 'Cold is the new cool, I'll have to remember that. I have to get this recorded. I've never heard anything quite like this before.'

'Now *that* is weird,' went Constable Cartwright. 'It seems as if the entire pub has gone sub-zero. All except for the band. And the band—'

And the band.

In a blur. As if accelerated. Many times any normal speed. Above and beyond. Impossible. Jonny Hooker's fingers flew across the fingerboard. Tom's fingers a blur, drumsticks moving too fast to be seen. The bass notes of Paul, a high-pitched whine. And heat. And superheat. And rush of fire and shriek and a terrible rush of power and from afar and growing louder and louder, the sounds of what might that be?

Laughter?

Terrible laughter?

And fingers fingers fingers.

And small hairy fingers, tearing the plugs that powered the amps from the wall sockets.

And implode.

38

Jonny Hooker awoke to the sound of Bow Bells.

These were not, however, those very Bow Bells that the cockneys rejoice in the hearing thereof. Rather, these Bow Bells were an approximation, an impersonation, an imitation, a vocalised rendition that issued from the black pursed lips of Mr Giggles.

And to this Jonny Hooker awoke.

In his cosy bed, in his cosy room, in his house, which although not altogether cosy, boasted at least an inside toilet and a view, on a clear day, from the rear, clean over the graveyard to the M4 flyover beyond.

Jonny Hooker awoke.

He yawned and made tut-tuttings with his mouth and shushed at Mr Giggles. He snuggled down and pulled his cosy blanket, or 'blanky' as he had called it when a child, close up about himself, to enjoy that final bit of snuggling down that precedes the getting up.

'Rise and shine, thou sleepy head,' cooed Mr Giggles.

'Shut up and leave me alone,' said Jonny, reply ever ready.

'Yes, you are right,' said the Monkey Boy, and, doffing his fez, he did a small gig and called, 'Sleep on, sweet prince,' from the foot of the bed.

Jonny Hooker made a rumbling-bottom sound.

Which *is* permissible, when you're in your own bed.

Sunlight flowed in upon Jonny, between curtains that should have been closed. Jonny nestled lower, pulling blanky over his head.

And then Jonny Hooker flung back the covers and jerked to a sit in his bed.

'What am I doing *here*?' he asked.

'Sleeping?' said Mr Giggles.

'But *here*?'

'I fail to understand the question. Oh, what a beautiful day.'

'Yes, it *is* a beautiful day.' And Jonny Hooker squinted. Rubbed his eyes and squinted once again. 'I'm home in my bed,' said Jonny. 'Home in my bed, right here.'

'As ever the master of deduction,' said Mr Giggles, replacing his fez and adjusting his colourful waistcoat. 'Did I ever tell you where I acquired this waistcoat?' he asked. 'It's a fascinating tale and one, should you ever wish to pen your autobiography as a cautionary tale of misspent youth, that you might wish to include, to enliven almost any chapter.'

'What am I doing here?'

'The eternal question. The question that elevates Man above the animals. But why are you asking it now?'

Jonny Hooker scratched at his head. 'And what has happened to my hair?' He arose and did stumblings to the dressing table. He had never wanted it in his room in the first place — it was far too girlie — but his mother had insisted that there was no place else to put it, her bedroom being packed to the gunwales with war–surplus field rations that she was hoarding as a hedge against a forthcoming Apocalypse.★

Jonny stumbled to his dressing table and viewed his image in the bevelled mirror that surmounted its rear. 'What *has* happened to my hair?' he asked once again, although with a greater emphasis upon the word '*has*' this time.

'Is it thinning?' Mr Giggles asked. 'For if it is, be grateful. Girls really do go for men with thinning hair. It makes them feel superior, you see. They just hate men with big hair, especially men who are prettier than they are.'

'Will you please shut up!'

'I thought you wanted to talk about your hair?'

'I do — what's happened to it?'

'I give up,' said Mr Giggles. 'What has?'

'Well, it's all gone flat on the top, as if I've been wearing a cap. And I *never* wear a cap. And blimey, what's happened to my face?'

'I give up,' said Mr Giggles once more.

'It's got at least about a five-day growth of whiskers.'

★ Very probably the same Apocalypse predicted from the Kleenex reading.

Mr Giggles did exaggerated startlings and equally exaggerated starlings. He cocked his head upon one side and cupped his hirsute chin in one hand. 'You have at least five hairs *on* your chin,' he observed. 'If that is what you mean.'

'It is,' said Jonny. And he examined this sparseness of beard. 'Do you think I've got a bit of a goatee going on here?' he asked.

'No,' said Mr Giggles. 'I don't. You might want to put some cream on that and have a tomcat lick it off. As we used to say in the navy, when I was flying bombers with Monty at the Somme.'

'Hm,' went Jonny and scratched once more at his head. 'I do feel rather odd.'

'Hangover,' said Mr Giggles. 'What a night you had last night, eh?'

Jonny Hooker peered at his own reflection. It had a distant quality to it. A certain vagueness. A certain lack of clarity. 'Last night,' he whispered.

'Pardon me, speak up,' said Mr Giggles.

'Last night,' said Jonny. 'I can't remember anything about last night.'

'Lucky you.' Mr Giggles bobbed about, sparring with the air. 'All that drink and bad behaviour. You're barred from The Middle Man by the way, for a week. O'Fagin said that he will shoot you dead if you show your face before a week is up.'

'Barred for a week?' said Jonny. 'Tell me, what did I do?' said Jonny. 'What on earth could I have done to get barred for a week?' asked Jonny, too.

'He caught you making the beast with two backs with his missis.'

'He never did!' Jonny Hooker did gawpings at his reflection. 'I had it off with O'Fagin's wife?'

'Apparently so,' said Mr Giggles. 'I didn't look.'

'Golly,' said Jonny, giving his reflected self an admiring grin. 'She's a damn fine-looking woman, Mrs O. It's a pity I can't remember it.'

'It sort of balances it out, that, doesn't it?' said Mr Giggles. 'The times you might get lucky while drunk and actually have sex with a good-looking woman and then not be able to recall it in the morning. As against the times when you'll be drunk and have sex with a really ugly woman, and remember that *all too well* in the morning. Once you sober up.'

'And that's another odd thing,' said Jonny. 'If I got *that* drunk last night, then how come I don't have a hangover this morning?'

'You're complaining about *that*?'

'I'm not complaining. I'm just puzzled. I always get a ripping hangover when I've been out on the lash.'

'Well, let's just hope it will kick in later, if that will cheer you up.'

'And I should be hungry.' Jonny Hooker felt at his belly. 'Ah,' he said, 'I *am* hungry.'

'Then why don't we just go down and have breakfast?'

'Because,' said Jonny. 'I appear to be naked.'

'Well observed,' said Mr Giggles. 'Put on your dressing gown, why don't you.'

Jonny Hooker glanced all around and about. 'And where are my clothes?' he now asked.

'Will you stop with the questions, already?' Mr Giggles turned up his pinky palms. 'Have some breakfast. Have a cup of tea. Lighten up.'

'I'm perplexed.' And Jonny shook his head.

Mr Giggles made further Bow Bell sounds, interspersed with Big Ben chimes and small change being rattled in the pocket of a Protestant.

Jonny shook his head more at these untoward noises.

But he did put on his dressing gown.

And he did go down to breakfast.

Jonny's mother was bothering eggs with a chamois on a stick. 'Good morning, Jonathan, my son,' said she, raising her head from the bothering-bucket and clicking a further good morning in Morse with her dentures.

Jonny Hooker sat himself down in his own special chair by the stove. A knife and fork and spoon were laid out before him on the table. On top of a pink gingham tablecloth. And there was a glass of orange juice and an empty cup that surely awaited coffee. Jonny Hooker viewed this spectacle.

'What is this shit?' he whispered, slowly and under his breath.

'How would you like your eggs?' asked his mum. And then she giggled. 'The vicar once asked me that when he was chatting me up. And do you know what I told him?'

'You told him that you'd like your eggs unfertilised,' said Jonny.

'Uncanny,' said Jonny's mum. 'It's almost as if you were there yourself. Which you *were*, if truth be told, but half of you was still inside the vicar.'

'Stop now, please, Mum,' said Jonny.

'So, boiled or fried? I can recommend these boiled ones – I almost have them defragged with this chamois.'

'Fried, thank you, Mum.'

And Jonny Hooker's mum took to fussing at the stove. 'You can read the paper if you want,' she told Jonny.

Jonny gave his head a shake. 'Paper?' he whispered. 'This is getting weirder by the moment.'

But the newspaper was there, folded upon the tablecloth. So Jonny Hooker unfolded it and gave the front page a good looking over.

The paper was Brentford's *Sunday Mercury*. The headline shouted

CRISIS IN MIDDLE EAST

WORLD STANDS TREMBLING UPON THE BRINK OF WW III

CAN TOP-SECRET TALKS SAVE PLANET FROM THREAT OF TOTAL ANNIHILATION?

Jonny Hooker viewed this paper. 'This is Sunday's paper,' he said.

'Ah,' said his mother, turning partially from the stove. A kind of half-hip swivel, with ankle-turn accompaniment.

'That would be,' said she, 'because today is Sunday.'

'Sunday?' Jonny Hooker mulled this concept over. 'Today is Sunday,' said he. 'Sunday?' he queried. '*Sunday?*' he questioned. 'SUNDAY?'

'The sabbath,' said his mother, who was considering the taking up of a religion to augment her already chosen hobbies of crown-green bowls, knitting and mayhem. 'The day of the Lord. The seventh day, upon which God rested.'

'Sunday?' said Jonny. 'Sunday, hang on.

Mr Giggles said nothing.

'How can it be Sunday?' Jonny asked.

'It's a weekly thing,' his mother explained. 'I love it when you ask me questions that I can actually answer.'

'Yes,' said Jonny. 'But it can't be Sunday. It must be—'

And then he had a bit of a think. And something seemed to be missing. 'It must be ... Hold on.' He scratched once more at his head.

'What have you done to your hair?' asked his mother.

'I don't remember,' said Jonny.

'Well, that's just careless. You should always put haircare at the very forefront of your thoughts. People see your hair coming before they see you. Well, they do if you're walking backwards, anyway. Which way up is an egg?' she continued, holding one before her.

'No,' said Jonny. 'I *don't* remember about days. My last recollection is of last Monday, I think. I had that farmer's-market-in-the-loft thing again. But it passed and I'm better now. But that's the last memory I have. And now it's Sunday. That can't be right.'

'Now that you mention it,' said Jonny's mum, half turning once more, although this time employing a double-knee manoeuvre, 'my memory seems to be somewhat on the blink also. How did you manage to grow that magnificent beard overnight, by the way?'

Jonny Hooker stroked at his chin. 'Something is *not* right here.'

'Well, if it's not right here,' said his mum, 'then it must be somewhere else.'

Jonny Hooker looked bewildered. Jonny Hooker *was* bewildered. 'I have hat-hair,' he said, 'and a five-day growth of beard, and about five days missing out of my life.'

'I have a pair of surgical stockings,' said Jonny's mum, 'a dropped womb and a Dutch cap that I haven't used in a decade. And you think *you* have problems.'

Jonny Hooker rose from the breakfasting table. 'Something is wrong,' he declared. 'Something is *very* wrong.'

Mr Giggles' voice spoke at his ear. 'Everything is A-OK,' said Mr Giggles. 'You're just having an episode. Say nothing more to your mother. You wouldn't want her to have you banged up in the loony bin again, would you?'

'No,' said Jonny. 'I wouldn't.'

'Wouldn't what?' asked Jonny's mum, who was now fully turned and contorted into such a curious leg-linkage affair that it looked possible that she might remain in this fashion for evermore.

'Nothing,' said Jonny, making as to leave.

And then somehow tangling parts of his lower self amongst the tablecloth, with the result that it was torn from the table, tumbling cutlery and crockery and orange juice in a glass, the Sunday paper and the cornflakes packet also. Although the cornflakes packet had not previously been mentioned, and the maker's name was mis-spelt.

The previously unmentioned cornflakes packet struck the linoleum floor. Which prompted a remark from Jonny's mother that men were a bit like linoleum, in that, 'If you lay them right the first time, you can walk all over them for the next ten years.' Nice.

'And I'll thank you to clean that up,' she continued.

'Sorry. All right,' said Jonny.

'No, sod her, don't,' said Mr Giggles.

'I made the mess, I'll clean it up,' said Jonny.

'Precisely,' said his mum.

'Don't,' said Mr Giggles.

'Don't be silly,' said Jonny.

'What?' said his mum.

Jonny found the dustpan and brush and took to dustpan and brushing. 'Nothing,' he said.

'Stick it in the pedal bin,' said Mr Giggles.

'The pedal bin is *always* full,' said Jonny. 'Pedal bins are *always* full. The only time they're empty is when you buy them.'

'Why are you saying this?' asked Jonny's mum, trying in vain to untangle her legs.

'Sorry,' said Jonny. 'I'll put all these swept-up cornflakes in the dustbin.'

'Don't you do it,' said Mr Giggles. 'Stick up for yourself, you little wus.'

'Little wus?'

'Who are you calling a marsupial?' asked Jonny's mum.

'No one, not me,' said Jonny, and he vacated the kitchen.

'Don't do it!' said Mr Giggles.

Jonny was in the alleyway now, the one that ran down the side of the house. The one with the dustbin in it.

'Toss it to the four winds,' said Mr Giggles. 'Let the squirrels eat it.'

'I am reliably informed,' said Jonny, 'that squirrels are just rats with good PR.'

'You'll probably get sued for that,' said Mr Giggles. 'Let's go to the mall and play "Poo, You're a Smelly One" with the old folk.'

'Oh, behave yourself.'

And Jonny lifted the dustbin lid.

And Jonny beheld.

And Jonny fell back.

And Jonny cried, 'Aaaaaaagh!'

And Jonny nearly fainted.

39

And what was the cause of this how-do-you-do?
  This all-falling-back and near-fainting?
  Why, 'twas the sight of what lay within
  The bin, and it weren't no oil painting.

What?

Jonny Hooker peered into the dustbin's innards, cast aside the lid and delved in. There was a park ranger's uniform, complete with a cap lined with tinfoil. There was a laptop, a slim metal cylinder that appeared to be a whistle of some kind and a lot of what looked to be used Elastoplast dressings.

'Plague, plague!' cried Mr Giggles. Loudly and somehow into both of Jonny's ears at the same time. 'Don't touch those dirty things – you'll get polluted. You'll get the lurgy.'

'I think not.' And Jonny Hooker snatched up the cap and rammed it onto his head.

And back in a great tsunami wave thoughts came crashing back, breaking over damns and breakwaters, sea defences and sandbags. The memories of the days gone before. Of all that had gone before and all that had happened to Jonny.

And, 'Ow!' cried Jonny, clutching at this cap.

'You silly boy,' said Mr Giggles.

'*Silly boy?*'

'I did it for *you*. To save *you*. To spare you.'

'You tricked me.' Jonny was pulling out the park ranger's uniform. He had torn off his dressing gown and was now standing all nude in the alleyway. 'Somehow you got me to take off this cap with the tinfoil lining. And then what? How was it done? The Air

Loom Gang beaming messages into my unprotected head? Wiping my memory? That's what happened, isn't it?'

'I did it for *you*.'

'I hate you,' said Jonny. 'I really hate you.'

'I did it for you. To keep you out of danger.'

Jonny's head was all banging about.

He scrambled his way into the trousers, put two legs down the same leg hole and fell all down on his sorry naked arse.

'See what I mean?' Mr Giggles jigged about on his furry feet. 'You fall over and hurt yourself. You're better off with me looking after you. Caring for you. Seeing that you come to no harm.'

'See this hat?' said Jonny, floundering about yet pointing to his cap with unerring accuracy. '*This* is going to stay upon my head, come what may, for as long as it takes.'

'As long as it takes to do *what*?'

'The talks!' cried Jonny, making it to his knees and doing up his uniform trousers. 'The *secret* talks in the Big House at Gunnersbury Park. The *secret* talks that could determine whether the world lives or dies.'

'Oh, those,' said Mr Giggles.

'Yes, those,' said Jonny, and he fished the park ranger's jacket from the dustbin.

'Keep out of that, that's my advice.'

Jonny glared daggers at Mr Giggles. 'I don't care about your advice,' he told the jigging Monkey Boy. 'I know enough now to know what must be done. Those secret talks, amongst the controllers, the secret council that really controls the world – I know that there are others who would control them: the Air Loom Gang.'

'Huh,' went Mr Giggles.

'Not "huh", no!' Jonny fished into the jacket pocket and drew out the brass key. The brass key with the date of 1790 upon it and the words ACME AIR LOOM COMPANY also.

'Real,' said Jonny. 'All real. Not some figment of my imagination.'

'Like me?' said Mr G.

'I don't know what you are.' Jonny Hooker was now fully uniformed. 'I don't know what you are and I do not care. I *do* now know what my purpose in life is: it is for me to ensure that the secret talks go ahead unmolested.'

'They might well still lead to us all getting blown up.'

'I think not,' said Jonny, taking up the laptop and examining it. 'James Crawford's laptop, with the recording of Robert Johnson's thirtieth composition upon it. When you had me bunging all this in the dustbin – and how did you do that, by the way? While I was drunk, I suppose, easy meat then, eh? "Take off your cap and sling it away, Jonny boy, it's ruining your hair." I can just imagine. Anyway, when you made me bung all this in the dustbin, you should have had me smash up this laptop. Very careless of you, there.'

'Hm,' went Mr Giggles. 'You could have had your breakfast *without* spilling the cornflakes. Then all would have been well.'

'All *will* be well,' said Jonny, tucking the laptop into the poacher's pocket of the park ranger's jacket, 'when I have dealt with everything.'

'*You?*' went Mr Giggles. '*You?* You're Jonny Hooker, no-mark loser. Who do you think you are? Jonny Hooker, saviour of Mankind? You're not, you're no one – stay out of it, it has nothing to do with you.'

'Oh,' said Jonny. 'Oh.'

'I didn't mean it,' said Mr Giggles. 'It just slipped out, sorry.'

'You meant it.' Jonny was now sticking the used Elastoplasts back onto his face.

'No, please don't do *that*. That's disgusting. That looks really naff.'

'I don't want to be recognised. I'm working undercover – Jonny Hooker, secret agent.'

Mr Giggles groaned.

'And I'm not talking to *you*.'

'I only did it to protect you. I don't want any harm to come to you. It's all got too dangerous. Too many people have died.'

'Well, I *am* involved. And I'm staying involved.'

'So what do you think you can do?'

'Thwart the plans of the Air Loom Gang.'

'There is no Air Loom Gang. Get real, Jonny, please.'

'I have the key.' Jonny flourished it. 'And the whistle.' Jonny flourished this also. 'Although I don't as yet know the significance of the whistle. But these items are all the proof I need. The Gang exists and they will try to influence the speakers at the secret talks. And I will thwart their evil schemes. This is my purpose. This I now know is what my life is for. The reason for my being, my existence. I will wage war upon the forces of evil that seek to control, indeed possibly even to annihilate, Mankind. War, I say, and I alone will wage it.'

'Get a grip, buddy boy.'

'And don't you "Buddy Boy" me!'

'Well, will you listen to yourself. You're not James Bond, you're Jonny Hooker, nice chap really, but a little misguided. Go back inside, have breakfast, read the Sunday papers, go down to the pub and have a pint at lunchtime and—'

'Pint?' said Jonny. 'At the Middle Man?' said Jonny.

'Yes, why not?'

'Because I understood from you that I was barred from there for knobbing O'Fagin's wife.'

'Ah,' said Mr Giggles. 'Well—'

'And I now recall that she ran off with a traveller in tobaccos,' said Jonny. 'You wanted to keep me away from there because you knew that O'Fagin would say stuff to me that might make me remember what had happened over the last few days.'

'Not a bit of it,' said Mr Giggles. Crossing his heart and hoping not to die.

'And this cap—' Jonny pointed to the item in question. '—This cap and its foil lining are *all* the proof that *I* need. With it on, I remember everything.'

'And with it off?' Mr Giggles mimed the removal of Jonny's unfetching headwear.

'No way,' said Jonny. 'It's staying *on*. It blocks out the Air Loom broadcasts that are directed at my head. *I* know that and *you* know that.'

'I know no such thing.'

'I'm not talking to you any more,' said Jonny. 'I am going to get this job jobbed all by myself.'

'Paul might like to help,' said Mr Giggles, 'if you're adamant.'

'I'll do it on my own. I will endanger no one else's life.'

'You'll never get back in the park, Jonny boy. It's ringed around by policemen with big weapons. They've dug landmines into the pitch-and-putt and everything.'

'And how would you know *that*?'

'I might be guessing,' Mr Giggles suggested.

'Yes, you might.' Once assured that there was nothing else pertinent lurking around in the dustbin, Jonny replaced its lid.

'So,' said Mr Giggles. 'Breakfast, the papers, then a pint.'

'No,' said Jonny Hooker, girding his loins as had the biblical heroes of old. 'It's war, this is, and war it be, and I am the chosen warrior.'

Mr Giggles gave another groan.

'War!' cried Jonny Hooker.

40

Inspector Westlake awoke from a curious dream.

It was a musical dream. Which was to say that there *was* some music involved. Within this dream, the inspector found himself to be no longer an inspector. Rather he was an itinerant musician who travelled from town to town, playing in pubs and town squares. A kind of wandering troubadour, with his little banjolele and a penchant for singing the blues.

And in this dream he had set up his amp and his speaker in The Middle Man's saloon bar, upon the small stage where bands were wont to play. And having done the setting up thereof, he had made away to the gents, caught short, as it were, to take a leak before he began his performance.

And if indeed it was not odd that he dreamed himself a musician, for in truth he had always harboured a desire to sing the blues, it *was* odd indeed, when his peeing was done and he took himself over to the washbasin to rinse his hands and beheld his reflection in the mirror above it.

For the reflection of a young black man gazed thoughtfully back at him. And the inspector, staring thoughtfully himself, and apparently without surprise, recognised at once that this young man was the blues legend known as Robert Johnson.

And then he found that someone was tinkering with his trousers and suddenly awoke to behold the face of Mrs Corbett smiling from the pillow next to his. With her fingers going fiddle-fiddle-fiddle.

'Well, da-da-de-da-da,' said the inspector, 'and pardon me, please, madam. It would appear that I have walked in my sleep and settled myself down in the wrong bed upon my return.'

'Well, da-da-de-da-da right back atcha!' purred the lady of the house. 'That's a new excuse, I do declare.'

And she gave a certain part of the inspector's anatomy a playful tweak.

'Oooh,' went Inspector Westlake. And then, 'Damn,' as memories returned to him in a hop, a leap and a great big jump.'

Not too far away from the inspector, in a storeroom beneath the Big House at Gunnersbury Park, a transperambulation of magnetic flux angled through the ether from the glass conducting cylinders atop the Air Loom, dispatched by the keyboard manipulation of the Glove Woman. This flux, attuned to the magnetic signature unique to Inspector Westlake, who had been magnetized by a certain boarding house landlady the previous night during a particularly frantic session of that much-loved sexual favourite, 'Taking Tea with the Parson', now coalesced into an audiogram within the inspector's skull, one that effected a selective erasure of his short-term memory. Which, given what he had read, and indeed tried to play upon his little banjolele, from a piece of paper that could be dated to the seventeen nineties and which had thrown him into fear and concern for the future of Mankind, being things of an Apocalyptic nature, generally, was not, in itself, such a bad thing.

But.

Inspector Westlake could remember everything else, which was to say the days previous, in all of their dire entirety.

Every annoyance, every lack of communication, every thwarting of his wishes, every ignominious everything.

They had not been good days for Inspector Westlake.

They had been *difficult* days.

And what had made them so difficult, was the fact that he was quite unable to put his finger on *why* they had been so difficult. But it somehow seemed that no matter what orders he gave regarding the security measures at the park, these orders somehow failed to be carried out.

It was almost as if Thompson of Extra-Special Ops had taken over the running of the entire operation himself and was not allowing Inspector Westlake as much of a foot in the door.

Difficult, it was, and frustrating.

There was certainly no lack of security. The park had been closed to the general public for the weekend, which had itself caused unparalleled distress to the members of the various sporting fraternities that normally played their matches there. And the men in the black uniforms were, as one might put it, *entrenched*.

Electric fences ringed the park around.

At one-hundred-yard intervals, watchtowers bristling with slightly-beyond-the-present-state-of-the-art weaponry loomed with menace. Frogmen bobbed in the ornamental pond, surface-to-air missiles rising and falling with the ripples. A machine-gun nest nested between the columns of the Doric temple.

There were slit trenches in the Japanese garden.

Once in a while, a squirrel ventured across the pitch-and-putt to be vaporized by a landmine.*

Within the Big House, the Gunnersbury Park Museum, the location of the secret talks, several constables came and went, in and out of visibility.

It *was* all *very* impressive.

But it *wasn't* being done the way Inspector Westlake required it to be done.

His way.

The men in black from Special Ops spoke into their little face mics and received their orders through tiny earphones embedded in their lugholes. They did *not* respond to the inspector's orders.

And whenever Inspector Westlake tried to get on the blower to Thompson, Thompson, it seemed, was unavailable for comment.

Inspector Westlake knotted his wounded fists and fumed in the landlady's bed.

'I *do* like a man who's *intense*,' cooed Mrs Corbett. 'As it's Sunday morning, how about getting a little adventurous? More tea, vicar, as it were.'

'Unhand me, *madam*!' Inspector Westlake rose from the bed. Then returned to it in haste, still handed. 'I have things to do, madam!' he further protested. 'Matters of national, indeed global, impact.'

'As James Bond once said,' said the lady of the house, 'best not to go off half-cocked.'

Inspector Westlake ground his teeth, checked his wristwatch,

* Obviously not the same squirrel each time.

stroked at his chin and then said, 'I suppose there's always time to "Take Tea".'

Mrs Corbett grinned the kind of grin that one generally associates with roadkill. 'The *full* Parson,' she whispered in Inspector Westlake's ear.

'Whisper to me, people,' came the voice of Thompson through many a tiny earphone into many a lughole.

'Whisper?' went Constable Cartwright, twiddling at his invisibility controls and somewhat surprising himself to discover that whilst his upper body had regained visibility, his legs were nowhere to be seen.

'It's a security thing,' whispered Constable Cassidy, 'so we don't appear to be talking to ourselves.'

'*I* knew that,' said Constable Cartwright. 'I am in charge, after all.'

'Why don't you have any legs?' asked Constable Rogers.

'And where's your head gone, Rogers?' asked Constable Milky Bar Kid.

'By the numbers,' came the voice of Thompson. 'Sound off.'

And all over the park, and all through the Big House, blackly clad Special Ops fellows, a few apparently lacking for bits and pieces, sounded off.

'I want this whole thing done by the numbers,' Thompson repeated. 'I want nothing – *nothing* – to go wrong.'

'Sir,' said Constable Cartwright, 'might I just ask—'

'Good question, Constable. Now carry on.'

'A right carry-on and no mistake,' said Constable Paul to Constable Justice. These constables wore the blue, and Paul envied those in the black. These constables in blue were on double time as it was Sunday, but had only got as far as the Gunnersbury Park car park before being halted by those constables in the black and told that they could go no further.

'Are you tooled-up?' asked Constable Justice.

'Eh?' said Constable Paul.

'Are you packing heat? Are you carrying an unequaliser?'

'Surely it's an *equaliser*,' said Constable Paul.

'Not if you're packing what I'm packing.'

'Ah,' said Constable Paul.

'I say we should blast our way in.'

'Right,' said Constable Paul. 'Yet strange as it may appear to you, I veer towards precisely the opposite view.'

'Does that involve any weaponry?'

'No,' said Paul. 'It involves you and me making away to whatever is left of The Middle Man for an early Sunday lunchtime pint. We're on double time here and if these sods won't let us into the park, let's go and guard the pub instead.'

'Do you think there might be someone at the pub who needs shooting?' asked Constable Justice.

'Bound to be,' said Constable Paul, reversing Inspector Westlake's car out of the car park, into the road, across the path of oncoming traffic and then slowly, but slowly, cruising it off to the pub.

'There are times,' said he, to Constable Justice, 'when I really do love being a policeman.'

'Do you love your Order and do you love your country?' Candles burned in a secret place, a dark and deep such place.

Heads went nod in the candlelight, heads both quaint and odd. A dusty periwig was to be seen, and an antique female coiffure.

'And are we loyal to our calling, we of the Secret Order that is beyond the secretest of all other Secret Orders?'

'We are loyal,' went those addressed. A gloved hand or two were raised.

'I feel,' said the speaker, 'that today the triumph will be ours. But not ours per se, you understand.' And mumble-mumble-mumble went the assembled company. 'But for the good of all, the greater good.'

And the man who spoke these words stepped out from the shadows and into the wan light cast by the candles' flames. A long and gaunt tall figure was this, in a black frocked coat, with a high-collared shirt and a flourish of frills and fancies, and a buckled shoe and a stockinged calf and rings that finger-twinkled.

And this fellow's cheekbones were angled and sharp, and his eyes deep-set and all a-glitter. And his beard, long and black, wore ribbons of silk and hid the wry smile on his lips.

'Oh, my brethren,' intoned this body, 'my brothers, and sisters, too,' and he offered a bow to the ladies. 'We of the Order beyond all Secret Orders have been summoned from our time once again, brought here to perform our duty. Oh, how we shall triumph. Oh, how we shall bring our pneumatic arts to a pretty perfection.'

'So shall that be, my brother,' quoth a fellow grey of hair and known as Jack the Schoolmaster, though dressed as a ringmaster, he. 'So we shall and our souls shall be blessed for it.'

'Blessed for it, yes.' The body in black with the great black beard cackled laughter.

As one will do when one is a villain.

'Yes!' cried he, affecting a pose that was noble and arrogant both. 'Today we do as we have done before. We set the world to rights. We do the doings and make it so, for such is what we do.'

Heads here and there nodded in mostly darkness.

'We *will* succeed.' And he of the long black beard laughed. 'Or my name is not Count Otto Black. And we are not the Air Loom Gang.'

Golly gosh.

41

'Golly gosh,' said the coal-black chap
  Who drove the limousine.
  'A fine to-do. An odd one-two,
  As strange as I have seen.'

'Now *that*,' said the voice on the other end of the telephone line, 'is something you should have done sooner.'

'Excuse me?' said the chauffeur.

'I *am* talking to Black Betty Bam-a-Lam, am I not?'

'You certainly are,' said the Black Betty in question. 'Note if you will the triple-barrelled surname. One of the Sussex Bam-a-Lams, I'll have you know.'

'Excellent,' said the voice. 'Then I have the right Black Betty Bam-a-Lam. What I meant when I said that *that* was something you should have done sooner was the speaking in rhyme. You might have established an interesting part for yourself. A black male chauffeur with a girl's Christian name, a triple-barrelled surname and a penchant for verse-improv. Given how dull some of these blighters are, you could have got yourself star billing.'

'Who *is* this?' asked Black Betty.

'I told you, I am the chief exec. of a top London theatrical agency and I'd like to hire your services for today to chauffeur that fine character actor John Hurt to a private film festival in Penge.'

'Penge?' said Black Betty. 'I've heard that it's a really nice place, although I've never actually been there.'

'A veritable Eden,' said the voice on the end of the line.

Although it wasn't really 'a line', because Black Betty was speaking into the handset of his car phone as he drove his black stretched limo along.

'Well, hum and hah and fiddle-de-de,' said Black Betty.

'Excuse *me*?' said the voice.

'Merely voicing my versatility. Did you say John Hurt?'

'I certainly did, star of both *The Naked Civil Servant* and *The Elephant Man*.'

'Not to mention *Hellboy*.'

'*Hellboy*?'

'I told you not to mention that!'*

'Most amusing,' said the voice.

'I thought so. But no, I regret that much as I would adore to be privileged to drive, as I believe it is now, *Sir* John Hurt—'

'If it isn't, it should be.'

'But anyway, I cannot. And the reason that I responded to your question in rhyme is this: as the chauffeur, and indeed owner, of this here black limousine, it is sad to report that for the most part nowadays I have to hire myself out, nay, *prostitute* myself, by taking hirings from ghastly chav girls for hen nights. Yet, yet, and here I feel that there *is* a God, and a God who sometimes smiles upon black chauffeurs with girly Christian names and unlikely triple-barrelled surnames. This very week, which is to say on Friday, and today, which is Sunday, I have been employed by some decent clientele. To whit, on Friday I conveyed a certain Andi Evans, heavy metal music entrepreneur, to a pub called The Middle Man in Ealing, where he made a recording. And from there, in the company of a can of audio tape, to London Airport, where, to quote Mister Evans he intended to "make away with the prize of a lifetime, because *I* deserve it". He boarded a plane for Los Angeles, I believe. And today—'

A yawn came from the other end of the phone 'line'.

'And today,' continued Black Betty Bam-a-Lam, 'today I am driving, at this very moment, to Buckingham Palace to pick up none other than Her Majesty the Queen, to take her to a secret location, which naturally I will not divulge.'

'Naturally,' said the voice. 'Then perhaps, if you are so engaged, you could give me the name of another limo-hire company whose credentials you could vouch for?'

* Alas Spike Milligan, sadly missed.

'Would that I could,' said Black Betty, 'but I regret to say that I cannot. I think you will find that all the top-notch limo-hire companies are busy today.'

'Doing *what*?' asked the voice.

'Chauffeuring dignitaries,' said Black Betty. 'Mister Mull, of Kintyre Cars, is at London City Airport picking up Ahab the A-rab.'

'The sheik of the desert sands?' sang the voice.

'The same. And Mister Jones, of We'll Keep a Welcome in the Hillside Motors is in Neasden, picking up a Mister Bagshaw.'

'Bagshaw, Bagshaw, stick it up your jumper?' sang the voice.

'Not as such,' said Betty the Black. 'Then there's Mogador Firesword, of Dragonslayer Car Hire, who is frankly often rather difficult to get on the phone. He, I know, is doing a pick-up from Battersea Dogs' Home – a chap known as Bob the Comical Pup.'

'How much is that doggy in the window?' sang the voice.

'You're not far short of the mark there. And the remaining top-of-the-line-stretch-limo-hire-out-jobbie-person would be Mister Esau Good, of Smack My Bitch Up Motors. And he's at Brize Norton Airport picking up Elvis Presley.'

There was a bit of a silence then.

'"Heartbreak Hotel?" said Betty. "Jailhouse Rock"?'

'But Elvis is dead, surely?'

'If you say so. Don't ask me, I'm only a black chauffeur.'

'And are all these, what shall we call them, *celebrities*, bound for the same place? Her Majesty the Queen, Mister Bagshaw, Ahab the A-rab, Bob the Comical Pup and Elvis Presley, the King of rock 'n' roll?'

'Such I believe to be the case,' said Betty.

'But you can't tell me where that is?'

'More than my job's worth. I'm sorry.'

'Are they dropping off, *waiting*, then picking up? Or are they dropping off, returning to base in case of a job in between, then returning to pick up?'

'The latter, I believe.'

'So where would they be waiting, were they intending to wait, which clearly they are not?'

'Gunnersbury Park,' said Betty. 'the Big House, Gunnersbury Park.'

'Thank you,' said the voice. 'And I'm sorry to have wasted your time.'

'No problem.'

Black Betty replaced the receiver of his car phone.

The owner of the voice switched off his mobile phone and tucked it away into the breast pocket of his jacket.

A jacket that was not without interest.

Although to whom must remain uncertain.

'Exactly what I wanted to know,' he said.

And having said this, he turned away, took himself over to a small wall mirror and grinned into it. The small wall mirror was barely to be seen amidst the stacks of army field rations that were piled up against the walls of what appeared to be a rather untidy bedroom.

The door of this bedroom now opened and a woman of middling years adorned with a quilted nylon pink gingham housecoat and matching slipperettes entered the bedroom.

'I'm sorry to have kept you waiting,' she said, grinning inanely. 'I had to get Jonny's breakfast. And pretend, like you told me, that I didn't know anything about what has been going on for the past few days.'

'You did very well, my dear,' said the owner of the voice. 'You deserve some kind of reward, I believe.'

'Well,' said Jonny's mum, for who else could it be but she? 'It *is* Sunday, so we might engage in something sexually adventurous.'

'Indeed we might. Shall we "Take Tea with the Parson"?'

Jonny's mum did some of that roadkill grinning. 'That would be lovely, Mister O'Fagin,' she said.

'Wake up, O'Fagin,' called Paul, and he did some thump-thump-thumping upon what was left of The Middle Man's saloon bar door.

'This place is in almost complete ruination,' observed Constable Justice. 'Did someone take it out with a heat-seeker?'

'On the contrary,' said Constable Paul. 'Things got rather cold. We played a gig here on Friday night and my mate Jonny played Robert Johnson's guitar. Most of the audience got sucked into a parallel continuum – there was some kind of transperambulation of pseudo-cosmic anti-matter or something.'

'Sorry I missed it,' said Constable Justice. 'So, good gig, then?'

'Better than usual. Mostly the audience just chuck stuff. Friday night, both Jonny and me got blow jobs.'

'You blew each other?'

'From *girls*,' said Paul, and he banged some more on the door. 'And we got a record contract. Although we haven't actually got it as such, but it's in the bag, as it were.' Constable Paul banged even more.

'It's only nine o'clock,' said Constable Justice.

Constable Paul gave him the Old-Fashioned Look.

'Oh yes,' said Constable Justice. 'We're policemen. There are no such things as licensing hours when you are a policeman and you fancy a drink. How did I forget *that*?'

'Because you're always thinking about shooting people.'

'Like you're *not*!'

Constable Paul knocked even some more. 'He's not here,' he said. 'Or he's asleep.'

'Or "Taking Tea with the Parson" with someone's mum.'

'Why would he be doing *that*?'

'I don't know,' said Constable Justice. 'He did it with *my* mum. Shit! He might be doing it with my mum right now!'

It is very unlikely that the Queen Mum ever 'Took Tea with the Parson'. She was far too sweet and cuddly and everything. And she was always Britain's favourite granny and everything. Mind you, Queen Victoria used to take a lot of 'tea' with that Scotsman.

But *not* the Queen Mum.

Although there's really no telling just what she *might* have got up to. According to the Illuminated One, David Icke, Her Madge, the Queen Mum and most of the royals generally are in fact reptilian shape-shifters who regularly engage in human sacrifice and the consumption of infants.

But probably *not* 'Taking Tea with the Parson'.

And of course the Queen Mum *is* dead now* and it isn't right to speak ill of the dead.

---

* Finally!!!

★

'One is dead chuffed,' said Her Majesty the Queen, speaking to her regal reflection, cast back at her from an IKEA wall mirror in her private billiards room. Where the Royal We keeps her extensive collection of Space Invaders machines, handbags and the mummified prepuce of Christ (which was a present from the Pope).

'One is dead chuffed,' the monarch said once more, reading from the card, which was printed with BIG LETTERS so she didn't need to wear her glasses. Because, let's face it, they *do* make her look old. 'Dead chuffed to attend this secret conclave, as chairperson and casting vote and—'

And a knock came at her chamber door

'Who troubles one?' she enquired. (Real class!)

'The car's here, Ma'am,' a menial (or lackey, or cat's-paw) replied.

'Is that Betty driving?' asked the sovereign.

'As ever,' the other replied.

'Bitchin',' said Her Majesty. 'Just love that bad-ass, Betty.'

42

It was clear to those in the know, though those in the know numbered two, that a degree of easy intimacy existed between a certain Black Betty who drove a black limo and a certain Royal Betty, who ruled the British Isles.

That the monarch, gliding down the front steps from Buck House with a sprightliness surprising for one of her advanced years, customarily greeted the chauffeur with much use of the 'N' word, which had long worn out its welcome for either shock value or a cheap laugh; whilst he, patting the regal butt as it entered his auto, responded with such words as, 'Yo, my sweet pussy,' and, 'You can kiss my OBE anytime.'

But as there were no witnesses to this, no definite proof can be found that it actually happened. And well it might be that this unlikely exchange was nothing more than wishful thinking. Although whether upon the part of Black Betty, Royal Betty or some third party, it is fruitless to speculate.★

The long, black limo slid away over the gravel and out through the main gates of Buck House, scattering Japanese tourists before it, much to the mirth of the monarch who made soul-fists with her waving hand.

Perhaps.

Mr Mull, of Kintyre Cars, was not one given to familiarity with his clients. The conveyance of the public was in his blood: five generations of Mulls had plied their trade in the great metropolis before him, His great-great-grandfather driving one of the original hansom

---

★ And as one who does not wish for one's books to go the way of Jade's perfume *Ssssh!,* in my personal opinion it *never* happened!

cabs. His name was Morris Mull and he was the first cabby to coin the phrase, 'I had that [fill in as applicable] in the back of my cab the other day'. But this only to a fellow cabbie and never to a client. *He* was a professional, and such was his great-great-grandson.

And so when Mr Mull, of Kintyre Cars, reached the secret rendezvous point where he was to make contact with and pick up a certain Ahab the A-rab (the sheik of the desert sands), he arrived early and waited patiently, reading a Sunday paper whose headline spoke fearfully of escalating trouble in the Middle East and the strong probability of an ensuing nuclear holocaust. And, whilst doing this, he chewed on a Google's gob gum (of a type one rarely sees nowadays) and gently tapped a highly polished boot heel in the dust.

The dust was that of the dockland persuasion, of that area of London dockland that is always threatened with redevelopment but somehow always manages to remain undeveloped. And disgusting, and desolate, and depressing. And other things that begin with the letter 'D'.

The limo was parked on a dock that was to be found upon a bit of bay. And it would have been of interest to fans of soul music to note that this was *the* very dock of the bay that Otis Redding had sat upon nearly five decades before.

And watched the ships coming in.

And the ships going out.

And things of a maritime nature generally.

The sound of a bosun's whistle alerted Mr Mull, who folded away his newspaper, spat out his gob gum, buffed his toecaps on the rear of opposing trouser legs, straightened his cap and saluted as a Thames lighter, piloted by a Thames lighterman, drew up alongside Otis's sitting area, and a bosun, all spiffed up in formal but outmoded livery, piped ashore a swarthy gentleman in the full Arabic attire: flowing robes, dishcloth hat and fan-belt wraparound.

Ahab the A-rab drew London breath up his nostrils and spoke with timbre through his beard. 'You are Mister Mall?' he enquired.

'*Mull*,' said Mr Mull. 'Mister *Mull*.'

'Mull,' said Ahab the A-rab. 'That is satisfactory. I was unreliably informed that I was to be collected and driven by a Jedi.'

'I *am* a Jedi,' said Mr Mull. 'At the last national census, it was discovered that more than twenty per cent of the nation listed their religion as Jedi.'

'The English,' went the A-rab, and he laughed. 'No wonder you never win the cricket.'

Mr Mull smiled professionally and nodded politely. Had such a remark been made to him in a pub, however, by some bloody camel-jockey that he wasn't being employed to drive, Mr Mull would have employed his Dimac and struck the blighter mighty blows to the skull.

As naturally one would.

But, smiling and nodding, he now swung open the rear door of the limo and did a little bowing of the head also as he aided his client into the car.

A similar, in fact all but identical limo, stood double-parked in Neasden, in a tiny cul-de-sac that it was going to be difficult to reverse out of. This limo was surrounded by small boys with sticky, inquisitive fingers and orange-juice mouth-masks (whatever they might be).

The driver of this car, a Mr Jones, of We'll Keep a Welcome in the Hillside Motors' was no lover of small boys. Of small girls, yes, and of sheep, of course, for he was Welsh.* Mr Jones owned a stick for such occasions as this (and a tube of lubricant for other situations).

In the manner, indeed, of a Jedi (for curiously enough this *was* the faith of Mr Jones) he flourished this stick Jedi-fashion, swirling it in great Lightsabre arcs to a lack of alarm and distress of the sticky-fingered lads.

Whilst he awaited his client.

His client, Mr Bagshaw, was saying goodbye to his mum. Although aged thirty-seven and with good prospects in the field of account-ancy, Mr Bagshaw (Billy, it would have been to his mates, but mates Mr Bagshaw had none) still occupied the bedroom that had been forever his, in the family house that he had grown up in. As well as having no friends, Billy, as he would have been called if he had, had also never owned to a girlfriend. Had never kissed a woman.

This might have been due in part to the slightly odd looks of Mr

* According to Anne Robinson. Allegedly.

Bagshaw. There was something about his head. The size of it. The dimensions. That head was much too big. It was a bit of a Gerry Anderson head. It made Mr Bagshaw look very much like Brains from *Thunderbirds*.

Not that all women are necessarily put off by a huge head.

Many women have no objection to any part of a man's body being huge. As long as it's clean.

And Mr Bagshaw *was* very clean. His mum had scrubbed his neck that very morning. And behind his ears. And made him clean his teeth *twice*, as he'd missed some hard-to-reach plaque the first time, which his mum had espied with the aid of a dentist's mirror that she'd won at a WI whist drive in Crawley.

Mr Bagshaw's clothes were clean. His tweed going-out jacket, with the leather patches on the elbows, was *very* clean. As was his checked shirt and knitted tie. And his light-brown corduroy trousers and his polished Oxford brogues.

Mr Bagshaw's mother did unnecessary straightenings of her son's tie, then licked a corner of her gingham housecoat and worried at his chin with it. Then lightly kissed him on the cheek, warned him against associating with liquor and loose women (as so many mums will do, because they care) and sent him on his way.

Mr Bagshaw stepped lightly down the garden path, for his mother had cautioned him many times against dragging his feet – 'It looks slovenly and it plays havoc with your Stick-a-Soles'. He swung open the nineteen-thirties sun-ray-style gate and made his way towards the waiting limo.

Mr Jones waved frantically with his stick.

Mrs Bagshaw closed the front door without slamming it.

Mr Bagshaw gazed at the sticky lads.

The sticky lads caught Mr Bagshaw's gaze.

Some of these lads immediately pissed their pants.

Others, with stronger constitutions, did not.

But *all* before the gaze of Mr Bagshaw fled immediately and as fast as they could.

'Shall we away?' asked Mr Bagshaw of Mr Jones.

And Mr Jones, holding on to himself, nodded and said, 'Yes, *sir*.'

Mogador Firesword, of Dragonslayer Car Hire (he had recently changed the name to avoid confusion with the breakfast cereal), never called any man 'sir', but for Lord Gort Phnargos of the Bloody Axe, who slew Rimor Gartharion on the Plain of the Guckmo Plit, neath the Mountains of Mahagadoom, where might be found, but never entered, the Cave of the Hideous Cagoules.

And so on and so forth and suchlike.

He called no man '*sir*'.

And he wore chain mail beneath his chauffeur's uniform.

And now he was *here*! On a *Sunday morning*!

Come to pick up—

A *dog*!

'A dog?' said Mogador Firesword to the very pleasant-looking lady who womanned the reception desk at Battersea Dogs' Home. 'I am apparently here to pick up a dog.'

'Then you've come to the right place,' said the not-altogether-ungorgeous young woman. 'For this is a dogs' home.'

'I understand *that*,' said Mogador Firesword. 'I'll bet you have hundreds of dogs here, don't you?'

'Hundreds,' said the beautiful lady. 'Sometimes thousands.'

'And I'll bet you don't find homes for all of them.'

'Sadly not.'

'So you have to snuff them out, I suppose.'

'We *put them to sleep*. That is the term we prefer.'

'But it amounts to the same thing.'

The stunning creature nodded.

'Do you chop their heads off?' asked Mogador Firesword.

'No, we certainly do *not*.'

'Would you like me to do it for you, then? I do have my own sword. I call it Soul Freer the Second'

'Soul Freer the Second?'

'Soul Freer the First got nicked at a gamers con in Hinkley.'

'Would you please leave the premises before I am forced to call the police?' asked the veritable goddess of a bird.

'I have a chitty,' said Mogador, flourishing same, 'for the dog. And you'll have to fill in another chitty, taking responsibility and to cover any cleaning bills if it craps in my limo.'

The Battersea Venus examined the chitty. 'Ah,' she said knowingly. 'You want Bob. I understand.'

'More than I do, my pretty,' said Mogador, leaning over the desk a little to cop a glimpse of cleavage.

'Bob,' said the wondrous one. 'Bob the Comical Pup.'

'That's what it says on the chitty.'

The breasts before him withdrew. 'Wait here and I will fetch him for you. But before I do, you have to fill in one of *our* chitties.'

'Why?' asked Mogador Firesword.

'Because Bob the Comical Pup is not just any young comical pup. He is a pup of outré abilities.'

'Outré, what?'

A chitty on a clipboard was thrust before him and Mogador Firesword gave it a cursory once-over.

'What's this?' he asked. 'Promise Three: *I vow that I will take to my grave any confidences confided in me by Bob the Comical Pup*? And I have to sign the Official Secrets Act?'

'I told you he's not just any young comical pup.'

Mr Esau Good of Smack My Bitch Up Motors was not at Brize Norton Airport to pick up just any old King of rock 'n' roll.

He was there, in the company of many, many official chitties, and high-security passes, and special military intervention, to pick up *the* King of rock 'n' roll.

Being flown in on a chartered Hercules via a complex route that evaded the defensive radar systems of twelve separate countries. Point of departure, unregistered. Point of arrival, Brize Norton.

Mr Esau Good had also had to sign the Official Secrets Act and he had been given an implant at the base of his skull. He had been assured by the masked surgeons who had performed this procedure against the will of Mr Good that should Mr Good mention the name of the gentleman that he would be conveying to Gunnersbury Park, even in passing, the voicing of this name would trigger the implant and blow his head clean off his shoulders.

Mr Good was somewhat upset by this circumstance, especially as he was something of a fan of the Big E and not averse to purchasing the occasional compilation disc or latest exploitation hit single.*

Christmas shopping was going to be tricky this year.

* Elvisploitation?

★

The Hercules Transport loomed in the heavens. Drew nigh unto Brize Norton and descended. Taxiing was done, steps were wheeled out to it, a door swung open.

And *he* stood framed by the opening.

And *he* wasn't that fat anymore. He was, if anything, slender and trim. His hair, the jettest of blacks, his sideburns superb and his cheekbones as killer as ever. He *did* wear the jumpsuit, though – the white rhinestoned number with the black diamanté belt. But then he *would* wear that, wouldn't he? Because he *was* Elvis Presley.

Mr Esau Good lifted his bum from the bonnet of his limo and made his way towards the grounded aeroplane.

There were many of those Men in Black types present, with the black suits and the sunspecs. And many high-ranking military personnel. And what surprised Mr Good, if anything *could* now surprise him, was the fact that all those present were so unsurprised.

That Elvis was alive and well and looking good surprised them not.

But then, come on now, none of us *really* believes that he's dead. Do we?

Mr Good had never believed it. He knew that something fishy had gone on that day, in that bathroom, at Graceland.

Rumours abounded and no more so than within the hire-car profession, where chauffeurs are apt to 'accidentally overhear' all manner of sensitive information and a certain underground grapevine spreads this info up and down the land. The word was out that Elvis' death had been faked because the King of rock 'n' roll was engaged in work of national importance and that the President himself had sanctioned the deception.

The word was out on the underground grapevine that Elvis was capable of travelling through time, aided by an alien vegetable that had taken up residence in the back of his head. Barry the Time Sprout, this vegetable was called.

And who would be inclined to doubt this?

Elvis descended from the plane, pressed palms with assembled personages and was led to the limo.

'Good day, sir,' said Elvis to Mr Good.

'Good day, Mr——' and he almost said it.

Elvis Presley entered the limo and was driven away.

43

Driven.

As in a driven soul.

When, in the early eighteen hundreds, John Haslam, the doctor in overall control of St Mary of Bethlehem Asylum, interviewed the inmate James Tilly Matthews regarding his extraordinary claims that his mind was under almost constant assault by magnetic emanations delivered to him via the medium of an Air Loom, Mr Matthews was able to supply Mr Haslam with a wealth of specific information.

He explained to Haslam that 'the apparatus, called by the assassins that manipulate it an Air Loom machine or pneumatic machine, might be said, in part, to resemble a kneehole or partners' desk, although magnified in size. In bigness it would appear some nine feet in length, six in height and another seven in depth. Large drawers to either side of it and between something like piano-forte keys, which open tube valves within the Air Loom to spread or feed the warp of magnetic fluid. To either side of these keys, levers by which the assailed is wrenched, stagnated, and the sudden-death efforts made upon him.

'Above, are a cluster of upright open glass tubes, which the assassins term their *musical glasses*. These are of extreme importance, for within these the magnetic fluxes condense and are dispelled. I am given to understand that these glasses are of a fragility and a volatility wherein explosive forces are pent. I could never ascertain what the bulky upper parts were, although I discerned paddle – or windmill-like attachments, but the barrels I saw distinctly, witnessing the famous gooseneck retorts, which supply the Air Loom with the distilled gasses, as well as the poisoned magnetics.

'The preparations within these barrels are of the most dreadful content. Sexual fluid, both male and female, effluvia of copper, ditto of sulphur, vapours of vitriol and aqua fortis, belladonna and hellebore, effluvia of dogs, stinking human breath, putrid effluvia of mortification and the plague, stench of the cesspool, gaz from the anus of a horse, human gaz, gaz from a horse's greasy heels, Egyptian snuff (this is a dusty vapour, extremely nauseous), poison of toad, otto of roses.'

He also furnished Haslam with a catalogue of terrible torments that the manipulators of this hellish contrivance were able to visit upon their sorry and magnetized victims, via the medium of a flux projected through the ether from machine to unfortunate target.

Space forbids the inclusion of all, but a sample should be sufficient to convince the reader of the horrors involved.

Fluid-Locking: A locking or constriction of the fibres of the root of the tongue, whereby the readiness of speech is impeded.

Stone-Making: The sensation that a precipitation exists within the bladder, as it were a stone or obstruction.

Kiteing: This is a very singular and distressing mode of assailment, much practised by the Gang, in which ideas that are alien to the victim are kited, or floated, into his head by means of the magnetic impregnations. The idea that is kited keeps waving in his mind and he becomes incapable of concentrating upon any other.

Lobster-Cracking: The external pressure of the magnetic atmosphere surrounding the victim is increased in order to stagnate his circulation, impede the vital motions and produce instant death.

Other equally terrifying torments include: **Stomach–Skinning, Lengthening the Brain, Thought–Making, Bladder–Filling, Gaz–Plucking, Bomb–Bursting, Apoplexy–Working, Thigh–Talking** and **Cutting Soul from Sense**.

It has been argued with vigour, by those who value the currency of present-day psychiatry above that of intuition, that Matthews was a paranoid schizophrenic who had created a delusional architecture of considerable detail, sufficient indeed to convince anyone other than the doctors who attended him, but was nonetheless, to these doctors, a stone bonker when it came right down to it.

Hence Mr Matthews's twelve-year incarceration in Bedlam,

regarding which it was fairly stated that, 'If you're not mad when they commit you, you soon will be.'

So, some things never change.

Logic informed the keepers of Bedlam that a device such as the Air Loom could not possibly exist. And the reason that such a device could *not* exist was because a device such as an Air Loom could not possibly exist.

These doubters of the Air Loom's reality based their doubts upon a number of premises. The technology to create an Air Loom did not exist. The madness of Matthews was, however, a symptom of an age of wonders, an age of scientific breakthroughs, of new and awesome machines. Of the animal magnetism of Mesmer. Of electrical experimentation. Of a general paranoia sweeping the nation, its flames stoked by the French Revolution. A fear of spies. The 'Reds Under the Beds' of the day. The fear of the new.

Everywhere were quack doctors and crazy scientists. Experimentation – magical, magnetical, metaphysical.

Why, it was enough to drive the sanest fellow mad.

There was just too much of it about.

And so Matthews, a somewhat excitable fellow by nature, had got an electrical, magnetical, pneumatic bee in his bonnet. He had gone off the rails.

He was, indeed, a stone bonker.

And what made James Tilly Matthews memorable was that he was the first recorded mental patient who claimed that voices were being put into his head through the medium of an Influencing Machine.

When it comes to paranoid-schizophrenic conspiracy-nuts, James Tilly Matthews was Patient Zero.

So that explains that, really.

In a nutcase, as it were.

'As it were.' Count Otto Black pulled out one of the organ-stop jobbies atop the piano forte keyboard of the Air Loom, adjusted something that might very well have been a flux capacitor and trotted out a well-loved chestnut kind of jobbie: 'The greatest trick the Devil ever played,' said the count, with a suitable cackle, 'was to convince Mankind that he doesn't exist.'

His partners-in-crime nodded grimly. Jack the Schoolmaster muttered obscenities and the Glove Woman placed a sheet of what might have been music on a stand above the organ stops and fluttered her gloved fingers over the Air Loom keyboard.

'We have the music, we have,' she said. 'And we will play, so we will.'

'And triumph,' said the count. 'As I may have mentioned.'

A knock came at the storeroom door and this knock went unanswered. A knock came again, a coded knock. A dwarf in a feathered bonnet answered this.

'I crave entrance,' came a female's voice.

'Under whose star?' came the reply from the count.

'Under the Master's star, which is Sirius in the ascendant.'

'Enter, Sister, and be recognised to all.'

The female entered the underground chamber. A somewhat crowded chamber, this. 'You have all that you require?' she enquired of the count.

'We could do with some beer,' said Jack the Schoolmaster.

'And crisps,' said the Glove Woman.

'I'll send out for both and more.' The female smiled upon the assembled company. The female had a certain air about her. As of authority. And she was a good-looker, too, what with the very nice breasts, the gorgeous green eyes and the really sweet nose.

'The barrels, I see, have arrived,' said Countess Vanda. And she wafted over to Count Otto and kissed him tenderly.

'Indeed, my countess,' said that man. 'Filled to the specification of formula, as I requested, I trust.'

'Indeed, yes. Heavy on the gaz from a horse's anus. Not to mention the toe jam.'

There was a pregnant pause, there was, but no one mentioned the toe jam.

'Lovely,' said the count, and he took Countess Vanda in his arms and kissed her passionately.

'I'd like a little of *that*.' Jack the schoolmaster smirked .

A dwarf tittered into his hand.

Count Otto Black turned upon Jack, whose face took fear in the candlelight.

'We will be done here this day,' said he. 'And when we're done we'll stay done for another century if need be, till we're called on again once more to do our duty. Oh, but tonight we shall dance and make merry and drink and imbibe strange drugs and lie together in filthy congregation.'

'I shall not nay-say to that,' said Jack.

'But for now know your manners, my lad.'

'I will, sir, my lord, sir, I will.'

'Just so.'

Countess Vanda smiled up at Count Otto Black. 'The Parliament of Five are on their way here,' she said. 'They should arrive within the hour. The talks are scheduled to begin at twelve. The Loom will be in full operating order by that hour, I assume.'

'How could it be otherwise, my love?'

'Nicely, nicely,' said the countess. 'This must all be done to a nicety. And none must know of our doing.'

'None *ever* know,' said Count Otto. 'And those who do are declared mad and committed to the madhouse. Such as it ever was, for some things never change.'

'Nicely, nicely,' said the countess once more.

'For how could it be otherwise?' said Count Otto Black. 'We control those who control the controllers. Bliss that is and the way it should be. And who—'

And he raised his voice and did laughings.

'Who might there be who can stop us?'

44

Jonny Hooker made some shapes and one heroic pose.

'And what, pray tell me, is *that* supposed to be?'

Jonny Hooker ignored Mr Giggles and flexed a muscle or two.

'And *that*? What was *that*? What are *those* supposed to be?'

'Those are muscles,' said Jonny, giving his arm a bit of a squeeze and only flinching a little. 'And I am throwing, as it were, a heroic pose.'

'Right,' said Mr Giggles. 'And for why?'

'You know for why – because I am going into battle against the forces of evil. A lone warrior. Heroic, and alone.'

Mr Giggles wrinkled his nose. 'And more than just a bit niffy,' he observed.

Jonny Hooker did armpit sniffing. 'It didn't help, you having me put this uniform in the dustbin,' said he.

'It's not a good look,' said Mr Giggles. 'And the sticking plaster all over your face. And that cap doesn't suit you at all. At least take off the cap.'

And Jonny Hooker made the face that says, 'Yeah right.' And continued to make it as he marched out of the alleyway, down his garden path and out of his front garden.

'You won't get in,' said Mr Giggles, diddling about with his fez and padding along beside Jonny. 'Into the park. You won't get in. There's far too much security. Blokes in black uniforms, guard posts, uniforms, gun nests. Let's go down to the pub.'

'The pub won't be open,' said Jonny.

'And how could you know that?'

'I know *that*,' said Jonny, 'because, even as we speak, O'Fagin the landlord is upstairs in my house, knobbing my mum.'

'Oh, please,' said Mr Giggles, hiding his face with his fez. 'Not an image I want imprinted upon my soul. But you can't know *that*, surely.'

'I saw him sneaking in,' said Jonny. 'I think he and my mum have been doing the nasty for quite some time. I'm sorry that I didn't really get to shag his wife.'

'Why don't we go back and listen at the bedroom door?' asked Mr Giggles. 'Perhaps I was a little hasty. It might be fun.'

'I think I'll just get on with the fighting the forces of evil,' said Jonny. 'If it's all right with you.'

'It's *not* all right with me. You know it's not all right with me.'

'You go and listen at the door, then. I'm off to Gunnersbury Park.'

'But,' went Mr Giggles. 'But-but-but—'

'But me no buts,' said Constable Justice.

'I wasn't going to,' said Constable Paul. 'Why did you think that I would?'

'I thought you might have some objection to me breaking down the door to the saloon bar and us helping ourselves to O'Fagin's beer.'

Constable Paul did shruggings. 'You won't find me complaining about *that*,' said he. 'I'll have my usual, a Guinness without the head.'

'You'll do no such bloody thing.' A hand fell upon the shoulder of Paul. Another on that of Constable Justice. The left shoulder, it was. The hands adjoined arms (separate arms). These arms terminated at shoulders. These shoulders belonged, as did all the other bodily bits and bobs (one bob in particular was now a trifle sore as it had recently been engaged in the sexual pursuit known as 'Taking Tea with the Parson') belonged to a certain Inspector Westlake.

The Inspector Westlake, in fact.

In case there was any confusion.

'Any confusion?' asked Inspector Westlake.

'None whatever, sir,' said Constable Justice.

Constable Paul just nodded.

'Good,' said the inspector, 'because there will be no on-duty drinkies this morning. We are on duty, for Queen and country. We have business that awaits us in Gunnersbury Park.'

'But we just came from there, sir,' said Constable Justice, edging himself away from the inspector's hand. 'Those bastards from Special Ops won't let us into the park.'

Inspector Westlake made a face that was both grim and determined. A forceful combination. 'As long as I have breath in my body,' he declared, and he placed a hand upon his heart, 'I shall defend this green and sceptical island of ours. We *shall* enter that park. We *shall* do our duty.'

'And I shall do mine,' whispered Jonny, who lay in hiding near at hand and had overheard the conversation.

'And you think that if you follow these nitwits, you might be able to sneak into the park?' Mr Giggles didn't whisper. He shouted very, very loudly.

'Will you shut up!' Jonny shushed him into silence. 'They might not be able to get in, but they might create a diversion sufficient for me to slip by.'

'It will all end in tears.' And Mr Giggles mimed weepings. 'Let's just head for the hills.'

'The hills are alive with the sound of music,' sang Mogador Firesword who, when not either driving the limo or fantasy gaming, numbered amateur theatricals and light opera *and* the history of musical cinema amongst his interests. The latter being the subject he hoped to specialise in if he ever got the opportunity to appear on *Mastermind*.

'Put a sock in it,' called Bob the Comical Pup.

Mogador Firesword put in the sock. And a chill ran down his spine. That dog really *did* speak. It wasn't some ventriloquist's dummy, or remotely controlled toy, as he had supposed when finally, his many forms filled in and signed, he'd been allowed to receive Bob into his company and accept that the Comical Pup was now under his personal protection. And should anything happen to the pooch – the beautiful young woman behind the reception desk had drawn her finger across her throat and mimed death. And she did it with a great deal more conviction and skill than Mr Giggles mimed weepings.

Although Mogador wasn't to know *that*.

So Mogador Firesword put in the sock and got a bit of a sweat on.

'Are we nearly there yet?' asked Bob, bobbing up and down on a rear seat. 'Only I really need to lift my leg and it would be a shame to taint your upholstery.'

'Not far now,' said Mogador Firesword. 'Less than half a mile. It's just past that wrecked pub on the right.'

'About half a mile and closing.' The voice of Thompson was in the ear-bead jobbie of Constable Cartwright. Constable Cartwright and Constable Rogers now sat in the big truck that had conveyed them from Mornington Crescent. The truck with the very special SatNav.

'I see them,' said Constable Cartwright, tinkering with this very special SatNav. 'Five limos approaching along Pope's Lane. And yes, I can see the heat signatures of the occupants. Who's in the first one, though? A driver and what? A tiny person in the back?'

'It's a dog,' said Thompson.

'Perhaps it's Bullet,' said Constable Rogers.

'Bullet?' said Constable Cartwright.

'Roy Rogers' dog. He had a horse called Trigger and a dog called Bullet.'

'He never did. I thought Rin Tin Tin was his dog.'

'Not a bit of it – Rin Tin Tin was very much his own dog. A bit like the Littlest Hobo. Same make of dog, the ever-popular Alsatian, or German shepherd as it's now known. Now that it's not so ever-popular. Although I don't think the one in the back of the limo looks anything like a German shepherd. Don't they wear leather shorts with bells on?'

There as a moment of silence.

Eventually this moment passed.

'Constable Rogers,' came the voice of Thompson into the ear of Rogers.

'Yes, sir?' said that constable.

'Never mind,' said Thompson. 'How are the invisibility suits, by the way? Everything hunky-dory?'

The headless Constable Rogers regarded his legless colleague. 'Working a treat, sir,' was all he had to say.

★

Jonny Hooker said nothing. He had watched the five limousines pass The Middle Man. He felt it reasonable to assume that they were heading for Gunnersbury Park.

Jonny now watched as the traffic lights at the crossing ahead turned red and a lady in a straw hat, dragging a packing case behind her, took to crossing the road. And then Jonny ducked down as Constable Paul, Constable Justice and Inspector Westlake took off towards the rear limousine at the hurry-up.

'And hurry up, do,' said Inspector Westlake. '*I* am in charge of security. *Me*. I.' And he urged the constables forward. Across the pavement, into the road.

And he tore open the passenger door of the nearest limo.

'Westlake!' he shouted at the passenger within. 'Head of Security. These are my constables. Get in, lads.'

And with that he was in.

Just like that.

Much to the great surprise of Elvis.

The lady in the straw hat really was having a great deal of trouble with that heavy packing case. And when the lights turned green, the drivers of the limos took to hooting their horns. And then a couple of them got out and gave her a hand.

The lady thanked them very much and bade them the best for the day.

'What was all *that* about?' asked Mr Giggles the Monkey Boy.

'That was what is called a fortuitous circumstance,' said Jonny Hooker. 'Fortuitous circumstances do sometimes occur when good people require them to.'

'They are a stranger to me,' said Mr Giggles.

'And formerly to me,' said Jonny, 'but as you can see, or in fact *cannot* see, on this occasion the fortuitous circumstance has served me well.'

'Indeed I *cannot* see,' said Mr Giggles, 'what with it being so dark in here and everything. Inside the boot of the very last limo in the line, which you slipped into whilst the fortuitous circumstance on the crossing was diverting attention, as it were.'

And Jonny Hooker smiled.

To himself. And in darkness.

And the limos rolled on. And turned into Gunnersbury Park. Passed through the security at the North Gate and rolled forward to stop in a nice neat line outside the Big House.

And Countess Vanda stepped out from the Big House to welcome the Parliament of Five. The Secret Government of the world.

And she solemnly greeted and solemnly shook the hand of each in turn. Or the paw, in the case of Bob the Comical Pup.

And when the greeting and the hand/paw shakings were done, the Parliament of Five entered the Big House for their secret meeting. In the company of Constable Paul, Constable Justice and Inspector Westlake. Whose hands had also been shaken by the countess.

And each of them who entered the Big House now had a hand (or a paw) that was thoroughly magnetized.

And Jonny Hooker bided his time and kept a cool head on his shoulders. And when he felt that sufficient time had elapsed for it to be safe to do so, he flipped up the boot lid and stepped from the limo.

To be met by an array of fearsome guns.

All of which were aimed at his head.

45

Jonny Hooker was genuinely scared. As well he might have been, considering.

Considering that he now found himself in one of the coal cellars beneath the Big House, tied naked but for his cap and Elastoplast face furniture to a bentwood chair and under interrogation.

And under interrogation, it appeared, by two supernatural beings.

Devils, or angels? Ghosts or divers booger men? Jonny wasn't certain. But he was a-feared.

The monster without the legs, who just sort of floated about, appeared to be the leader. The headless horror was pretty scary, too. Scarier, really, because *he* didn't have a head.

'Cough up, you Islamic rotter!' demanded the headless one. Somehow. 'Where have you hidden the explosives?'

'Explosives?' asked Jonny. 'Islamic?' asked Jonny. 'Are you the living dead?' he also asked.

The creature without the legs smiled at Jonny.

'Special Ops,' he said. 'Hence the state-of-the-art camouflage.' He pointed to the visible part of himself. He had lots of little solar-panel jobbies all over this. 'And you'll never get your fundamentalist fingers on any of it.'

Jonny Hooker didn't know what to say.

'Have you swallowed them?' asked the legless being.

Jonny Hooker *still* didn't know what to say.

'The explosives! Are you a walking bomb?'

'Only one way to find out,' said the headless entity. 'Cut him open and check out his guts.'

Jonny Hooker now knew what to say. 'No,' he said. Indeed, he wailed this word. 'I'm not a terrorist, if that's what you think I am. I'm a park ranger. I work here.'

'A likely tale,' said he without a bonce. 'We copped you on our special state-of-the-art SatNav, sneaking into the rear of the rear limo. You're dealing with the A-Team here – nothing slips by us.'

'Are you alive?' Jonny asked.

'Of course we're bloody alive. What is the matter with you?'

'Probably drugged up,' said another fellow, this one also in black and with the little solar-cell jobbies all over his person. 'They snort Es and rub crack into their genitals to give them courage. There's a website about it.'

There was another of those silences.

'I found it by accident,' said Constable Cassidy, for it was he. 'I was looking for porn. Honest.'

'You're policemen,' said Jonny.

'Of course we're policemen,' said Constable Cartwright. And, 'Ouch,' he continued, as he bumped his invisible knee into a visible table. 'I keep doing that.'

Constable Rogers tittered. 'The question that troubles me,' he said, 'is whether I have my helmet on, or off.'

'I thought you wore a cap,' said Constable Cartwright. 'I know I do. Although I'm no longer certain what colour my socks are.'

'You're definitely policemen,' said Jonny.

'We are Special Operations policemen,' said Constable Cassidy, 'and we'll get the truth from you if we have to torture you to death first.'

'*Definitely* policemen,' said Jonny, with some relief.

'So,' said Constable Rogers, 'do you want to tell us where the explosives are hidden, or should I apply my cigarette lighter to your private parts?'

Inspector Westlake was in parts private. He was inside the Big House, which was something. And he *had* met Elvis, which was *really* something. But he did have a job of work to do and as yet he was still getting *no* cooperation.

'*You* know I'm in charge, don't you?' he asked Joan.

Joan was on the reception desk in the entrance hall, which looked all spick and span again, because the late Henry Hunter's assistant had worked really hard on it.

'I normally don't work Sundays,' said Joan, and she yawned,

'because if I've struck lucky during Saturday night's clubbing, I usually spend Sunday morning banging away like there's no tomorrow.'

Inspector Westlake raised an eyebrow.

'And don't come all that with me,' said Joan. 'Mrs Hayward is a good friend of mine, and she phoned me earlier to tell me what you and her had been up to this morning. Which is a Sunday, please note.'

Inspector Westlake groaned.

'Exactly,' said Joan. 'Would you like a cup of tea? I've brought my flask.'

'No tea.' Inspector Westlake made fists. 'I'm supposed to be in charge of this secret operation.'

'Did you see that funny little pup that came in here?' Joan asked. 'Dogs aren't normally allowed, you know.'

'I saw the dog,' said the inspector, 'and I saw the Queen. I was commissioned to take on this responsibility by the Queen.'

'And isn't Elvis looking well?'

'Oh, so *that's* who he was,' said Constable Paul. 'I thought it was Gary Glitter.'

The sun went behind Heartbreak Hotel and a hound dog howled in the distance.

But it wasn't Bob the Comical Pup. He was having a nap.

The Queen had Bob asleep on her knee. The Queen and the other members of the Parliament of Five were in the antechamber next door to Princess Amelia's sitting room, where the secret talks were soon to be held. It was where VIPs drank cuppas before big talks got going. The Queen was having a cuppa. Mr Bagshaw was having a cuppa. Ahab the A–rab was having a cuppa. Elvis Presley was having a cuppa, and he had no sugar in his.

'I have to be careful of sugar,' he told Mr Bagshaw. 'And fatty acids, of course. And anything that isn't high in polyunsaturates. And I always use that L'Oréal on my hair, because I'm worth it.'

'Of course you are,' said Mr Bagshaw.

'*Your* hair looks very clean, sir' said Elvis.

'Head and Shoulders,' said Mr Bagshaw. '"Frequent use" – it contains its own conditioner. So I can just wash and go, as it were. It's ideal for a playboy about town such as myself.'

'I see,' said Elvis. 'But I suppose it must take quite a long time for you to wash your hair, what with you having such a huge head and everything. No offence meant, of course, sir.'

'None taken, I assure you.'

'We have Our own special shampoo,' said Her Majesty, tickling the sleeping Bob's earhole, 'made for We by a little man in Piccadilly. It's very exclusive, contains virgins' milk, and the poo from a wooden horse, and hens' teeth and all that kind of business. And of course We don't have to pay for it, because We never carry money.'

Elvis made with the nodding head.

Mr Bagshaw, too.

'I *never* use a shampoo,' said Ahab the A-rab. 'We dodgy, swarthy Middle Eastern types have little truck with hygiene, as you better-educated Western folk must all know. When we're not out buggering the Bedouin, we're to be found at home in our tents hating Americans and watching reruns of *Father Ted*.'

Elvis Presley nodded again. 'Do they dub *Father Ted*?' he asked, 'or do you have subtitles?'

'Dubbed,' said Ahab, 'by the Islamic TV service. Some of the jokes about George Bush are a bit near the mark, but the overall message that there is no God but Allah never fails to hit the spot.'

'I once met the lady who plays Mrs Doyle,' said Her Majesty the Queen. 'She's much younger in real life and she doesn't have those moles on her face.'

'The moles aren't real?' said Ahab.

'Stuck on,' said Her Madge. 'Made of Maltesers, or something.'

Ahab the A-rab stroked at his beard. 'You have sorely disillusioned me,' he said, sadly and sorely, in a disillusioned tone. 'The moles are my favourite bit, after the sayings of Muhammad, peace be unto His name.'

'More tea?' asked Countess Vanda, moving amongst them with the teapot.

Those who wanted more signalled in the affirmative.

Those who didn't did not.

'Any more of those custard creams?' asked Mr Bagshaw.

★

'Any more of those custard creams.' Count Otto Black mimicked the words of Mr Bagshaw. Count Otto Black and his Air Loom Gang saw all. Saw all and heard all and soon would control all. 'Magnetized as ripe as ninepence,' said the count, pulling out an organ-stop jobbie or two, twiddling a dial, adjusting a stopcock on a barrel and giving a slender glass conducting tube a gentle rap with his knuckle. 'Soon they will move to the conference room and we will adjust their thoughts to our choosing.'

His evil cohorts clapped their hands.

'I never got my crisps,' said Jack.

'I never have been, am not now and never will be a terrorist,' said Jonny Hooker. 'Please don't toast my nuts. I'll tell you anything you want to hear. Anything. And if I don't know an answer I'll make one up.'

'I don't think that's how it's supposed to work,' said Constable Cartwright.

'I think it's pretty much how it always works with torture,' said Constable Rogers. 'Your torture victim is usually in such great pain and under such mental duress that they'll say anything to stop the agony.'

'So what is the point of torture?' asked Constable Cartwright.

He didn't see Constable Rogers smile. 'The fun of it,' he heard him say.

'Listen,' said Jonny, 'I'll own up. I'll tell you everything.'

'Don't be too hasty,' said Constable Rogers. 'You wouldn't want to give up without a bit of a fight, surely.'

'I would,' said Jonny. 'I know when I'm licked.'

There was another moment of silence.

But it soon passed.

'Tell us everything,' said Constable Cartwright.

'Fair enough,' said Jonny. 'But could I have my uniform back first?'

'When you've told us everything.'

'All right.' And so Jonny began. And Jonny told the constables everything. Every single thing. Right from the very beginning. About the Da–da–de–da–da Code that he thought he could crack. How it had left a trail of headless corpses behind, and how he had learned that the Air Loom (which he had to explain about in considerable detail because none of the constables had ever heard of such a thing) was going to be put into operation, to influence the dignitaries taking part in the secret talks. And every single other thing that Jonny could possibly think of that might have any relevance at all. Including how he had got to play Robert Johnson's guitar.

And when he was done with all this, there was another silence. And quite an intense silence it was.

And when that silence was finally broken, it was broken by the sound of policemen's boots upon a cobbled coal-cellar floor. Leaving at speed. Leaving Jonny all alone.

'I don't really think they believed a word of what you told them,' said Mr Giggles to Jonny.

'Apart from the last bit,' Jonny said.

'Oh yes, they went for the last bit. About how you were an undercover Special Operations policeman disguised as a park ranger, who had followed Inspector Westlake, who is really none other than Osama bin Laden with his beard shaved off, to this very park, this very morning.'

'Well, it was a bit remiss of them not to notice on their SatNav two constables and an inspector appear inside that other limo.'

'And Inspector Westlake *is* a bit of a twat.'

'That too. So do your stuff.'

'My stuff?' said Mr Giggles.

'Your metaphysical stuff,' said Jonny. 'Untie my hands so I can make my escape.'

'I can't do untyings,' said Mr Giggles. 'I'm a non-corporeal companion.'

'Yet you pulled the plug from the amps on Friday night, to spare myself and the band from being sucked into – where? Hell? For playing Robert Johnson's final song.'

'I did nothing of the kind,' said Mr Giggles.

'Oh yes you did,' said Jonny. 'Now untie my hands and I promise I'll leave the park at once and never return.'

'You promise?' said Mr Giggles. 'Scouts' honour? On your mother's life and may your nads be nailed to a butcher's block if you're telling a porkie pie?'

'Would *I* lie to *you*?'

46

There was some unpleasantness, but then there always is. An unpleasantness born of misunderstanding, or more often misinformation.

The constables from Special Ops had clearly been misinformed. They had been misled, set on a wrong'n, led up the garden path, smoked like a kipper and told a porkie pie.

And when they set out to apprehend the debearded Osama, they went in a gung-ho fashion. And when they encountered the world's-most-wanted himself, chatting away at the reception desk, it seemed odds-on that a capture/detain/torture-to-extract-information/shoot-whilst-trying-to-escape scenario was well on the cards, as it were.

But this was not to be the case.

There was indeed some unpleasantness. Born indeed of misunderstanding. And also misidentification.

Constables Paul and Justice were more than just taken aback by the fellows in black who stormed out upon them. Fiends from the bottomless pit, as loosely predicted through the accurate reading of Kleenex tissues, Constable Paul supposed. What with the missing bodily bits and everything.

And there had been something of a firefight.

And it had come as something of a surprise to Constable Paul in particular just how powerful a bit of fire power was in the possession of Constable Justice.

It came as an even greater surprise to Constables Cartwright, Cassidy and Rogers, who took to an almost simultaneous surrender.

There was even more unpleasantness when Inspector Westlake ordered the blackly clad constables to divest themselves of their invisibility suits and pass them to *his* constables.

And it was with some degree of glee that Constables Paul and Justice put them on.

Then there was the matter of interrogation. Inspector Westlake demanded to be told exactly *why* he was being faced with a capture/detain/torture-to-extract-information/shoot-whilst-trying-to-escape scenario, when Constables Cartwright, Cassidy and Rogers had been introduced to him the previous day and each and every one had found each and every other's credentials to be of the A-OK persuasion.

The trail led back to Jonny Hooker.

And then there was even more unpleasantness when the constables in black led the other constables, who now came and went in their commandeered invisibility suits, along with Inspector Westlake, to the coal-cellar interrogation cell.

And when this cellar door, a substantial steely affair, was unlocked, it revealed nothing more nor less than an empty chamber.

Voices were raised again and smiles were not to be seen.

Jonny Hooker was smiling. But then Jonny Hooker had made good his escape. And he had done so, as might well have been expected – at least to those who had been following Jonny's adventures – via the medium of another secret passage.

'Free at last. Free at last. Sweet Tesco we are free at last,' sang Mr Giggles, somewhat enigmatically.

'Free for now,' said Jonny, 'but caution must be our watchword from now on.'

'Have to correct you there,' said Mr Giggles. 'Escape must be our watchword. Indeed our only word. Until we utter later words of the "that was a successful escape" variety.'

'Possibly so, when the time comes,' said Jonny Hooker. And he edged along another secret passage.

'Ah, no,' said Mr Giggles. 'It's up and away, my darling fellow. Like unto how you promised.'

'Oh, that,' said Jonny and edged along further.

'Yes, that,' protested Mr Giggles. '*That.* You swore. You promised—'

'I lied,' said Jonny. 'Get over it and move on.'

'I … I … I—' went Mr Giggles.

'You've lied to me often enough. I am merely returning the favour, as it were.'

'That doesn't make any sense, but no, *you* can't lie to *me*. That's not the way our relationship functions.'

'Our relationship does *not* function,' Jonny whispered. 'You manipulate me without shame or conscience. Now you have performed a service for me. We are even.'

'That is nonsense. That doesn't compute.'

'You can stick around and bother me, or you can leave me alone,' said Jonny. 'I no longer wish to communicate with you on any level. If you have my best interests at heart, which is to say *your* best interests, I would suggest that you depart at once. Your verbal meanderings may well distract me when I need my concentration to be at its most acute. This could easily result in my death at the finger of some trigger-happy constable. What think you of this?'

Mr Giggles made grumpy noises.

'I will not be distracted, or dissuaded,' said Jonny.

'But—' went Mr Giggles.

'I'm *not* listening.'

'But—'

'Are you going, or what?'

'I think I'll just stick around a tad longer,' said Mr Giggles.

'As you please.'

'So what are you going to do next?'

But Jonny didn't answer.

'Let Us answer the Call,' said Her Majesty the Queen, finishing her cuppa, dusting bickie crumbs from her chin and gently awakening Bob.

The Comical Pup did comical yawnings, dear little fellow that he was.

'Might I lead the way?' asked Countess Vanda.

'You do that, dear,' said Her Madge. 'It's all but twelve o'clock.'

The ormolu mantel clock chimed on the ormolu mantel. It had been a present to Sir Henry Crawford from Napoleon Bonaparte. It still kept perfect time.

The clock and the mantel were now to be seen as the lights had gone up in Princess Amelia's sitting room. Countess Vanda's desk and accoutrements had been removed to make way for a mighty conference table.

Surrounding this were five chairs. At the head of the table, Her Madge for the use of, a gorgeous gilded throne-type jobbie, which had been known to bums of royalty for more than two hundred years.

The Parliament of Five entered the room. Elvis cast longing eyes towards Her Madge's throne. For, after all, he *was* the King. Ahab the A-rab was rather taken with Sir Henry's mantel clock because, as he might have put it, 'We are simple desert people and such marvels of the West fill us with wonder.'

Bob the Comical Pup noted all the wastepaper baskets, reasoning that if he was caught short, at least he wouldn't be forced to piss on the carpet.

There were named place-setting cards upon the great table so that there would be no confusion, nor scrambling for particular seats.

Her Madge sat at the table's head, which was to the north.

To her left, on the eastern side of the table, Elvis, then Bob.

To her right, on the western side of the table, Ahab, then Mr Bagshaw.

At the southern end of the table, to read the minutes, take dictation, pop out for coffee, sweets, dog biscuits, etc., Countess Vanda.

When the Parliament of Five were seated, Countess Vanda closed and locked the door and took her place at table.

'Your Majesty,' she said.

Her Majesty nodded and smiled that smile of hers. The one she had been taught to smile by her mum. 'Thank you, dear,' she said and plucked from her cardigan sleeve a slip of paper. And then, she cleared her throat and read from it.

It was not the speech that she had been rehearsing earlier. This was a later, honed-down version, passed to her as she left the palace.

Why? Who can say?

Parliament of Five, (she read) we are gathered
here today upon matters of the gravest
import. Our intervention in world
matters we keep to the necessary

minimum. We steer the course of
nations by means of the influence we
can exert over those of high office
who we have placed there to act
in our interests. Which are to
say, the interests of all.

'Here, here,' went Mr Bagshaw.
'Where?' went Bob the Comical Pup.

'At present, (Her Madge continued) there exists in the
Middle East a state of tension.
There is fear and there is menace.
There is the ever-present danger of
escalation. That the spark might
ignite the powder keg and bring
about global confrontation. Indeed,
the possibility of global
extinction. The destruction of
the human race. We, the
Parliament of Five, must settle
this situation once and for all.

'Are we agreed upon *this*?' she concluded
'On *that* we are no doubt all in agreement,' said Ahab the A-rab.
'It is the manner in which this situation is to be settled that might be
a cause for disagreement.'
Mr Bagshaw went, 'Ahem.'
Her Madge said, 'Mister Bagshaw? Take the floor as you will, so
to speak.'
'Thank you, Ma'am.' Mr Bagshaw cleared his throat. 'Brother
Ahab, I believe, has some fears that we might consider a radical
solution a tenable option.'
'A radical solution?' queried Her Madge.
'A nuclear solution,' said Mr Bagshaw.
'Damn and tootin' right,' said Ahab. 'And naturally as a humble
tent-dweller with little or no education, ill-versed in the ways of
Western sophistication and force-fed a diet of vegetarian McDonald's

and kipper fillets, I concur that on the face of it, it is probably the best thing to do.'

'Oh,' said Mr Bagshaw. 'You do?'

'I have my mobile with me,' said Ahab. 'It's a Tesco mobile, and as a valued customer I have a free voicemail facility for three months. I can phone the Nuclear Command Centre in Baghdad and have a nuke shot over to wipe out Israel in less than half an hour.'

'Nuclear Command Centre in *Baghdad*?' said Bob the Comical Pup.

'It's a US thing,' said Elvis, and he curled his lip in a manner that Her Madge found most appealing.

'A US thing?' said Bob. 'You mean the Americans have placed nuclear missiles in Baghdad that are aimed at Israel?'

'Tut tut, Bob,' said Her Madge. 'Could *you* think of a better place to put them? No blame could possibly attach to the West if they are ever fired.'

'Might I just raise my hand here?' said Mr Bagshaw.

'Need the bog?' said Bob, a pup to whom the appellation 'comical' seemed more in the realm of irony.

'Are we sanctioning the nuclear destruction of Israel?' Mr Bagshaw enquired. 'I'm not objecting, you understand, I'm only asking.'

'It's an option,' said Her Madge. 'One amongst many that we can discuss.'

'Not *too* many, I hope,' said Ahab. 'I've brought my satellite TV – *Father Ted* is on at three.'

'Then we'll try to get done by two.' Her Majesty brought out her knitting from somewhere and click-click-clicked with the needles.

'My guys,' said Elvis. 'Which is to say, my army. Which is to say the American Army, are keen to be home by Thanksgiving. I could have them pulled out in a couple of weeks. Then Israel could be nuked, and in the forthcoming nuclear retaliation, none of my guys would get hurt.'

'That's fair,' said Ahab. 'My family, of course, would all die.'

'You can't make a peanut and banana flapjack without breaking eggs,' said Elvis. 'Is it time for lunch yet?'

'I'm peckish,' said Her Madge. 'Lunch might be nice.'

'Might I read through the notes so far?' asked Countess Vanda.

'You do that, dear,' said Her Madge.

'Full-scale American troop withdrawal from Iraq, followed by nuclear assault on Israel launched from Baghdad, followed by nuclear retaliation from Israel resulting in the destruction of Iraq—'

'And Iran,' said Elvis. 'To be on the safe side.'

'And Lebanon,' said Mr Bagshaw. 'And Libya. Take out the entire Arab world as a whole, mess cleared, job done—'

'And time for lunch,' said Her Majesty the Queen.

The Parliament of Five now left the secret meeting room. A pair of eyes that watched them leave went blink-blink-blink behind them.

This pair of eyes had peered through the eyeholes in the portrait of Sir Henry Crawford. The pair of eyes belonged, of course, to Jonny Hooker. The pair of ears, one to either side of this head, did also.

Jonny Hooker replaced Sir Henry's canvas eyes and stood in the darkness.

'*You* heard all that, too, didn't you?' he said.

And there was silence.

Then the words, 'You mean *me*?'

'I mean you, Mister Giggles,' said Jonny, 'You heard all that in there, didn't you?'

'Yes, I believe I did.'

'They're going to nuke the Middle East.'

'Seems so, yes.'

'The Queen,' said Jonny, 'Elvis Presley and a talking dog.'

'Don't forget the camel-jockey and the bloke out of *Thunderbirds*.'

'They're insane,' said Jonny. 'They'll destroy us all.'

'I'm sure there's method in their madness.'

'What?'

'I'm sure they know what they're doing.'

'I'm sure that they don't.'

'So what do you propose to do about it?'

'I'll expose them,' said Jonny. 'I'll expose them to the world.'

'Oh, right,' said Mr Giggles. 'You'll tell the world that Her Majesty the Queen, Elvis Presley – the dead King of rock 'n' roll, and a talking pup named Bob are plotting to instigate a nuclear war.'

'Hm,' went Jonny Hooker.

'Hm indeed,' went Mr Giggles. 'Don't you see, Jonny? Don't you understand how this works?'

Jonny Hooker shook his head in the darkness.

'I'll assume that was a shake,' said Mr Giggles. 'It works in this fashion. Each and every one of us has a little bit of the conspiracy theorist in us. Even if it's only a tiny bit. At one time or another we've each felt that we're not being told all of the truth. Even on a minor level, by our doctor, or our accountant, or our lover—'

'Because we're *not*,' said Jonny.

'Quite so. But usually it's trivial, just the usual lies that folk tell each other. And we all do it. But when you are in charge of a nation, a continent, the lies can get quite big. Big and important. And the theory that there is something else going on behind the scenes, that there is some big secret that we're not being told because it *is* a big secret, which is why we're never going to be told it – well, now you know it's true. But now you also know, you can do absolutely nothing about it, because *no one* will believe you. Because the truth is so ludicrous, so fanciful, so outré, so whacked-out, that no one will ever believe it. Which is why it is true. Which is why it works.'

'But we can't let these loonys kill millions of innocent people.'

'Who is innocent?' asked Mr Giggles.

'Don't give me *that*.'

'Fair enough,' said Mr Giggles. 'Let's away, then. We'll leave the park, then you can phone up the *Sunday Sport* and tell them everything you know.'

'That sounds like a plan,' said Jonny.

'Top man,' said Mr Giggles.

'But I can do better than that,' said Jonny. 'I can broadcast my story.'

'Not quite following you there,' said Mr Giggles.

'No,' said Jonny, 'but I have a plan. And with my plan, if all works out, I'm going to save Mankind.'

47

Inspector Westlake had a plan.

And this he now explained.

He sat in the cab of the big Special Ops lead truck, in the crowded company of Constables Paul, Justice, Cartwright, Cassidy and Rogers. 'Play it back again,' he told Constable Cartwright.

Constable Cartwright tinkered with the super SatNav.

'There,' he said, and he pointed. 'You see how he slipped into the boot of the last limo. That didn't slip by me – we arrested him as soon as he stepped from the boot.'

'And those–' Inspector Westlake pointed to the glowing shapes of three other men. '–Those would be myself and my two constables, entering another of the limos. But you failed to notice that at the time.'

Constable Cartwright grunted in the affirmative.

'Can you bring it up?' asked the inspector.

'Not quite following you there, sir,' said Constable Cartwright.

'The image of the terrorist in the boot. Can you expand the image?'

'I think *I* can do better than that,' said Constable Rogers. 'I've been having a little tinker with this jobbie whenever I've had a free moment, and it can do all kinds of party tricks. You're hoping to identify the terrorist, I suppose.'

Inspector Westlake nodded.

'Then just watch this and prepare to be impressed.' And Constable Rogers took to tinkering. The SatNav image of the body in the boot zoomed in and a fuzzy image of a man's face filled the screen. Then a grid formed about it, twisted at ninety degrees and a three-dimensional model appeared. Then the screen split, with the facial image to the left and a blur of faces to the right as the computer skipped through the central database in search of a match.

Constable Paul watched it searching. He knew that sooner or later, and probably sooner rather than later, it would find its match. Amongst the inmate files of the Special Wing of Brentford Cottage Hospital.

'Oh dear me, Jonny,' whispered Constable Paul beneath his breath. 'You are in *so* much trouble.'

'Bingo,' went Constable Rogers. 'Jonathan Hooker. Local boy. Escaped mental patient.'

'Escaped mental patient and serial killer,' said Inspector Westlake. 'And I thought he was dead.' And he tapped his finger against the SatNav screen. 'I'll have you, my lad. I will.'

'You mentioned something about a plan, I believe, sir,' said Constable Justice.

'Whoa!' went Constable Paul. 'His head's all vanished away again.'

'Keep the suits switched *off*!' said the inspector. 'I *did* say something about a plan, yes, and I am going to outline this plan to you right here and now, so there can be no confusion when *we* put this plan into operation. Do I make myself understood?'

'So far,' said Constable Cartwright. 'You're not going to have us prosecuted for shooting at you and trying to arrest you and all those other little mistakes? Sir?'

'No,' said Inspector Westlake. 'Not as you've been trying *so* hard to impress me by being *so* helpful. Not if you can help *me* to pull off *my* plan. Firstly, I want you to go and collect every earphone and mic from every Special Ops operative in the park. *I* am in charge of this operation, not Thompson.'

'I'll do that,' said Constable Cassidy. 'I like a nice walk in the park.'

'Jog,' said the inspector. 'Throw all the earphones and mics into the pond and then return to me.'

'Yes, sir,' said Constable Cassidy, and he squeezed his way from the cab.

'What do you want us to do?' asked Constable Cartwright.

'I want you to impress me some more with this SatNav gizmo. I want you to use it to locate the whereabouts of Mister Jonathan

Hooker, serial killer and would-be assassin. Train the SatNav on the Big House and let's flush the blighter out.'

'That's very clever,' said Constable Cartwright.

'Very clever, *what*?'

'Very clever, *sir*,' said Constable Cartwright.

'That does sound like a rather clever plan,' said Mr Giggles the Monkey Boy. 'Would you care to run it by me just one more time, in case I missed anything?'

'No, I wouldn't,' said Jonny.

'Oh yes you would, you really would.'

'All right,' said Jonny. 'It's very simple. I am going to use James Crawford's laptop, which I have here in the poacher's pocket of this ill-smelling jacket, to record the rest of this afternoon's meeting. It has a webcam jobbie on it and a mic for sound. I'll put it up to the eyeholes of the portrait and record the proceedings. Then I'll e-mail it to every news agency in the world.'

'And you can really do *that*? With that little laptop computer?'

'That and a whole lot more. It's a pretty smart plan, is it not?'

'It is,' said Mr Giggles, with a somewhat thoughtful tone in his voice.

'I'll have them,' said Jonny. 'Ludicrous and impossible as though they may be, I'll expose them to the entire world. When people see them with their own eyes and hear them with their own ears and watch the situation in the Middle East coming apart exactly as the Parliament of Five have orchestrated it, they'll believe me then.'

'Yes,' said Mr Giggles. 'I do believe they might.'

'I've got them,' said Jonny. 'I'll bring them to justice. They'll pay for their crimes against Mankind.'

And Jonny Hooker rubbed his hands together. 'They are in *so* much trouble,' he said. 'Just wait 'till they get back from lunch.'

Count Otto Black was having his lunch. He'd had to send out a dwarf to pilfer Special Operations field rations, but he was enjoying this lunch all the same.

The Glove Woman sat at the keyboard of the Air Loom, flexed her fingers and clicked her long neck from side to side. 'Phase one is a success,' said she.

'Oh yes,' said Count Otto. 'Phase one. Our magnetised Parliament of Five dance to the tune of the Air Loom. As puppets do they dance, bereft of their own wills, made slaves to the magnetic flux beamed upon them. And how humorously so. The opening theme you played so well upon the keyboard – I so enjoyed the Arab, such false modesty, such subtle innuendo.'

'I am honoured that you appreciate my technique,' said the Glove Woman. 'A little trill of my own, here and there, to take the edge off the brutality of the message. To inject a little humour, a little joviality.'

'Oh sweet, sweet,' crooned the count. 'They are our puppets, they dance to our tune.' He approached the infernal machine and ran a long and slender hand up and down one of the tall glass tubes. Dangerous energy swirled within; magnetic fluxes fluxed. 'Oh yes,' the count continued. 'Oh sweet, sweet, sweet. We shall indeed prevail.'

48

At somewhat after two of the afternoon clock, the Parliament of Five returned to Princess Amelia's sitting room. They could have returned there sharp upon two, as folk will do after having their lunch hours, but this *was* the Parliament of Five, for dearness' sake, the secret rulers of the world. The controllers who control the controllers. If they chose to be late back from lunch, who was going to tell them off?

Jonny watched them through the eyeholes of Sir Henry Crawford's portrait. 'Swine,' he whispered to himself. 'Filling their evil guts and I'm starving.'

'You should have brought a packed lunch,' said Mr Giggles. 'Forward planning is everything. You'll pass out from the hunger if you're not careful. Let's go down to the pub.'

Jonny did not dignify this with an answer.

Her Madge settled herself back into her gilt and throne-like at the head of the table and bade the others take their seats. But all had done so already.

'Round two,' said Her Madge. 'Ding ding, seconds out and all that kind of caper.'

'"Kind of caper"?' said Bob. 'Does the Queen say things like "kind of caper"?'

'It's what being Queen is all about,' said the Queen. 'We would not say "kind of caper" in front of the plebs, of course. We just waves We's hand and smiles We's special smile.'

And she smiled her special smile in demonstration.

And all agreed that it *was* a special smile.

'Where were we up to?' asked Her Majesty the Queen of Countess Vanda at the table's end.

Countess Vanda ran through the notes and while she did so Jonny diddled about with the late James Crawford's laptop. The mic and the webcam jobbies were on extendible wires and Jonny extended these. He poked the mic through one eyehole of the portrait and the webcam through the other. Then he wiggled them about until perfect sound and vision were to be heard and seen in the laptop screen department. 'Damning evidence take one,' he said as he fingered keyboard keys and got the whole thing up and running.

'Look at that,' he said to Mr Giggles. 'Lovely image on the screen, eh? And perfect sound quality. The ultimate reality show. What would you call it? *I'm a Celebrity and I Secretly Rule the World, So Don't Get Me Out of Here?*' What do you think?'

'On past experience,' said Mr Giggles, 'I think it will all end in tears. But let's look on the bright side – you're all hidden away in a secret passage where you can't really get yourself into any trouble for the moment and no one is likely to find you, so that's something, isn't it?'

'That's something,' said Inspector Westlake in the constable-crowded vehicle. 'What *is* that something?'

'That something,' said Constable Cartwright, 'is Joan on the reception desk. She's a bit of all right, that Joan, isn't she?'

Inspector Westlake cuffed the constable lightly on the ear. 'We are supposed to be discovering the location of the serial killer,' he said. 'Impress me, if you will.'

'Will do, sir,' said Constable Cartwright. 'Now here–' and he did pressings of buttons '–Is an architectural schematic of the Big House that I downloaded from the central database. The only people inside the Big House should be the six atendees of the secret meeting—'

'Secret meeting?' said Constable Cartwright. 'What secret meeting is this?'

'You mean you don't know about the secret meeting?' asked Constable Rogers. 'What do you think we're all doing here anyway?'

'That's what I kept asking,' said Constable Cartwright. 'Again and again I asked.'

'Ah yes,' said Constable Rogers. 'And you never did get an answer, did you?'

'No, I bloody didn't.'

'Language,' said Inspector Westlake.

'Well, sir, it's not fair.'

'So what *is* the secret meeting for?' asked Constable Paul. 'No one's told us either. Is it to organise a come-back concert for Elvis?'

'Elvis?' said Constable Cartwright.

'We came in with him in that limo,' said Constable Paul. 'Nice chap. I don't believe he really has Barry the Time Sprout in his head.'

'*Barry the Time Sprout?*'

'Enough.' Inspector Westlake raised a fist and, the constables cringed at its raising. 'For your information and your information alone, or at least for those of you who don't already know, a secret meeting is being held in Princess Amelia's sitting room – a secret meeting of heads of state to sort out the troubles in the Middle East.'

'And Elvis Presley is a head of state?' asked Constable Justice, for he hadn't said anything for a while.

'Slightly puzzled about that myself,' said Inspector Westlake. 'I saw Her Majesty, a shifty-looking Arab, a bloke who looked like Brains out of *Thunderbirds* and a dog.'

'A dog?' said Constable Paul.

'There is a dog,' said Constable Cartwright, pointing to the screen of the advanced SatNav. 'It's sitting at the table in Princess Amelia's sitter. Six around the table. Including a dog.'

'That would be the secret meeting,' said the inspector. 'Now scan about a bit and let's see if we can zero in on our serial killer.'

Constable Paul chewed on his lip, but kept his thoughts to himself.

'Ah,' said Constable Cartwright, 'here's something.'

Inspector Westlake looked on.

'More people,' said Constable Cartwright. 'In fact, another five. But they're not our men because there are none of our men left in the Big House.'

'*None* of your men?' said Inspector Westlake.

'You arrested us,' said Constable Cartwright. 'We were the Big House secret security team.'

'Just the three of you?'

'There were more.' Constable Rogers crossed himself. 'But the invisibility suits, they sort of—'

'Sort of *what?*' went Constable Paul.

As did Constable Justice.

'Sort of blew up one after another. It's all been a bit stressful really,' said Constable Cartwright. 'Which is why we didn't really mind handing our suits over to you blokes.'

Constable Paul was now struggling to remove himself from his suit.

'Keep it *on!*' said Inspector Westlake. 'We may have need of it.'

'But, sir—'

'Keep it on. And pay attention. If there are no security forces in the Big House, who are the other people registering on the SatNav?'

Constable Cartwright twiddled further knobs. 'I'm getting a big reading here. Five people,' said he, 'in the basement,' said he, 'in one of the storage rooms,' said he also. 'And—' And he paused.

'And?' said Inspector Westlake.

'There's something more, sir. There's something down there with them and it's chucking out a lot of radiation.'

'As in heat?'

'As in magnetic, sir.'

'Magnetic?' Inspector Westlake tried to give his head a scratch, but it *was* very crowded, so he only succeeded in scratching Constable Justice's.

'Thank you, sir,' said Constable Justice. 'But are you thinking what I'm thinking?'

'Probably not,' said Inspector Westlake. 'But pray do tell what you're thinking.'

'Nuke,' said Constable Justice.

'No,' said Inspector Westlake. 'You are not going to nuke anyone. I know how much you love your weapons, but—'

'No, sir, not *me* nuke, sir. In the basement. Something big, giving off magnetic radiation. I remember reading in *Jane's Megaweapon Catalogue* that the new Apocalypse Three Thousand (Gamma Knubnub Kill-the-lot-and-let-God-sort-'em-out, one-size-slays-all) bomb, the one that can fit into a suitcase, gives off magnetic radiation when it's about to ... ' Constable Justice's words trailed off.

'Explode?' asked Constable Paul.

★

'Boom!' went Elvis. 'Then boom, boom – how many booms did you say there'd be, Mister Ahab the A-rab, sir?'

'Six should be enough.'

Mr Bagshaw nodded his great big head. 'We will lose all of the Middle Eastern oilfields,' he said as he nodded, 'but this will not present any difficulties as the Russian ones we are presently opening up can more than cover the shortfall. Or if not, we can always resort to the MacGregor-Mathers Water Car.'

'What in the name of glory is that, sir?' Elvis asked.

'It's a car that runs on water, rather than, as you colonials put it, gasoline.'

'I want me one of them,' said Elvis.

'And you might well get one. We've been holding back the patent for decades. At a pinch we could put them into production.'

'One with fins,' said Elvis. 'And weather-eye air conditioning.'

'And a litter tray,' said Bob. 'Although that's really a pussy thing, but I do get caught short sometimes.'

'So, are we all agreed?' asked Her Madge, clicking away with her needles. 'Boom boom boom and all that kind of caper?'

'Sounds good to me,' said Mr Bagshaw. 'Positively inspired, in my opinion.'

'Oh, how splendid,' said Her Madge. 'We can all be home in time for tea. Well, at least I can, because I only live up the road.'

'I love it when a plan comes together,' said Ahab the A-rab. 'That's off *The A-Team*, by the way. We get that, too, dubbed as well. That Mister T is a bit of a character, isn't he? I love the way he endorses Islamic Jihad every week.'

'Well,' said the Queen, 'then I don't think we need to spend any more time on this matter. The solution is indeed inspired. In fact, I have to say that I personally do not feel that I can take credit personally, personally, as it were.'

'How so, your loveliness?' asked Bob.

'Well, dear,' said Her Madge, 'as you know We *are* English, and We *are* the Queen, so naturally enough We *are* greatly loved by God. But We have to confess that He rarely, if ever, speaks to We personally. So when, during the course of this meeting, He has been singing away in We's head telling We what to say, then that is what We mean by inspired. Divinely inspired.'

'You've been hearing the voice of Allah?' asked Ahab the A-rab.

'Well—' said Her Madge.

'Because so have I. Although at first I thought it was Father Ted.'

'I thought it was Colonel Tom,' said Elvis.

'I thought it was my mum,' said Mr Bagshaw.

'I thought it was your mum, too,' said Bob. 'But if it was God, well, so much the better for it, I say.'

'The *voice* of God?' Jonny Hooker gazed at the screen of the laptop. '*The voice of God?*'

'Just like Joan of Arc,' said Mr Giggles.

'No,' said Jonny. 'Not like that at all. Don't you get it? They haven't been making those terrible decisions. It's not them.'

'It looks very much like them,' said Mr Giggles.

'It's *not* them,' said Jonny, 'making the decisions. It's the Air Loom Gang. The Parliament of Five have been magnetised. They think they are being inspired by God, but it's not God, it's the Air Loom beaming words into their heads. How could I have been so stupid as not to realise what was really going on?'

Mr Giggles didn't answer.

Mr Giggles was silent.

And sometimes silence can say so much.

And this was one of those times.

49

Cometh the hour, cometh the man.

And things of that nature, generally.

'Evacuate! Evacuate!' Inspector Westlake comethed.

'Evacuate who?' asked Constable Paul.

'To where?' asked Constable Justice.

'The Queen first, I think. We have to clear the area.' And as there was just room for him to get his hand upon the truck's ignition key, and as he *was* sitting at the steering wheel, Inspector Westlake keyed the ignition, put the big truck into gear, *brrmed* the engine and let that trucker roll.

'Sir?' went Constable Cartwright. 'Sir, can you actually drive this vehicle?'

'Out,' cried Inspector Westlake. 'Constables Paul and Justice stay in this truck with me. Other constables out – alert the Special Operations unit to make away from the park at the hurry-up.'

'To where?' asked Constable Cartwright.

'Perhaps Brighton,' said Inspector Westlake, swinging the wheel and ploughing through a rather lovely flower bed that had been designed by the late Henry Hunter, based upon that of Francis Dashwood.

'Out then, out!'

Constables Cartwright and Rogers took to tumbling from the truck.

'I think we should probably evacuate, too,' said Constable Justice, preparing to join the evacuating constables. 'Live to fight another day, eh?'

'Not a bit of it my lad. You will aid me in disabling the nuclear device and making the arrest, or possibly the termination of the suicide bombers.'

'Termination?' Constable Justice mulled that one over. It *would* be a risky business. In fact, it *was* a risky business. The bomb could go off any minute. But terminate ...

'Would that be terminate with extreme prejudice, sir?'

Inspector Westlake nodded, hunched low over the wheel and swerved the truck through further flower beds (somewhat unnecessarily, in Constable Paul's opinion) towards the Big House.

Wherein.

The laptop was back in the poacher's pocket.

Jonny Hooker was making haste along a secret passage.★

'We're off to the pub now, aren't we?' asked Mr Giggles. 'Or is it an internet café?'

'It's neither,' said Jonny. 'I have business here.'

'But no weapons,' said Mr Giggles. 'No big laser cannons or atom-blasting ray guns, or anything.'

'I'll manage, somehow.' Jonny bumbled on in the darkness. But he bumbled with determination. A man on a mission, as it were. Cometh the hour, cometh the man, and all that kind of caper.

As Her Majesty might have said. But she wasn't saying it now. She was having another cuppa and dunking a custard cream, in that antechamber next door to Princess Amelia's sitter.

'You can come round to my house for tea,' she said to Ahab the A-rab. 'You can *all* come round, if you want to.'

'If you'd just like to sign the official documents,' said Countess Vanda. 'I've had them printed out on the photocopier. If you'd sign two copies each, one for yourself, the other for the PM and the President – you all know the drill.'

Biros were brought to bear, signatures were signed.

'If it wasn't for the fact that it's all down to God,' said Bob, 'we could all give ourselves pats on the back. Would someone like to pat my back anyway – it does get me really excited.'

★ Exactly why it was that Jonny hadn't showed up on the advanced SatNav was anyone's guess. Perhaps Count Otto's gang showed up because there was more of them. Yes, that was probably it. (Phew!)

Elvis turned away and dunked his biscuit.

The Queen gave Bob's little back a pat.

And then things got a bit confusing, as there was suddenly a lot of shouting and bustling-in as an inspector and two constables, one of whom had a very large weapon, made an unexpected, unwarranted and quite unwanted police presence.

'Emergency situation,' panted the inspector, who'd got a bit puffed on his way up the stairs. 'Have to ask you all to evacuate the premises immediately.'

'Before we've finished tea?' asked Her Madge.

'Best to,' said the inspector. 'I have reason to believe that a nuclear device is primed and ready for detonation in the basement of this building.'

'Perhaps not my London house, then,' said Her Madge. 'Perhaps Balmoral.'

'If you would be so kind, Ma'am,' said the inspector. 'my constable here will lead you down to your car.'

'I can see right through your constable's stomach,' said Her Madge. 'Is that right?'

Black Betty (Bam-a-Lam) knew what was right.

And proper.

And taking on other jobs when you were waiting to pick up a celebrity client was neither.

Black Betty sat in his limo, listening to a rather depressing programme on Radio 4 all about the crisis in the Middle East and how if talks weren't held soon and problems ironed out, it looked like kiss-your-arse-goodbye time for the denizens of Planet Earth.

Except for the cockroaches, of course. Because, as everyone knows, they will survive a nuclear war.

Next to Black Betty's limo there was only one other limo. The other three limo drivers having slipped away with their limos to fit in other jobs.

And the remaining black stretch limo parked next to that of Black Betty (Ram-a-lam-ding-dong-da-da-de-da-da) was lacking for a driver.

Its driver, Mr Esau Good of Smack My Bitch Up Motors had gone off to take a walk by the ornamental pond and feed the ducks.

And tell himself again and again and again that he must not, for fear of that exploding implant, ever again mention the name of Elvis Presley.

'Mister Presley is leaving the building,' said Elvis as he was ushered down the stairs, through the entrance hall and out onto the drive to where the only limo possessed of a driver was standing. Quietly.

And joy of joys, there was *no* unpleasantness.

Because Black Betty (Boom-bang-a-bang-loud-in-your-ear) was a professional. And a gentleman. And so he ushered each and all into his limo and drove away in the direction of Scotland.

'And let *that* be a lesson to you,' said Inspector Westlake to his two constables.

'A lesson in *what?*' Constable Justice asked.

'In evacuation. There'll be medals in this, if we pull it off properly.'

'Are there any medals that have black ribbons?' asked Constable Paul.

'It is very black in here. How do you know where you're going?' asked Mr Giggles the Monkey Boy.

'I know exactly where I'm going and exactly what I'm going to do.'

'Do tell.'

In the darkness, Jonny shook his head. 'You knew,' he said. 'You knew that the people at the meeting upstairs were being manipulated by the Air Loom Gang. You knew!'

'So did *you*,' said Mr Giggles. 'The manipulating *is* what all of this is about, surely.'

'I was misled,' said Jonny. 'Or fooled, or confused, or—'

'Well, don't go blaming *me*.'

'I'll fix this,' said Jonny. 'I'll fix all of this. I have that bunch upstairs recorded on the laptop, and as for the bunch down below—'

'Yes?' said Mr Giggles. 'Go on.'

'You'll see.'

★

'I can still see you,' said Inspector Westlake. 'Can you still see me?'

He and his constables were once more in the entrance hall of the Big House.

'Is this a game anyone can play?' asked Joan. 'Like "hide the sausage".'

'Madam,' said Inspector Westlake, drawing his attention away from Constable Justice, 'you should not be here. You should have evacuated the building.'

'Why?' asked Joan. 'When?'

'Because there is a bomb in the basement. And *now*.'

Joan shrugged. 'There, you see, you have it,' she said. 'A complete lack of continuity. I must have been sitting at this desk when you hustled Her Majesty and Elvis and the rest down the stairs, right past my desk here and out to the limo. But did *I* get told to evacuate? No. It was just as if I didn't exist. Complete lack of continuity. Appalling.'

There was another of those silences.

And the sun *did* go behind a cloud.

And a dog *did* howl in the distance.

'So, *can* anyone play?' asked Joan.

'Madam—' said Inspector Westlake.

'Call me Joan,' said Joan.

'Joan,' said Inspector Westlake, 'it is very possible that a nuclear bomb, which has been secreted in the basement of this building will shortly be detonated. So I suppose that it matters not whether I call you "madam", or "Joan". 'So, *madam*, I was just checking, with my constable here, as to whether our invisibility suits are working.'

Joan shook her head.

'You're shaking your head, madam.'

'That is because *you* are not wearing an invisibility suit. Just your constables. The continuity is all over the place, I'm telling you. And as for a nuclear bomb in the basement.' Joan laughed. Loudly.

'You are laughing, madam,' said Inspector Westlake, 'and I am finding all this talk about continuity somewhat alarming.'

'As well you might.' The receptionist leaned back in her receptionist's chair, stretching her arms up above her head and giving her bosoms that special thrust out. 'There is no bomb in the basement,' she said. 'No bomb at all.'

'There isn't?' said Inspector Westlake.

Joan arose from behind the desk, came around to where Inspector Westlake was standing and took him by the hand. She smiled up into his eyes and gave his hand a firm gripping.

And then she did the same to Constables Justice and Paul respectively.

'Madam,' said Inspector Westlake, 'whatever are you doing?'

'Just giving you all a little handshake,' said Joan. 'A little touch of something special, as it were. Although you have already had a little touch of it back at your lodgings. A little touch of something special.'

'Something special?'

'Very,' said Joan, all a-smile. 'A bit of, how shall I put this? Animal magnetism.'

'Magnetism?' Inspector Westlake stared at his hand.

'Oh, there's nothing to be seen,' said Joan. 'It has to be passed on through a handshake. As it has been for centuries. As it is passed from one generation to the next by those who are members of the special brotherhood.'

Inspector Westlake said, 'What?'

But already he was somehow becoming unclear about exactly why he was standing here in this entrance hall talking to this woman.

A little voice inside his head seemed to be saying, 'There's nothing for you here. Take your constables down to the pub for a drink.'

'Well,' said Inspector Westlake, 'I don't think there's anything for me here. Shall we adjourn to the pub, Constables?'

Constable Paul looked at Constable Justice.

And Constable Justice looked at Constable Paul.

And both seemed to come to a simultaneous conclusion that indeed there was nothing for any of them here and yes, indeed, it would be a really good idea to simply go down to the pub.

'Would it be all right if I joined you?' asked Joan.

And three heads nodded.

So she did.

50

And then there was only Jonny.

Which seemed rather a shame.

Rather an anticlimax, somehow. What with the comic possibilities of all those ludicrously armed Special Opperations personnel and the landmines on the pitch-and-putt, and the chauffeurs with the humorously named limo-hire companies, and Elvis and Bob the not so Comical Pup and Ahab the A-rab and Her Madge and Inspector Westlake and two invisible constables, and the lovely Joan, all vanished away.

As it were.

Leaving just Jonny Hooker.

Shame.

Not that Jonny would have seen it that way, of course. Although he probably would have appreciated some sort of armed back-up, to guarantee some big-gun action, if required, even if it did mean lots of Gunnersbury Park Museum getting blown to boogeration in the process.

But it was not to be. There was only Jonny and Jonny marched on along a secret passage, pushed upon a secret panel and entered an underground storeroom.

To be greeted by someone within.

'Count Otto Black, I presume,' said Jonny. 'Deathless supervillain and Master of the Air Loom gang?'

'Welcome, Jonny Hooker,' said the count.

51

Dust and musky odours. Antique leather, fabric, burnished brass and lacquered wood, a candelabrum, and there in uncertain light, the gang of villains, large as life and not too easy on the eye. And, as it were, a dreamscape, shifting shadows, shining bulky, the terrible Air Loom, as it were some mighty cabinet. Its board with keys of ebony and ivory. Its barrels with their polished nozzles and their gleaming turncocks. And its great glass conducting tubes, huge and glowing from within, where plasma vortexes of magnetic flux swirl sinuously, energised, sensitised, awaiting the touch upon the keyboard, the notes, the chords to send their forces forth, like wicked messengers. Swirl and flow, flickering candle flame, curious faces, ancient powdered wigs, queer frocked coats with quilted sleeves. Outré. Strange. Unreal.

Jonny Hooker gave a little bow, as somehow this seemed appropriate. 'And so you know my name,' said he. 'Although I must confess that I am not surprised.'

'Your name,' said Count Otto, and he fished from his cloth-of-gold embroidered waistcoat an antiquated timepiece and held its face towards a candle's flame. 'And you are on time. To the minute, to the second, probably. As expected.'

'Well, that is a happy happenstance.'

And Count Otto Black now bowed. 'And all respect to a worthy opponent. You played your half of the game with vigour and with dedication. And you know my name. I am impressed.'

And by the twinkle of the candle's flame, the Air Loom Gang applauded Jonny. And Jack the Schoolmaster said, 'Well done, that man.'

Jonny Hooker bobbed his head to this applause. 'Please save your handclappings,' he said. 'The final act has yet to be played out.'

Count Otto Black cocked his head on one side and ran a knuckle slowly over his forehead. 'You do appear to be somewhat unaware of your dire predicament,' he said. 'You *do* know that I now must kill you?'

'You're certainly welcome to try,' said Jonny. 'We'll see how things work out.'

'Such bravado. Such braggadocio. But Jonny, see, you are alone. All alone. The soldier boys have gone away. Everyone has gone away, as we arranged it. As we played it.' And he mimed a little keyboard trill. And very well he mimed it. 'There is only you left, my dear boy. Only you, to do what? To save Mankind, just you?'

'Whatever it takes,' Jonny said. And he put his hands in his trouser pockets and did a little boot-heel-scuffing on the dusty floor.

'My dear, dear boy,' said the count. 'All alone like a poor orphan lad. You are here and we are here. But still you do not see it, do you? *Why* you are here? Why you, out of the thousands of millions alive on this planet? Why you?'

'Don't know. Don't care,' said Jonny, tracing his initials in the dust.

'So you don't think it, how shall I put this, *odd*?'

'*Odd*?' And Jonny Hooker laughed. 'Odd? I should say it's odd. But I've been coming to terms with odd. Odd and me have few secrets any more.'

'We enjoyed you,' said the count. 'You did everything that we'd hoped you'd do. You didn't let us down. You didn't disappoint us.'

Jonny Hooker stood his ground.

'You see, you were chosen,' said the count. 'Or rather, you chose yourself.'

'The Da-da-de-da-da Code,' said Jonny.

'How charmingly put. But of course. We needed someone in order that we might test our defences. We never leave anything to chance. No cost is too great in the cause.'

'No cost,' said Jonny. 'No lengths you will not go to. Which include murdering your own in order to cover your tracks.'

'Not all of our own.' The count ran his slender fingers gently up and down one of the tall glass conducting tubes. Little cracklets of magnetic energy sparked between the glass and his fingers.

'Everything had to keep pace, to be achieved in the right order. Our interventions in the ways of Mankind are infrequent. When we *do* intervene, we leave no loose ends, no evidence of our comings and goings. If it is necessary to sacrifice some of our own to the greater good, then so be it. No nobler fate could there be. James Crawford was not one of ours and he needed to be silenced. He knew far too much and was a man who might have been believed. And he was immune to the powers of the Air Loom, as was his ancestor Sir Henry before him. They could not be controlled and so—' And Count Otto drew a finger accross his throat.

'You mad, murdering bastards,' said Jonny.

'What must be, must be. Your little imaginary friend explained so much to you, regarding how conspiracy theorists are always thwarted. Because those in ultimate control are so ludicrous, impossible and unlikely that no one in their "right mind"–' and Count Otto did that finger thing to mime inverted commas '–No one in their "right mind" would ever believe such nonsense. It would take someone like you, who has never really been in your right mind, to believe in the Parliament of Five, or the Air Loom Gang.'

'I have seen both with my own eyes,' said Jonny.

'Yet no one would ever believe you. Because *you* are a certified stone bonker.'

'So you'll be letting me go, then.'

'No, we'll be killing you. I thought I had made that clear.'

'I hope I made it clear that you can *try*. But tell me this,' said Jonny. 'You *always* win? You never ever lose, is that right?'

'This is what wins.' Count Otto Black ran a loving finger over the Air Loom. 'This impossible piece of technology. This fantasy. This stuff of dreams. This paranoid, schizophrenic, delusional architecture, or whatever the fashionable phrase of the day is coined to describe it. The impossible Air Loom. *This* is the truth. *This*, reality. What the world believes unreal, is real. And probably the other way about. As for myself and my companions here – what are we? Who are we? Shades, ciphers? Can you pin us down? Do we have real origins, birth certificates? No, *we* are the stuff of rumour and myth. The Air Loom is the reality. Its music orchestrates history. Its music is the background music to life itself. And much more than that. Me, my Gang – we are nothing. We fade to grey, become as crumbling mummies. In an instant we are here and then in another we are gone, to be replaced by others. The final chords have been played and now the curtain falls upon Mankind.'

'So *that*,' said Jonny, and he pointed to the Air Loom, '*that* is the truth?'

Count Otto Black smiled and nodded. 'Beautiful, isn't it?' he said, stroking up and down a tall glass cylinder. 'Exquisite. The perfect work of genius. An instrument capable of influencing people's minds, controlling these minds, putting thoughts into these minds that are so compelling that they must be translated into actions. And this instrument, this controller of controllers – what powers it, do you think?'

The count now pointed to the great polished oaken barrels. Brazen tubes rose from the centres of their sealed tops and penetrated the Air Loom's side. 'Powered by what?' cried the count, with some degree of animation. 'Powered by shit! Bullshit. Cow shit, horse shit, human shit. *Shit!* Isn't that a treat? Isn't that the ultimate irony? The ultimate cosmic joke? Bullshit baffles brains – that's a present-day saying, isn't it, Jonny? And how true that is. It is all shit, Jonny. All of it. Everything run by, powered by shit. And somehow, in your heart of hearts, you just knew that, didn't you?'

'You're shit,' said Jonny. 'Everything about you is shit. The way you treat people. The way you have treated me.'

'Cruel,' said the count, 'but it is what we do. There always has to be a Jonny Hooker in the equation. It's part of the game. The Count of Saint Germain, Handel, Moreschi the castrato and Robert Johnson. And yourself. And in common, what? Always a musician – that is the common bond.'

'Tell me about the music,' said Jonny. 'Please.'

'It is always the music and always the musicians. It is all around you, Jonny. It always has been, but never so much as now. You cannot escape from music. It plays in your lifts and your supermarkets, your shops and malls and pubs and clubs. It is everywhere. And behind it, unseen, the Air Loom. The Glove Woman tickles the ivories and the music plays. The messages are sent. We're here, we're there, we're everywhere. But when? Where? Who knows? What messages are being sent? Vote for this man. Do this, do that.'

'And it always goes "da-da-de-da-da",' said Jonny.

'And you cannot escape from it. This here and now. Today. *This* is a very special occasion, beyond the everyday. Today is history in the making. Today is the beginning of the end. For ever.'

'I see,' said Jonny. 'Well, I see some, if not all. In truth the big question might be, *why* do you do it? If it is only the Air Loom that has true reality, as it were, what is the point? Do you obey a machine? Does the Air Loom have some kind of sentience? Does it command you?'

'Oh no no no.' Count Otto shook his beard. 'We take our orders directly from our Master.'

'Ah,' said Jonny. 'Your Master. And I really don't need to ask who your master is, do I? The God of this world? The Orchestrator? The One who wants this world destroyed, returned to chaos.'

'You are thinking, perhaps, Satan?' said Count Otto Black.

'I am,' said Jonny.

'Then alas, you are incorrect. There is no Satan, never was and never will be. There is another, a lover of, how shall I put this, pandemonium? Music, Jonny, it's all to do with the music. The solution to the code that goes "Da-da-de-da-da". Three notes, Jonny, as in the three-chord trick, as in the three letters that spell out the name of our god. PAN, Jonny – our god is the god of music, the god of pandemonium. Our god is Pan.'

'Pan,' said Jonny, slowly. And suddenly it all made sense.

Well, at least to Jonny it did!

'And there you have it,' said the count. 'But we have spoken enough. The final overture must now be played. The concert will soon be done. The world will shortly return to chaos, destruction and chaos, the way it was when my Master ruled it. Before another brought order out of chaos.'

'God,' said Jonny.

'Well, obviously God. But we have talked enough. The Glove Woman must now play out the final chords. The Parliament of Five have signed their orders. And now they must die.'

'Die?' said Jonny. 'You're going to kill the Queen, and Elvis, and that dog?'

'All those in the car,' said the count, 'including Countess Vanda. Whom, you might be either pleased or not so pleased to know was, as you might put it, is one of the good guys, influenced by the Air Loom. All of them must die. It will be a terrible motor car accident. The chauffeur will drive them off a flyover. Foreign chauffeur? Suicide chauffeur? Outrage! War! Nuke those foreign bastards! But of course not, that's not the British way. Troops out of Iraq. Then that unexpected nuke. All preordained. Pre-planned. Pre-programmed, by us. And *boom*!' And Count Otto mimed this boom.

'Boom,' said Jonny.

'Boom,' said the count.

'No,' said Jonny.

'No?'

'No.' And Jonny shook his head. 'I'll have to stop you there,' he said. 'I can't have you assassinating the Queen.'

'It has to be,' said Count Otto. 'Soon she and those in the car will be beyond the Air Loom's range. They will awaken from their trances, as it were. We can't have that, now, can we? All would have been wasted.'

'All is wasted,' said Jonny. 'You and your miserable crew and that unspeakable bit of apparatus are finished. You are not going to assassinate the Queen, nor draw the whole wide world into a nuclear war. I will not permit it.'

'*You* will not permit it?' Count Otto Black gave a villainous laugh, pulled a flintlock pistol from his pocket and pointed it at Jonny. 'The show's not over till the gloved lady plays,' said Count Otto. 'Madam, play that long loony note and let it float.'

And the Glove Woman's hands hovered over the keyboard.

And Count Otto Black's thumb cocked the hammer of the flintlock.

And it looked as if that was that.

'No,' cried Jonny, 'please.'

'No time,' said the count. 'Goodbye.'

'No, please, please, please. At least a last request.'

'It will have to be a quick one.'

'Really, really, quick I promise. This is all about music, yes? Then please let me end it with music of my own. Just a little, please.'

'A little music?' And Count Otto Black looked baffled.

'A tiny little hymn to Pan. It's all I ask, it won't take a moment.'

'A tiny hymn to Pan? Then so you may.'

★

And Jonny Hooker took from his pocket a certain something. A certain something that had come from the pocket of a mummy. A certain something that Jonny had blown in the saloon bar of The Middle Man.

With devastating consequences.

And Jonny Hooker hastily put this slim, brass, cylindrical certain something to his lips.

And blew it as hard as he could.

52

And then there *was* an explosion.

Which was something.

This explosion was *really* something.

It was a kind of simultaneous explosion as the tall glass conducting tubes atop the Air Loom erupted into fragmented chaos and the twisting, swirling plasma vortexes tore out into the underground storeroom with crackling tongues of energy. Like the electrical outpourings of Frankenstein's laboratory, they arced from the Air Loom, striking the Glove Woman and the count and Jack and the others of the Gang.

But not Jonny, though, for he had ducked away.

And there came the most horrible sounds, discordant sounds, abominable sounds, born of no human throat and which had never been played by Man. And Jonny crouched, cross-eyed, his hands pressed over his ears, as mighty forces tore all about in the storeroom. And with a sound that for all the world seemed to be that of Niagara Falls disappearing down a bathtub plughole, Count Otto and the Glove Woman, Jack and the others were sucked away into the Air Loom, which then sucked away itself.

With a bang.

Not a whimper.

Right down the Pan.

As it were.

53

Jonny awoke in darkness.

Utter darkness, as of the grave.

He floundered about somewhat, felt his way here and there, eventually located a light switch and gave that light switch a tweak.

A neon tube guttered and stuttered into life. Illuminating a storeroom that had been stripped of stores, and contained nothing else.

The storeroom was empty, but for Jonny.

'Hm,' went Jonny. 'A job well jobbed, as it were.'

The sun was rising over the park as Jonny emerged from the Big House. He had the whole park to himself, it seemed. A bit like a childhood fantasy, that. The playground all to yourself. The ornamental pond, with its paddle boats, and you the only paddler and no one to call, 'Come in, number twenty-seven, your time is up.'

Jonny Hooker walked in the park.

It *was* a beautiful morning.

Jonny Hooker flexed his shoulders, clicked his joints and grinned. He wandered to the ornamental pond and sat down on a bench.

'What a lovely morning,' said Jonny.

Mr Giggles didn't reply.

'Nothing to say?' Jonny said.

'I suppose you think you're very clever.'

'Actually,' said Jonny, 'I do. *I* saved the Queen from assassination. And once beyond the range of the Air Loom she would have wakened from its spell and cancelled those orders. I expect the Parliament of Five will be having another meeting soon, one that will lead to a happy conclusion.'

'Don't be too sure of that.'

'Actually,' said Jonny once more, 'I *am* sure. They're gone. The

Air Loom and the Air Loom Gang, gone, as if they never existed. As if they were nothing more than a figment of a madman's imagination.'

Mr Giggles made growling sounds.

'Keep them to yourself,' said Jonny. 'I know what you are and who the Master is that you serve. Satyr, Pan's little helper and the last of your kind.'

'Yes,' said Mr Giggles. 'And you may have thwarted my Master's plans, but *I* am not done with you. Not a bit of it. You will atone, you will serve My master. You will build a new Air Loom. You will recruit a new gang. You will bring forth the mayhem that will return my Master to rule this miserable planet.'

'No,' said Jonny. 'I think not.'

'And *I* think *so*. A wanted serial-killer, so you are. And if you wish to remain at large, you will do what *I* tell you to do. I have been far too lenient with you. We will both learn from our mistakes.'

'No,' said Jonny. 'I'm done. All finished.'

'You're far from done, buddy boy. You're only just beginning. You will be a loyal servant. A good and faithful servant.'

'No,' said Jonny Hooker. 'I won't.'

'You will,' said Mr Giggles. 'You will.'

Jonny Hooker rose from the bench and took himself over to the pond.

'Fancy a paddle?' asked Mr Giggles.

'Something more than that, I think.' And Jonny stepped into the pond.

'What is this?' asked Mr Giggles.

'This is goodbye,' said Jonny. 'We won't be seeing each other any more.'

'Thinking to drown yourself? Forget that. You wouldn't be able to do it.'

'No, probably not.' Jonny Hooker reached into the poacher's pocket of his now *very* smelly jacket and brought out the late James Crawford's laptop.

'What are you going to do with *that*?' asked Mr Giggles.

'I think you know.'

'Throw it in the pond?'

'Not that.' Jonny Hooker opened the laptop. Keyed in the

password – 'Da-da-de-da-da'. 'Time for a little music,' said he.

'Oh no,' cried Mr Giggles. And he was in the water too, now, clearly visible to Jonny, splashing about something wicked.

'The last Robert Johnson recording,' said Jonny. 'That thirtieth recording. The one with your Master's laughter on it. The laughter that is too much for any human brain to bear. That none may hear without dying. Robert Johnson never sold his soul to Satan, he sold it to Pan, the god of musicians. So now it's time for me to listen to the laughter of your Master. But this time the joke will be on him, for you are the last of His little helpers, the last true believer, and as pretty much everyone knows, when the last true believer of a particular god dies, then that god dies with them.'

'But why, why?' crooned Mr Giggles. 'You don't want to die. You're young.'

'I'm twenty-seven,' said Jonny. 'Same age as those iconic rock stars were when they died. And I've done everything I needed to do. I've played the music. I've saved Mankind. I have lived my life. What more can any man ask?'

'For a longer life. For more life.'

'With *you*? I will never be free of you. And you might just win in the end. So better now, I think, than later.'

'No,' cried Mr Giggles. 'This is absurd. Ridiculous, ludicrous.'

'Unreal?' said Jonny. 'Impossible? Fantastic? Unbelievable?'

'Yes, but—'

Jonny Hooker tapped at the keyboard.

Let the music play.

'I'm happy now,' said Jonny Hooker. 'And at least I go out on a song.'

'No no no, please, Jonny, please.'

'Goodbye, Mister Giggles.'

Da-da-de-da-da-de—Album

It is now sixty years since the Roswell Incident and forty years since Sergeant Pepper and the Summer of Love. And so, to celebrate the anniversaries of these momentous events, those wonderful people at Orion have agreed to release a CD of music to accompany this book. And free of charge, too.

This CD acts as a soundtrack and companion piece to the novel. It features real musicians and I, Robert Rankin, will be forever in their debt. Their web addresses are listed below and I heartily recommend that you check them out.

Headless in Gunnersbury
Music: High Rankin
www.myspace.com/highrankin

Soundscape. Opening title sequence. The literary camera pans across Gunnersbury Park to reveal the headless body of twenty-seven-year-old musician Jonny Hooker floating in the ornamental pond.

Burning Rope
Lyrics/vocals: Robert Rankin
Music: High Rankin

Jonny's father (now presumed dead) took Jonny, when he was a child, to many museums and told him many wondrous tales. Dads are gods to small boys. Mine was.

Still is.

Da-da-de-da-da
Music: High Rankin

Mr Giggles the Monkey Boy says, 'Da-da-de-da-da'. It's there, that riff, in all popular music. You can't escape from it. There's a lot of it about. And there's a very great deal of it on this track.

Smart Hat Jonny
Lyrics/vocals: Robert Rankin
Music: High Rankin

Jonny Hooker disguises himself as a park ranger. It works like that, you see. Put someone that you know well into a uniform and a cap and you won't be able to recognise them. Really. Truly. I mean it.

Dance of the Sugar-Plum Technofairy
Arrangement/all instruments: Lady Raygun
www.ladyraygun.com

The Devil's Interval, or tritone, a halved octave, was banned by the church for centuries. It was considered to be the original Devil's Music. For its length, there are more Devil's Intervals in 'The Dance of the Sugar-Plum Fairy' than in any other piece of classical music. Why? Good question.

The first of two classical pieces recorded specially for this album. Played on steel pan by Europe's top female soloist, Lady Raygun.

Pelted with Stones
Lyrics: Robert Rankin
Music/vocals/all instruments: Jon Hooker
whatinfothereis@btinternet.com

Punk musician, living legend (and real person) Jonny Hooker took time out from his rock 'n' roll lifestyle to record this for the album. Give him gigs. Give him groupies. Give him a record deal.
And as for, 'pelted with stones on the common because of my new-style hair-do–' we've all been there.

We haven't? Shame on you.

Some Call Me Laz
Lyrics/vocals: Robert Rankin
Music/all instruments: Phil 'God made me do it' Cowan
Backing vocals: The Woodbinettes
www.myspace.com/philcowanmusic

The only piece of music that was not specially recorded for this album. This little gem was produced in 1978 at a London studio owned by Gary Glitter's drummer. It was rejected by every major record label, because they were 'unable to find a niche for it'. It receives its first ever release here. Which proves that it was indeed nearly thirty years ahead of its time.

Note, if you will, the riff that runs all the way through the track. It goes da-da-de-da-da.

Whatever happened to those lovely Woodbinettes?

Sides to a Story
Dry Rise
www.myspace.com/dryriseband

Top Brighton metal combo Dry Rise (Dry Rot) perform this mini-masterpiece, which says what it has to say and means it. And even makes mention of my kidney stone. Check out their website, catch their gigs and buy their CDs.

And note, if you will, Constable Paul's bass beating out a mighty da-da-de-da-da at the end of the number.

Brilliant stuff.

Apocalypse Blues
Vocals/lyrics(some)/harmonica: Robert Rankin
Music: Lady Raygun

Lady Raygun put together a steel pan version of the blues which consists almost entirely of Devil's Intervals. Which is why it sounds so freaky. This was put through a phaser, as were the vocals, which are for the most part lifted directly from the Book of Revelation. And there really is a line in Revelation that goes 'I heard the sound of harpers, harping with their harps'.

Check it out if you don't believe me.

Lobster Cracking (Air on a Loom)
Vocals: Robert Rankin
Music: High Rankin

The hideous pneumatic sounds of the dreaded Air Loom, as the evil Count Otto Black and his gang of assassins broadcast its sinister magnetic flux to assail their victims. The words belong to James Tilly Mathews, taken down in 1812 at St Mary of Bethlehem Hospital.

They fair put the wind up me!

Requiem for Jonny
Handel
Arrangement/all instruments: Lady Raygun

Ombra mai fu, largo from *Xerxes* by George Frederic Handel. The story goes that Moreschi, the very last castrato, sang this piece before the Pope in the Vatican in 1902, where it was recorded on a wax cylinder. It is said that his rendition was so beautiful that it touched the angels in Heaven and one of them descended to Earth to join him in the final chorus. The recording of this is, of course, hidden in the Vatican archives. A hauntingly beautiful piece, recorded exclusively for this album by Lady Raygun. Class act, eh?

Here endeth the album